# 21 Rangers West

## All for Texas

**Donald Knott Jr.**

*21 Rangers West*
Copyright © 2019 by *Donald Knott Jr.*

ISBN: 978-1-949231-56-4

All rights reserved.

No part of this publication may be reproduced, distributed, or transmitted in any form or by any means, including photocopying, recording, or other electronic or mechanical methods, without the prior written permission of the publisher, except in the case of brief quotations embodied in critical reviews and certain other noncommercial uses permitted by copyright law.

For permission requests, write to the publisher at the address below.

Yorkshire Publishing
4613 E. 91st St.
Tulsa, Oklahoma 74137
www.YorkshirePublishing.com
918.394.2665

The streets of Austin were a buzz. People were gathered in small little huddles while some one read from the newspaper, the Austin Gazette. At the same time, there was much talk and debate. The headline read: WAR! TEXAS SECEDES FROM THE UNION, March 2, 1861 Texas to join her southern neighbors to the Confederacy.

"That's good enough for me. YEEEHAAA! I'm goin' now and joining up!" whooped one of the young men who stood nearby.

"Hold on, Willy, I'm right behind ya. How about you, Caleb? Come on, we'll have those Yankees whipped good and proper in six months. Come on!" shouted Harry White.

"Go on, Harry, I'll be along. I've got something I need to do first," said Caleb.

Caleb walked out of the dormitory and started walking down Main Street to the livery stables. "Can I help you, young man?" asked a tall muscular man with blue eyes, brown hair and broad, thick shoulders and a friendly smile.

"I'm looking for the owner."

"That would be me."

"Good. Have you any horses for rent? Say for a week?"

"Got two. Are you traveling far?"

"I'm riding to Uvalde."

"Then you probably want Dusty here. He's a fine gelding and can go all day. Who should I make the bill out to?"

"Captain Andrew Parker Texas Rangers."

The livery owner's eyes grew wide. "The Andrew Parker? From the Pena Ranchero?"

"Is there more than one?" Caleb was trying not to be rude but he was in no mood for idle chitchat.

"Ha ha ha ha, of course not, forget it. You know, on second thought perhaps you would prefer Jack, that buckskin yonder."

"Either, or. I just need a horse. I'm riding to Uvalde not going to a race."

The livery man's feelings were vexed but he tried hard not to let it show. "Right you are. That'll be 15 cents a day."

"Here," Caleb handed the man a five dollar gold piece. "Keep the change."

Caleb saddled the horse. The horse sensed the urgency as Caleb cinched the saddle tight. The old buckskin was ready to go. Caleb straddled the horse and rode out southeast toward Uvalde.

The following afternoon was business as usual at the Pena Ranchero. Children were running here and there around the small houses that were homes to the married ranch hands and vaqueros. To his right was a fair sized gathering of hands standing along the fence rails of the corral cheering and shouting. A young man of about 16 or 17 was riding a wild, fiercely bucking and twisting white horse. Caleb smiled at the sight. The young man looked in Caleb's direction and suddenly became airborne, landing a mere foot from the corral fence. He quickly stood up, climbed the fence and then waved. "Hey, Caleb!" The boy ran up alongside Caleb's horse, his hand outstretched. "Boy howdy, ain't you a sight for sore eyes! You here to stay a while?"

Caleb looked down at the young man and studied him for a moment. "Johnny? Johnny Caldwell?"

"That's me. Only it's Pena now. Johnny Caldwell Pena."

"Why, you are nearly a man now!"

"Nearly? Yes, I reckon you could say that. But just don't say in front of the hands." Johnny blushed.

"I see," said Caleb. He smiled. "Done deal."

"What brings you to Uvalde? You joining back up with the Rangers?"

"Not quite, Johnny. But I am here to see the captain. He here?"

"You bet. Only he ain't the captain anymore. Whiskey Jack's the captain now."

"What happened to Capt. Parker?"

"Nothin'. Just that ole "Rip" Ford done went and made him Major Parker now."

Caleb whistled out well. "Major!"

A voice in the corral hollered, "Hey, Johnny, you quitting? What's the matter? Is ol' Tornado too much for ya?"

Johnny smiled. "I best be getting back to work. Pa, Whiskey Jack, I mean, doesn't take kindly to loafing around," Johnny slapped Caleb's knee. "I'll see you at supper time." Then he rushed back over to the corral.

Caleb rode up to the hacienda and dismounted and tied his horse to the hitching rail.

"Can I be of some assistance, young man?" came the voice of an old but authoritative man.

Caleb turned slowly and looked at the white haired man. He wore a blue Spanish vest and a white shirt with a black bow tie that hung low at the ends. The vest was adorned with golden thread scroll that flowed and wound in an almost musical type of pattern. His pants were also blue but a shade darker than his vest with a black stripe down the side of each leg. The old man held a glass of red wine and a cigar between the fingers of his right hand which also held a glass of wine.

"Yes, sir. I assume that you are Don Miguel Pena?"

"That would be correct. And you are?"

"Caleb, sir. Sgt. Caleb of Capt. Parker's Company D.

"So! At l last I get to meet the young man that my grandson has spoken so proudly of!"

"Me, sir?"

"And modest too. Please come inside. We have much to talk about."

"Talk, sir?"

"Yes, talk. After all you do also carry the name Parker, do you not? And since I am Andrew's grandfather I suppose that gives me some entitlement. Would you agree?"

"Yes. I reckon it does," Caleb chuckled.

"May I offer you a glass of wine?"

"Don't mind if I do, sir."

Don Miguel poured a glass of wine and said, "Andrew is out on the ranch with some of the men. They are hunting a cougar. I had thought they were all gone but in the past few weeks we have lost several young calves to one. He may be back tonight or it could be several days."

"I see," said Caleb.

"I could send one of my vaqueros to get him if you wish."

"No, sir, I'm in no real hurry. I just want to talk to him."

Don Miguel could sense that something was troubling the young man but opted not to press the issue. At least not now. "Andrew tells me that you are in school studying to become an attorney."

"Yes, sir. That is part of the reason I'm here."

A squeal came from across the room. "Caleb! Mama! Mama! It's Caleb! He's here!" It was the voice of young Sally. She came running and nearly knocked the wine glass from his hand, tackling Caleb with a big hug.

"Sally! Why look at you. You have grown! You were this high when I last saw you." Caleb held his hand at waist level.

"Oh, Caleb! Have you come here to live?"

Caleb did not have time to answer. Marjorie came walking into the room. She said nothing at first just strolled over to him and kissed him on his cheek. "We have missed you. You're looking well. A little thin but well."

"I think he looks just wonderful!" said Sally.

Marjorie laughed. "Yes, dear, just wonderful."

"The young man has come to speak with Andrew. He said it is important," said Don Miguel.

"That might be some wait. He's hunting."

"Yes, ma'am. Don Miguel told me. A cougar."

"All the better. We will have more time with you. But right now I'll bet you would rather have a nice bath and something to eat. Caleb, come, let's see what we can do." Marjorie took Caleb by the elbow and began to lead him down the hallway.

Caleb could not argue. He was hungry when he left Austin. He was in such a state of bewilderment that he forgot to bring anything to eat along the way and a hot tub sure did sound inviting.

When Caleb returned to the large space where he had been with Don Miguel there was quite a gathering. Don Miguel, Senora Kataryna, Marjorie Stanton Parker, Sally, Mary Caldwell Parker, Johnny, Capt. Whiskey Jack and his sister, Jenny. Caleb stopped and stared in disbelief.

"Welcome home!"

Caleb blushed, “I don’t know what to say.” His eyes did not go toward Jenny as she had hoped but rather fixed on Whiskey Jack.

“Captain. It’s mighty good to see you.”

“And me? Oh, Caleb!” Jenny ran to her big brother and threw her arms around his neck.

“Yes, my dear sister. I am thrilled to see you. I thought you were in Uvalde at the mission. I heard you are teaching school now.”

“Not quite yet. I am helping Marjorie teach. I am her assistant.”

“Well, now that qualifies in my book,” said Caleb.

“That is just what I said. But I am afraid an old man’s word isn’t what it used to be,” teased Don Miguel.

“It isn’t that at all. Why, you are still Don Miguel Pena! Truth is, Jenny still has another year before the Town Council will allow her to teach her own classes. She must graduate herself then she can teach and study to become a licensed teacher,” said Senora Kataryna.

“Teaching, teaching! Let Sergeant have some breathing room. I am sure he would love to catch up with all of us. But not all on the first day.” Whiskey Jack held his hand out to Caleb and they shook hands. “Welcome home, Sergeant.”

“Thanks, Captain.”

“Now, let us all sit down to eat before it gets cold. Juanita has worked hard to prepare a special homecoming meal for young Caleb here,” said Don Miguel.

Supper had ended and everyone had retired to the large living room. There was much talk of days past and laughing. Whiskey Jack and Caleb drank a toast.

“To Billy Spears,” said Whiskey Jack.

“To Billy Spears,” said Caleb.

As the night drew on the women had all retired to their rooms and only Whiskey Jack, Don Miguel and Caleb remained. Johnny had excused himself as he had to tend to mending a fence and needed to start while it was still cool. “I’ll see you tomorrow, Caleb. Welcome home. Buenos noches, Don Miguel. Buenos noches, Pa.”

“Buenos noches,” replied Jack.

Jack watched Caleb with discerning eyes. "So, are you going to tell me what's wrong?"

"Wrong? What makes you think there's something wrong?"

"You're gonna play it like that, eh?" said Jack.

"No disrespect, Captain, but I think I'd rather wait until Capt. Parker returns. I mean, Major Parker."

"No disrespect taken. Only don't always say there's nothing wrong. I've known you for too long and let's not forget I have a whole company of rangers I look after. I'm good at reading faces and yours says you are holding a pair of jacks against a full house."

"You're right about that. I'd be more than happy to discuss the matter with you and Don Miguel. But only when Major Parker is here as well."

"My boy. You have my deepest respect. I am pleased that you value my grandson's wisdom so highly. I will not pursue the matter any further," said Don Miguel. "Now if you two will excuse me I will retire for the night."

Don Miguel left the room and the two rangers just sat quietly for some time.

"It's good to see you, boy," said Jack.

"Good to see you, Jack."

Morning came and Caleb got up from his bed and walked over to the large window of his room and splashed his face with water from the large porcelain basin that sat on the table in front of the window. He was drying his face with a small towel that hung on the side of the table. A familiar voice from behind him growled. "About time you woke up."

Caleb turned around. Fighting back an urge to cry, he answered, "Morning, Capt. I mean Major, sir."

"Caleb." Major Parker held out his hand. "Sure is good to see you."

"And you." Caleb took Major Parker's hand.

"You're late for breakfast and Senora Kataryna threatened to fire Juanita if she didn't hold a plate aside for you. So if you're hungry-"

"Hungry? I'm starved!"

"Well, then, let's go. You don't want Juanita to lose her job do you?" smiled Drew.

Caleb smiled, "No, I surely do not."

Caleb ate his breakfast as Drew Parker sat across from him enjoying a cup of coffee.

"Did you get him?" asked Caleb.

"I beg your pardon?" said Drew.

"That cougar. Did you get him?"

"Her. Yes. I'm back, aren't I?"

"You are at that," Caleb said with a chuckle.

"We have some horses to round up and drive into Uvalde. You wanna come along?"

"Do I? No offense, Major, but I've been looking for a reason to escape for a few hours."

"No offense taken. I grew up here. Remember? I know just how you feel."

The hard work and sweat did Caleb a world of good. He hadn't worried about anything all day. He felt good."

"We'll drive them into town first thing in the morning. For tonight, we'll just camp here," said Drew.

Caleb was going to question why but acquiesced. He was enjoying the change in activity. He never knew how much he missed a hard day's work. Being in school had started to soften him. "Sounds great. I'll fetch some wood for a fire."

They sat around the fire that evening. For quite some time no one spoke a word. A young vaquero sat with his back against the tall mesquite and played a slow and sad melody. Soon another vaquero began to sing. It was about a young man and woman so far apart yet so much in love. In the song, he lay dying after being caught in a stampede. In his pocket is a picture of his beloved. As he gazes upon it, he asks his compadres to tell her, as they had always vowed to each other, he would see her at the gate.

Caleb lay back on his bed roll and his head upon his saddle for a pillow and gazed up at the night sky. Drew sat next to him using a log for a seat and sipped a cup of coffee not saying much at first. He had been told before the drive by his mother, Senora Kataryna, that the young man was troubled and had ridden all this way solely for his counsel.

But Drew was not one to press. It wasn't his way. He knew that in good time and in his own time that Caleb would work his way up to it.

"Unusually calm tonight. Comfortably cool air," said Drew.

"Mmmhmm. I was just thinking back. I never knew how much I would miss being on the trail," said Caleb.

"Well, I suppose. But I would hardly call this being on the trail. More like a camping trip," Drew chuckled.

"Maybe so. But nonetheless, it brings back memories. One thing is sure. Coke is nothing like Juan. Good Lord! That man could cook!"

"I'll be sure to tell him you said that. He speaks of you often. All the men do."

"I'd like to see them again myself. Bunch of hooligans," Caleb said with a smile.

"I suppose you will be here when the baby comes?" asked Drew.

Caleb sat up right as if yanked by his shirt collar. "Baby? What baby?"

"Marjorie is going to have a baby. I thought you knew," said Drew.

"No, I didn't. I didn't even notice any change. She looks like Marjorie. I mean, shouldn't she look like it?"

Drew laughed. "It's only been a couple months. She'll be showing it soon enough. But some women hardly ever do and others show early."

Caleb smiled and laughed as well. "Roll me in cow poop and call me stinky! Oh, baby. Boy or girl?"

"One of the two," said Drew chuckling.

"Sorry. Silly question, wasn't it? Congratulations, Dad."

"When I first found out I thought what lousy timing. But then I thought about Don Miguel. It will be a blessing for him and for Mother."

"Lousy timing? I don't follow."

"Don't tell me you haven't heard the news? Surely being in Austin you would have heard before us."

"That news. Yeah." Caleb became sullen once more and lay back down. "A baby."

The town of Uvalde was almost at the point of chaos and rioting when the men came driving their horses through town to the holding pens by the livery stables. An occasional fist fight would break out but soon ended as one of the town's deputies would step in and break it up. There were shouting matches and lifelong friendships ended in the blink of an eye and new alliances were formed in some cases with lifelong rivals. Men held newspapers up high above their heads so that all could read the headlines.

SAM HOUSTON REMOVED FROM OFFICE!

"What did that say?" A man was waving a newspaper above his head and shouting. Drew reached and grabbed the paper from the man. The man shouted. "Hang the coward!" Drew read the paper. He hung his head and shook it, distraught. Caleb read the paper as well. "An avalanche. That is a good description. Only I would say that to all the states. An avalanche of morals crumbling into the abyss. Does anyone yet know the real reason for war?" said Caleb.

"We aren't at war yet," said Drew.

"May as well be. Otherwise, why secede from the Union? Surely states rights can be resolved. If this is what it's really about and if it's over industrializing the South because of a few bales of cotton. Then by God Almighty we are being led by a pack of fools. Let those politicians fight on the front lawn of the Capital rather than have good men on both sides die just so that they can sit back on their fat asses sipping brandy and smoking cigars getting rich at others cost and blood! Blessed Savior in Heaven, forgive this nation. I sure as hell cannot," said Caleb.

"What's the matter, son, you too yella to get into a little scrape? I say hoorah for Texas and damn the Yankees. By God, I fight to preserve Texas!" said one of the men.

"Mister, if you knew who you were speaking to you'd not ask that question. This is Sgt. Caleb of Company D Texas Rangers and believe me, he is no coward," said Drew.

"And just who the hell are you, another lover of Yankees?" said the man.

"I am Major Drew Parker Company D Texas Rangers and whether or not it is a matter of being a lover of Yankees is a fool question. I am a Texan. Yet it is not unreasonable to question why Texas will be sending her sons to die. Or have we become so enamored over the thought of killing that reasons do not matter? If that is the case, then by your own words I need no more reason to blow your head off here and now!" said Drew as he drew his revolver and pointed it at the man.

"Whoa whoa now! You can't do that. Why it would be cold-blooded murder. I ain't done nothing to get killed for," said the man who was now suddenly sobering.

"My point and the point of the Sergeants here exactly. No one wants to die without at least knowing the reason."

"But there's honor! The honor of Texas! Doesn't that matter?" asked the man.

"Yes. But with that honor is purpose and with that purpose, dignity. One son of Texas is worth a thousand Yankees. Don't send her son out to fight and die for no reason," replied Drew.

Soon people were quieting and walking away. Caleb looked at Drew and asked, "Do you have mixed feelings about this as well?"

"I'm a Ranger, son. Fighting outlaws, Indians or even Yankees I wouldn't kill any man without a just reason. Never have, never will," said Drew.

"I feel exactly the same way. But that fellow was right about one thing. The honor of Texas. I owe Texas and I owe the Rangers. If not for you and the Rangers I may have ended up with my face on a wanted poster," replied Caleb.

"Maybe. But somehow I doubt that. Some men through divine providence are destined to be lawmen. I believe with all my heart that you were such a man."

Caleb smiled. He knew now what he wanted. He looked at Drew and said, "Thanks. You know, you're pretty smart for a Texas Ranger."

Drew laughed as he said, "So I've heard, so I've heard. When the time comes, the right thing to do will come to you."

"It's a comfort to know you have friends who more times than not have more confidence in you than you have in yourself," said Caleb.

"We best get to selling those nags before some jack of apes steals them all," said Drew.

"I wonder which side?" Caleb questioned as he sat on his horse and stared at the herd in the corral.

"What was that?" asked Drew.

"Which side will end up with those horses. Them or us?" asked Caleb.

"Good question."

A short four days later Caleb was standing outside on the veranda enjoying the evening's cool breeze. When Senora Kataryna came strolling up behind him. As she gently placed a hand on the back of his shoulder she asked, "You will be leaving us soon?"

"No," Caleb turned to face her. "I'm in no hurry. At least not yet."

"It is a terrible thing, this talk of war. I hate it!" she said.

"I'm not too fond of it either. I just wish I knew who was right if, in fact, anyone is even right at all," replied Caleb.

"You must follow your heart. Where do your allegiances lie? Where do you call home?"

"Si, but what if home is on the wrong side?"

"That is a quandary, isn't it? Would I believe if one serves his country with love and purity in his heart, that man is never wrong even when those who lead him may be. Our Lord tells us to obey those in authority over us. You have been given a great blessing. You still have time to decide which authority to serve. I believe before this is all over many will lament at brother against brother and father against son. It is prophesied. There is an old Spanish saying "El peor enemigo es el que fue una vez un amigo." The worst enemy is he who was once a friend."

"Maybe so. But who is truly my enemy? I mean I could see both sides and agree with both on so many subjects," replied Caleb.

"I do not wonder who will be the enemy during the war. It is after the war that must be considered. Now, I'm getting a chill. Shall we go inside?"

Caleb looked at Senora Kataryna and smiled. "You are an amazing woman; do you know that?"

Senora Kataryna shrugged her shoulders. "If you say so."

As the two walked into the hacienda the large room was filled with people. Drew, Jack, Don Miguel and Johnny were standing around a large billiard table. The women were all seated and having idle chitchat.

Sally was seated on a large pillow and reading. Everyone stopped what they were doing as Caleb and Senora Kataryna entered the room. Drew walked over and took his mother's arm in his and proceeded to lead her to a chair. "I love you but I am quite able to seat myself," she quietly chided him.

"Si. I was just overcome with jealousy seeing you in the company of this young man."

"Young man is right. Such a handsome one too," said Senora Kataryna.

Jenny laughed, "Why Caleb! I do believe you are blushing."

Caleb said nothing. He just glared at Jenny with a look that would melt glass. Jenny laughed again.

"I do believe you are correct, Jenny. Just what were you two doing out there, young man?" Don Miguel said with a humorous look in his eye.

"Dancing!" exclaimed Senora Kataryna. "He is a wonderful dancer."

Johnny broke in and asked, "Hey Caleb, you were there. Tell us about that big buckskin mare the Major broke back on the Pecos River. Was she really as rough as I've been told?"

Drew laughed and said, "You must excuse Johnny here. He has been trying to make a name for himself with the hands as a top bronc buster. Seems one of the Rangers told the story about that mare and ever since Johnny feels he has something to prove."

"Naw! That ain't so. It's a goal I have set for myself. Why Pa always says a man has to have a goal. Topping the Major isn't my goal at all. It's matching him," said Johnny.

"Well, Drew as I recall that was one tall horse. All the boys stayed shy of her. Said she was a man killer," said Caleb.

"But the Major rode her down?" asked Johnny excitedly.

"That's right, Johnny. He rode her until she was prancing around like a lipizzan," replied Caleb.

"Golly! I wish I could've seen that!" exclaimed Johnny.

"Well, I wish I could take bragging rights on that but can't. You see, that isn't quite the way it went down. Sure I rode her. But the truth be known I really had no choice." Drew looked into space, remembering.

A mischievous grin on his face, he said, "I had watched the men as they were breaking and choosing their mounts for the remuda. I should've been paying more attention than I had. But I was preoccupied with thoughts of the gang of outlaws we were chasing. I looked at that buckskin and I immediately decided she would be mine and quick. Because the others had been pretty fair judges of horse flesh. Better than I had assumed. So I went up to her and slowly covered her head with my jacket. I saddled her and climbed on and when I removed my jacket." He laughed. "I thought I had saddled a keg of dynamite by mistake." He laughed again. "That mare leaped so high! And came down like a spinning top. She bucked, oh she bucked! First her head was so high I couldn't see over her then so low I thought she was gonna bore a hole through the earth straight to China! Then she sprang on all fours high into the air and sunfished. Twice she came down on her side. She was up and bucking so fast. I tell ya I was scared – scared to let go, scared to stay on. I hung on for dear life. I reckon the others had thought it was determination but it wasn't. It was survival. When it was finally over, I suppose you could have called it a draw. So you see, I didn't break that horse. We just came to a mutual agreement. In exchange for food and grooming, she would allow me to ride her. Perhaps that is why she won't allow anyone else on her."

"Nice story, hermano, but I am not buying it. Everyone from here to Laredo knows that you are top bronc buster and always had the fastest horse. Why, Drew here is still unbeaten at the Hondo annual rodeo and horse race," said Whiskey Jack proudly.

"Now, there's a goal for you, Johnny. I haven't been at the Hondo in years except for in official capacity," said Drew.

"Break your record? I don't know, Major."

Sally interrupted. "Oh, my! I've never been to a rodeo. Johnny, you can do it! I know it!"

"Well, you surely have time to practice. The rodeo is not until the 4th of July. Our vaqueros always went to Hondo rodeos. You have good company, that's for sure, and you're a Pena so you have yet another advantage," said Don Miguel as he put his arm over Johnny's shoulders.

"Gracias, Abuelo. I will do my best," said Johnny.

Johnny Caldwell Parker would not get his chance at the Hondo rodeo for another five years.

## April 19, 1861

Since 5 o'clock in the morning, Caleb along with Drew, Whiskey Jack, Johnny and nearly all of the vaqueros and cowboys of the Pena Ranchero had been rousting steers out from dry washes, cacti, deer brush and mesquite so thick you could barely walk through let alone ride a horse through it. The job was made somewhat easier with the aid of two Spanish sheepdogs that Don Miguel had purchased as puppies from a Basque Spanish sheepherder he had met while in Galveston. Don Miguel had gone to Galveston originally to collect some new grapevines he had shipped all the way from Barcelona, Spain. He purchased the pups and trained them specifically for herding cattle. It was a complete success. An angry two-year-old calf was giving Johnny a fit by playing a cow's version of peekaboo and hide and seek. The dogs would push them out of the brush but as soon as the calf saw Johnny's horse he would charge back in and the chase was on again.

Caleb rode over to assist him with the calf. Johnny saw Caleb riding his way. When Caleb sided Johnny, Johnny spouted, "Dern calf! I've half a mind to leave him there and good riddens!"

"Ha ha ha! Perhaps two men are needed. I'll hang down here and you ride on up ahead a ways. When that dog brings him out again, I'll throw a rope on him and then you do the same. By golly, we'll drag him if need be. Truth is, I just think he's playing. He thinks that dog just wants to have a game. Has nothing to do with you."

"Heck, you know, I never even thought of that! I bet you're right," said Johnny.

They were just getting set to rope the calf when suddenly the sound of gunfire and shouting caught their attention. "Now, what would that be?" asked Caleb.

"Rustlers?" Johnny said to Caleb.

"Let's not sit here like two frogs on a log. Let's go!" said Caleb.

Caleb and Johnny rode up to assist the others against the rustlers, their guns drawn poised for battle. But when they got to the rest of the men, everyone was shouting and slapping each other on the back and firing their weapons into the air. One of the vaqueros who had been working at the ranch house was waving a newspaper.

"What's going on?" asked Caleb.

"What's going on? Here read for yourself. Yeehaw! We're at war boys!"

Drew came galloping into the crowd. Apparently rustlers were the same deduction that Caleb and Johnny had. Drew sided Caleb. "What in thunderation!!!"

Caleb hung his head low and handed the paper to Drew. "Oh Lord. They went and done it, didn't they? They couldn't wait for the other fella. They had to start it themselves."

On March 4, 1861 Abraham Lincoln was inaugurated as the President of the United States. In an address to his cabinet he took the stand that no state in the Union had neither the power nor the legal right to separate itself from the United States and that the United States had the power to govern over them. Yet the states that had seceded and formed the Confederacy charged that all United States Union troops will leave the Confederate territory immediately. But they did not leave. Union forces occupied Fort Sumter in Charleston Harbor, Charleston, South Carolina. A demand for their surrender and evacuation of the Fort went unheard. The Union commander at Fort Sumter refused. On April 12, 1861 Confederate forces took control and allegedly fired upon Fort Sumter.

On April 14,1861 Confederate forces took full possession of the Fort. On April 15, 1861 Union President of the United States, Abraham Lincoln declared war against the Confederacy. Drew continued reading.

"That's enough, Major. Drew, I get it. We are at war. May the God of host have mercy and forgive us all!" said Caleb.

Drew yelled out for one of his vaqueros, "Antonio!"

The vaquero rode up to where Drew and Caleb were sitting. "Si Patrone."

"Have the men push the herd in to the holding pens. We aren't going to get any more work done today it seems."

"Si Patrone," said Antonio.

The next morning after having breakfast and said goodbyes to everyone Caleb rode to Austin. As he mounted the rented buckskin mare and was about to leave, Senora Kataryna cried out, "Wait!" Then she went inside the hacienda. When she returned she placed a hand up on his knee and looked up at him. I have something for you. It will bring you comfort in troubled times." She handed him a Bible and placed a rosary in his hands.

"Senora," he began.

"Ssh ssh, I want you to take it and please do not call me Senora. You are a part of this hacienda and this family. You are as dear to me as my own sons. I want you to call me Grandmother, Abuela. You will write often?"

"Yes, ma'am. This means a lot to me. Pray for me for I will have all of you in my prayers as well."

**June 26, 1861**

My dearest family,

May this letter find you in good health and high spirits. Upon my arrival to Austin I was met by none other than old Capt. Charles Welch. Needless to say he was very perturbed by the idea of war as he was going to retire. But the good Governor Francis R. Lubbock had in his convincing way talked ol' Charlie to remain in office. I would tell you what Charlie said in his own words but I made a promise to Abuela to live a Christian life so I will not say. Charlie will be liaison to the 1st Regiment Texas Mounted Riflemen. Controlling a line of defense from the Red River to the Rio Grande. Window-dressing is how Capt. Charlie refers to it. As he said he can't see anything from an office in Austin with no windows.

As for me I have been assigned to the 8th Texas Cavalry under Col. Benjamin Franklin Terry. I have been graciously given the rank of

Second Lieutenant I did not want. I would have preferred to be just a regular soldier. But the Col. said there were not enough qualified men who came from West Point and considering my being with the Texas Rangers was the next best thing. That and a recommendation from ol' John "Rip" Ford himself. I was obliged to accept. Shanghaied really.

My days are simple. In the morning we go to breakfast, then truant to lunch, then drill until supper. After supper we drill some more.

I miss you all.

Yours affectionately,
Second Lieutenant Caleb Parker
8th Texas Cavalry

**September 12, 1861**

Caleb had been given his first furlough since becoming a soldier in the Confederacy. He decided he would find a nice café in town and reacquaint himself with real food. It will be nice to sit at a real table with linen and fine dishes and silverware for a change.

He was crossing the street to a place called Holidays fine food and drink. "All right. I'll try," he said to himself. As he stepped up onto the board walkway someone shouted, "Hey! Soldier boy!" Caleb turned around and was taken aback. "Well, I'll be as I live and breathe! Hamelton O'Toole!"

"Sgt. Hamelton O'Toole." O'Toole turned proudly showing off his Sergeant stripes. Then he became aware, snapped to attention and saluted. "I beg your pardon, Lieutenant!!"

"Knock it off!" said Caleb. "How about joining me?"

O'Toole held his salute.

"I told you knock it off. We're friends. Fellow Rangers."

"No, sir. Not until you return my salute, sir!"

Caleb returned his salute. "Now will you join me?"

"Unfortunately I can't. Regulations you know?"

"For God's sake, Hamelton."

"Look, Caleb, I'd love to. But you're an officer and I'm an enlisted man. I could get you in big trouble. It's called..."

"I know what it's called, thunderation! Okay. Tell me who you are with."

"The 8th sir. Col. Terry's outfit."

"Well, don't that beat all! So am I. Wonder why I haven't seen you before now?"

"I'm pretty busy training the new recruits in the fine art of horsemanship. I don't get away much," said O'Toole.

"I'm going to have to make it a point to swing by your way," said Caleb.

"They are a fine bunch of boys. Big strong men. Yes, sir, a fine bunch!" replied O'Toole.

Caleb was about to say more when O'Toole snapped back to attention. "Begging the Lieutenant's pardon sir. But I must be on my way. The men are waiting for me at the saloon."

Caleb snapped a return salute. But before he left O'Toole smiled and jabbed Caleb in the arm. "Good to see you Caleb." Then O'Toole skittered away.

Seeing Hamelton O'Toole made Caleb's supper go down a lot easier. Somehow it brought back a sense of being home and purpose. Suddenly he got an idea. Tomorrow he would check the enlisted roster at the Austin headquarters. "I wonder how many of the boys have enlisted and if any are in the 8th?"

The next morning Caleb managed to steal away for a few hours by volunteering for courier duty delivering dispatches and formal letters to headquarters.

"Here you are, Lieutenant. Every enlisted man in the 8th as well as the 1st Texas Mounted Riflemen," said the clerk.

"Thank you, Corporal."

Caleb began finger tracing every line. He mumbled to himself "O'Toole I know." Then began reading all the names:

1. Private Brown, John. Eighth Texas Cavalry
2. Cpl. Crawford, Thomas. Eighth Texas Cavalry.
3. Private Todd, Terrence. Eighth Texas Cavalry

"Hmm that's all? How about the 1st Texas Mounted Riflemen?"

1. Pvt. Collins, Daniel
2. Pvt. Collins, Martin
3. Pvt. Oaks, Jerolde
4. Pvt. Riley, Jubal
5. Cpl. Riley, Sampson
6. Pvt. Wiggins Kyle

"Well, I'll be. The 1st Texas Mounted Riflemen Regiment. I reckon the Rangers couldn't spare any more men." That evening after supper Caleb went to the tent of Col. Benjamin Terry and rapped on the post.

"Enter," boomed Col. Terry's voice. Caleb cautiously and timidly entered the tent and snapped to attention and saluted. Second Lieutenant Parker requesting an audience with the Colonel. Sir!"

Col. Terry promptly returned the salute. "Audience? Now that's a new one. What is it you are inquiring Lieutenant?"

"Colonel, as you well know before all of this I was a Texas Ranger."

"You can drop all formalities, Lieutenant. Just say Colonel and forget all the rest. Yes, I am aware of your service with the Texas Rangers and I must say I am very impressed. I wish I could have a dozen more like you. What does this have to do with your coming to see me?"

Caleb smiled a mile wide smile, "Colonel, I can't promise you a dozen but will three more do you?"

"Three? Just what are you boiling in that pot of yours?"

"Colonel, we have three of the finest, shootingist, fightingist, best horsemen you ever saw. Texas Rangers right under your nose. But sadly there is a hitch. They are in Lieutenant Col. Lubbock's outfit. But then again, Colonel, with all due respect, and I mean it too, Lt Col Lubbock, they are in the 8th and you command the 8th, sir."

Col. Terry began laughing as he tried to light his pipe. "Good Lord, Charlie Welch warned me about you! Ha ha ha. I'll just bet that you feel that these three men would be better use of their skills if they were in company C. Is that what you are saying, Lieutenant?"

"Absolutely Col. Why we need our very best up front. To strike a devastating and decisive blow at the forefront of every engagement. I'm not saying that Lieutenant Col. Lubbock's men aren't good men. Why, sir, that's the best man in the Confederacy or from Texas. Everyone knows that. But everyone also knows that none but the best of the best make it into Company C."

Colonel Terry studied Caleb with a twinkle in his eye and a wolfish grin on his face.

"You were studying law before all of this insanity, weren't you Lieutenant?"

"Yes, sir."

"Don't stop. I have a feeling some day you are going to be a very good attorney. If your closing arguments are anything like that speech you just gave me."

"Actually Colonel that was my opening statement," said Caleb.

"Lieutenant Parker, have those three men out in front of my quarters at 0700 in the morning. I want to see what the finest, shootingist, fightingist horsemen in Texas look like."

"Yes, sir. Will that be all, sir?"

Colonel Benjamin Terry could hardly refrain from laughing. "That is all, Second Lieutenant Parker. Dismissed."

**THE NEXT MORNING 07:00**

"Gentlemen, you are probably wondering why I had you called here. It has come to my attention that the three of you are, as it was so eloquently stated to me, the finest, shootingist horsemen in all of Texas."

"Damn right," muttered Private Terrence Todd.

"Quiet in the ranks!" ordered the Sergeant.

"That's quite all right, Sgt. That is why you are here today. Gentlemen, if you will – at ease. If you look off to your left, you will see three horses, furthermore you will see an array of various targets laid out in an obstacle course. Your objective is to, one man at a time, saddle any horse of your choosing, choose any rifle or pistol and make two passes through that obstacle course scoring as many hits as possible."

Cpl. Crawford spoke up. "Sir, with all due respect, can we use both or are we limited to only one weapon?"

"You may use both if it pleases you," said Col. Terry.

"One more question, if I may, sir?"

"Yes, Corporal?"

"Do we have to use those nags, sir? Why, we had better mules in the Rangers, sir."

"Ha ha ha ha. Yes, Corporal, I do agree we most certainly did. Just who did you men serve with as Texas Rangers?"

"Why, Capt. Drew Parker, sir. The best Texas Ranger ever given birth to, or ever will. Present company excluded, sir!"

"A very fine man indeed. I would have loved to have him in my command. But Texas will still need peace officers. So your Capt. Parker, now Major Parker, will have that burden to bear."

The three former Texas lawmen of the Texas Rangers of Company D showed their skills in brilliant fashion. Col. Benjamin Terry was so impressed, he gave them the horses of their choosing that day. "Bravo! A finer show of shooting and horsemanship I have never seen. It would appear that the rumors of you men were no exaggeration. But I do have just one question. That is not a regulation emblem of the Confederate Army up on your hats. Why, pray tell, did you opt to use the star of the Texas Ranger?"

"Because sir, that is what we are. We were told we would be in the 8th Texas Cavalry. They are calling us Terry's Rangers. So it just seemed fitting," said Cpl. Crawford.

"Well said, Corporal. I would like to see that star on every hat in my regiment. Lieutenant!" said Col. Terry.

"Yes, sir. Here, sir." Much to the surprise of the three soldiers the Lieutenant was Caleb.

"Lieutenant, see to it forthwith that every hat in this regiment bears the star of the Texas Rangers. Understood?"

"Yes, sir. Right away, sir.

"Oh, and Lieutenant, you were right. They are the finest, shootingist horsemen I have ever seen. Well done, men, well done!"

**September 26, 1861**

My Dearest Family,

You will never guess who I ran into in these past few days. Our dear friends from Company "D" Rangers, Hamelton O'Toole, Johnny Brown, Tom Crawford and Terrence Todd. Hamelton is now Sergeant Hamelton O'Toole. Ol' Tom Crawford is now Cpl. Tom Crawford. Terrence Todd and John Brown are Privates Todd and Brown. All in the 8th cavalry. It looks like this war is starting to shape up. I have also discovered that many from the old outfit are now with the 1st Texas Mounted Rifle Regiment. We have received our orders today. We are setting out for Kentucky in three days. Tell Jenny not to worry. I can't be in better company. My dearest Abuela, I have been doing as you asked. You are right it does bring much comfort. Major, the boys here all send their howdys and wish you and Mrs. Marjorie the best. O'Toole says he's betting his first months pay that it's gonna be a boy. Abuela, I suppose I should let the cat out of the bag. The boys and I thank you for the horses. Johnny, I hope you've learned to stay on one by now.

Yours Truly,<br>Second Lieutenant Caleb Parker.<br>8th Texas Cavalry<br>aka: Terry's Rangers.

"He sounds like he is adjusting. You know it was a hard thing for him to enlist. Even better for Charlie Welch to recommend him for a commission. A man of his caliber just wouldn't do well as a non-com," said Drew.

"What's a non-com?" asked Johnny.

"It means non-commissioned officer. Like a Sergeant or Corporal," said Whiskey Jack.

"But wasn't Caleb a Sergeant in the Rangers?"

"That's very true. But the Rangers and the Army are two different worlds."

"Caleb would have done well regardless. He is an honorable young man," said Don Miguel.

"I will ask that their names be mentioned at mass this Sunday," said Senora Kataryna.

"Don't worry, Jenny," said Johnny. "Why the war will be over in a year. Especially with the Rangers in the mix. Caleb and the boys will whup 'em good."

"I hope you're right. I don't know what I'd do if..."

"Now there will be no talk of that. Don't even think such ideas," interrupted Senora Kataryna.

"With all of this attention towards the war it's making easy pickings for rustlers and bank robbers lately. Seems a gang of four or six men held up the bank in Eagle Pass. My guess is they probably crossed over into Mexico. Anyway, we've been called on to investigate and make arrests if possible," said Drew.

"That's it. No particulars?" asked Jack.

"If you mean dead or alive, the letter didn't say. I don't think we are expected to catch them. Formalities I suppose," said Drew.

**EAGLE PASS**
**Two days later**

One would never have known that the town of Eagle Pass had just had its bank robbed not more than a week ago. But it was a small town made up mostly of Mexicans. The town's population was a whopping 312 people not including the goats, pigs, chickens and two burros. The burros belonged to Pedro Allee. Pedro Allee is the town's loafer who occasionally would go out into the Mexican desert searching for rare and precious stone turquoise being the most frequently found.

The town's only sheriff is Wayne Appleton. A middle-aged man of fair stature with green eyes and brown hair with strands of silver growing through it. But he still had the quickness and alertness of men half his age.

"Only the two of you? Well, I reckon the Governor considers us a minor trifle. What with the war and all. But you're gonna need help, if the two of you can catch them at all."

"How much money did they get away with?" asked Major Drew Parker.

"Ha ha ha. That's the puzzling part. The bank only had $1500. This is a small town Ranger. We rarely have that much money in the bank ever. Why this town is so peaceful and out of the way, the banker George Lewis part times as bartender. We've never been robbed before now. How they knew about the money I just don't know," said Sheriff Appleton.

"How is it that your bank came to have so much?" asked Captain Whiskey Jack.

"A fella came by a while back with a herd of horses, fine animals too. He was here two or three days when this big mean looking fella with dark hair and a mustache rode in. Finely dressed I mean his clothes had that just washed and ironed look to them. Well, he rode in with about eight other men and took possession. He paid of course, which accounts for the $1500 you see. Then the next day they rode off taking the herd with them," said Sheriff Appleton.

"Did you happen to pay any mind to which direction they went?" asked Drew.

"No, not really. I mean they rode east out of town. But after that, no. I gave it not another thought."

"And this fellow who sold the horses do you remember his name?"

"Chet Marrow. Funny thing about him, he rode out with the rest. Now why would someone sell horses then ride off with them like some hired hand?"

"Could be that he was," said Whiskey Jack.

"What? I don't understand," said the sheriff.

"I have a feeling that this was all for show. Maybe the money was stolen. So this well-dressed buyer, who was probably the leader of the gang of outlaws, gets one of his men, Chet Marrow, if that is his name, to pose as a cattleman. The transaction and the sale are legally noted and in the bank. Now the money as far as anyone is concerned is legitimate. This Chet Marrow has opened an account in your bank as a legitimate cattleman. No one would suspect otherwise. Now all he has to do is to make regular deposits. Like you said, this is a small town and out of the way. No lawman would give it a second thought as an outlaw's nest egg. It could also be that Chet Marrow is the real leader and not the well-dressed man," said Drew.

"When they find out that their money has been stolen from them there's going to be trouble. They will tear this town apart. Thinking it was a local inside job," said Whiskey Jack.

"Exactly. Which is why we have to find those bank robbers," replied the sheriff.

"We? You can't go, Sheriff," said Whiskey Jack.

"And why is that? This is my town, is it not?"

"Sure, but someone needs to be here for the town."

"I don't know, hermano, maybe we should all stay," said Whiskey Jack.

"Stay? And let those fellas get away scott free?" exclaimed Drew.

"The way I see it, they already have. But what if Chet Marrow or whoever he is and his gang return with another deposit or worse for a withdrawal?" said Jack.

"Ya, I see what you mean."

"Hermano, I hate to say this. Can we get our hands on $1500 muy pronto?" asked Jack.

"Oh, no, no, no, no sir!" replied Drew.

"We'll give it back," said Jack.

"Uh huh, just suppose it's what you said. Instead of a deposit, they make a withdrawal? No!" Drew reiterated.

"It's our only insurance to saving this town. If they do make a withdrawal, they won't be the wiser. If not, once we take down their gang, we take back the money. One thing is certain. The original $1500 is most likely never going to be recovered. Our only hope is some cheese for the rats," explained Jack.

"Rats?" said the sheriff.

"Whoever took the money has a man on the inside. If whomever it is learns of another large deposit he may tell his friends and they may just be bold enough and arrogant enough to try again," said Jack.

"That's one hell of an expensive piece of cheese, Jack!" said Drew.

"Whatever we do, it better be before our cattleman Mr. Chet Marrow returns," replied the sheriff.

Against his better judgment, Drew sighed and said, "All right, but you are going to get it. I am staying here with Sheriff Appleton. But you better hurry. I don't know if we may already be too late."

"Who? Me? All right, I'll go. Coward, you always do this to me," said Jack.

"Hey, it was your idea," laughed Drew.

When Whiskey Jack returned four days later the town looked just as he had left it. Children played near a water trough, splashing one another. An old woman was sweeping dust and dirt from the front door of her house. Several young women were sitting in the shade of a lean to weaving baskets and talking. A middle-aged man, presumably the butcher, apron stained with blood and holding a meat cleaver was staring out the door of a small building. As Jack neared the sheriff's office, Drew stepped outside and waved him on toward the bank.

"So far, so good," said Drew in an even voice so low as not to be overheard.

"I'm not sure if that's good or bad," said Jack.

"I'd say up till now it's been a good thing seeing that we didn't have the money yet," replied Drew.

"I suppose you're right," said Jack.

They put the money in the bank and then proceeded to let it be known by speaking casually and openly about it in the cantina and dining house. They were hoping to draw out any informants and then follow them to their hideout. So far nothing had happened.

About three days after Jack had arrived with the money, something did happen. Mr. Chet Marrow showed up in town. He checked himself in at the only hotel in town, Amy Long's Boarding House, then proceeded to the Eagle Pass cantina. He found a table far in the back of the cantina which offered him a full straight on view of both the front door and the rear door of which was more or less a side entrance actually. One by one, Drew, Jack and Sheriff Appleton entered the cantina each trying to make their arrival look as casual and non suspicious as possible. It was during the noon time and lunch was being served.

Chet Marrow was no fool. He had spotted the three lawmen almost immediately upon arriving into town. That and the fact that he had seen Drew leaving the sheriff's office from the boardinghouse window as he was checking in. Also, he had made it a point to discreetly check the register for names of any other boarders. "Ha ha, you're good fellas but not good enough." Chet chuckled to himself. He noticed Drew approaching in his direction and pretended to be oblivious to Drew's movements. He read the menu that had been placed upon his table.

"Excuse me, you mind if I sit down? I'm a stranger in town and I hate to eat alone," said Drew.

"No, no. Not at all! As a matter of fact I would welcome the company. My Spanish isn't that good. So, as you would guess, conversation has been a might thin," said Chet Marrow.

"Yes, I suppose it would be. Nice quiet little town though, wouldn't you say?" said Drew.

"Just the way I like 'em. Don't like big towns myself. Never seem to be able to get a good night's sleep as compared to towns like this. My name is Chet Marrow."

"Pleased to meet you. I am Drew Pena. My father was Mexican."

"Can't hold that against you. We have to have a father, right? Besides I'm not the prejudiced type. I have a lot of Mexican friends," said Chet.

"You're right there. Besides I found that to judge a man by his family can be very misleading for lack of a better word. It's the company a man keeps that gives them away," said Drew.

"True, so true. Would that we would all feel that way," replied Chet. "Uh, menu?"

"Yes. Thanks. Hmmmm, not the same as yesterday's. They must change up every so often. Good food though."

Drew was reading the menu when Jack walked through the front door. He glanced around acting innocent and smiling. He scurried over to the table were Chet Marrow and Drew were sitting.

"Hey! Good morning, Drew. Who's your friend here?" asked Jack.

Drew looked up from the menu and smiled. "Good morning. This is Mr. Chet Marrow. Chet, Whiskey Jack. Chet and I were just getting ready to order something to eat."

"Sounds like a plan to me. Mind if I join you?" replied Jack.

"I don't know. You will have to ask Mr. Marrow."

"No, no, please. The more the merrier." Chet was having a good time with the two men in their little game of deception.

Unexpectedly, much to the surprise of Drew and Whiskey Jack, a third man walked into the dining hall. He was clean shaven, his clothes, though obviously not new, were clean and well pressed as if he had just put them on after a Chinese laundry. His dark hair was combed and parted on the left. He wore high topped, shiny, black riding boots. His shirt was a lavender color with a black bow tie.

"Hello, Chet," said the man.

Drew glanced up to see who it was and nearly fell backward in his chair. He stood up abruptly.

"Captain! I mean Colonel. What brings you to Eagle Pass?"

The man laughed heartily, "Relax, Drew. Chet Marrow, I see you've met."

"The infamous Major Drew Parker? Yes, sir, I have. We were having a little fun playing button button," laughed Chet.

"You mean you already knew who I was? Why, you scoundrel you!" laughed Drew.

"Yes, I recognize you from your description. That and I saw your name on the boardinghouse register. You know, you're quite famous in the halls of headquarters and the governor's mansion. Your exploits are already examples for new Ranger recruits," said Chet.

Humbly Drew replied. “Awhh, come on now! I wouldn’t go that far.”

“Him, famous? Why, I’m the real brains in this outfit,” said Jack.

“Now, Jack, you’re right up there with him. Although the governor is reluctant to agree. But in headquarters you and Drew are high examples of what Rangers should be,” replied Colonel John “Rip” Ford.

“Colonel, what’s going on here? You know, we had you figured for a couple of outlaws and horse thieves. I guess I should tell you. Shortly after Chet here had deposited that $1,500 someone robbed the bank,” said Drew.

Drew was explaining the events that had taken place up to this point when Sheriff Appleton walked in as well.

“Sheriff, let me introduce you to Colonel John “Rip” Ford and...”

“Sergeant Chet Marrow.”

“Sergeant Chet Marrow. Our notorious outlaws,” said Drew.

“Santa Maria! Now I’m as dizzy as a man on a three day bender. Colonel “Rip” it sure is a pleasure to meet you. Yes, sir! So now what? Seems we’re back where we started,” said Sheriff Appleton. The men sat and talked for several hours.

“Colonel, what I can’t get a grasp on is why of all places in Texas, you chose Eagle Pass to buy and sell horses? Surely you could have chosen one of the ranches around here. Many have good reputations and stock. Why here?”

“That’s a fair question, Drew. But I’m afraid I can’t tell you. Military secrets and all that. That fifteen hundred dollars was supposed to go to buying provisions to be picked up at a later time. Our masquerade was meant to prevent any unwanted attention obviously. No one would suspect someone making such small deposits. Especially here,” said “Rip” Ford.

“So the fifteen hundred was one of several deposits to be made. Gradually building a stock pile of revenue?” said Whiskey Jack.

“Does this have anything to do with the 1st Regiment of Texas Mounted Riflemen and the Texas line of defense?” asked Drew.

“How did you come to hear of that?” asked Sergeant Chet Marrow.

“Many families have loved ones in the Army, Sergeant. Plus you forget, I am a Texas Ranger,” replied Drew.

"Ya, I know. The famous Captain..."

Drew interrupted. "Major Drew Parker."

"Yes, Major Drew Parker," replied Sergeant Chet Marrow.

"I'm sorry, Sergeant, did I offend you or something?"

"No," Sergeant Marrow excused himself and left the room.

"Touchy, ain't he?" said Jack with a slight chuckle in his voice.

"He's strong-willed and bullheaded but is a good soldier. He'll grow out of that I can do anything you can do attitude in time. If he lives that long. Don't let him get to you," said Col. "Rip" Ford.

"May I suggest something, Colonel?" asked Drew.

"Why most certainly and I thank you."

"I've been mulling over this, that and the other. Could it be that you have an informant in your ranks?" said Drew.

"Oh, Drew, come on now! This is Colonel John "Rip" Ford you're talking to," said Whiskey Jack.

"That's quite all right, Jack. Drew could be right. Seems I may have crossed all of my 'T's' but one. T for traitor!" exclaimed Col. John "Rip" Ford.

"It's just a thought, Colonel, but what if I'm right?" asked Drew.

"That Maj. Parker, I will leave to the Texas Rangers to find out. Of course, I will do my own investigation but this is a civilian matter. If the man or men you find responsible happen to be mine then and only then will I step in," stated Col. John "Rip" Ford.

About a week later Drew had just stepped out of the barbershop after having a haircut and shave. He was putting on his hat when he thought he saw Sgt. Chet Marrow talking to Pedro Allee next to a small corral at the end of town. Drew stepped back into the darkened corner in an alley between the barbershop and a small house. He watched as Chet Marrow and Pedro Allee talked. Pedro nodded profusely and had a nervous look about him and was pointing to the South. What was actually being said Drew could not hear. Drew decided to keep this to himself. For all he knew the Sgt. might be conducting an un-official investigation of his own. Drew felt it prudent to keep silent, watch the Sergeant and to see where it led. When Sergeant Marrow left Drew decided that he would follow Pedro and see what came of it.

"Whatcha doin'?" Drew was startled and turned quickly around with his right hand hovering over his revolver.

"Jack! Don't ever sneak up like that. You of all people should know that!"

"Heck, hermano. I thought you heard me coming."

"Did it look like I heard you?"

"You're getting slow. Unless you have had something else on your mind real bad. You've been off your game for some time. I was going to let you ride it out, but..."

"But what? I'm just fine!"

"Sure you are. It's Marjorie and the baby, yes?"

"No. Well, maybe a little. She wasn't feeling well when I – when we – left. I told her I could pass this assignment on to someone else but she said, "I see the need to go in your eyes. You're a Ranger and you miss it. Maybe this will get it out of your system for a while?" Dang my fool hide! I should've stayed home," said Drew.

"Was she right? Were you missing it?" asked Jack.

"I don't know. Maybe a little," replied Drew.

"She's a wise woman with an army of help. She'll be fine. Mother and Don Miguel will make sure of that," said Jack.

"Perhaps you are right."

"What were you staring at?" asked Jack changing the subject for Drew's sake.

"I thought, no, I'm certain I saw that Sergeant Marrow down at the corral. He was talking to Pedro Allee and Pedro didn't look too happy either," said Drew.

"Could you hear them? What did Sergeant Marrow have to say?"

"No, I couldn't hear. Pedro kept pointing to the south whatever that meant," said Drew.

"One way to find out. The ride might do you some good. You think better when you're in the saddle," said Jack.

The Rangers followed Pedro Allee's trail at a slow and even pace. Allee had traveled south along the Rio Grande. For most of that day the ride was tolerable and not very hard on the horses. They had been on Allee's trail for nearly six hours. Once Allee stopped and built a small fire, most likely to prepare something to eat and coffee. The Rangers didn't want to apprehend Allee, just see where he was going and who he was meeting up with. Soon the terrain started to become more difficult. The trail grew rockier and dipped in and out of dry washes and ravines making travel difficult without being heard. They had traveled about 14 miles when suddenly the trail dipped down the face of a cliff some 800 or 900 feet along a switchback trail that zigged and zagged on the way down to a canyon floor. On either side of the canyon stood rock walls and crags that jutted out angrily. The Rio Grande flowed lazily through a mile long canyon. Then they saw Allee. Allee was not aware he was being followed and moved along steadily. He was astride a gray colored horse and riding bareback.

"There he is," said Jack.

"I see him," said Drew. At the end of the canyon the land grew flatter with only a few sparse signs of vegetation.

"Reckon he'll across the river?" asked Jack.

"If he does, we can't follow. It's a wasted day," said Drew.

"Look!" exclaimed Jack, "Up in those hills."

Drew looked where Jack was pointing and saw a flash of light. "Probably from a pair of binoculars or a rifle barrel," he said, "He'll never hear us from here. If we get in a hurry we might injure one of our horses. Let's hope whoever it is hasn't seen us as well."

The Rangers rode on, keeping a safe distance and pace. If they got in a hurry whomever was on that cliffside might see their movements or their horses could kick up dust clouds and they might be spotted.

"Do you think it's an ambush? Or could he be meeting someone?" asked Jack.

Drew replied, "I'm not sure. But I don't want to ride into it either. Let's hold up here. If it is an ambush, we'll hear. We'll wait about 10 minutes or so and ride on. I want to see what's up there."

"I wonder where he got a horse and what became of the two burros?" asked Jack.

"Good question. Another reason to see what's ahead," said Drew.

They waited and watched. Pedro Allee was out of sight and all was quiet.

"I haven't heard anything. Didn't see any smoke from a rifle shot either," said Jack.

"Which probably means we can't go any farther or else we'll get spotted. If we haven't been already," said Drew.

"So what now?" asked Jack.

"We wait, what else?"

"Wait where? Can we build a fire for coffee? I'm a might hungry as well."

"I saw a spot aways back near the river. It looked hidden enough to have a small fire and we'll be near the water. The horses will like that," said Drew.

"Sounds good. I was afraid of a cold camp. I'm so hungry I could eat a skunk," said Jack.

"When aren't you hungry?"

"Hey! What can I say? I'm a growing young man," replied Jack.

"You're growing all right. But in all the wrong places," chuckled Drew.

"What are you trying to say, hermano?"

"I'm saying you're getting fat."

"Fat!" exclaimed Jack.

"Yes. Fat."

They set up camp in a low pocket that was shielded by 6 to 8 feet tall walls on either side. Cacti and mesquite brush along with a few scrub oaks lined the top of the walls and river banks. A small thirty foot clearing made up the bank of the river.

"Nice spot. Surprise you even noticed it," said Jack.

"I probably wouldn't have but I thought for a moment that Pedro was going to cross the river here. But he must have changed his mind."

"San Rodrigo River, Nava, Piedras Negras, Zaragoza," Jack was mumbling and thinking out loud.

"What was that you said?" asked Drew.

"Hmmm? Oh! Nothing really. I was just trying to remember what was over on the other side. I mean towns, villages and such."

"You think there could be Union spy camps there?" asked Drew.

"No, I doubt Mexico would allow Union anything. Mexico is more sympathetic toward the South," replied Jack.

Drew held out an empty cup in one hand and a pot of steaming hot coffee in the other. "Coffee?"

"Gracias," said Jack.

"How much do we know about Pedro Allee? I mean family wise: wife, children, parents?" asked Drew.

"As far as I know he's just an old bum, a drifter. Folks back at Eagle Pass really didn't tell me much on that matter anyway. Seems they tolerated him and that's all. He hasn't been in any trouble that I know of. Why?"

"I'm not sure. Just curious," said Drew.

Morning came. The sun was casting orange and yellow streams through the darkened morning clouds. A slight misty fog hovered over the river. A slight breeze drifted south by southwest. The water in the Rio Grande glided slow and lazy barely making a sound. If not for an occasional piece of driftwood one would not even notice the water movement at all. A dove cooed softly in the distance.

Drew knelt down and dipped the small cast-iron pot into the water. Then using the small pot as a wash basin, he took his neckerchief and soaked it in the water. He washed his neck, face and arms. Then slowly poured the water from the pot over his head and washed his hair. After rinsing his hair several times, he reached into his shirt pocket and took out a comb and combed his hair. Then he put his hat back on, rinsed the pot out, refilled it. He walked back toward the campsite.

Jack was stirring in his bed roll. He sat up, yawned and stretched his arms out wide. "Coffee smells great. Whatcha got cooking there?"

Drew lifted the lid from the large cast-iron skillet and answered, "Biscuits, boiled jerky and grits."

"Boiled jerky?"

"To soften it then I mixed it with the grits," explained Drew.

"I'm so hungry I'm not going to complain. Besides it smells pretty good. Did you hear anything this morning?" asked Jack.

"Nope, not a thing. Except for your snoring, it was a peaceful watch."

"Snore? I do not snore!"

"If you say so."

"I say so!"

Suddenly Drew heard the clacking sound of horse's hooves upon rock and gravel.

"Sshush! Do you hear that?"

"I hear it now. Someone is coming," said Jack.

Drew quickly poured the remaining coffee from the coffee pot onto the fire putting it out.

"Saddle up. Could be trouble," said Drew.

The two Rangers quickly saddled their horses and led them on foot to the side of the small trail. They mounted their horses and waited. Drew had his rifle laying across the pommel of his saddle. Jack pulled his revolver.

"One or two?" whispered Jack.

Drew looked at Jack and shrugged. "Hard to tell with all that echoing from the canyon."

They remained quiet and waited. It was Pedro Allee on the same gray he had ridden on the day before. He was leading a pack mule that was lightly loaded with some burlap sacks and other goods. The burlap sacks full of something lumpy and round. Pedro was not expecting to meet anyone on the trail. As far as he knew, he was one of the few people that even knew the trail existed. He and whomever he was secretly meeting.

As he rode up to where the two rangers were waiting, Drew spurred his horse out into the middle of the trail in front of Pedro. Jack circled behind him.

"Hold it right there, Allee!" commanded Drew.

"Madre e Dios! Quien dice eso?" said Pedro.

"Texas Rangers. Don't move. Hands up in the air high. Now! Ahora mismo!"

Pedro looked around and behind him and there he saw Jack. "What is this? I have done nothing."

"Just stay still and you will be all right. Jack, check him for a weapon," commanded Drew.

"I have no gun. No weapon," said Pedro.

"Maybe not a gun. In his boot, Jack, a knife. Get it. What's on the pack mule, Pedro?"

"Nothing to concern you. What's this all about?" asked Pedro.

"Where's Sergeant Marrow? We know you met with him. Where is he?" asked Drew.

"I don't know what you are talking about. I don't know any Sergeant Marrow."

"Don't lie to me, Allee. We saw the two of you talking near the corral in Eagle Pass. But if you want to hold to that story, that's fine. Jack, search the mule. I'm afraid we are going to have to confiscate that mule and all that is on it. Your horse, too. "

"Confiscate? What is meaning of confiscate?"

"It means we will have to hold it as evidence until after the hanging. Or a firing squad," explained Drew.

Said Jack as he searched the packs on the mule, "The Army doesn't do any hangings. They just shoot you."

"Ha ha ha, you don't scare me. I'm not a soldier. No one is going to shoot me."

"Oh, I think you are working for the Union Army. That makes you a mercenary soldier. Held to Army rules and regulations. Worse yet, you are a spy. So you'll face a firing squad just the same as Sergeant Marrow," said Drew.

"Nothing in the packs except for some clothes. The rest is food supplies and utensils and such," said Jack.

"Spy clothes," said Drew.

Allee began to get nervous, angry and somewhat frightened.

"Please, those are not spy clothes. They are for my family."

"I'm sorry to hear that, Pedro. Just tell me where to take them and I will," said Drew.

"You will take them? What does that mean?"

"Well, you will be dead. If you want to write down any parting words. I will take that to them as well," said Drew.

Jack was searching through Pedro's coat that had been rolled up and tied behind his saddle. "Well, my, my, my. Will you look at this?" Jack held up a small yellow leather pouch. "There must be at least $100 here. Mostly in gold coin. Reckon how he got his hands on this?"

"Part of the money stolen from the bank in Eagle Pass most likely," said Drew. "All right, enough of this. We best be on our way. Colonel "Rip" Ford will be interested in all of this as well."

------------//------------

The bell in Eagle Pass was ringing. Music was coming from the cantina. There were at least a dozen horses tied up in front. Four horses were in front of the bank and four more in front of the sheriff's office.

"Army horses? What's the Army during here? I thought Colonel "Rip" Ford was going to leave this up to us?" said Drew.

The Rangers escorted their prisoner into the sheriff's office. Colonel "Rip" Ford was sitting at the sheriff's desk. He lifted his head up from the letter he had been reading when Drew and Jack entered.

"Major Parker, Captain Jack, I've been expecting you. Who is this hombre with you?"

"From all appearances, Colonel, I would have to say a spy and a bank robber," said Drew.

"Spy? You don't say. And Marrow?"

"We were not able to apprehend him this time. But we will," said Major Drew Parker.

"Not alone. Next time I'm sending help," said Colonel "Rip" Ford.

"With all due respect, Colonel. I thought you said that this was a civilian matter and that you were going to leave this to the Rangers," said Drew.

"Yes, I did. I also said unless I have proof of Marrow's guilt. Or something to that effect."

"That's true enough but we haven't any proof and this fella here isn't talking. At least not enough to point fingers in Sergeant Marrow's direction. What's got your feathers ruffled up?" asked Drew.

"Sergeant Marrow has been AWOL for over three days. Either he has deserted or has got himself into some trouble. Take that into consideration and adding the bank robbery I'd say I had reason enough to suspect him as being a traitor or spy. If nothing else at least a deserter," said Colonel "Rip" Ford.

"I don't claim to know military matters, Colonel, but I'm going to have to say, no thank you," said Major Drew Parker.

"If Sergeant Marrow is one of those who robbed the bank, and I suspect he is, then you are going to need help. Marrow is not going to be easy to apprehend. He is bound to have a fair number of men with him. Most likely Union soldiers. That makes it an Army matter," said Col. "Rip" Ford.

"Again Colonel, with all due respect, I decline any offers of help. I have never been afraid of the thought of dying. But I'm not anxious to get the job done either. If your Sergeant Marrow is with those who robbed the bank, we will get him. I promise you that. But I will get him my way. I also do not want to carry the thought that I may have been the reason for a bunch of soldier boys being massacred," said Major Drew Parker.

"What do you mean, massacred?" asked Col. "Rip" Ford.

"We followed Pedro Allee to a canyon along the Rio Grande and saw signs of look outs posted along the rocks and mesquite along the canyon wall on our side of the river. If anyone were to try to go through that canyon, they'd be cut to pieces. They would not stand a chance. You'd do well to just stay here and mind the town. Jack and I will get your man, I promise. If you truly want to help, you can start with getting Pedro there," Drew pointed to the jail cell in the back of the sheriff's office, "Question him and get him to tell what he knows."

"All right, if you insist but I think you're making a mistake by rejecting my offer of help," said Colonel "Rip" Ford.

"Maybe so, Colonel. But it would be my first. Jack and I know this territory and should we get killed it's much better and acceptable than some of the men. But we won't get killed. You are setting up headquarters here in Eagle Pass, Colonel?"

"Not exactly. Although we are commandeering the town. Eagle Pass is to become one of the many outposts for the 1st Regiment Texas Mounted Riflemen. Which reminds me. They could use men like you two. So have you given thought to join the ranks of the Confederacy?" asked Colonel "Rip" Ford.

"We had, Colonel. But the governor got to us first. What with nearly every Ranger already enlisted, the Texas Rangers are all but none. Texas will need peace officers more than ever now. Every undesirable walk of life will see the towns and those who remained in them as easy pickings. The local sheriff and town marshalls will most certainly be limited in manpower and experience enough to form any decent opposition to protect the towns while other men have gone to war. So you can see how we were obligated to take the job. We will be attached to the frontier Regiment," said Drew.

"Yes, yes. I suppose you're right," said Colonel "Rip" Ford.

"If it is all the same to you, Jack and I will be leaving in the morning."

"Very well then. I wish you luck. But I still think you'd do well to take some of my men along with you."

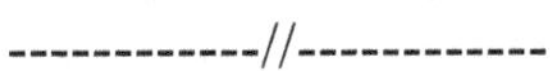

About 25 miles south of Eagle Pass along the Rio Grande was a small village by the name of Casas Siete made up predominantly of Mexican farmers. It was the idea of the two Rangers to travel south by-passing the approximate location of where they had lost sight of Pedro Allee and had seen the look out posts along the canyon wall. They wanted to approach from the south in the hope of a more open line of vision and surprise their quarry. All of this hinged on the idea that the terrain flattened out at the canyon's end.

Riding to the tiny village of Casas Siete they received a cold welcome. In fact, they got no welcome at all. With the exception of three middle-aged men who stood under a straw canopy of the one and only excuse for a cantina which bore no name. The three middle-aged men were standing and talking most likely about the usual, the weather, crops and livestock. Their conversation came to an abrupt halt as Drew and Jack drew near. One of the three farmers looked up with wide and curious eyes and a wide toothy smile.

"Hola, senors. Como esta? Por favor, sit. You thirsty and maybe hungry. We have beer, tequila, plenty beans and rice and chicken."

"Gracias, amigo. That sounds good right now," said Jack as he slid down from his pony.

The two Rangers were no strangers to such small villages as Casas Siete. South Texas was full of them the farther south one went. They were shy people at first with the exception of a few old-timers whose time and wisdom were more open to reading strangers. They knew there was little a man would want from a small village such as this except maybe food and lodging. Chances were they would move on in the morning.

"Disculpa, por favor. Que camino es el corral?" (Excuse me, please. Which way is the corral?) asked Drew.

"Ir al derecha. Quiero que te muestre el camino? (Go right. Want me to show you the way?)," asked the proprietor of the cantina.

"No, no. Gracias, I think I can find it," said Drew as he led his and Jack's horses to the corral. When Drew returned, Jack had already taken a seat at a table and had ordered food and drink for himself and Drew. As he approached, he noticed Jack eating as if he hadn't eaten in a week.

"You better slow down or you'll choke. Dios mio!" said Drew.

"I'm hungry! And this is the best chicken I have eaten in months!" said Jack.

The proprietor of the cantina strolled over to their table holding a large clay pitcher. "More beer for you, senors? Will you two be staying the night?"

"Si. Mas cervesa para mi. Cuanto es habitacion? (Yes. More beer for me. How much is a room?)" replied Drew.

"For both of you? Cinco pesos. That includes the food," said the proprietor.

"Cinco pesos? That is mighty kind of you. I would also like a bath. I will pay extra. Puedo ver su casa de banos? (May I see your bathhouse?)

"There is no charge. Please, por favor, you are at home and you may do as you please. There are fine towels, soap and a dish and other things you may need at your service."

"You are a fine host. Be careful though. You do not want to spoil us. We may never leave," laughed Drew.

"Por favor, disculpa. I do not wish to pry into what is not my business, but are you...?"

Drew cut the proprietor short, "In trouble? No sir. Nor are we outlaws. May I ask your name? Como se llama usted, por favor?"

"Alberto Sanchez. Como se llama usted, Señor?"

"I am Drew Parker and this is mi hermano, Jack. Do you have trouble with bad men coming here?"

Alberto's face flushed and he stared into space as if contemplating an answer. Then, making up his mind, he answered, "We have had other visitors, si. Gringo visitors. If they are outlaws I do not know but I do not trust them. Why do you ask?"

Drew decided to confide in Alberto. They would need an ally in Casas Siete. "Alberto, mi amigo. We are Texas Rangers. I would ask that you tell no one of this. We are on the trail of some hombres muy malo. One hombre in particular. Maybe these men are the same ones."

"Dios mio! I knew it. I knew you were good men the second I saw you. I have prayed to the Blessed Virgin and she has sent you," Alberto said as he made the sign of the cross over himself.

"Please tell no one. We are just out of work vaqueros. Comprende?"

"Si."

"Is there anything else you want to tell us, Alberto?" said Jack.

"Aye chihuahua! Si. It is my daughter, Consuela. She is fond of one of these men. I have told her he is no good. But she does not believe me."

"Does this gringo have a name?" asked Jack.

"He calls himself Chet. That is all I know."

"His name is Chet Marrow and he is a very dangerous and unpredictable man. He is also a spy and a traitor to the Confederacy as well as being a bank robber. He and some of his friends robbed the bank in Eagle Pass."

"How can I be of help? She is my only daughter and my prize in life," pleaded Alberto.

"Relax, Alberto. We will protect you and your daughter. All we need from you is to tell us when they are coming or how often they visit," said Jack.

"Please do not be offended but how can two men protect us from 30 or 40 men?" asked Alberto.

"We only want Chet. Maybe we can capture him without having a shootout with the rest. Besides we are Texas Rangers," Drew said with a smile.

"Well, I don't know about you two hombres but I'm getting sleepy. So if you will show me to our room," yawned Jack.

"Of course. This way." Alberto showed the two men their room and bid them good night.

Two days had passed since the Rangers arrived in Casas Siete and in those two days they had taken the time to learn the countryside and to talk with Consuela Sanchez. It was hard for Consuela to consider that the young man she was sweet on could possibly be a bad man. "But he is always so polite and he has never done anything to go beyond being a perfect gentleman toward me. How can this be?" she sobbed.

"It is all true, Consuela. Believe me, we have no reason to lie and would not do anything to purposely break your heart. This Chet Marrow has been trained in the art of deceiving. He is a Union Spy and a traitor toward the Confederate Army. He and some of his friends, probably Union soldiers as well, robbed the bank in Eagle Pass. We do not wish to kill him. Only to capture him and take him back to Eagle Pass for trial. Then he will be turned over to the custody of the Confederate Army," explained Drew.

"But does not the Army shoot deserters and traitors?"

"Yes, that is true but Chet Marrow is the kind of man who is true to no one. To protect himself, he would think nothing of harming the people of this village and you. He is a Judas of the worst kind. I do not enjoy telling you this."

"I cannot believe such a thing of him. He said he loved me," Consuela began sobbing uncontrollably.

"No, I suppose you don't. Has it ever caused you to wonder where and how he gets his money and where he goes for such long times?"

"He say he is a cattleman. That he works for a ranch north of here is all I know. But I believe him and I love him too."

"I see. Consuela, do us a favor. Say nothing of this to him when he arrives. If what you say is true then we will not bother him. But for the sake of your father and the people of Casas Siete, let us do our job. Can you promise me that?"

"Si, for a little while." Consuelo looked at her father and at the Rangers then walked away. Drew could see that this was going to be no easy task. If Consuela could not keep her promise everything could blow up in their faces and possibly get many people hurt or even killed.

"We're going to have to nab Chet Marrow before Consuela has a chance to see him. I'm afraid her love for him will not allow her to keep her promise," Drew said looking at Jack and then at Alberto.

"Si," Alberto sighed. "I think what you say is true. But there is a way, I think."

"Oh? How is that?" asked Drew.

"Always, when he comes, he has a drink and then a bath. He always take a bath before seeing Consuela and having su comida," said Alberto.

"That could work! Is there any chance your daughter might get word to him first and spoil our chances at capturing him?" asked Jack.

"Si, so I will send her with some of the women who are going to the mission in Laredo. She will protest I'm sure, but she will go. Even if she decides to come back to the village, it will be too late I hope," said Alberto.

Alberto was correctly predicting Consuelo's protests but she went just the same. As far as she knew, she would be back before Chet Marrow and his men ever arrived. As fate would have it or call it divine providence Drew and Jack were just preparing to do some more scouting of the countryside, when one of the three men who were at the cantina on the day they had first arrived came walking hurriedly to the cantina and began talking to Alberto and pointing to the west and at the two Rangers. Alberto motioned for Drew and Jack.

"What's the trouble?" asked Jack.

"Bernardo say he see them coming. He was working in his field and saw their dust down the trail. Maybe a mile or maybe two. But they are coming."

"We have to hide our horses, Alberto. They will see them in the corral," said Drew.

"Just north of the village is a large thicket of scrub oak and mesquite. You would do well to hide them there," suggested Alberto.

"Good. Jack stay here. Find a place in the back and keep out of sight. I will hide the horses and circle around and come in from behind the cantina," said Drew.

"Right," agreed Jack.

Chet Marrow was followed by four other men. "Hola, Alberto. Como estas? Uno cervesa, por favor."

"Coming, Senor Chet. Hola! Como estas?" said Alberto.

"Hot, dry and thirsty. How about a hot tub?" replied Chet.

"As always, Señor, I will get it pronto."

"Say, where is everyone? The village looks deserted," said Chet.

"Hey, amigo! How about some grub?" shouted one of the men.

"Si, it will be done," Alberto answered the man then looked back at Chet. "No, Señor Chet. Not deserted. The women take some of the children and go to Laredo. To the mission. There they will enjoy the Mass at Church. Then they will shop and be on their way back in two days."

"Two days? What a pity. We will be gone," said another of the men.

"Never you mind. We haven't the time to celebrate on this visit anyway. We have a job to do," scowled Chet. "Now, about that tub?"

"Right this way. There are clean towels on the chair next to the tub," said Alberto.

Alberto led the way to the bathhouse and then turned back toward the cantina. As he nervously started down the little corridor, Drew signaled his attention. "Pssst! Alberto."

"Dios mio!" hissed Alberto, "Don't do that, Señor Drew. I almost made water on myself!"

Drew chuckled. "Sorry, amigo. Where is Chet?"

"He in the bathhouse."

"Bueno. Now go about your business. Keep the others entertained. As far as you know, Chet is still in the tub. From here on you know nothing. Comprende?" Said Drew.

"Si, si. And that is how I want it. Good luck and vaya con Dios," said Alberto.

Chet Marrow was settling in his tub of hot bath water as the two Rangers sneaked around the bathhouse to the rear entrance. They paused long enough to hear Chet Marrow splashing around. Drew looked at Jack and whispered, "You or me?"

"Flip you for it. Heads or tails?" said Jack.

"Heads."

Jack flipped the coin and let it land in the sand. "Heads it is. He's all yours. Be careful, hermano."

"Every second," said Drew.

Drew was just about to enter into the bathhouse when he and Jack were startled by a rustling sound coming from behind. Jack turned around just in time to see Consuela. She started to let out a warning yell and Jack, not knowing what else to do, struck her with a strong right fist in the jaw. Consuela folded like a limp dish towel. With a what was I to do look, Jack shrugged. Looking at Jack, Drew shook his head. Then quietly and slowly he eased the back door of the bath house open.

Chet Marrow must have had soap in his eyes when he felt the draft of the door being opened and assumed that it was Alberto. He called out, "Alberto, more hot water, por favor."

Drew answered by walking behind Chet Marrow and placed the barrel of his revolver in Chet's right ear. Chet froze like a marble statue.

"One sound and you're dead," Drew threw a towel at him. "Now slowly stand up and dry yourself off then get dressed," commanded Drew.

"What? You're crazy. Loco!" said Chet.

"Shut up and get dressed. I'd just as soon take you in dead as alive. You're under arrest, Marrow. For robbing the Eagle Pass bank and for desertion from the Confederate Army and whatever charges Colonel Ford has in mind."

Chet stared at Drew for a moment and then replied. "I remember now. You're that Ranger. Parker, ain't it?" Chet Marrow was trying to ease his way over to the wooden peg in the wall that held his holster and revolver. He froze in mid-step when he heard the ratcheting of Jack's repeating rifle.

"Two of you? You'll both be dead soon!" Drew struck Marrow with a heavy chopping blow above the temple and Marrow collapsed to the floor. He was unconscious.

"Oh, great, hermano! What will we do now?" asked Jack.

"Carry him out behind the corral. I'll get the horses and meet you there," said Drew.

Jack started to argue. "How about you carry him?" He noticed he was alone. "Darn it! He always does this to me!"

They made their escape and were about two hours on the trail north back toward Eagle Pass when Chet Marrow regained consciousness. He had been draped over his saddle and tied. Marrow groaned. "Ummmph, aaahh! Hey, untie me. At least let me sit upright. My guts are churning like a riverboat wheel."

The Rangers stopped and allowed Chet Marrow to sit upright in his saddle.

"Only going to say this once. Don't get any ideas of escaping. We'll just shoot you," warned Drew.

"Ha ha ha. I ain't gonna escape. I ain't gonna run. You ain't gonna kill me either. My men will be on top of us before nightfall and you and your brother here will be my prisoners. I'll just enjoy the ride."

"That remains to be seen," said Jack.

"Even so, it wouldn't be a bad idea if one of us doubled back and checked the trail," said Drew.

"You or me?" asked Jack.

"Doesn't matter. Though I'd rather stay in case ol' Chet here decides to make a run for it," replied Drew. Jack turned his horse and started off.

"You sure all fired up anxious to put a bullet in me. Why?" asked Chet.

"Because you sicken me. There are a lot of good young men now wearing the uniform of the Confederacy. The same uniform you wore.

But you disgraced that uniform. You wouldn't make a patch on the long johns of the lowest private," replied Drew.

"Don't tell me. A brother? Couldn't be a son. He wouldn't be old enough," said Chet.

"No brother. No son. If he had been my son, I'd be proud. A young Lieutenant. One of my Rangers before all of this insanity," said Drew.

"And you? Why is it that you're not in dress grays?" Chet sneered.

"I would have gladly put on the uniform but the governor needs us here to protect the innocent from vermin like you." Drew was about to say more when Jack came riding up.

"Didn't see anything, hermano, but just in case we should leave the trail for a while and skirt the higher ground while we still have some. We'd be able to watch our backs a lot easier and if we have to put up a fight, I'd rather be looking down at them than up," explained Jack.

"Military man?" questioned Chet Marrow.

"No. Rangering and fighting Comanche, Kiowa, Apache, Comanchero and scum like you. I would say I had plenty of practice," said Jack.

"You ain't got no call to lump me in with the likes of no red skin or Comanchero!" protested Marrow.

"You're right. I apologize. Comanche and Apache and Kiowa deserve more respect than that. Thank you for putting me straight on the subject," said Jack.

"It's getting dark. We may as well look for a good place to set up camp for the night. They won't be following us in the dark. It hasn't rained for a while and the ground is too hard for them to read signs without daylight," said Drew.

An hour before first light, the two Rangers and their prisoner were on the trail. Once more it would appear that providence was on the side of the Rangers. Hidden within some mesquite and scrub oak, they had stopped to rest their horses and were looking down from a high hill when in the distance they could see Chet Marrow's fellow Union soldiers. As luck would have it, at the same time they could also see a band of Comancheros. Whether the Comancheros figured the civilian clothed Union soldiers were a posse no one will ever know. Or whether the Union soldiers believed the Comancheros were an enemy patrol. The Comancheros opened fire and charged headlong into the Union soldiers. The shooting was so intense, it sent the union soldiers scrambling for cover.

Chet Marrow looked on with widened eyes. "Do something! They'll be slaughtered! You have to do something! Don't sit there! Go help!"

Jack looked at Chet and then at Drew and almost spit out a laugh saying, "Let the two dogs fight. I say let's get the hell out of here muy pronto!"

"I agree, let's ride," said Drew.

"You can't be serious! They'll die!" said Chet Marrow.

"Reckon they will. But they are the enemy. Yankee soldiers. If we helped them, it would be betraying the Confederacy. Maybe we'll get lucky and they'll kill each other to the last man," said Drew.

"My God, you are a coldhearted bastard!" replied Chet.

"They should have stayed out of Texas," said Drew.

Two days later after having taken the long way around north by northeast and then cutting westward and into Eagle Pass, the Rangers arrived with their prisoner. They had reached the town line when they heard a shout. "Halt! Who goes?! Advance and be recognized." A young man of 17 or 18 stepped out in front of them from behind an old buckboard wagon. He was dressed in gray trousers and a brown shirt and wore a gray Confederate cap. He was wearing a Private insignia.

"Easy, son! We are Texas Rangers. I am Major Drew Parker and this is Captain Whiskey Jack. We are here with a prisoner and to see Colonel "Rip" Ford."

"Sir, yes, sir! Major Parker, sir. Only the Colonel ain't here. He left about two days ago," replied the Private. "Captain Campbell left instructions that if a Major Parker of the Texas Rangers was to arrive to send him straight to Headquarters immediately."

"Where is headquarters, son?" asked Drew.

"Same place as before I reckon, sir, over at the sheriff's office."

"Very well, Private. I'll be sure to let Captain Campbell know what a fine job you are doing."

"Sir, thank you, sir!" The young private snapped to attention and saluted.

"Spirited young fella," commented Jack with a smile.

"Yes, but he'll get over that in time. If he lives that long," replied Drew. "What's with you, Marrow? I figured you'd be happy to be among your comrades in arms. I'm certain they can't wait to see you again. They probably have a big welcome home party planned for you."

Chet Marrow did not reply. Instead he rode with his head hung low and his hat pulled down near his nose. A big burly man with curly strawberry blonde hair and gleaming hazel eyes stood on the stoop in front of the sheriff's office. The big man stood inquisitively with a pipe clenched between his teeth.

"Can I help you gents?" He said as the two Rangers approached with their prisoner.

"Major Drew Parker and Captain Whiskey Jack to see Captain Campbell and to deliver a prisoner."

"Stay put. I'll inform the Captain of your arrival," said the big man.

A few short moments later a tall, thin man with shoulder length brown hair and a mustache that hung low on either side of his mouth came bounding out the front door. "Gentlemen, please, come in! I am Captain Morgan T. Campbell at your service. Sergeant Major! Don't just stand there. Take the prisoner into the jail and lock him up. Place two guards at his cell window and two guards at his cell door."

"Yes, Captain. Consider it done," said the big, burly Sergeant Major.

"Please, excuse Sergeant Major Bowman. He's somewhat unorthodox but a top notch soldier never the less."

"Unorthodox?" asked Jack.

"Lax you might say. Doesn't quite hold to Army etiquette. If he had his own way he would only wear his uniform at parades. But the men respect him and obey him. For that I am grateful. Now! Enough of that. What can you tell me about our guest? All I know is that he is a deserter and possibly a spy. That in itself should be enough but the Colonel is demanding a detailed report. Sergeant Marrow will be escorted to San Antonio and there tried and sentenced. Most likely, shot."

"There isn't much to tell but we will try. I must say right off we were not able to retrieve the stolen money. Whatever you took from Pedro Allee is all you get. Sorry," said Drew.

"We were afraid of that. But this is war and those things are going to happen."

The Rangers talked for nearly two hours with Capt. Campbell. When they were done, Capt. Campbell was satisfied with the report and filed it with the company Yeoman.

The following morning after having had a hearty breakfast, the two Rangers rode back toward Uvalde. There would be a report to file to Ranger headquarters. If the past few days were any indication, life as a Texas Ranger was about to become very interesting and very deadly. Not just for the Rangers but for all of Texas.

**Woodsonville, Kentucky**
**December 17, 1861**
**9:45 am**

"Company! Halt! Lieutenant Parker!" barked Colonel Benjamin Franklin Terry.

Caleb spurred his horse forward at a trot then siding Col. Terry answered, "Yes, sir, Colonel."

"Lieutenant, our scouts report enemy troops not more than two miles ahead. We haven't time to wait on General Hindman and his infantry. I doubt they are in much shape to do any good anyway. Lieutenant, take a small squad of men and proceed on our left flank. The enemy will have to go to our left flank if they flush. They will not want to chance the Green River. If they do, then Captain Bastrop's men will have to handle it. Lieutenant, that's the 32nd Indiana volunteers, Colonel Willich's men. They're fighters so when you hit them, hit them hard and swift. Once they break stay on them. Do not let up. We cannot allow them to regroup and get organized. Is that clear, Lieutenant?"

"Crystal clear, Colonel. You can count on us, sir!" said Caleb.

"I have every confidence. Dismissed," saluted Colonel Terry.

Caleb returned his salute and rode to the rear formation to inform the squad. "Boys, the Colonel tells me there are Yankees up the road about two miles. They are the 32nd Indiana Volunteers. Colonel Terry says they are real fighters. He wants us to cover the left flank and drive them back to Indiana. He wanted me to choose our best men. I immediately thought of you. What do you say?" said Lieutenant Caleb Parker.

"Caleb! I mean Lieutenant. You know we're with you all the way!" exclaimed Private Johnny Brown.

"Sergeant O'Toole, get the boys to collect as much ammunition and extra firearms as possible. Go to the rear and collect from those that are sick."

"Yes, sir. Lieutenant, I'm one step ahead of you," said Sgt. O'Toole.

"You always were and that is just how I like it."

**December 17, 1861**

Colonel Terry took the main body of the 8th Texas Cavalry and proceeded north into Woodsonville, Kentucky. At 12:45 pm a Union infantryman spotted the 8th and sounded the alarm. The 32nd Indiana Volunteers were in no way prepared for an attack.

The 8th Texas charged into the Union encampment at a full gallop. As predicted, the 32nd Indiana Volunteers flushed. Many of them to the left flank with Colonel A. Willich commanding. The Union forces were moving so fast to form a skirmish line that they never saw Caleb and his squad of men. Caleb was surprised as well for he hardly had the chance to sound the charge. They were 35 yards away. Caleb looked at Hamelton O'Toole, a look of elation and surprise on his face. "Okay, give 'em hell, boys. Charge!"

The Rangers of the 8th Texas Cavalry under the command of Lieutenant Caleb Parker rode headlong into the Union 32nd Indiana. Screaming and howling like Comanche, they waited until they were within 10 yards of the Union soldiers before firing. They began with revolvers but soon they were so close they started firing their shotguns. The battle lasted about forty-five minutes. The Union lines broke and they retreated out of Woodsonville. That was the first of many battles that the 8th Texas Cavalry would be engaged in and the first of their many victories.

Shouts and cheers rose up all about but the victory celebration was to be short-lived.

A rider came galloping up to Caleb's squad. "Lieutenant! Lieutenant! Sir, come quickly. Colonel Terry has been killed."

"My God in Heaven! Corporal, are you sure?"

"Yes, sir, shot in the head. But he lived long enough to see you boys in action. He pointed and smiled. Then he went to be with the Lord," said the Corporal.

The 8th Texas Cavalry lost four men and three were wounded.

The Union losses were much higher. Seven prisoners were picked up as they had lost their bearings in the thick brush and briars that the Union soldiers walked smack dabbed into the camp of the 8th Texas Cavalry. They were promptly disarmed and sat down to be given hot food and coffee.

"We bear you no malice but you are our prisoners now. Behave and you will be treated fairly," said Lieutenant Caleb Parker.

"You boys can sure fight. I'll give you that," said Sergeant Major O'Toole.

"Apparently not good enough. We're your prisoners," laughed one of the Union soldiers.

O'Toole laughed and pointed at the young Union soldier. "Reckon you have a point there."

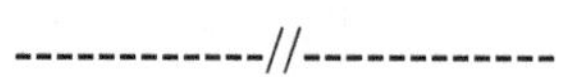

The death of Colonel Benjamin Franklin Terry was a hard blow to the 8th Texas Cavalry. He was highly respected by all of his men and equally loved. Colonel Terry was the 8th Cavalry. In the eyes of his men, an equal they would never find. It would be hard even for the governor to fill his boots. Lieutenant Colonel Thomas Lubbock was assigned to the daunting task.

"Well, someone had to take Colonel Terry's place. I reckon ol' Tom Lubbock is about as close as you can get." said a Confederate soldier. Caleb was taking a late evening walk around the campsite and had overheard the men talking. The soldier looked up. "How about you, Lieutenant? What's your take on all of this?"

"There's nothing to take on or from. Colonel Thomas Lubbock is Commanding Officer plain and simple. We will obey his commands," said Caleb. solemnly.

"Yes, sir. That's true enough. But do you think Colonel Lubbock has the same grit as Colonel Terry did?"

Caleb paused, stared into the dark of night and sighed. He wanted to speak truthfully. But the truth was he was an officer and knew what he must say in spite of himself.

"I suppose so. I suppose any man willing to ride out in front of his men in a hail of lead is worthy of some respect. That's enough grit for me. I'd follow a man like that."

"Yeah, reckon so but the 8th will never be the same without Colonel Terry. No disrespect meant. That's just my take on it is all," said the soldier.

Caleb smiled. "I suppose Col. Lubbock is of the same opinion. But it doesn't have to be that way. It could be better. After all, we are still Terry's Rangers and every battle we are in should be to bring honor to that name and of Col. Terry. I don't suppose Col. Lubbock would take a bit of offense to that."

"That's my kind of officer too, Lieutenant. Anything is better than being laughed at especially when it's the enemy doing the laughing. I swear I could hear them Yankees laughing for ten miles when the Colonel died. Ol' Jimtown Harrison, that's who I am afraid we'll get. I ain't fighting for a man who tucks tail and runs."

The young soldier was not alone in his resentment and distaste for Major Thomas Harrison. At Jamestown, Kentucky every Ranger, even those sick with dysentery and malnutrition, was ready to rain down Texas terror on Union forces in Jamestown. But Major Harrison, feeling he had inadequate forces both in numbers and in health, chose to retreat after having ordered troops to every flank spreading them out too thin. It was because of his haphazardness coupled with his reluctance to put up an actual fight that earned Major Harrison the nickname 'Jimtown Major'.

"I am not at liberty to give my opinion of Major Harrison but I can say Colonel Lubbock is a fighter," said Caleb.

The Rangers were kept busy through the month of January. They had been assigned to Brigadier General Hindman's brigade. Their jobs were reconnaissance and to wreak havock on enemy troops. It was during one of these missions just a few miles southwest of Nashville that the 8th came face-to-face with a Union Army patrol both infantry and artillery. Union forces were moving north. There were 40 Rangers on this reconnaissance mission and the Union numbered nearly 200. Being accustomed to Indian fighting, the Rangers were not deterred by numbers. Indian fighting had given them the edge they would need in combating superior numbers.

"There they are men. About 200. We can take them if we can take out the artillery unit. Lieutenant Parker, this time you will lead the attack. We will split up into equal units. I will be waiting a mile ahead up the road. My unit will be on both sides of that road and we will catch the Yankees in the cross fire. But we will wait on your unit to attack that artillery in the rear. Your attack will be our signal to attack. Are you prepared to lead the attack, Lieutenant?" asked Colonel Lubbock.

"Colonel, the boys and I have been waiting for some payback. We owe ol' Johnny Blue for Colonel Terry. Sir, we're ready. I'm ready, Colonel. This one is for Colonel Benjamin Franklin Terry. You need not worry about us. You just keep your men shooting straight."

"Good man! Proceed on your mission, Lieutenant. May God ride with you." Colonel Lubbock saluted and Caleb returned his salute.

"And with you, sir!" said Caleb.

The Union artillery came marching up the road and was now with their main body of infantry caught squarely between Lubbock's men, who had taken position on either side of the road. Colonel Lubbock was impatiently waiting for Lieutenant Caleb's attack.

"Come on, boy. What's keeping you?" Colonel Lubbock said to himself. He was nearing the end of his patience and was almost about to order his attack when he saw an unbelievable sight. Lieutenant Caleb Parker and 10 of his men had quietly slipped in behind the entire Union artillery detail and they were riding as if they were part of it. But their little prank was short lived. One Union soldier looked back and spotted Caleb and his men.

"Rebs! Rebs! On our rear!" That was the last words that poor soldier ever spoke. Private Terrence Todd let loose with both barrels of his shotgun. The young Union soldier was lifted off of his feet by the blast and his body flew backward landing on top of an ammo caisson for the artillery. Before the Union soldiers had actually grasped what was going on, more firing came from their flank. As the rest of Caleb's unit came swooping down upon them, screaming and shooting like wild demons from hell, Colonel Lubbock's men began their attack. The attack came so swiftly that the artillery unit had no choice but to run, surrender or die. Up ahead Col. Lubbock's men were having similar success. Some of the infantrymen chose to make a stand of it but were quickly persuaded to lay down their arms.

It was during this time of success that Col. Lubbock, enjoying such a swift and exact victory, was sitting upon his gray stallion, rallying his men. "That's the way, boys. That's how it's done! Bravo!"

A young Union soldier had climbed an oak tree and positioned himself on a limb halfway up the tree taking a sniper position. The shot came like a cannon booming. Colonel Lubbock was struck square in the chest. The bullet tore through his heart. He died instantly. The brave Union soldier had done his duty with honor but vainly so. Fourteen Rangers opened fire in unison answering his shot with a volley of rifle and pistol shots.

On February 20th,1862 Union forces had destroyed General Albert Sidney Johnston's line of defense. The Texans reluctantly retreated into Mississippi along with Johnston's Army. The 8th Cavalry served to protect Johnston's rearguard as the Army made its way into Corinth, Mississippi. During their stay in Corinth, the 8th Texas cavalry received new recruits. Among them was Clinton Terry, the brother of Col. Benjamin Franklin Terry.

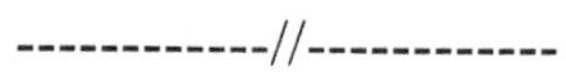

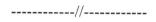

**April 9, 1862**

My Dear Family,

I am doing well. Tell the Major that the boys all say howdy. I suppose you may have heard the news. We have lost Col. Lubbock. I swear our next commander I will forcefully dress as a woman. It seems Yankees love shooting officers. The good ones anyway. How I wish I were home. I suppose the East is a fine place and certainly I have seen some beautiful countryside. But it isn't home. It isn't Texas. I suppose that is why God created so many types of creatures. The East is a fine place if you're a duck. I miss the smell of sage, mesquite and juniper. Most of all, I miss you. Abuela, I am still saying my prayers. Jenny, I think of you daily, little sister. Pray that this insanity ends soon.

Lieutenant Caleb Parker

Caleb, having been assigned as Officer of the Guard, was walking about the camp perimeter checking on the sentries who were on duty at that time. As he strolled across the camp, he was halted by a small group of men sitting around the fire, enjoying coffee and oatmeal cookies that had been supplied by the ladies auxiliary and temperance league. Among the group of men was Private Terrence Todd.

"Hey there, Lieutenant!"

Caleb walked on over to where the group of soldiers were sitting. "What can I do for you men?" Caleb asked.

"Figured to offer you a cup of coffee and some of these cookies. They are mighty good. Compliments of the ladies here in Corinth. How about it, Lieutenant?" asked Pvt. Todd.

"You know I would. Thanks fellas," said Caleb.

"Say, maybe you can help us with another problem," said another one of the soldiers. "Well, not really a problem problem. But the fellas and me.."

"The fellows and I," Caleb corrected the soldier's grammar.

"Uh, yes. Beg your pardon, sir."

"That's all right. Bad habit of mine, I guess. So what were you going to ask me?"

"Well, the fellows and I were thinking of our own special rallying call. Seems every unit has one 'cept us. The 8th Cavalry. You know? Something with spirit and fire to rally the boys together. Something that."

"I've got one," another soldier interrupted. "How about Help!?" The men around the campfire began to laugh loudly.

The soldier continued to joke. "Works for me. I holler help and folks seem to rally around me."

"Very funny. Seriously, got any ideas, Lieutenant?"

"Well, it seems to me that such a matter of a rally should come natural. Or perhaps by accident or just on their own. For example, whose idea was it to call us Terry's Rangers? Surely it was not Col. Terry. He was too humble a man to be naming an entire regiment after himself," said Caleb.

"I see what you mean," said the soldier.

"Besides, we're Terry's Rangers. That's a rally enough for me. Plus I don't think a rally call should be decided on like buying a new saddle," continued Caleb.

"Then Help! it is," laughed the other soldier.

The time spent in Corinth, Mississippi did volumes for the morale of the men of the 8th Texas Cavalry. When the order to pull out came, the men were in high spirits and well refreshed. From Corinth to Shiloh and on in to Chattanooga, Tennessee, the Rangers proved their metal. But not without losses. At Shiloh, General Albert Sidney Johnston was killed.

"Lord have mercy! We keep losing commanding officers. Who will they send next?" complained a young Cavalryman of the 8th Texas.

"Maybe Mrs. Whittington from the Corinth ladies temperance league," said another.

"If that would ever happen, it would be a glorious day for the Texas 8th Cavalry," spouted Sergeant Major Hamelton O'Toole.

"What's that supposed to mean?" asked one of the soldiers.

"It means that maybe some of you tumbleweeds might actually take a bath or the temperance league might get the job done," chuckled Sergeant Major O'Toole.

"Ha ha ha. Very funny, Sarge. I'll have you know I took a bath when we were in Corinth. How's them apples?" said a scraggly cavalryman of about 27 years old.

"I commend you on your effort, Private Poorman. But that was in April. It's nigh unto July and the air ain't getting any fresher," laughed O'Toole.

The Rangers were ordered under the Command of Brig. Gen. Nathan Bedford Forrest. They had been on the move since the loss of General Albert Sidney Johnston and had been in several skirmishes. Sad though they were, the 8th Texas Cavalry mourned each and every loss, counted themselves fortunate and the losses acceptable. They left Chattanooga on July 7th heading northwest into Murphreesboro, Tennessee. It was now July 12th. Ahead of them waited 2700 Union soldiers under the command of General Crittenden. Their presence spelled disaster for the Confederate supply shipments and the railroad from Nashville to Atlanta, Georgia.

## July 14, 1862 OFFICERS CALL

"Men, we have a full day's work ahead of us. General Crittenden's men are yonder." Brig. Gen. Mason Bedford Forrest pointed. They were positioned at the top of a small mountain. "Just below and on the other side of that meadow. We are going to crush that brigade or by God in heaven, we will die trying. Every last one of us. Gentlemen, the Confederacy's hopes of winning this atrocity they call a war, depends on the security of the railroad to carry supplies into Atlanta, Chattanooga and into Nashville. Not only for the Army but for the civilian citizens as well. Now, I am of the opinion that the Army can persevere but I cannot say the same for the women and children of Murphreesboro. General Buell's men will do their part. But I am a son of a jackal if I am going to be the reason children go hungry and cold! No, sir. I will not carry that on my conscience. Lord knows I have enough to answer for already come Judgment Day. Col. Walker, how are you feeling today?"

"Fine as snuff and twice as dusty, General Forrest, sir!" said Lieutenant Colonel John G. Walker.

"And you, Colonel Wharton, you ready for a long day?"

"Yes, sir! But I sure could use a drink right now. My rheumatism, sir."

"Are my lieutenants and sergeants ready?"

"Ready, sir! So are the boys!"

"Very well then. Assemble your men. Is that Padre still around?" asked General Nathan Bedford Forrest.

"I'll fetch him, sir!" said one of the sergeants.

The Confederate forces spread out about a half mile wide swatch and quietly proceeded down the mountainside until they reached the edge of the meadow. The 8th Texas Cavalry would lead the charge. The Rangers mounted their horses. Colonel Wharton gave his instructions. Lieutenant Col. Walker would be on the right, Capt. B. C. Wooten on the left. Caleb was assigned to Capt. Wooten on this charge. They would cross the meadow in a side by side, shoulder to shoulder formation. When they reached the midway portion of the meadow, Col. Wharton and the center would fade back slightly and the formation would assume a half-moon configuration allowing Col. Walker on the right and Capt. Wooten on the left positioned to prevent Union forces any chance of flanking maneuvers.

The 8th Texas Cavalry surprised the Union forces with such swiftness that some did not have the opportunity to get to their weapons. The Rangers came screaming and whooping and shooting with such fierceness that one soldier stood watching and peeing himself. Later he would say, "I thought the gates of hell were opened."

The attack would be a trademark for the Rangers and a style of fighting they would adopt for the remainder of the war. At the end of the attack, Confederate losses were nearly too few to mention. Of the 8th Texas Cavalry two losses and one wounded. The dead were: Private John J. Adaley; his horse stumbled and Pvt. John J. Adaley was thrown thus breaking his neck. Capt. B.C Wooten; mortal bullet wound to the heart. Lieutenant Colonel Wharton; gunshot wound to the left thigh.

Union prisoners – 1400 of General Crittenden's U.S. Army. Among the prisoners of war was Brig. Gen. Crittenden himself.

In true gentlemanly fashion and in regard to a fellow officer of West Point, Confederate Brigadier General Nathan Bedford Forrest offered a parole to General Crittenden. But Crittenden refused. "I will not bargain with a guerilla and a terrorist," stated Brigadier General Crittenden.

No one can deny Nathan Bedford Forrest of having a sense of humor. Nathan Bedford Forrest knowing his adversary very well promptly placed General Crittenden under guard. But not just any guard. Corporals Cotton and Smoot, two of the biggest, burliest men in the regiment. Their talk and teasing of General Crittenden was naturally all in fun but General T. T. Crittenden, believing that the two corporals secretly planned to kill him, reconsidered and accepted Brigadier General Nathan Bedford Forrest's offer of parole.

The supplies that were confiscated from the Union forces were much needed and well used. A man true to his word, Brigadier General Nathan Bedford Forrest rationed the food supply and sent most of it to the town of Murphreesboro.

As war raged in the easternmost part of the United States and the Texas 8th Cavalry were making themselves renown as the most effective and feared Army Regiment in the Confederacy, a small force of volunteers were struggling to keep the Texas borders and towns secure and also adding needed support to the Army.

The Texas Frontier Regiment was kept busy not only with repelling Union Army forces but also struggling to keep the Comanche and Kiowa as well as the Apache Indian raids to a minimum at best. Outposts were formed from Eagle Pass north to the Red River. Among one of these outposts was the Breckenridge outpost, Captain Howard D. Coaker commanding. Among the 26 men that usually occupied each outpost that were between 20 to 30 miles apart were former Texas Rangers of Company "D": Pvt. Daniel Collins and his brother, Pvt. Matthew Collins, Pvt. Jerolde Oaks, Pvt. Jubal Riley, Cpl. Sampson Riley and Cpl. Kyle Wiggins.

Since their conception at the onset of war in 1861, the Frontier Regiment had battled Comanches, Kiowa, Comancheros and Anglo outlaws with great success. But try as they might, they could not keep the folks at Elm Creek protected.

In October 1864, the air had cleared and the survivors were busy with the task of burying their dead and cleaning up the debris from the Comanche and Kiowa raid. Sixteen dead and seven women and children captured. The dank smell of charred lumber and flesh still lingered in the air.

"My God in Heaven! We have failed. We are too late. May God and the folks of Elm Creek forgive us," said Captain Howard D. Coaker.

A young boy, probably 13 years old, stood over the site of four graves. He raised his head. His eyes were bloodshot from crying his lips were trembling. "They're gone. They're all gone. What will I do? Where will I go now?"

"I am truly sorry. I swear to God, I am truly sorry," said Captain Coaker.

"Captain, do you want me to take a few of the boys and help with the burials?" asked Cpl. Kyle Wiggins.

"No, Corporal, that is something reverent and should not be intruded upon unless asked. I fear it could offend some of the folks, us showing up after the fact, only to bury folks. I know it would me."

"Yes, sir."

Corporal Sampson Riley, his brother Jubal and four others came galloping into town and reined next to Captain Coaker.

"Followed their trail out of town, Captain. Looks like most of them headed north toward the Canadian River. Others had turned west toward New Mexico Territory. They are most likely Kiowa or Apache," said Corporal Sampson Riley.

"Very good. We will rest our horses or a day or two and help the folks of Elm Creek."

"I say we get after them murdering Red Devils and kill them all!" said Jerolde Oaks.

"Twenty six men against three hundred? Not good logic, son," said Captain Coaker.

"All due respect, Captain, but we're Texas Rangers. Numbers never bothered us before. Especially Major Parker. Sir."

"That may be so but this is not the Texas Rangers. And I am not Major Parker."

"You can say that again," mumbled Jerolde Oaks.

"What was that?" asked Captain Coaker.

"Nothing, sir. Nothing at all."

Pvt. Colllins walked over beside Jerolde Oaks. "You take chances, Jerry."

"What's the worst he can do to me? Bust me down to private?"

"Well, watch it anyhow. You're too out spoken sometimes."

"Maybe so but it's true. Major Parker would have chased them down. You know that to be true yourself."

Danny Collins stared at the ground. "Ya," he replied then spat.

The following morning the regiment was awakened by the ringing of a church bell. The sun was shining through the boards of the livery barn walls. A rooster announced the arrival of a new day. Private Jubal Riley stepped out into the air outside of the barn. Oddly and to his wonder, the morning appeared clear and crisp. Everything about him including the trees, the building, the corral fencing, the sound of birds and even the livestock seemed bolder and more pronounced.

"Good morning, Private Riley," came the voice of Captain Coaker.

"Good morning, Captain. What day is it, sir?"

"I believe it is Sunday," replied Captain Coaker.

"That's what I figured too. With all due respect sir I would like to go to services. I believe we all have much to be grateful for and much to be forgiven for. Speaking for myself of course, sir."

"I'd be honored to go along with you. If you don't mind?" said Captain Coaker.

"Yes, sir, of course. The honor would be all mine."

Capt. Coaker, giving to each man to his own conscience and conviction, the opportunity to pray and attend Sunday services. Then after a late breakfast, they rode north toward the Canadian River.

The 1st Regiment Texas Mounted Riflemen followed the Comanche, having short skirmishes along the way. The main body of the Comanche never stopped to engage the Regiment. "Perhaps they consider us too few to be a real threat. Just enough of a nuisance to send an occasional scouting party to slow us down and to keep distance between us," said Capt. Coaker.

"Perhaps it could also be that there are military patrols around. Whether Confederate or Union, they might be trying to slip through the lines as quietly and quickly as possible," suggested Cpl. Riley.

"That's a very astute observation, Corporal," replied Capt. Coaker.

"That's just how I would do it if I were leading the Comanche."

"Who is leading this bunch, Captain? Is it that Chief Dancing Crow?" asked Private Marty Collins.

"Dancing Crow? He may be with them but he is not leading them. I hear tell it's a young buck named Yellow Pony," replied the Captain.

"I've heard of him. He's muy malo," said Private Carlos Montoya.

"Could be that Kiowa Chief Santana. I doubt any Kiowa would be involved without his approval or participation. But I could be wrong," said another private.

"Does it make any difference? Our job is to stop them and that's what we're going to do. Or bust a cinch trying," replied Captain Coaker.

There was no more talk for the rest of the day until they had made camp that evening.

"I don't get it. We're supposed to be protecting the people of Texas and the Confederacy and here we are with the Comanche and the Kiowa running rampant, killing and riding at will and we stop for coffee and biscuits?" said Private Jerolde Oaks in disbelief.

"Beats me. But the Confederacy is lost. Ever since they made slavery an issue to continue the war. As for the Indians, I will fight them as long as they continue to raid and kill. But I think we will have no problems worse than the Indian to worry about in the future. Since this was started I have thought hard about why we fight it and why it started. Wasn't over Negro slaves. Bet if they could answer, those that have died would agree. Only the rich and high and mighty could afford slaves anyhow. I wouldn't have any. Don't believe in it. But I'll tell you this. Not to say that there weren't any mistreated, God knows that some were. The poor devils. But them that I have seen had a better life than me. I say we should have freed the Negroes first then fought the Yankee. Lincoln's wife owned slaves. For that matter, so did many a Yankee. My Pa used to trade horses with William Tecumseh Sherman before the war and even he owned slaves. That's one murdering son of a hypocrite there. Yet many have the unmitigated gall to call the Indian savages and heathens. In Atlanta, Georgia Sherman burned alive over 260 women and children simply because they would not evacuate their homes. So he had their houses torched with them still in them. The Sacred Heart of Mary orphanage was torched, 87 orphans and three nuns burned alive. One of the nuns begged Sherman to spare the orphanage asking where could they go and with what would they feed them since Sherman's men confiscated all their food. Gen. Sherman laughed at her and said "They could eat slop and go to hell. Then he ordered the orphanage burned," said Private Matthew Newsome.

"Good God Almighty! Is that for true?" asked Cpl. Jubal Riley.

"As true as water is wet. Still have the letter from my sister Abigail. She was a nurse in Atlanta when Sherman set it afire. I'll let you read it if'n you want. We're going to be doing the same thing to the Indians. Seems to me their reasons for fighting are an awful lot like ours. Or were. At least that was my feelings when I first joined this insanity. But I took an oath and I will honor it. May God forgive me," said Private Newsome.

"May God forgive us all. Seems there will be enough on both sides to answer for when we give our accounts. But then there will be no lying to the Almighty, will there?" said Capt. Coaker.

"Is that why you are so reluctant to chase after the Comanche, Captain?" asked one of the men.

"Partly but mostly because of what you men have forgotten. There are Union Army patrols in the area. Our first duty is to fight the Yankee and I do not wish to fight two foes at the same time. We have done our duty as I see it and have driven the Comanche back into Indian Territory. I see no need to pursue them farther."

"But that's just it, Captain. We really didn't drive them anywhere. They were already going," said Cpl. Sampson Riley.

"If it will make you feel better you can say we escorted the Comanche north into Indian Territory," said Capt. Coaker.

"I meant no disrespect, Captain. Only I can't get Elm Creek out of my head. But I reckon that's why you're Captain and I'm just a Corporal."

"None taken, Corporal. In fact, I have seen many a corporal I would rather have led me in battle than commissioned officers. It only makes you less accountable to any mistakes. I wish sometimes that were the other way around. You're a good man and I'm proud to have you with me."

**November 24, 1864**

The afternoon sun was beating down like sunlight through a magnifying glass. The wind blew like a blast of heat from a furnace as he came out of the west. The grass crumbled beneath the horses' hooves with every step.

"Storm coming up, Captain," said Private Carlos Montoya.

"Nawh! Too hot. Besides there isn't a cloud in the sky," replied the Captain.

"I'm tellin' ya, it will be storming by nightfall. New Mexico blowing in," replied Private Montoya.

"Sand storm?"

"Si. Best look for cover muy pronto. It's going to be a long night."

"We can't be too far from Adobe Walls?"

"About a four hour ride to the west. Give or take. We might get there in time, sir."

**November 25, 1864**

Kiowa, Comanche and Mescalero Apache led by Chief Santana of the Kiowa raided Adobe Walls. Union troops led by Kit Carson were attacked. Over 350 soldiers and the opposing Indian forces were at nearly 3000. The battle lasted close to five hours. Union Army forces were beaten back, suffering heavy casualties.

"Adobe Walls, Captain! Straight ahead," yelled Private Montoya.

"And just in time too. Looky yonder! Here it comes. 'Bout an hour out," said Cpl. Kyle Wiggins. They rode into Adobe Walls only to find another surprise.

"Holy mother-of-pearl! What happened here?" said one of the soldiers.

"Place is deserted. Looks like another Indian attack," said Private Jubal Riley.

"Not quite. Over here, Captain!" Private Marty Collins was kneeling on the ground supporting the head of a young Union soldier and giving him water from his canteen.

"Is he conscious? Can he talk?" asked Capt. Coaker.

"Just barely, sir. He's hurt powerful bad," said Private Collins.

"Some of you men fetch him inside this old building. Get him out of the open," ordered Capt. Coaker.

The young Union soldier looked up through bloodshot eyes. His face was ashy gray.

"What happened here, boy?" asked Capt. Coaker.

"Indians hit us at sun up. Where were you?"

"Son, we just got here. When sun up? Today sun up or yesterday sun up?"

The soldier groaned in pain. "Maybe it was yesterday. Can't remember. Must be yesterday."

"How is it you made it out alive? I see several graves behind a trading post," said Capt. Coaker.

"Reckon I got overlooked. They never would have left me behind. They wouldn't."

"No, I suppose not. It's a good thing we came along when we did. We'll get you fixed up."

"So's I can be your prisoner I suppose?"

"We ain't got time to tend to any prisoner. We'll send you on your way," said Capt. Coaker.

The soldier coughed and shivered. "Cold," he complained.

Capt. Coaker looked around. "Someone get this brave young man a blanket."

"No need," said Private Marty Collins. "Captain, he's dead."

------------//------------

**September 30, 1864**

The 8th Texas Cavalry had been busy to say the least. They had caused havoc all the way. Their job was to harass and slow down Union forces until General Longstreet's Army would advance into Chickamauga. There they would intercept and stop Union forces under General Crook.

"Begging your pardon, Lieutenant, but don't you think we should attack? Them boys are getting mighty close," said Sergeant Major Hamelton O'Toole.

"Dang it, Ham! Will you please and for the love of mercy, quit calling me Lieutenant? And I don't think we should attack yet. I told Lieutenant Pierce of Hood's brigade that I would give him time and that's just what we're going to do. Besides the closer the better," said Lieutenant Caleb Parker.

"Okay. And I can't help it! You are a Lieutenant and should be addressed as such, sir," said O'Toole.

"Yes, maybe when subordinates are around but it's just you and me here. We were Rangers together. Doesn't that count for anything?"

"Yes, sir, and even then you outranked me," chuckled Sergeant Major O'Toole.

"Only because you wouldn't accept the promotion. You scalawag!"

"Oh! So now you're using nautical terms. I thought we were in the Cavalry."

"Whatever. I don't know how to cuss in Irish," said Caleb.

"The same as you do in American. Only with a lovelier accent," said O'Toole.

"Get ready, Lieutenant. Pierce is almost in position," said Caleb.

"Boys, check your weapons. If anyone has to pee, do it now!" said Sergeant Major O'Toole.

"We will open fire just before the Yanks have a chance to reach that bridge. Hood's boys will cover their rear to prevent them retreating on the road. We must catch them here, Ham, we must!" exclaimed Caleb.

"Aye, boy. We'll stop 'em. You can count on the men. They'd charge Satan himself if you asked them to," said Sergeant Major O'Toole.

"Just Yankees today, Ham. That's close enough to Satan for me. Take your positions."

"Take positions, boys, get ready," said Sergeant Major O'Toole in a low voice. "Pass the word."

The 8th Cavalry Texas charged the Union forces with such fierceness and velocity that the men under General Crook's command hardly had the time to reload after their first volley of firing. Screaming like Comanche warriors, Texans raced down the wooded hill firing revolvers, shotguns and rifles at such close range Union forces could see the color of their eyes. As the Union soldiers scrambled to gain composure, they were suddenly attacked at their rear flank by the Texans of General Hood's Old brigade. Sergeant Major Hamelton O'Toole was shot in his shoulder while protecting a young David Brown, the newest recruit and the youngest at age 16. Private David Brown's horse was killed from underneath him and Brown was thrown into a pack of angry Yankees soldiers. Sergeant Major O'Toole spurred his charger to rescue Private Brown. With his reins in his teeth and a double barrel shotgun in his left hand, he raced into the swarm. Sergeant Major O'Toole held out his left hand for Private Brown to grab and Private Brown swung his right leg up into the air over the charges and landed safely behind Sergeant Major O'Toole.

As this was happening, an anxious and frightened Union soldier fired at Private Brown. He missed but struck Sergeant Major O'Toole in his left shoulder. At the same time Lieutenant Caleb Parker and most of the rest of the 8th Texas Cavalry were converging on the fleeing Union soldiers assisting the charging Texans of Lieutenant Pierce and General Hood's Old Texas Brigade.

When it was over, General Crook's brigade was fully humiliated and terribly whipped. The 8th Texas Cavalry was victorious. General Crook's men suffered nearly 150 dead and several wounded including General Crook who was mortally wounded.

The 8th Texas Cavalry went on to build and uphold the reputation as the dreaded 8th Cavalry of Texas. Whether or not it is true, it has been rumored that Union officers would become terribly ill or develop dysentery just before going into battle. If the 8th Texas Cavalry was even mentioned the Union enlisted would desert or become missing in action.

On October 11 the 8th Texas Cavalry had chased the Union Army all the way to Decatur, Alabama. The 8th Texas Cavalry never ceased to attack, attack, attack. During this relentless pursuit, the 8th Texas Cavalry would suffer its largest loss of men: 30 killed and 20 wounded or MIA.

**October 12, 1864**

In a small town three miles east of Decatur, Alabama the 8th Texas Cavalry became vigorously involved in an evident flow skirmish with Union forces. During the battle a fire had broken out caused by the wadding from the rifles. The foliage had become extremely dry due to a lack of rain and extremely hot weather. Wadding was presumed because it had been known to happen as at Cold Harbour and at Chickamauga. The fire started to spread rapidly and the wind was blowing in the direction of the Union forces sending them fleeing. The Union fleeing the fire as well as the 8thTexas Cavalry. It was shortly after the fire had burned itself out that Cpl. Tom Crawford and Private Terrence Todd, searching for Confederate and Union wounded, heard an odd sound coming from an outhouse untouched by the fire.

"Did you hear something, Terry?" asked Cpl. Tom Crawford.

"I thought that was you coughing," replied Private Terrence Todd.

"It came from that direction," said Tom Crawford.

The two soldiers began to search again. They were just about to give up the search when they heard coughing, gagging and choking sound.

"By cracky its' coming from that outhouse," said Cpl. Tom Crawford.

Terrence Todd walked over toward the outhouse and said, "All right. Come on out. We know you're in there."

"Can't. You'll have to come and get us, Johnny Reb."

"What you mean us?" questioned Terrence Todd. He opened the outhouse door. What he saw made him gag as well as made him laugh. In panic, three Union soldiers trying to escape the rushing fire had sought refuge in the outhouse. They were now not just in the outhouse but in the bottom of the outhouse.

"Don't you be laughing. It was better than being barbecued. It could have just as easily been you, Johnny Reb."

"How on earth did you manage to get down there anyway?"

"Ripped the lid off. It's wet down here and wet don't burn."

Todd fought back his laughter and said, "Ya'll come on out now."

"Can't. It's too slippery," said the Yankee soldiers, embarrassed and scared, sobbed.

They fetched the Union soldiers out of the outhouse and promptly marched them to a small creek to let them bathe and wash their clothing. For both sides, it would be a story to tell their grandchildren.

**December 4, 1864**

"And you want to write and tell everyone you are coming?" asked Sergeant Major Hamelton O'Toole.

"No, Sergeant Major, I don't see the logic in it especially when we might get there the same time the letter would. Besides it would be the perfect surprise," replied Lieutenant Caleb Parker.

"Surprise? Seems like a cruel joke if you ask me."

"Sure! Don't you see? It's nigh onto Christmas time. If we ride steady and don't spend much time in any towns, we might make it on time."

"What? No getting drunk? Caleb, laddie. We've just come out of four years of fighting. Don't you think we've earned it?"

"Now it's Caleb, laddie? No Lieutenant, sir? I see what you're doing and it ain't gonna work. Trying to get on my soft side?"

"But, sir. Not even three or eight or twelve? I've built up a powerful thirst these past few years. Have a heart, laddie."

"Awh! You were born with a powerful thirst. It's the Irish in you. I wonder what this Rose O'Shea would say if she heard you talking that way?"

"Aye, yes. A fine figure of a woman she is. But the fact is, she's there and we're here and I'm thirsty. Besides, we ain't married."

"Yet," added Caleb, laughing, then handed O'Toole his canteen.

"No, thanks," said O'Toole.

"But you said you were thirsty, Irish!"

"Darn tooten and don't you be forgetting it neither," smiled O'Toole.

With the war looking as though the South may lose as General Lee had been beaten at Gettysburg on July 4th,1863 and the burning of Atlanta on September 1,1864 the Texas Senators Louis Wigfall and William Oldham insisted Confederate President Jefferson Davis began dismantling the Texas brigades which included the 8th Texas Cavalry. Caleb received his transfer orders into the 2nd Texas Cavalry Regiment under Colonel John Salmon "Rip" Ford as did Sergeant Major Hamelton O'Toole.

"Sure wish we could've brought back all the boys. That surely would have been a grand thing, it would," said O'Toole

"Ya, it sure would have," answered Caleb.

"Awh! They'll do all right, I'm thinking. They're good, smart, tough boys. I've a feeling we'll be seeing them before too long," said O'Toole assuredly.

"About two days more, we'll be there," commented Caleb. He was concerned about the others as well. He was feeling a sense of guilt and remorse over leaving the 8th and not bringing the rest of the boys home with him. But he was under orders. There was little he could do. It was a double-edged sword. He was coming home. He felt glad, that was true enough. But the sense of guilt and betrayal over leaving the others behind was heavy. At the same time, he was not in control. Hamelton O'Toole could almost read Caleb's mind. After all, he had been with Caleb since he was a young boy.

"You know it's not your fault?" said O'Toole.

"What's not my fault?" asked Caleb.

"This is the Army, son, not the Rangers. Things are done much differently. So don't be beating yourself up."

"Can't help it, Ham. I know that what you say is true but I can't help it."

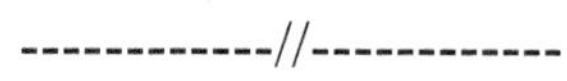

**Uvalde, Texas**

"No, no, no. The garland is all wrong. It should be lower and flowing!"

"Flowing, Senora? How can this what-you-call-it flow?"

"It's called garland, Manuel, and it should be lower and looping. Like waves and curls in a young woman's hair. Comprehende?"

"Oh, si! A woman's hair," Manuel said with a look of confusion.

Senora Kataryna Louisa Pena Parker was busy with her most favorite time of the year decorating for Christmas.

"Mother-in-law, please, take a break. I can take over for you for a while," insisted Marjorie Parker.

"I am fine, my dear. Everything has to be perfect. The children will be here in two days and we haven't even prepared the piñata's yet. And where are the candy canes?"

"You might as well give up, love. My mother has been doing this every year for as long as I can remember. She has her own special way of doing things. You don't want to stand between her and the baby Jesus. You should know that by now," chuckled Drew Parker.

"Mother, Marjorie is right. The hacienda could not be more beautiful. I am certain that the Padre and all the children will be more than happy," said Drew.

"Drew, mijo. When will everyone learn? I do not do this just for the Padre nor the children. Although they are very dear to me. I do this for our Blessed Virgin mother and our Lord and Savior, Jesus Christ," gushed Senora Kataryna.

"Si, muy bueno, aye chihuahua! Have it as you wish, Madre. But if our blessed Savior were here now, He would be more than pleased," said Drew.

"Do I hear my grandson crying?" scowled Senora Kataryna.

"I'm going. I'm going. Oh, by the way, the tree is crooked," chuckled Drew as he was walking away. His mother turned and studied the position of the tree.

The next morning was Christmas Eve. Senora Kataryna, along with others at the Peña hacienda, waited impatiently for the arrival of the new padre, Father Bernardo Sanchez, and the children of the orphanage.

"Mother, what is wrong? You look unhappy. Everything is just as that you planned it. Or are you worried that the new Padre will not like it?" asked Marjorie.

"The Padre! The Padre! I am not concerned over the Padre. Only one thing will make this a true Christmas."

"Yes, I know. You have said that every Christmas for the past four years. We all miss him and I am sure he would not want us to spoil Christmas doting over him," said Marjorie.

The escort for the Padre and the children arrived around 5:30 PM. The excitement of all the children was so great that Señora Kataryna had little time to worry about Caleb not being there for yet another Christmas. Little Miguel Andrew Parker was having a grand time.

It was nearly time for the reenactment of Joseph and Mary and the Nativity. Little Miguel was to be the baby Jesus. The procession through Bethlehem was just about to begin when Whiskey Jack's stepson, Johnny Caldwell Peña, and several call hands and Vaqueros came charging into the hacienda grounds, shouting and shooting pistols into the air. Not sure just what to make of this raucous, Drew rushed inside and came out with his holster and a pistol strapped on and a rifle in his hand. "What is it, Johnny? Trouble? Yankees or Comanche?" asked Drew excitedly.

"Lordy, no, sir. Worse than that. Texas Rangers, sir!"

"Texas Rangers? What are you talking about? Texas Rangers? I am a Texas Ranger," said Drew angrily.

"Yes, sir, you surely are. But these Texas Rangers are dressed in gray. Confederate gray. Looky and see!"

Señora Kataryna began weeping uncontrollably as the two Confederate soldiers rode to the front of the band of the Vaqueros.

"Praise be to our Blessed Virgin and our Lord most high," cried Señora Kataryna as she briskly walked to Caleb's horse and took his hand.

Caleb slid down from his horse and removed his hat. "Abuela, I have come home. Merry Christmas!" Then he hugged her. "I have brought a guest."

Sergeant Major Hamelton O'Toole removed his hat as well. "Señora Kataryna, it is good to see you again. Merry Christmas."

"Folks! I hate to interrupt this glorious reunion and no one is more excited as I am but our baby Jesus is going to be too tired to perform if we don't get a move on," pointed out Drew.

For the remainder of the evening, it would have taken a raid from Yankee soldiers or Comanches too pry Caleb away from Señora Kataryna. As the evening's activities came to a close and all the children were put to bed, the women reluctantly said good night themselves. The men all retreated into the big room.

"Well, now that Mother has released you from her grasp, I want to welcome you, Caleb. A young man who is not only like a son to me but is also my first Ranger. Welcome home."

The men all raised their glasses in a toast. "Here, here. Welcome home." Drew continued, "Let us not forget Hamelton O'Toole, Sergeant Major of the 8th Texas Cavalry and one hell of a Texas Ranger. Here, here. To Sergeant O'Toole. Welcome home."

"Thank you, Major, Capt. Jack, Abuelo, Johnny. But I'm afraid it is only a short stay. You see the Sergeant Major and I have been reassigned to the 2nd Texas Cavalry under Colonel "Rip" Ford."

"The 2nd Texas? Maybe we will see you from time to time at least," stated Whiskey Jack.

Don Miguel spoke, "Gentlemen, I regret to say though I am most happy and proud to see two of our finest Rangers and friends return to us safely but I shall say good night. Welcome home, men."

"Good night, Don Miguel, sir," said O'Toole.

"Good night, Abuelo," said Caleb.

Christmas had come and gone. The Padre and the children from the orphanage in Uvalde were given the traditional send off and escorted by a dozen Vaqueros and cowboys of the Peña Ranchero.

"Mother, I swear. There are few if any like you. If the Lord in heaven doesn't reserve a special place for you then he is unjust," stated Drew.

"Andrew Parker! Watch your tongue. If our blessed Lord sees fit that I sweep the streets of heaven it will be enough! It is not how we serve only that we serve as He has commanded. I am surprised to hear you talk so."

"I apologize. I meant nothing by it."

Drew was sharply cut short. "You have already said too much, my fine son. You will accompany me to mass next Sunday."

Drew laughed. "Si, Mother. I am 40 years old and she still thinks she can boss me around."

"Thinks? I say she did a bang up job of doing it," laughed Caleb.

"Not you too?" said Drew with a smile.

Caleb reached into his coat pocket and pulled out the rosary beads Senora Kataryna had given him the day he left to go fight the war. "Hey. It sure helped me," he said with a mile long smile.

**January 5, 1865**

The time had come for Lieutenant Caleb Parker and Sergeant Major O'Toole to leave. They were to report to Col. John Salmon "Rip" Ford who was now in Gonzalez.

"I hate to see you go. You were gone for so long and I'd nearly forgotten what you look like. Now you're leaving again. It isn't fair," wept Jenny.

"It has been a long time but, who knows, maybe we will be passing through this way soon," soothed Caleb.

"Take care, boy," said Drew as he held out his hand.

"You bet," answered Caleb.

"Sergeant Major, you always have a home here. You look after him?"

"Yes, sir, but he's done a fine job of looking after me and the others. He's become a hell of a man. You can be proud of him."

"Yes, he has. I was afraid he would end up like so many others. Hard and callused."

"When you raise them right, they rarely forget," said O'Toole.

Señora Kataryna could barely contain herself. She hugged and kissed Caleb. "I have packed, for the two of you, some sandwiches. You should eat well while you can. Please come home." Then, weeping, she turned briskly and went inside.

"Vaya con Dios," said Don Miguel. The two soldiers rode off.

**January 7, 1865**
**Gonzalez**

It was nearing daybreak and a warm breeze was blowing from the east. Smoke from the Army campfires was creating a grayish haze down the main street of Gonzalez, Texas. The Confederate flag of the South was fluttering lazily in the breeze.

"Smells like beans and bacon cooking," said Sergeant Major O'Toole.

"That's not the impression that first entered my mind. But now that you mentioned it," chuckled Caleb.

A sentry posted at the end of town hollered out, "Halt! Who goes there?"

"At ease, Private! I am Lieutenant Caleb Parker and this is Sgt. Major Hamelton O'Toole reporting to Colonel Ford."

"Yes, sir. Advance and be recognized. Colonel Ford's headquarters are just yonder at the old mission," said the sentry.

Activities by both civilian and military persons in Gonzalez may have been a bit lax but the headquarters for the Col. John S Ford and the 2nd Texas Cavalry could not have been busier. Telegraph keypads were tapping away. Men were bustling from room to room. A short, skinny, balding Sgt. with a long drooping yellow mustache barred their entry. "Excuse me, Lieutenant, sir. May I asked the nature of your business?"

"Lieutenant Caleb Parker and Sergeant Major Hamelton O'Toole to see Colonel Ford."

"Wait here, sir."

After waiting a very long time, Sergeant Major O'Toole said, "What is he doing in there, reciting Shakespeare's Hamlet?"

"Relax, Sergeant Major. Maybe they are preparing a surprise party to welcome us," kidded Caleb.

"Ha ha ha ha. Not funny, sir," said O'Toole.

The Sgt. returned with a wide smile on his face. "The Colonel will see you now."

"Don't ask me why but something in me doesn't like that man," said O'Toole.

Caleb teased, "You're just jealous!"

"Of what?"

"He has more hair than you do."

**Northwest Texas**
**February 2, 1865**

Just a few weeks earlier on January 8, 1865, a war party led by Kiowa Chief Santana had engaged in a harsh battle with Confederate militia. The battle lasted well into the evening. By nightfall Santana's Kiowa had killed nearly 40 Confederate soldiers and many others wounded. The Kiowa did not lose as many men. But fearing there may be more Confederate troops nearby they fled into Mexico. Meanwhile the Comanche were being systematically starved to death by whites.

Quanah Parker, seeing his desperate situation and trying to keep the old and the women and children fed and alive, had entered into a truce with the whites understanding that food rations would be supplied regularly. As corrupt Indian agents and politicians would find more profitable ways of using the food rations promised to the Indians, it would turn out that this would not be true.

On February 2, 1865 Quanah Parker could stand no more and with 700 warriors led a raiding party from the Canadian River south to the Colorado River and west into New Mexico. They escaped then to the north. He would lead his people into Oklahoma Indian Territory. During this raiding expedition, Quanah would attack Confederate supply wagons and wagon trains taking food, guns and ammunition. They removed blankets and coats from the dead soldiers. But not without a price. Though Confederate militia losses were many, Quanah Parker will lose over a third of his warriors.

"What do you suppose we do? The Army needs those supplies. Moreover, we are in severe need of ammunition," said a militia man of the frontier brigade.

"I think we should just count our blessings and let them be," said Private Oaks.

"Let them be? I'd like to get that Quanah in my gun sights. I let him be all right. I let him be dead. I lost two good friends in that raid," ranted the militiaman.

"And, if we go chasing him, you could lose more. Or even get killed yourself. Don't you see? Quanah doesn't want war. He has no choice. His people are starving and freezing to death. The ones I'd like to get in my sights are those stealing from them. They're the true devils. Not the Comanche," said Private Oaks.

"He's right, boys. Chasing Quanah now would be pure suicide. They're angry, hungry and desperate. For one of them to die in battle would be to them a noble death filled with nothing to lose," said Cpl. Sampson Riley.

"I hate to admit it but the Corporal is right and I don't believe we will be having any more trouble from Quanah. Not for a while anyway.

He's gotten what he wants. I'm sort of glad he got away," said Capt. Coaker.

"Glad? Sir, I don't understand," said a young private.

"All he wanted was to feed and care for his people. The old and the women and children especially. Otherwise, we'd all probably be dead," said Cpl. Riley.

"But he has killed. Maybe we were just lucky or maybe we were too much for him," replied the private.

"Yeah, kid. That's what it was. All 26 of us. We were too much for 700 Comanche," said Private Newsome.

"All right. Lay off. Give the kid a break. Yes, they have killed before. But this was Quanah Parker leading this raid. The others were led by that hot head Yellow Pony. Him and that Kiowa with Chief Santana. Quanah has been trying to listen to Dancing Crow but like any good man would do seeing his people starving and freezing to death he took what should rightfully have been his in the first place. I agree with Captain Coaker. Let him go."

"I'll take that even one step farther. Why are you fighting this war?" asked Capt. Coaker.

"Why? That's easy, Captain. To stop the Yankees from taking what's ours. Oh, I see what you're saying, I reckon," said the militiaman.

"Kind of ironic, ain't it? When the white man's doing the killing, it is justified in the name of progress and prosperity and call it all in the name of God. When the Indian is doing the killing, fighting back, we call 'em devils and savages even. Yet they were here first," said Capt. Coaker.

"Then why can't we all live in peace leaving each to his own? There's plenty of space for us all, ain't there?"

"We were. For a while that is. We were living in peace. Until the bankers, politicians and bureaucrats in the east and in Washington stuck their nose in," said Marty Collins.

"Like I said before, the ones we should be chasing after are them that are stealing from the Indian. If'n you ask me, I'd say they're the ones most guilty for killing all them settlers and Army soldiers. Not the

Indian. Hell, if it meant seeing my young'uns get full bellies and be warm in the winter, I'd do some killing of my own," said Jerolde Oaks.

------------//------------

**April 9, 1865**
**Secondary headquarters of Col. John Salmon "Rip" Ford**
**Commanding Officer**
**2nd Texas Cavalry**
**Gonzalez, Texas**

The morning air was brisk and cool. The Confederate flag of the South popped like pistol shots in the air. The smell of coffee drifted down the streets from the individual soldier campfires. Somewhere in the mix of tenants and soldiers someone was playing "My Wild Irish Rose" on a harmonica. Caleb couldn't help but wonder and chuckle to himself why it is that the prettiest yet saddest songs are all Irish tunes. He was nearing his tent when he heard some commotion just beyond. Some men were laughing and a young boy was protesting and cussing. As Lieutenant Caleb Parker drew near he could more plainly make out some of the talking and laughing.

"Hot dog but ain't he perty? Wouldn't you say this was the perttiest toy soldier you ever did see, John?"

"Boy howdy, Bob, I'll say. Where'd they get you from, sonny? I want to buy one just like you and mail it off to my little boy. He'd really love seeing the likes of you. Ha ha ha ha ha!"

The soldiers were teasing and laughing and spinning a young boy round and round, poking and prodding and roughing up his hair.

"Get your hands off my hat! Greasy son of an ape! Awh, come on, fellows! Leave me go. I ain't no toy soldier. I'm a soldier just the same as you!" shouted the boy.

"Is that so? Does your mama know you're out here, boy? You best run along, Toy Soldier."

Upon approaching the scene, Caleb could not help but want to laugh himself but held it inside. "What seems to be the situation here, men?"

"TennShunn!!" shouted one of the soldiers.

"At ease. Now what seems to be going on here?"

"We found us a real live toy soldier, Lieutenant. Pretty uniform with braids and shiny buttons and looky here, he even has pretty red Cpl. stripes and a little toy drum."

"It ain't no toy drum and I ain't no toy soldier. I am Cpl. Jeffrey Boxer Drummer Corps. Knob headed jackass!"

"That will be quite enough of that, Cpl. Boxer. Now state your business," commanded Lieutenant Caleb Parker.

Corporal Jeffrey Boxer snapped to attention and rendered a salute. "I was instructed to report to the 2nd Cavalry Texas Cavalry. I was told to find a Lieutenant Parker, sir."

Caleb returned the salute. "Well, sonny, you've found him."

Cpl. Boxer handed Caleb a folded paper that he had tucked into the waistband of his trousers and handed it to Lieutenant Caleb Parker. Caleb read the paper and grew flush in the face. "There must be some kind of mistake, Cpl. Boxer. I am the aid to Col. Ford sure enough but this is a cavalry unit. Not a marching band."

"Marching band? Begging your pardon, Lieutenant, but I'm a fighting drummer."

"Come, Corporal. Let's get to the bottom of this."

"Where we going, sir?"

"To see the Colonel. Fighting drummer indeed."

"Everything looks in proper order. Welcome to the 2nd Texas Cavalry, Cpl. Boxer," said Col. John S Ford.

"Where are we going to put him, Colonel? We haven't room for a youngster. The men would surely eat him alive. We can't bunk him with one of them," stated Lieutenant Caleb Parker.

"Ya. I thought about that. Which is why I'm bunking him in your quarters, Lieutenant."

"My quarters, sir?"

"Your quarters. Do you have a problem with that, Lieutenant?" It was more of an order than a question. The Colonel knew that Jeffrey Boxer would be well protected and more comfortable in officer quarters than with the hard, cruel and vulgarness of the enlisted men. Their play could get quite rough and not be understood by a young boy of 13 years old try as he may to pretend to be just as tough and grown up.

Caleb had been sitting on his bunk bed polishing his boots when Cpl. Jeffrey Boxer walked into the tent and laid down on his bed. He laid there for a few minutes staring up at the tent ceiling.

"You don't like me much do you, Lieutenant?"

Caleb froze. He was stunned and surprised at the question. Actually, he had not given the matter a second thought since the young drummer was quartered with him. Had he really been that standoffish and mean to the boy?

"What kind of question is that, Corporal?"

"Just a question sir. I understand if you don't. Officers ain't supposed to fraternize with the enlisted. But I think it's more than that. With all due respect, sir."

"Well, I give you credit for not taking the long way around to getting to a place. You sure come straight to the point."

"I don't know any other way," said Jeffrey.

"I'm sorry if I gave you that impression. I reckon I've been alone for so long I just got used to it. I think you're a fine boy. I apologize."

"That's just it. You look at me like a boy. Rather than a soldier. Just because I'm a drummer. I can shoot too, you know?"

"I reckon you can. I'm not doubting your moxie. It's just your age, Jeff. This damned war."

"My age, sir? Why I hear tell there are fellas younger than me in this war farther east."

"True. Maybe that's what's been eating at me. It's for you and young men like you that this war should be fought. So that you won't ever have to do this in the future. You shouldn't be on the battlefield, Jeffrey. You should be in school or playing marbles or fishing. Not here, son."

"That may be but I never got anything for free and I don't want what I ain't earned. So I reckon I have that right coming to me, Lieutenant."

"I suppose you have a point, Jeffrey, but that doesn't justify sending young boys to war. Where do you call home?"

"Beaumont was home."

"Was. I don't understand?"

"My family was from Beaumont. Then Pa went off to war. When he was killed, my mom changed somehow. She was strange to me. Like she was always fixing to go somewhere. Then one day we went into town. She took me to the barbershop to get my haircut. When I came out, she was gone. I'd see her some. I was homesick and should be there. I waited for four days. I knew I had to do something or starve. Since the war, there have been few jobs. So I went and joined the Army. The sergeants said they could use me in the Drummer Corps. I figure it's better than starving."

"Where did your Pa die? If you don't mind my asking."

"Nawh. I don't mind. It helps sometimes for me to talk about them. We were real close my Pa and me. He was with the Texas 14th Infantry. He died in some place called Newmarket, Virginia. That's about all I know. When they post the listing of missing and dead, they don't explain a whole lot. Maybe it's best that way. I hate to think he suffered."

"I'm truly sorry, Jeff. He must've been a heck of a good man if you're any indication."

"He was. I miss his laugh. He used to laugh and when he got to laugh real hard and long he would remind me of a donkey braying. Ha ha ha. And fish! Lordy! No one could out fish my Pa."

For the next couple weeks, Caleb and Jeffrey became almost inseparable. He was probably the only friend the boy had since the loss of his father. The rest of the enlisted men gradually stopped their teasing. But still Jeffrey maintained the nick name Toy Soldier. After a while, even Jeffrey got used to it. Aside from his duties as drummer, sounding officer call and mail call as well as general assembly, Jeffrey was also messenger boy and self appointed stable Captain since he spent so much time caring for the horses. "Someday I'm going to own my own horse ranch and be the best breeder in Texas," Jeffrey aspired.

"No doubt you might. You sure have a way with them," complimented Sgt. Medley.

Sgt. Michael Medley also was fond of Jeffrey. "Reminds me of my own son. He has dark hair and blue eyes, too."

**May 9, 1865**

Cpl. Jeffrey Boxer was laying in his bunk bed resting from the midday heat when Lieutenant Caleb Parker entered the tent. “Grab your drum, Toy Soldier! Sound officer’s call. Come on. Hurry!”

Jeffrey sprang from his bed. “Yes, sir!”

“Officer’s call. Go on, boy!”

In the headquarters building, Col. John Salmon “Rip” Ford was pacing back and forth, chewing on his pipe and looking like a freight train struggling to climb a mountain.

“We move out in two hours. I want each man equipped with pistol and rifle, 75 rounds of ammunition. Capt. Sunday, you will see to it that each man has two extra horses in the remuda. You will then meet up with Capt. Bill Robinson somewhere north of White’s Ranch area. There you’ll combine forces and repel Branson’s Union forces. You will hold White’s Ranch until reinforcements arrive. Lieutenant Hill, you will move your men here.” Col. Ford pointed on a map. “Half a mile west of Capt. Sunday and Robinson. Here you will meet up with the 3rd Texas Cavalry under Capt. Refugio Benavidas and his Tejanos. Lieutenant Parker, you will assemble the rest of the 2nd Cavalry and proceed with me where we shall converge on the center. Lieutenant Dobbins, you shall bring up the rear flank with the cannons. This day, Mr. Dobbins, you are our artillery commander. Is everyone clear on what they should do? Any questions, gentlemen?”

“Yes, sir. No question, sir,” sounded from the officers.

“Very well. Dismissed!”

Caleb remained behind when the officers left the war room. “Yes, Parker. Is there a question? A problem?”

“No, sir. Uh, yes, sir.”

“Confound it, boy, which is it? Yes or no!”

“Begging your pardon, Colonel. No question toward my duty, sir. I know them all too well. It’s the boy, sir.”

“What boy?”

Caleb cleared his throat. “Toy Soldier, sir.”

“Oh! Yes, I completely forgot. Fine lad. What of him?”

"Well, Colonel, what do we do with him? Bring him along?"

Col. Ford paused for a moment and reloaded his pipe. He puffed on it for a moment. He looked at Caleb.

"Lieutenant, what would you have me do? He's a proud young man. He is also a soldier. Would you have me disgrace his whole life by leaving him behind? That would ruin him forever. I can see you are fond of the lad. Have him accompany the remuda. Better yet, the artillery. That will keep him far enough away from any close fighting while at the same time be in the fight. I'll leave it to you how you sell it to him."

Caleb rolled his eyes. "Gee, thank you, Colonel, sir." Then Caleb saluted and did an about-face and left. Col. Ford was softly laughing to himself.

Caleb was thinking of a way he could sell the idea to Jeffrey without hurting the boy's feelings. Then his eyes lit up. "I've got it! Remember you said you would leave it up to me," Caleb mumbled to himself devilishly. Caleb went to his tent and found a pen and paper. He sat down and began to write. "There! That resolves it just fine. Signed, Col. John Salmon Ford. Commanding Officer 2nd Texas Cavalry." Caleb folded the paper and stuffed it into an envelope.

Later that same day many heard,"Jumpin' catfish! My first set of orders. I am to assist the artillery and also given courier duty. What is that?"

"Courier is a French word meaning you'll be busy riding up and down behind the lines, taking dispatches messages from one unit to another," explained Caleb.

"Is that an important job?"

"Holy smokes! You bet. Did you know that entire armies have been destroyed because a courier failed to deliver a message?"

"Awh! You're joshing me now."

"No, sir. Never. Why look at Napoleon Bonaparte. He was destroyed at the Battle of Waterloo and all because of a courier."

"Golly! So why pick me? I'm just a kid."

"You're a soldier, aren't you? Maybe because you're the fastest rider in the 2nd Cavalry, a little shorter than the rest of us so you wouldn't be seen as easily. Of course, I could go back and tell the Col. that you refuse your orders."

"Geeeshh! No way! I'm mighty proud. Of all the men, he picked me. Who's the Toy Soldier now?"

"That a boy! I'm proud of you!" Caleb went on.

It was a sneaky thing to do and it might even get him in hot water with the Colonel. But Caleb had to protect Jeffrey and the Col. had so much as given him the permission to forge a letter. He did say "I'll leave it up to you how you sell it."

Caleb swore under his breath, "You best remember that, Lieutenant, upon your courtmartial."

On May 12,1865 the men of the Confederate 2nd Texas Cavalry Captains Sunday's and Robinson's detachments were beginning to have their breakfast when a sentry spotted Union forces converging upon the encampment just north of White's Ranch.

"Yankees! Yankees! Yanks on our front!"

The sentry then fired upon the oncoming Union forces and all hell broke out. Confederate forces of the 2nd Texas Cavalry hardly had time to mount a horse. Many charged on foot. From the vantage point chosen by the Confederates, they were in superior cover and mostly uphill from the Union forces. As the terrain was a rolling meadow in light, with sick deer brush, mesquite and small oaks the Union had less cover and were more in the open. Heavy volleys of lead poured upon the Union as if it were raining lead from above. That combined with the fact that the Union had been up most of the previous night and were exhausted. They started to fall back. The fighting went on for several hours. The Union suffered heavy casualties. The Union soldiers retreated toward White's Ranch and laid low licking their wounds. Cheers went up around the camp, "Hoorah! Hoorah! Texas! Texas! Hoorah!"

About 4 pm, Col. Branson's Union forces were reinforced by more forces of the 34th Indiana Infantry and an additional 300 men. With their numbers increased, the Union soldiers proceeded towards Palmito Ranch. Along the way constantly being harassed by Confederates from Capt. Robinson's cavalrymen chasing the Union to Tulosa.

"Let him go men!" shouted Capt. Sunday. "They've had enough and we're starting to spread ourselves too thin."

As evening grew longer and the sun was an hour from dropping over the horizon, Col. John Salmon "Rip" Ford arrived with his detachment: 200 men and eight cannons. By now the fighting had ceased but everyone knew that tomorrow would bring more fighting. Fires flickered bright orange and yellow and tiny sparks rose high in the sky like tiny fireflies disappearing into the dark sky. A chill hung in the air. A soldier sat sipping coffee. It was quiet with the exception of Private Kayle playing his harmonica softly. Cpl. Jeffrey Boxer strolled through the camp. He was looking for Lieutenant Caleb Parker. He could not help but look around and wonder why everyone was so quiet, distant and somber. It reminded him of how his mother looked before she ran off and left him.

"Hey, Jeff! Over here, boy," It was Caleb sitting on an old stump and looking like all the others.

"Whatcha doin'? You should be sleeping. Tomorrow promises to be a long day."

"It's too quiet. Couldn't sleep. What's wrong with everybody? Why, I walked on through the middle camp and not one of the fellows teased me or called me Toy Soldier. Why is everyone so quiet?"

"They tease you because they like you. This is your first fight. I reckon after tomorrow you will understand why but I'll tell you the short and quick of it. They're, all in their own special way, praying. Them that believe anyway. It's a hard thing to kill a man, Jeff. It stays with you forever. Like a broken bone heals some but you're never the same. Especially when you know that tomorrow could be your last day."

"But they're Yankees. Shouldn't they be glad to kill Yankees? Ain't that what we're here for? They should be glad we're whoopin' 'em and celebrating. At least that's the way I see it."

"Yes." Caleb smiled. "I'm sure you do. Four years ago so did many of them fellas out there. Until they had to actually do it. They've seen plenty of Yankees die. But they've also seen plenty of Rebs die too. Some of them best friends or brothers. Now all they want is to be done with it and go home."

"I suppose you're right. Only it seems that they are all sad like we lost or something."

"I know that right now you don't understand but in an odd yet sobering way, Jeff, we did lose. We lose something inside of us no matter who the victor is after a battle. You still lose. I cannot explain it to you any better. But I reckon after tomorrow you will understand and wish you hadn't."

"Shucks! I ain't scared. Besides I figured I owe it to them for killing my Pa."

"Jeff! I don't believe that and I don't believe your Pa would want to hear you talk like that. How many Yankees felt the same way about your Pa? Don't you think your Pa killed many a young man's father? Your Pa didn't kill out of revenge or because he enjoyed it. He did it because it was his duty. That's true for every man here and out yonder as well. We fight for what we believe in."

"Gosh, you sound just like him. That's just like something Pa would say. I reckon I best be getting back. It is sorta getting late." Jeffrey had that well chastised and forlorn look in his eyes.

"Why don't you stay here? You can have my bed. I have to be up anyway. It's my turn at officer of the day. I will wake you at first light."

Jeffrey yawned. "Okay. As long as you're sure. I don't want to impose."

"Offered, didn't I? Now get in there and get some sleep. And be sure to take off your boots."

Morning came too quickly. Far off toward the east, the sky grew dark, threatening rain. The wind blew from the east. It felt good and Caleb inhaled deeply. "Lieutenant, come quickly!" shouted Sergeant Major O'Toole suddenly.

"What is it, Ham?" asked Caleb.

"They're forming a line, sir. There to the east and there to the west. Quite a passel of them. They'll be making their charge anytime now," warned Sergeant Major O'Toole.

Caleb turned and rushed to his tent. "Jeff! Wake up!"

Jeffrey sprang to his feet, still half asleep. "What is it?"

"Hurry, sound assembly. We'll be knee-deep in Yankee blue before long. Hurry! Take my horse and go!"

Jeffrey hopped up upon Caleb's horse and took off at a gallop shouting all the way, "Yankees! Yankees comin'! Wake up you Rebs! Yankees!"

Men in gray began scrambling out their tents some of them still dressing as they stumbled and hopped to their horses. Soon they could hear the brrrump, brrrump, tappity tap tap tap, brrrump, brrrump, tappity tap tap tap from Cpl. Jeffrey Boxer's drum.

Colonel John S. Ford came trotting through the camp hollering, "Get to it! On the double! We got Yankees on our left flank! Come on! Boys, there's hell to pay for the Yanks!" As Col. Ford was rallying all the men, he stopped and looked down at Jeffrey and raised that his eyebrow. "Corporal Boxer, is it?"

"Yes, Colonel Ford, sir!" replied Jeff.

"Corporal, you have no boots on." Then the Col. spurred his horse into a gallop and rode to the front of his men.

"Lieutenant, Parker!" commanded Col. Ford.

Caleb came running. "Yes, sir, Colonel!"

"Lieutenant, why does Cpl. Boxer have your mount?"

"Well, I..."

"Never mind. Just get it and report back to me. Pronto, Lieutenant Dobbins!"

"Yes, sir!"

"Mr. Dobbins, bring up the artillery. I want three cannons covering the left flank there and there on the center. The remaining cannon held in reserve. Now! Dobbins! Now! Captain Sunday!"

"Here, Colonel!"

"I want that right flank pushed back. They will turn and have little cover to protect them there! Capt. Robinson!"

"Sir, yes, sir!"

"Mr. Robinson, when the Union soldiers began to break and run from the right flank you will punch straight across that field with Capt. Sunday's men covering from that point and you there yonder. You will act as a spearhead forcing them to their center. When their right flank reaches the center, Mr. Dobbins will bombard them with cannon fire," Col. Ford commanded as he was pointing to the right.

Caleb returned a little red in the face from embarrassment. "Colonel!"

"Good! Lieutenant Parker, you have the left flank. See that wash just yonder about a half mile out? Do not let them past or in that wash. You will take 50 men and charge the Union forces before they can reach that wash."

"Yes, sir!"

"Whatever you do, do not let them reach that wash. If the Yankees get in that wash they will be unstoppable and I will have our left flank at a disadvantage."

"You can count on me, sir. I'll stop 'em!"

"I have every confidence you will."

As Col. John Ford was instructing his men, a shout came from behind him.

"Here they come and they have their bayonets fixed too!"

Sergeant Major O'Toole ordered, "First squad, dismount! Form a skirmish line. Let 'em get close enough to see their shiny buttons then fire at 'em!"

The Union soldiers came within 50 yards and Sergeant Major O'Toole shouted "Fire!"

On the Union side the entire front line charged. "Keep moving men! We have them now!" shouted Union Lieutenant Corby. The Union soldiers kept coming.

"Okay, laddie's, here is where you earn your pay! Fix bayonets!" shouted Sergeant Major O'Toole.

The two armies clashed in a bloody hand-to-hand combat fight. They were a tangled, writhing mass of fists and bayonets when Col. Ford came leading a mounted charge of nearly 40 men of the 2nd Texas Cavalry picking their way through the heavy mass, rifles and pistols blaring.

"Fall back! Fall back!" shouted Union Lieutenant Corby.

"Cease fire!" shouted Col. John S Ford. "Let 'em go!"

"Hooray! Hooray!" shouted the men of Sergeant Major O'Toole's cavalry detachment. "Easy men! Don't celebrate too early. They'll be coming back as sure as you can say Sam Houston!" shouted Sergeant Major O'Toole.

"Good work, Sergeant Major! That gave them something to think about at the very least," said Col. John Salmon Ford.

"Aye, sir. And they're thinking of trying again! Look! Alright, boys, get mounted. We'll send them back to Corpus Christi this time and into the Gulf!"

At 2:30 in the afternoon, a detachment of nearly 30 Union soldiers under the cover of a small hill began crawling their way around the dry wash on the Confederate left flank. Colonel Branson's Union forces now reinforced by the 34th Indiana volunteers were preparing for a full frontal attack to the Confederate center.

Colonel Ford sent the dispatch to his right flank.

"Hey, Sarge! What in blazes is that?" asked a Union soldier pointing to a tiny figure on horseback that was racing to beat the devil across the horizon.

"I'm not sure. Why! It's a darn kid!" said the sergeant.

"Kid, my Aunt Betsy! That's a messenger rider. Kill him!" yelled Lieutenant Corby.

"You kill him! I ain't shooting no kid!" declared Union Sgt. Willis.

Cpl. Jeffrey Boxer came riding up to Capt. Sunday who was now commanding the right flank.

"What, Corporal?"

"Dispatch from the Col., sir!"

Capt. Sunday opened the letter: Attack at once! was all it read.

"Well, that's plain enough. Good work, Cpl. Boxer," said Capt. Sunday.

At 3:15 pm, Confederate forces of the 2nd Texas Cavalry led by Capt. John Sunday made their charge accompanied by Capt. Refugio Benavides and his Tejanos of the 3rd Texas Cavalry.

Cpl. Jeffrey Boxer was oblivious to the bullets whizzing over his head and all about him as he raced back to Col. Ford. "I got it to him, sir! He said to tell you all for Texas!"

Col. John S Ford smiled and said "Capt. Sunday always did have a flair for the dramatic. Take this letter to Lieutenant Dobbins and this one to Lieutenant Parker. Do you think you can do that?"

"Consider it done, sir!" replied Jeffrey.

Just as Col. Ford had predicted, when Capt. Sunday's forces attacked, the Union did collapse and retreated to meet up with Branson's forces in the center.

"Lieutenant Dobbins! Dispatch from the Colonel, sir!"

"Thank you." The dispatch simply read: Commence firing upon Union center.

As Cpl. Jeffrey Boxer rode on toward the left flank commanded by Lieutenant Caleb Parker, he could hear the boom of the cannons. The percussion from the cannons caused a vibration that shook him from head to belly. He was at full gallop when suddenly his horse folded underneath him sending him tumbling forwards. Shaken, and in a daze with his ears buzzing, Jeffrey stumbled around trying to regain his composure. Bullets tore up the ground all around him. Something whined past his ears as he bent over to pick up his dispatch case. Jeffrey began to run the rest of the way. A bullet tore a hole in his coattail.

"Jeff! Are you alright?"

"I'm okay. Dispatch from the Col., sir!"

"Now you choose to call me, sir?" Caleb teased.

"What?" shouted Jeffrey. "I can't hear you. My ears are ringing something fierce!"

Caleb read the dispatch. "Mount up. Get ready to charge!"

It was just then when a sniper's bullet struck Caleb and he collapsed to the ground.

"Caleb!" shouted Jeffrey. "Sergeant Major! The Lieutenant's been shot!"

Sergeant Major O'Toole came running over to where Caleb lay. His left leg and hip now red with blood.

"Sergeant Major O'Toole. You will have to lead the charge. Don't let them make it into that wash. And someone get that sniper! How did he get so close?"

"I see him, I see him! Over there! Next to that clump of junipers. Three of them!! Three Yanks!" yelled Jeffrey.

Seeing that their position had been discovered, the three soldiers fled immediately back to their unit revealing their position as well.

"We've got 'em boys! Mount up!" commanded Sergeant Major O'Toole.

Sergeant Major O'Toole led the charge and what was to be the closing of the battle of Palmito Ranch. As the cavalry detachment charged into the Union forces on the Confederate left flank, a small group of about 15 Union soldiers was making their way toward the wash unnoticed. A sniper who chose to remain in the junipers was taking potshots at Caleb's artillery cover. Jeffrey was watching the charge and became excited at the flight of the Union soldiers as they began running. He began shouting, jumping up and down waving his hat.

"Hot dog! That's the way! Put it on them! Yeehaw!"

As Cpl. Jeffrey Boxer was cheering the cavalry led by Sergeant Major O'Toole, the sniper shot and killed the man holding the torch used to light the cannon. The torch dropped to the ground. Cpl. Boxer picked up the torch and continued to watch and cheer on Sergeant Major O'Toole and the others. In his excitement, he began jumping up and down hollering as the Confederates made short work at chasing back the Union soldiers when he accidentally touched off the cannon. The cannon boomed and sent a canister round straight in the path of the Union soldiers advancing toward the wash. The cannon boom scared the daylights out of of Jeffrey. "Yeeeow!" Cheers rose up all around. "Hooray! Hooray! That a boy! Nice shooting!" No one but Cpl. Jeffrey Boxer knew that it was by accident. He tried to explain but was stopped.

"Nice shooting!" said Lieutenant Caleb Parker.

"But..."

Pvt. Stanley Harwood who used to tease Jeffrey grabbed him and lifted him up onto his shoulders. "Hoorah! Cheers for the best cannoneer in the 2nd Cavalry. Hooray for our Toy Soldier!"

Jeffrey never would believe that he would not only miss but be glad to be called toy soldier. It was then that he remembered Caleb. He ran over to where Lieutenant Parker lay propped against a large rock "Lieutenant, are you hurt bad?"

"I will be all right. Took a bullet in my hip though. Help me out, Corporal, will you?"

"Sure thing." As he was helping Caleb to his feet, Jeffrey began to exclaim, "Why! You've been shot in the butt! Ha ha ha ha ha! Beg ha ha begging ha ha your pardon, Lieutenant, sir!"

"I have not! It's my hip!" shouted Caleb.

"Looks like the butt to me! Ha ha! Oh boy! Ass shot!"

"Watch your tongue, Corporal! Besides, are you a doctor?"

"No, sir."

"Then I say it's my hip!"

"Sure. Ha ha ha. Whatever you say, Lieutenant."

**May 15, 1865**

The battle ended around 4:30 pm as Confederate forces consisting of the 2nd Texas Cavalry, the 3rd Texas Cavalry, Refugio Benavides' Tejanos along with artillery support cornered the Union near Boca Chica. The Union forces at the Battle of Palmito Ranch had been defeated. The Union losing nearly 230 dead or wounded and nearly 70 captured. Confederate losses amounted to only eight dead and 11 wounded.

Later that evening, Cpl. Jeffrey Boxer stopped in at the medical infirmary.

"Howdy, Lieutenant. How are you feeling?"

"Howdy, Jeff. I'll be all right. Right, Doc?"

"Why sure. A couple weeks in bed and I don't see why you wouldn't be as good as new," said the doctor.

Jeffrey picked up the clipboard that was hanging at the foot of Caleb's bed and tried to read it. "I don't see how anyone gets well around here. I can't make heads or tails out of this scribble."

"Just never you mind. You have no business reading that anyhow. That's property of the surgeon and my personal record. Emphasis personal," scowled Caleb.

"What's gluteus maximus mean, Doc?"

"What?"

"This right here. What's that mean?"

"I said just never you mind. Doc, please tell this little squirt that I was shot in the hip and that's all."

"Well, sure. I suppose you could write it down that way. The hip portion of the gluteus maximus," said the doctor.

"That means butt, don't it, Doc?" asked Jeffrey.

Caleb reached down to the floor and picking up one of his boots and tossed it at Jeffrey. "Get out of here, you little rat!"

Laughing, Jeffrey ducked. "I'm going! I'm going! See you tomorrow, Lieutenant." Jeffrey could not pass up the urge and stuck his head back into the tent. "It still means butt!" And then he was gone.

"You like that kid, don't you?" asked the doctor.

"Yeah, he's a swell kid."

"Too bad though for the young Corporal. Toy Soldier is what the men call him?"

"I'm not sure I follow you," said Caleb.

"How long do you think this war will last? Face it. Today's victory is great for the morale of the men of the 2nd and 3rd Cavalries. The fact is, much as it pains me to say, the South is licked. This war can't last much longer, son. Then what will become of that youngster?"

"I don't know. I really hadn't had time to think of that," replied Caleb.

"Right now the Army is all the family that kid has. He has warm clothes, he eats regular and aside from the jokes from the men, he actually has grown to like it. There isn't one man out there that wouldn't lay down his life for that boy. But the hard truth is once this war is over, everyone will go their own way. That leaves that young Corporal out in the cold. Right back where he started. Because then he won't be a young drummer boy Cpl. He'll just be a homeless hungry kid. Along with hundreds of other homeless hungry kids. He may end up on the wrong side of the law. Simply as a matter of survival," said the doctor.

Caleb was the last person to be told about the way of life. He himself had been down that road. Although it really had not been that long ago, six years, though it seemed an eternity ago.

The sad and tragic news reached the men of the 2nd Texas Cavalry. On April 9, 1865 Gen. Robert E Lee surrendered to Union Gen. Ulysses S. Grant at Appomattox Courthouse in Virginia.

"Dear God in Heaven! What have we done? All of those lives. Lost! And for what? Jesus, forgive us. Forgive us all, please," said Caleb as he watched the Confederate stars and bars being lowered for the last time.

**June 19, 1865**
**Uvalde, Texas**

"Reckon they'll like me, Caleb? I mean, what will they say? What will they think?"

"What kind of question is that? Don't you fret any. They will see you as you really are. My friend and a former soldier to the Confederacy."

"Not much of one. A toy soldier, remember? You were an officer."

"Toy soldier? Why Colonel Rip gave you his best horse for turning back half a Regiment with that cannon. You aren't a toy soldier anymore. Every man in the 2nd Cavalry would testify to that. Look at me, all I ended up with was a Purple Heart and a scar on my hip."

"You mean butt. Don't you?"

"Hey! Are we going to go through that again?" threatened Caleb.

"Nawh! I reckon not. Your secret's safe with me. Promise," smiled Jeffrey.

"Besides, we came out of the war equals. These shiny trinkets, don't really amount to much and we are alive," said Caleb.

"You make it sound like I'm riding into heaven with you," said Jeff.

The Peña Ranch and hacienda were unusually quiet as Caleb and Jeff rode on to the property and into the courtyard. A young girl was kneeling and pulling weeds from the flower garden in the courtyard center.

"Hola, señorita. Where is everyone?"

"They have gone to the burial," answered the girl.

"Burial? What burial?" asked Caleb.

"Señor Don Miguel. He died two days ago. They are all at the cemetery." Caleb gasped.

"Por favor, come in. Do you wish me to prepare you some food? You can tie your horses..."

"Gracias, señorita. I know where to go."

"Muy bien. I will fix you some food."

**Uvalde, Texas 1869**

"How can you even consider selling, Mother? This ranch has been in our family since the first Spanish conquistadors stepped foot on this continent."

"I know, mijo. But what am I to do? There is no demand for horses these days and those no good scheming carpetbaggers and land speculators are practically stealing every corner of the market. Oh, if only your grandfather were here. He would know what to do. The Jacobson's sold their land at $50 an acre! So sad."

"Yes, Mother. It is sad. But that was Lou Jacobson's choice. He did not have to sell and I know what Don Miguel would say. He would say no. He would never sell."

"Maybe so but things are different now. Even if we did try to sell off some of our horses and cattle we would never get a fair price. Those bankers and land speculators are more interested in scooping up as much property as they can. They would see to it that we would go broke. We would either have to sell or borrow from the banks and they would arrange it so that we could not make our payments then foreclose on us." The discussion between Drew Parker and his mother was not a new one.

"There might be one possible way," interrupted a now tall, lean, dark-haired, blue-eyed, 17 year old Jeffrey boxer.

"Oh? And what, pray tell, is that?" asked Drew.

"The Peña Ranchero controls much of the water to many of the ranches and homesteads around here. Isn't that right?" asked Jeff.

"Yes, it does but if you think we would stop the flow of water to save our necks while destroying everyone else in the process the answer is no. That is not Don Miguel's way."

"That's not what I am saying at all. I am suggesting a joint operation. We supply the water and help with getting the other ranchers and farmers cattle and produce to market in return for a percentage of what the others produce," said Jeffrey.

"That's quite an undertaking and a very huge gamble to say the least," said Drew.

"I am not so sure, hermano. The kid here makes sense. I think we should call a meeting. Have each of the ranch owners and farmers put it to a vote. It could work," said Whiskey Jack.

"I am in agreement with Jack and Jeffrey. But I believe we should send for Caleb. After all he is a lawyer and would be able to help us get around any loopholes. Much more if those Eastern businessmen try any legal or illegal tactics to stop us. Caleb would be a big help," said Mary Caldwell Parker Jack.

"I think that is a wonderful idea. I say we send a rider today and fetch him here right away," said Senora Kataryna.

"That's not any of my concern, Bartlett. You signed the agreement and failed to meet your end of the bargain. You have 48 hours to vacate the property or I will have no choice but to remove you. By force, if necessary."

"Ainsworth, you still have five days until I have to make any payment. You can wait five more days."

"That's not what your agreement says. Had you taken the time to read it thoroughly, your agreement clearly states that if at any time the

Asbury and Benson Association determines that you are in jeopardy of defaulting on your loan that Asbury and Benson reserves the right to terminate said agreement and assume full ownership of said property," declared Harvey Ainsworth.

"Oh, I read it. Page to page. Tell me something, Ainsworth, just how do you come about making that determination? Is that before or after my cattle are run off or six of my men are shot to hell? You know, Harvey. You are a very lucky man. Because if I were 10 years younger or hadn't lost full use of my right arm, I'd blow you right out of that saddle. You go back to Austin and tell Asbury and Benson, that I will take full advantage of my next five days. You'll have your money. And Harvey, if I see you or any of your vermin on my property during that time, I'll kill you and them," said Jack Bartlett.

Harvey Ainsworth started to reach for his revolver when he heard the unmistakable sound of a rifle being cocked.

"There are four men with rifles and shotguns and every one's on you, Ainsworth. Now, get the hell off my land!" said Jack Bartlett of the High Solara Ranch.

Harvey Ainsworth set up straight in his saddle, both his hands on the pommel, so as not to be mistaken for any aggressive movements and laughed, "Ha ha ha, okay. Okay. Five days, Jack. I'll give you that. Five days then you go. One way or the other."

The meeting at the Peña hacienda was akin to a congressional meeting. With some wanting to call for the hiring of armed men and some saying it was better to sell than to end up with nothing and others wanting to appeal to the governor.

"At this point there are no grounds to appeal to the governor. Asbury and Benson have taken great caution in protecting themselves. So far no one can conclusively pin any blame of wrongdoing on them. So far no one has caught one employee rustling or using strong arm tactics," said Caleb.

"So what are we to do? Bring in their bodies draped over a saddle?" asked Sam Laudermill of the Bar S Bar Ranch.

"Unfortunately, I think that is exactly what we will have to do. Which is why we summoned Caleb all the way from San Antonio to be here," said Drew.

"What about you, Major? You're a Texas Ranger. What can you do to help? Can we get a company of Rangers to patrol the area?" asked Tyler Beasley, a farmer.

"I wish we could. But ever since the end of the war, the Texas Rangers have been all but dissolved. Those of us that remain hardly have any more authority than a town marshal. There are petitions before the governor to reinstate the Rangers but there are those just as adamant about doing away with the Rangers altogether," replied Drew.

"So you honestly think this co-operation thing will work?" asked Sam Laudermill.

Senora Kataryna broke in. "I truly believe it will be the best way. Violence should be our last resort. As I am certain many of you have seen your fill of killing during the war. We must use our wits and do everything legally. Our hands must stay clean."

"Plus there is strength in numbers. Our drives and farm shipments are less likely to be attacked if under large escort," suggested Caleb.

"And while we are providing all this manpower and escorting cattle and produce, who will be protecting our homes and the rest of our property?" asked Charles Owens, a farmer.

"That's a very good point. You ranchers have the manpower to spread around. We do not," said Tyler Beasley.

Senora Kataryna stood up. "The Peña Ranchero will offer protection for the farmers provided there is an agreement to this co-operation."

The vote was unanimous. So began the Cattlemen and Farmer's Co-op Association of Uvalde, Texas.

The first trip to Austin was an escort of six tons of corn, one wagon load of apples and two wagon loads of onions from the Taylor and Owens farms and 700 head of Longhorn cattle from Jack Bartlett's High Solara Ranch.

They were seven hours north of Uvalde and only six hours more to Hondo. It was nearing high noon and the clouds began to darken from smoky gray to dark blue-gray with swirls of white clouds that resembled a stampede of horses running from the storm. Tiny puffs of dust popped from the road surface as the rain gradually began to pelt the ground. The cattle began to pick up the pace of their walking as if they sensed what the clouds meant. The air was filled with the smell of earth, rain and the scent of mesquite, scrub oak and cedar all mingled together pleasing yet strong to the nostrils.

"We best look for a place to bed these cattle down before the storm hits. Lousy timing, isn't it? For weeks we've needed rain and it chooses today to come," said Whiskey Jack.

"We're going to have to get a move on. If it hits before we pass D' Hanis, we're in big trouble. That old creek bed will have us at a standstill and if it goes to lightning and thunder, we'll have Longhorn scattered everywhere. There's an old, burned out farmhouse from the war just about a mile past it. I believe the old corral just might hold. If not, we will at least be past the riverbed and into clearer land. If they do bolt, we won't have such a hard time rounding them all up again," said Drew.

"Thinking it's a good place to make a stand if we are hit by rustlers, right?" asked Jack.

"That wasn't my original concern but now that you mentioned it. I was thinking that barn would be a nice place to stay dry. Plus it would help protect all of that grain from getting wet and spoiling," said Drew.

"You reckon those outlaws will try to hit us in this storm?" asked Johnny Caldwell Parker, Whiskey Jack's stepson.

"They might but I doubt it. It would be too much like working to them. They'll probably let us do most of the work for them. But I'll keep one eye open for them anyway," said Drew.

"Why? If what you say is true then we haven't anything to worry about."

"Because every now and then I'm wrong."

"Jumpin' catfish! Now I know it's going to storm. You? Admitting you're wrong?" teased Whiskey Jack.

"I never said I was wrong. I said every now and then I'm wrong. It has nothing to do with the here and now. Because I'm not wrong," replied Drew.

"You're an arrogant man, hermano. Arrogant," said Jack teasingly.

They had just arrived at the old burned out farm and pushed the last of the cattle into the corral when the sky lit up bright white. Crack! Boom! Lightning streaked across the sky. "Won't be long now!" yelled a Vaquero.

"You reckon that corral's going to hold 'em?" asked Johnny.

"It's going to have to. But if they break, they won't go far. The cover is sparce around here. So we won't have trouble getting them back," explained Drew.

That next morning, they found the corral had held and the cattle were fine. Huge puddles of water were everywhere. They resembled small fishing holes in the Beaumont region where Jeffrey Boxer had grown up.

"Looks like the bayous. Sort of makes me homesick," said Jeffrey.

"You think about going back?" asked Johnny.

"Shucks no! What would I do? Nope. I'm content right where I'm at."

"Glad to hear it," said Johnny.

Since the end of the war when Caleb returned to the Peña Ranch with Jeffrey, they had developed quite a friendship. They worked well together and enjoyed many of the same things. They were about four miles outside of Lytle, when two of the Vaqueros who had been assigned to ride the point came racing up to Drew and Jack.

"What's the rush, boys?" asked Jack.

"Better hold the herd and the wagons up here, Senor Jack. The bridge is out. The one that crosses the big creek just outside of Lytle?" said Stefano.

"And?" Jack could see on the other Vaquero's face that Stefano had not said everything.

"It looks like someone had taken an ax to some of the support posts but I can't say for sure," said Stefano.

"We had better hold up. Jack, you and I will have to go look. Stefano, Pedro, you two get with Caleb. Tell him what's happened. I want everyone on alert. This could be where those outlaws are hoping to spring their trap."

When Drew and Jack reached the old bridge, Jack slid from his saddle and scampered down the bank of the river and started to examine the posts. Then picking up several woodchips in his hand, he sniffed them.

"Someone has taken an ax to them all right. By how fresh these woodchips smell, I'd say this was done in the last day. Probably figured on a rise of the river and its current to do the rest of the job," said Jack.

"I agree but why here? This is not a place I would pick for setting up an ambush," said Drew.

"Me either. But then that depends on the kind of ambush," Jack paused for a moment then looked at Drew. "Hermano, I don't recall hearing or seeing any riders today or yesterday for that matter. And from the way this bridge is moaning and popping, I don't see it standing for very long."

"So, what are you suggesting, Jack?"

"Well," Jack removed his hat and brushed back his coal black hair with a calculating look. "Either this is meant to prevent us from going any farther or slow us down. Or the ambush, if there is to be an ambush, has already been set. What if they were waiting already and allowed us to pass them by only to hit us here at the river's edge?"

"Which would give us nowhere to go! Jack, you're a genius! I'm glad you're on our side. But, if you are right, then the others could already be in trouble. We better hightail it back."

The herd was lumbering along slow and steady. Caleb had placed out riders on both sides of the road. As he rode drag with the wagons. Each wagon had one man riding shotgun like that on a stagecoach. Drew rode up alongside of Caleb.

"Any sign of trouble?" asked Drew.

"Nope and it has me concerned. You know? I haven't seen one bird all morning. Not even a chirp from one have I heard."

"The bridge is useless and will most likely collapse before we get there. Jack and I believe that is most likely where they will strike."

"So what's the plan of defense?" asked Caleb.

"I'm still working on that. I had the load crest a small hill. We will stop the wagons at the top of that hill. It will give us an advantage. We will be able to see a long ways. If they are coming, we will see them and have more time to prepare for them," said Drew.

Jack and Stefano came trotting up to Drew and Caleb. "Hermano, Stefano here has an idea and I think it just might work."

"Let's hear it. I'm open to most anything to save the herd and all this grain and produce. Not to mention the men."

‘"Si, Senor Drew. When I was a boy I would often take rides. We would fish this creek. There used to be a big sand bed farther up the creek. There are some big flat rocks in the creek also. But I don't think we would have any problems with the wagons. As a boy, we could wade from one side to the other. If we cut north to that point, I think we could get across and then set our own trap," suggested Stefano.

"How long would it take to get to this sand bed?" asked Drew.

"One, maybe two, hour and the wagons would have no trouble."

"Sounds like it will work. Good thinking, Stefano."

"It is nothing. I am just glad I remembered."

Two hours later they crossed the wagons first, as cows would have created too much mud and would have bogged down the wagons. After the wagons were across then the cattle were crossed.

"Jack, I want one man to remain here on this side of the river. If the outlaws are trailing us they won't take long to pick up our trail and figure us out. When they cross, we will be waiting with your men preventing escape."

"My men. My eight men? What makes you think I want to have this side? How about you and eight men and me with a herd and wagons. Hmmmm?"

"Jack, it was your idea!"

"My idea?! You mean Stefano's idea."

"Yes, but you put it before me. It was you who said it would work."

"I said crossing would work. Not set some counter ambush. That is your idea, hermano."

"Okay, Jack. I'll stay if you're too worried about it. Fine, go. Just try not to have a stampede. We can't afford to be shooting it out with rustlers while at the same time stopping 700 head of Longhorns from scattering from here to San Antonio."

"So, now you're suggesting I'm scared? You'll never live to see that day."

"For crying out loud, I would never say that. What's up with you anyway? I'm just reminding you to be cautious, that's all. I'm more than happy to do this chore," said Drew.

Jack looked sternly at Drew. "Why do I have this feeling you're doing it to me again?"

"Doing what? Come on, Jack. Make up my mind. Do you want this chore or the other?"

"Ha ha ha! I'll take the wagons and the herd. See?! You thought you'd outsmart me again, didn't you? Ha ha ha ha! No, sir. Not this time."

An hour had passed. Andrew and eight other cowboys and Vaqueros waited in a large thicket of junipers and scrub oak. Soon they could hear the pounding of hooves. Fifteen men came riding up to the point of the sand bed where the wagons and cattle had crossed.

"They crossed here!" said one of the men.

"I'll be. Those dirty double-crossers," said another.

"Stop gawking and let's get after them," said the leader of the bunch.

The outlaws crossed the creek and took out in a direction for Jack and the others. Drew waited an hour then began to grumble, "What's keeping them? They should be breaking their necks trying to cross back over by now."

"You reckon we should follow after them, Major?" said one of the cowboys.

"No. We'll give him a bit longer."

Another 20 minutes passed. The sound of pounding hooves and gunfire started getting closer. "Here they come, men! Get ready!" shouted Drew. The outlaws busted through the brush on the opposite bank of the creek followed by the sound of shouting and shooting.

"Don't let them cross. Catch them in the water!" hollered Drew.

When the outlaws reached the creek, Drew began firing. Suddenly, there was shooting and shouting from every direction.

"It's a trap!" shouted one of the outlaws.

"Keep going. Don't slow down!" shouted another outlaw.

One of Drew's cowboys stepped out from behind a scrub oak in order to get a clear shot. As he stepped out into the open, he was spotted by one of the oncoming outlaws. The outlaws drew his pistol and fired. The cowboy spun around grasping his shoulder and falling to the ground. They kept coming. The injured the cowboy dove head first into a tuft of tall grass and bushes, came up on one knee and snapped off two quick shots using his good arm. The outlaw screamed as the bullet tore into him. Two shots just inches below his pocket and he flew backward over his saddle like a dog that suddenly reached the end of his leash.

"Dan! Are you okay?" yelled Drew to his wounded cowhand.

"Went clean through. I don't think it hit any bone," replied Dan.

An outlaw raised his pistol aiming at Drew. "Duck!'" yelled Dan.

Drew fell flat on his belly and rolled to his left out of the path of the outlaw's charging horse. There was the unmistakable sound of a double barrel shotgun. Drew looked quickly behind him in the direction of the shotgun boom. It was "Tiny" Harrison.

"Boy, am I glad you were there!" smiled Drew.

Boom went a shotgun again. "Gotta be somewhere," laughed Tiny. He had taken another outlaw out of the action.

"Let's get out of here!" yelled an outlaw on a tall black horse. "Come on, fellas!" As he started up the bank of the creek and riding up stream, Drew and his men began firing and chasing on foot.

"Let 'em go. They won't be back."

A young Vaquero was tending to Dan's wounded shoulder. "He will be alright, Senor Drew."

Tiny Harrison inspected the Vaqueros handiwork. "Antonio, not a bad job. Shoot, I bled worse from a razor cut."

"Si, only your razor is a Bowie knife," laughed Antonio.

"Major, we got three of them but I'm afraid they won't be talking anytime soon. At least not in this world," said another cowhand.

"Too bad. Saddle up, boys. Bring that trash with us," said Drew.

Drew and his men rode into camp where the rest of the escort had set up a small camp in the middle of a semi-circle made with the wagons.

"Damn! You got three of them," said Johnny.

"Johnny, feed and water the horses," said Drew.

"Yes, sir."

"Where's Jack?" questioned Drew.

"He had an errand to do," Stefano spoke up.

"An errand?"

"Si. He should be back soon."

"How many men did we lose?" asked Drew.

"None. The outlaws gave up muy pronto when they saw how many men we had. Some headed north and I guess you know where the others went."

Jeffrey Boxer came walking up to Drew. Now at 17 years old, he looked more like a man than a boy. He was 6 feet tall, with wavy dark hair and was forming the beginning of beard from too many days without a shave. He was broad across the shoulders and had thick arms and a muscular chest.

"Excuse me, Major, sir."

"What is it?"

"I don't want to seem presumptuous but something has been on my mind ever since those outlaws hit us."

"Not at all. How can you learn if you don't ask?"

"Yes, sir."

"So what's on your mind?"

"How did those outlaws know we'd be making this drive? I don't recall us telling anyone about this drive. Seems to me it was decided at sunlight. So to my way of thinking wasn't time for anyone to know about it, sir."

Drew raised an eyebrow. He hadn't considered that idea. "That's a good question. You're pretty smart. Even I had not thought about that. But now that you've brought it up..."

"It's just a thought, Major. I could be way off which is why I came to you."

Drew sat down next to the campfire. Using his saddle for a chair, he spread his blanket out on the ground and began to clean his Colt revolvers. Jack Bartlett came walking over to where Drew was sitting. He was carrying two cups of coffee and handed one to Drew.

"We were very lucky today. But I fear the next time they will have an army of their own," said Bartlett.

"I do believe you're right," said Drew sounding irritated.

"Did I say the wrong thing?"

"What? Oh, no. I'm just wondering where the heck Jack is."

"Well, he had an errand to do," said Bartlett.

"So everyone keeps saying. Just what kind of errand?"

"You didn't hear this from me. He threatened to shoot anyone who told you but he and some of the boys are out rounding up the herd. They bolted like shot from a cannon when the shooting started. Caleb told him he should put more distance between the herd and the wagons. But Jack said he felt better that he could see the wagons. When those outlaws hightailed it, he took some men to round up the herd and told everyone he'd shoot the first man to tell you about it," aughed Bartlett.

"Oh, I see. Ha ha ha. This is just too good to let slide. Thanks, Jack."

"Here he comes now. You want more coffee? I don't want to be within 20 feet of you two when the dust starts flying."

"Sure. Bring one for Jack, too."

When Whiskey Jack got down from his horse and walked over toward where Drew was sitting, he could see the "I told you so" on Drew's face though Drew had not yet said one word.

"I was..." Drew was stopped in mid-sentence.

"Hermano, if you say what I think you're going to so help me, I'll knock the wax clean out of both your ears," threatened Jack.

"What? Just wondering when you'd get back. Coffee?"

"Yes. Thanks," Jack took a sip of coffee then spouted. "Well, how was I supposed to know? Those ornery critters took off so fast, they were halfway to San Antonio before I knew they were gone!"

"You couldn't have known. Might have helped to distance them more from the wagons. But still that's no guarantee of anything."

Jack took a surveying look around the camp. "Lose anyone?"

"No. Dan took one but he'll be fine. Took three of theirs though."

"Recognize any of them?"

"No. They're buried over yonder." Drew pointed. "Jack?"

"Ya?"

"Do you recall anyone saying anything about this drive? I mean, besides the obvious people."

"Can't say that I do. Why?"

"Someone knew. Those outlaws had no reason to think or know that we were making a drive. So how did they know to plan the when and where to hit us?"

"That would make sense. But who? And how'd you come to suspect anything?"

"I didn't. It was young Jeff that brought it to my attention and it does make sense."

"Sure does."

"One thing we do know. It wasn't anyone from this bunch."

It was a warm windy day when they finally came into Austin. A misty rain blew east to west across the main street of town. Thunder boomed in the far distance, announcing the forthcoming of a heavier rain. Small dust tornadoes swirled about in the east end of town. Someone in a rush to get to dry shelter left their newspaper lying about and now the wind was scattering it all around.

"Get those cattle over to the feedlots down at the rail station and make sure the gates are locked secure when you are done!" ordered Drew.

The wagons containing the produce and grain had been quickly shuttled into Hathaway's feeding grain warehouse and barns.

"Looks like we've done it. We made it here all in one piece. No worse for the wear either. Thanks to you, Major Parker," said Charles Owens.

"We're here all right. But don't go thanking me yet. Remember, some of that outfit that jumped us may be here as well. If so, I'm certain they have told their employers the news. We may have made it but now we have to sell it and make money doing so."

"That should not be much of a problem for me as I signed an agreement with Charles last fall. I should make out all right. Six times of corn at three dollars a ton and apples at a dollar and $.75 a bushel is $1968. I'm not going to complain. At least I'll be able to keep my land. After all, this is just the first haul."

"What about Taylor? Did he make the same arrangement?" inquired Drew.

"I reckon he did. I can't say for certain. I think Charlie Hathaway offered everyone the same deal, far as I know."

"Just as a safeguard, I think we should post men to watch over things until tomorrow morning," said Drew.

"Think someone might start some trouble for us?"

"I don't know, Charlie. I just have this feeling."

The next morning Charlie Owens and Richard Taylor were in the office of the Hathaway feeding grain.

"What! Two dollars a ton! Charles Hathaway, we signed an agreement and you're going to honor it or else!"

"I'm really sorry. I am fully aware of our agreement, Charles. But the fact remains, I no longer own the feed and grain store anymore. Asbury and Benson own it now. It's just by grace that they continue to let me run the place. I work for them now. Sadly, any agreements I might have made are not valid anymore."

"I don't believe you, Hathaway! You're in cahoots with that bunch of swindlers and coyotes! Tell me it isn't so," demanded Richard Taylor.

"They came to me last fall. Offered me a loan to keep the place going. When I couldn't make the payments in full they deemed me a liability and foreclosed. Honest! There was nothing I could do. So there's the offer. At the price Asbury and Benson set. Take it or leave it," said Charles Hathaway.

At the office of Asbury and Benson, things were getting a bit tight. Harvey Ainsworth was sitting in a large mahogany chair with red velvet cushion seats. He was seated in front of William Asbury's desk.

"How many times do I have to tell you, Ainsworth? Put that infernal thing out now. This is my place of business. Not some cheap barroom."

Harvey Ainsworth leaned forward and snuffed out the end of his cigar on the heel of his boot. "You best start talking a bit more polite to me, Asbury. You need me. Remember that. You need me and my men. Not the other way around."

"Yes, I need you. Or at least someone like you. I pay you well for your services. But don't go getting greedy and think you can squeeze me for more money. I can replace you in a twinkling of an eye. You're a mercenary, Ainsworth. The country is full of them. Why, you botched your task at the Bartlett spread. Five days? I told you to kill him if need be. Just bring me the deed to the land."

"What your little informant didn't tell you is he had men with shotguns and rifles pointed right at us, and what's five days? He's never going to make that deadline anyway."

"Is that so? Tell me how it is that there are five wagons in the feeding grain warehouse and 700 head of Longhorn at the railyard in the feed lot eating my hay! Do you know who he has with him?"

"Sure. It's that has-been Texas Ranger. So what?"

"He is not only not a has-been, the governor has yet to disband the Texas Rangers. But Drew Parker is the grandson to Don Miguel Peña. Son of Senora Kataryna Louisa Peña Parker."

"Okay, let's say you tickled my curiosity? Anyway, Don Miguel Peña is dead. What's so special about this Peña Parker stuff? Who cares?"

"The Peña family is one of the oldest and wealthiest families in South Texas. Chances are they have already agreed to front the other ranches and farms. If that is the case, then I say you'd better care. Because Texas Ranger or no, Drew Parker is not someone to be trifled with. Not only that, but the Peña Ranchero has its own private little army you might say. With over 200 ranch hands, cowboys and Vaqueros. Each and every one loyal to Don Miguel and his daughter, Señora Kataryna. Senora Kataryna is Drew Parker's mother," stated William Asbury.

"Don't you worry about Drew Parker and the Peña Ranchero. My men and I know how to handle that problem. In six weeks, Major Drew Parker will be sitting here at this desk begging you to help him. Or selling out," said Ainsworth.

"So, what do you think? Do they have the legal right?" ssked Charles Owens.

"I cannot say until I have read the agreement. Judging from what you have told me so far, I'd say no. Have any of the other farmers or ranchers been given notice of Asbury and Benson's takeover of the

Hathaway feeding grain? Or of any price chart changes to said agreement?" asked Caleb.

The men were all talking around a long, wide table at the Austin Hotel and Diner. Jack Bartlett of the High Solara was particularly concerned.

"Well, I did get what I was asked for with the herd. The kicker is that the railroad agent wants double what it used to cost to haul them," Jack Bartlett was interrupted by the young waitress who approached their table.

"Gentlemen, may I help you?"

The men all ordered their meals and after the waitress had left, they resumed their talk.

"I hate to say it but it looks like they have me boxed in on all four sides. I'm not going to make the deadline," said Bartlett.

Caleb looked at Jack Bartlett then at everyone at the table.

"Not exactly, Mr. Bartlett."

"You can call me Jack. I prefer that my friends do. So what do you mean not exactly?"

"How do you feel about the Army?"

"The Army? Caleb, I'm afraid you've lost me."

"Jack, if you have any qualms dealing with Yankees, I just might be able to help you with your predicament."

"Right now, I'm fighting Asbury and Benson and their bunch of skunks. I'd almost deal with Satan himself. I suppose Yankees are the next best thing. What do you have in mind?"

"One thing I know for sure. Asbury and Benson don't own the telegraph office. That belongs to the government. If you will give me until morning?"

"Sure."

"Caleb. They might not own the telegraph office but they might own the telegrapher," said Johnny Caldwell Parker Jack.

"I hadn't thought of that," replied Caleb

"Don't you worry about him. If anyone can operate the key, I can distract him long enough for you to send any message," smiled Jeffrey Boxer.

"So what's your plan?" asked Whiskey Jack.

"I have an old classmate from law school who is at Fort Leavenworth. He can arrange to take those Longhorns at a much better price and the Army does not pay to have anything shipped by the railroad," said Caleb.

"Classmate? So why would a Yankee want to do a Reb any favors?" asked Jack Bartlett.

"Let's say he just owes me and vowed anything I asked."

"Favor, what for?"

"At Chickamauga. I let him live."

"Sorry I asked," said Jack Bartlett.

The telegrapher was sitting at his desk playing solitaire. When he heard the pap pap! from Jeffrey Boxer's revolver, he sprang from his seat and rushed to open the back door of the telegraph office.

"What's going on out here?!"

"Jeffrey was poking at the woodpile with a shovel in one hand and his revolver in the other.

"Rattlesnake. I missed him. I think he might have gone behind that crate there," said Jeff pointing at a wooden crate next to the woodpile.

"Rattlesnake? Good grief. We better get him. Sure don't want to get bit getting wood for the stove," said the telegrapher.

Jeff handed the telegrapher the shovel. "Here use this. Flip it over and I will shoot him."

"Sure enough," agreed the telegrapher. Jeff stood back with his revolver poised to shoot.

"Any time you're ready," said Jeff.

The telegrapher, shaking, took the shovel and flipped the crate over expecting a snake.

"Aaaaahhhh!" screamed the telegrapher as a large skunk sprayed him square in the chest. Jeff looked at the telegrapher with innocent unknowing eyes and shrugged.

"Who knew?" Jeff said trying his best not to bust out laughing.

"Thought it was a snake!"

Jeff cut the telegrapher short and holding his nose said, "I'll watch the place for you. Do you have the keys? I'll lock up."

The telegrapher tossed Jeff the keys and took off.

"Hahahahah, Caleb should be able to wire China with no problem now," laughed Jeff.

An hour before daybreak the next morning, the town of Austin, Texas was awakened to the sounds of yelling and the smell of smoke.

"Fire! Fire!" Someone was ringing the church bell. "Fire! Fire in the warehouse!"

Drew ran outside on to the hotel's front porch still putting on his shirt. "Oh, God, what next?" he said to himself. When the men from the hotel reached the warehouse, it was engulfed in flames. A bucket brigade had been formed and the Austin fire wagon pulled by four black horses was coming down the street ringing a bell. Drew reached the warehouse staring at the scene before him in disbelief. He turned to see Charles Owens running toward him. Drew reached out and grabbed Charles by his arm.

"Charlie! Charlie! Hold on! It's no good, man. It's lost. I'm sorry. It's all lost."

Charles Owens dropped to his knees. "Fifteen years. Fifteen hard backbreaking years! Years of sweat, going without, to build a home. We survived the war only to lose it like this. What am I going to tell Betty and the kids?" Charlie wept.

Drew could find no words. All he felt was anger and a lust for revenge.

"Don't go on so, Charlie. You're a good friend and neighbor and a Parker or Peña does not watch a friend go under. You'll keep your farm. I swear by all that's holy. You'll keep your farm."

The train pulled out of Austin on time at 2:00 pm. With 700 head of cattle and a 20 man Army escort. The escort was actually for shipment of arms and payroll money but it was unlikely that any harm would come to the cattle with soldiers on the train.

The door to the sheriff's office flew open with a crash when Drew kicked it, revolver drawn and poised to fire.

"Have you lost your mind?"

"The name is Drew Parker. Major Drew Parker, Texas Rangers. I want you to know my name before you die."

"Now hold on, mister. Think before you pull the trigger. The Rangers are done. If you pull that trigger it'll be murder and you'll become a common outlaw. Do you want that?"

"Sheriff, I'm thinking, why is the Sheriff sitting on his fat butt doing nothing as the warehouse burns to the ground? As for being a murderer, I'd say you have a lot to answer for. All those honest, hard-working ranchers and farmers and their wives and children. You've killed and destroyed their lives as sure as if you yourself had pulled the trigger. You're no good. You're a tin star bought and paid for by Asbury and Benson. No, Sheriff, killing you won't make me an outlaw. They may even elect me mayor of Austin. Maybe even the next governor for killing your worthless hide. But I'm going to give you a man's chance though you don't deserve it. I'm giving you until morning to pack your bags, saddle up and leave Austin. If I see your face tomorrow or any day after, I swear by Almighty God, I will kill you on sight. No warnings, I'll just kill you like you would a cockroach."

"You have some nerve," the sheriff stopped in midsentence as he heard the hammer on Drew's revolver click as it was being pulled back. "Don't push me, Sheriff," threatened Drew as he backed out of the office and walked away.

Along the Canadian River, in the Oklahoma Indian Territory, the fires were burning brightly outside of the teepees of the Comanche tribe. Children ran to and fro playing. The women were busy either jerking venison or beef or cleaning the fat and meat from hides to make into clothing or blankets. The night was quickly approaching as the sun painted the sky orange and pink. Inside the Council Lodge was not so serene and peaceful.

"I am sick of this waiting, How long?! How long will our people behave like a dog on a rope? I say we must take what is ours!" said Yellow Pony.

"Yellow Pony is without a doubt a brave warrior. He has proved that many times. But Dancing Crow is still our chief and has served his people well. I believe we should obey his advice and not go to war with the white eyes," said Quanah Parker.

"You, who led so many raids in the past, say no? Has Quanah become tired and sickly as well?" taunted Yellow Pony.

"Yellow Pony has always been at competition with me. For what I do not know and why I do not know. But do not make the mistake that I am weak. I do not wish to kill any one of my people. But to underestimate my ability as a man and a warrior, Yellow Pony would be greatly missed." It was a challenge as clear as the sound of the fire crackling. Yellow Pony did not answer. He only held up his hand as if to say forget it.

Quanah Parker stood up. "I have great respect and admiration for Dancing Crow. It was he who kept his people from starving when I was a boy. It was he who kept his people safe during the white man's Civil War. I also have great respect for Yellow Pony. Few warriors can best him. He is feared by the Kiowa and the Apache. If the time comes that there must be war, I want such a man as he to fight at my side. But do not make me choose between the two of you.

"It is not a matter of choosing me or Dancing Crow. Dancing Crow knows my heart. It was he who taught me the way of the warrior. It is a matter of choosing to live or die. My heart sinks and my gut churns at the site of our children and women and our old ones going hungry and nearly freezing to death from the winter cold. Quanah wants peace with the white eyes. This is a good thing to wish for. But time and time again the whites have proven to be untrustworthy. They take the green grass and the water. Then put the Comanche on a hill of sand and say, "Here, this is a good land for the Comanche to live." If it was such good land whites would have kept it. But when the Comanche makes that hill of sand fruitful the whites cry out, "It is not right for the Comanche to have that hill! The Comanche are standing in the way of progress." Always this is so with the white eyes. They are like the locust. They are like a wolf pup who will eat and eat until it's stomach bursts. They would set their own women on fire if they thought they could get a good price for the ashes! No, Quanah, I am not asking you to choose me or Dancing Crow to follow. For surely it is your rightful place in line to lead the Comanche," said Yellow Pony.

"Yellow Pony's love for his people cannot be overmatched by anyone. This I know to be true. He would gladly die to protect them. This too I know to be true. There are very few worthy to pull back his bow. But if our warriors keep dying fighting the whites soon we will have no warriors to fight! I say wait. Let us learn more of the white man's laws. Any great hunter will tell you, to first catch the bear you must learn the ways of the bear. This is true of the whites as well. Yes, we will fight. But let the warpath be our last resort. For knowledge is a powerful weapon too. Sometimes more so than the bow or the rifle. I say we should listen to Quanah. Let us not be the hand that takes the food from our children's mouth," said Dancing Crow. These words of Dancing Crow would haunt Quanah Parker all the days of his life.

**Austin, Texas**

The morning sun was making its debut over the eastern horizon. The gray-blue silhouettes of the clouds resembled the mountain ranges of the West Texas in Drew's mind. He longed for those days in a nostalgic way.

From down the street he could hear the ringing of the school bell. Drew was just finishing a plate of biscuits and sausage gravy and sipped a cup of black coffee. He was staring out the window when Caleb came walking across the hotel dining room floor to Drew's table.

"May I sit down?"

Drew looked up and almost startled. He waved his hand across the table and said "Yes. Please, Caleb, be my guest. What brings you over this early in the morning?"

"You. That wasn't very smart, Drew."

"What wasn't? What are you talking about?" asked Drew honestly puzzled.

"The sheriff. He went to the mayor who in turn went to the govenor because of your reputation as a Ranger and being the grandson of Senora Kataryna," said Caleb.

"I am still at a loss," replied Drew.

"You threatened to kill Sheriff Shepfield. Did you not?"

"I did and I will. Unless he heeds my advice to get out of Austin and out of Texas entirely."

"No doubt you had good reason but now the govenor wants to see you."

"Right now I suppose?" replied Drew.

"Yes," sighed Caleb. "I am afraid so."

Drew stood up and took his hat from the hat rack next to his table. He tossed some money on the table. "Well, let's not keep his Eminence waiting," replied Drew mockingly.

"Now hold on, Drew. I'm sure you feel uncomfortable having me especially come to get you and all. But let's not sharpen our horns for a fight with the govenor. Okay? I'm sure it isn't as bad as you might be thinking."

"Actually the govenor knew exactly what he was doing by choosing you as his messenger. For obvious reasons but whatever it is you think I may be thinking, I'm sure you are mistaken. I've been trying to figure out a way to see him anyway. Him with his so-called busy schedule and all. If I knew all I had to do was threaten the sheriff, I'd have done that a long time ago," said Drew as he smiled and put on his hat.

"The govenor will see you now, Major," said the woman at the receptionist desk as she looked him up and down appraisingly.

"Thank you, ma'am," said Drew.

Governor Edmund Jackson Davis was sitting at his desk reading a piece of paper and strumming his fingers on his desk. He looked up at the door opening to his office." Come in, Drew, come in. "

"You sent for me, sir?"

The govenor looked at the paper then cleared his throat. "Yes, I did. You know, Drew, I have always admired you. But I have also said that you have the temperament of an alligator. What in heaven's name were you thinking? Threatening to kill the sheriff? Drew, really. You know that there has been pressure on me from every angle to completely disband the Texas Rangers and now you've gone and complicated the matter even more by threatening to kill the sheriff of Austin! Have you lost your senses? Were you drinking? That's it. We'll just say you had too much to drink and were emotionally distraught over the fire and for your friends. That was it, right?"

"No, I meant what I said and if I see him again, I'll kill him. What's so hard to figure out?" replied Drew.

"What for?"

"You are familiar with a company called Asbury and Benson?" asked Drew.

"Yes, I have heard of them. I don't much care for them but they are a legitimate enterprise and could be good for Texas. Why? And what do they have to do with you wanting to kill the sheriff? Drew, you have got to enlighten me. Believe it or not, I am trying my damnedest to put the Rangers back in full force. I can't make any headway if I have them terrorizing local law enforcement such as Sheriff Shepfield," said the govenor.

"He's a skunk and he's on Asbury and Benson's payroll. How else can you explain that gun hand Ainsworth and his bunch for having so much liberty in this town and there's the fire? The entire warehouse was engulfed in flames and the local sheriff just sits on his duff and does nothing? Men like me are just what you do need before that disease makes its way into this very office. Can't you see what they are doing? Men like Asbury and Benson and all of those carpetbaggers are feeding on the miseries of good people! People who either have or nearly have lost everything they and their fathers before them fought and bled and toiled and sweated to rebuild what they lost because of the recent war. Officially and by all historical records, the war is over and that may be a good thing. But politically it still rages on. Instead of guns and cannons, they have been replaced with crooked politicians and bankers and lawyers. They won't be satisfied until they have everything that Texas and the South has to offer. They're still waging a war but it's a different kind of war. Not for any noble cause such as slavery either. Slavery! Do you really believe that's what it was about? Look at Chicago, New York, Philadelphia and all those other big Eastern states' cities. You'll find sweatshops hidden in every dark corner in those cities with children doing the work for them. And others as well. No, Governor, slavery was not the issue but they wanted to capitalize on it. But because

Lincoln chose that as a platform to get re-elected and end the war they have to find a new means of slavery. Bloodsuckers every one of them. The South should've done away with the slaves then started the war."

"That may be so, Drew, but people like Asbury and Benson are legitimate businesses. From what I can see they have followed the law," said the governor.

"By following the law, you mean hiring men like Ainsworth? Running off stock and destroying produce and grain shipments, burning down warehouses and killing good men? Men who are trying to rebuild their lives? That kind of law, Governor?"

"I can't act on hearsay, Drew. I have no proof. How do you know this to be true?"

"Bcause just a few days ago, I and my men as well as some other good people, all my friends, were attacked by those so-called legal employees from Asbury and Benson that's how! We were bringing produce, cattle and grain to Austin. It was for some their last hope from being foreclosed on by Asbury and Benson. Ainsworth is their chief enforcer. We killed three of them. Since we could not identify them by name, Asbury and Benson as well as Ainsworth could deny knowing them. So we buried them. I won't be so thoughtful next time. Next time, I'll be sure to take some alive. Believe me, I'll find out who's running this dog and pony show," said Drew.

"Let's not have talk of vigilantes! You've already done enough with Sheriff Shepfield. Can't you see him trying to help? I'm on your side and the side of the Texas Rangers. Help me help you," said the governor.

"Sure, but remember I'm also a rancher and anything I do in defense of my land, my cattle, my family and my friends will be in that capacity and not as a Ranger. As the patriarch of the Peña Ranchero I also will act in that capacity. So while you're doing whatever you have to do to protect your social standing, I will be doing what I have to do. You said you wanted to help? Let's start seeing it. Until then, Governor, stay out of my way!"

Drew turned and stormed out of the governor's office. It was a gamble to call the governor's bluff in that way but Drew knew that the only way to get the governor to act was to put another dog in the fight. The Peña family held a lot of clout and influence with the people of South Texas. Influence that could determine whether or not Edmund Jackson Davis got re-elected or not. Drew also knew that Texas needed the Rangers now more than ever. Since the beginning of the war and up until it's end, the Longhorn cattle had gone feral and roamed the ranges. Now with the war being over for nearly five years, ranchers and ambitious young men wanting to build a new life and start over were rounding up as many of the Longhorns as they could handle. This was also a tumultuous time as many a dispute over whose cows were whose constantly flared up on the range resulting sometimes in deadly gun battles. Then there was a rustler who would let the honest men do all the work then steal his cattle. For as long as they had no brand there was no proof of ownership. The worst were men like Asbury and Benson who would front many of these rustlers. Remaining behind the scenes never getting their hands dirty and buying law enforcement, judges and politicians. Texas Rangers were indeed needed. Drew knew this and he also knew Gov. Edmund Davis knew it as well.

Caleb was waiting in the lobby as Drew came down the stairs from the Governor's office. "I take it that all went well. At least he didn't shoot you," said Caleb.

"Only time will tell for certain," replied Drew.

"I suppose you will be rounding up the men and starting back in the morning?"

"I better before I get myself in trouble. How I miss old Charlie Welch. There was a man for you. He knew how to handle the likes of the Honorable Edmund Jackson Davis. I'm just no good at diplomacy. Things are either right or wrong with me. I just can't see things differently. Now Charlie would have had that governor in the palm of his hand by now," said Drew.

"Maybe so. Am I going to see you before you go?" asked Caleb.

"How about breakfast. Say 5:30?" said Drew.

"Sounds good. I'll see you in the morning," said Caleb.

"You're not going to walk with me?" asked Drew.

"I promised Mr. Owens and Mr. Taylor that I would look over their new contracts with Asbury and Benson. Luckily, I got them to honor the original but that was the last of it."

"I'm sure you will get them the best deal possible. See you in the morning, Caleb."

Drew sat in the chair next to the bed in his hotel room staring out the window. His thoughts were of home, Marjorie, his wife, and Sally and his son, Miguel Andrew.

A knock came upon the door to his room and it opened slowly. Whiskey Jack stuck his head into the room and called in a low voice into the darkened room. "Hermano, you awake?"

"Yes, Jack. Come on in but don't light the lamp."

Whiskey Jack walked over to the edge of the bed and sat down. "You all right, hermano?"

"I'm fine. I just want to sit in the dark. The light hurts my eyes. Headache."

"I see. How did it go with the governor?"

Drew cracked a light smile and chuckled. "I don't think he'll be sending me any Christmas cards this year."

"Told him off, didn't you?"

"I wouldn't say that. I just let him know what boot went on what foot."

"Hermano, one of these days you're going to stub your toe kicking at the wrong rock. You thinking we should be heading home in the morning?"

"Seems the thing to do. Only I hate leaving and seeing Charles Owens and Richard Taylor go home empty-handed. That damn fire. Jack, I can't accept that it was an accident. Someone set that fire. I'm sure of it."

"Suppose you're right. Who would be the culprit? Do you really believe that Asbury and Benson would burn their own warehouse? Why?"

"I don't know, Jack, but the thought has crossed my mind that they did. Or at least paid someone to do it for them. I'm going to the bank in the morning and we're going to buy those notes to their farms."

"Whose farms?"

"Charles' and Dick's. Weren't you listening?"

"Without talking it over with Mother? Are you taking a gamble that she won't disapprove?"

"She won't. Besides I'm the new patriarch, responsibility falls on me regardless. I know that's what Don Miguel would have done."

"That's a very noble thought from you, hermano, but don't you think you should talk it over with Charlie and Dick first? After all, you know what they say Presta dinero y perder a tu amigo. Lend money and lose your friend," said Jack.

"Yes, I know," replied Drew. "What else can I do?"

"Do nothing, Drew. These are proud men we're talking about. You could offend their manhood and pride by offering to pick up their debts. Your heart is in the right place. Let them come to you so that they can save face at least a bit."

"You do have a point there. But they've been our neighbors for years. You and I grew up with Charlie. There has to be something we can do."

"All the more reason to step back and let it be. Knowing Charlie the way we do, he'd rather cut off his right arm than take the handout and Dick's the same way," said Jack.

"Pride! Damned pride. I'm thinking about their wives and kids not just Charlie and Dick."

"I'm sure. But you're just as prideful. You'd take it as an insult just as quickly as they would and you know it. I pray to God that the Peña Ranchero can last. It would surely kill Mother. That house is not just her home, it is her. She is the Peña Ranchero," said Jack.

"I've given thought to that too," Drew sat and stared out the window in silence for a moment then he shot Jack a look. "What about the cattlemen's and farmer's association?"

"What about it?"

"Suppose we call a meeting. I have this idea that just might work," said Drew.

"You scare me, hermano, whenever you get like Moses leading the Hebrews across the desert way. Whatever it is, I don't want to know until Mother has heard it as well. Go to bed. Your brain is smoking," said Jack.

"I suppose you're right. I am probably overthinking things. I can't help being me, hermano," said Drew.

"Si, and a finer man I've yet to meet. But you can be frightful obsessive over matters too. Hermano, you can't save the whole world. Sometimes it's all a man can do to save himself. Good night, hermano." Jack stood up and patted Drew's shoulder. "Get some sleep. I'll see you in the morning."

"Good night."

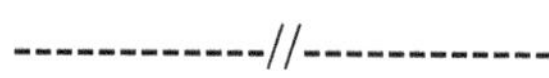

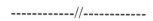

**Uvalde, Texas**

The casual visitor would never know that anything was wrong at the Peña Ranchero. Children were laughing and running and playing as always. The cowboys and Vaqueros who had stayed to look over the ranch were at their normal everyday routines as Drew and Jack and the others came riding on to the ranch.

As they neared the hacienda, Drew and Jack reined their horses to a halt and looked at each other with puzzlement. Three unknown cowboys were bringing in a small herd of steers numbering about 60 head and doing a good job of it as well.

"Ours?" asked Drew.

"Must be. Or else they're mighty dumb rustlers," replied Jack.

"Let's ride over and give them a hand. Johnny! You and Jeff see to it that everyone gets settled in and help Charlie and Dick with those wagons," Drew ordered.

"Yes, sir," repled Johnny.

As Drew and Jack got closer to the riders they were again amused. It was Marjorie, Nancy and Sally pushing the herd.

"Well, roll me in cow poop and call me stinky!" laughed Drew.

Marjorie raised a hand and waved. "Well, don't just sit there gawking. We've got cows to move!" she yelled.

"Yes, ma'am!" said Drew. "Where did you ladies learn to do this?"

"It isn't so hard when you have smart horses and a few lessons from some of the boys," said Nancy. "But this isn't what you should be concerned with right now. We've got troubles."

"What kind of trouble?" Jack asked his wife.

"Someone salted the watering hole on the east range. Paco found four dead heifers. He pushed the rest of the cattle away from the water then rode to tell us. By the time we got there, the cattle were back at the watering tank. They seem to be okay so far. But we started driving them off that part of the range immediately," Nancy said.

"So what in blazes are you doing out here? You should have sent some men to do the job," Jack said.

"We did just that. They are about a mile behind us and for your enlightenment, Mr. Whiskey Jack Peña Parker, we women are as much a part of this ranch as you men. We saw what needed to be done and we did it," declared Nancy sternly.

"Yes, ma'am, I reckon you did." Jack chuckled as he leaned forward in the saddle and kissed his wife hello.

Drew and Marjorie along with Sally came trotting up alongside Jack and Nancy. "Did you hear?" asked Drew.

"Ya, someone salted the water. Any idea who?"

"We can't prove it but got a list of about fifty," said Drew.

"Did Paco and the boys look for any tracks of who may have done this?" Drew asked Marjorie.

"He said between the wind and the cattle, their tracks were destroyed. But Paco thinks it was the job of just one man. He said it was unlikely that cows would have wiped out all the tracks had there been more than one," answered Marjorie.

"Makes sense and if Paco couldn't find the trail, we probably won't either. He's one of our top hands and a darn good tracker too," replied Drew.

**Mule Shoe, Texas**

Hamelton O'Toole was coming down the stairs of the newly built Paradise Hotel. As he approached the hotel's check-in counter, he was summoned by the hotel clerk.

"Mr. O'Toole! I have a letter for you. The stagecoach brought the mail early this morning," said the clerk.

"Letter? Who do you suppose would be sending me a letter?"

"I'm not sure, sir. But it's from Austin. A Mr. Caleb Parker, Attorney at Law," replied the clerk.

Hamelton O'Toole took the envelope from the clerk. "Thank you, Dave."

O'Toole carried the envelope over to a table in the hotel's dining room and sat down. A young waitress came to his table. "May I take your order, Mr. O'Toole, or will you have the usual steak, eggs, fried potatoes, biscuits, grits and gravy?" smiled the young woman as she filled his coffee cup.

O'Toole looked up at the woman and smiled. "Yes, Anne, that will do just fine. Thank you."

"It'll be about ten minutes," said the waitress.

O'Toole was sipping his coffee as he opened the letter. "I wonder what he would be writing about to me?" O'Toole read the letter and gazed at it for a long time. The letter simply read:

> Sergeant Major, Come at once. You are needed. Trouble.
> Caleb Parker
> Attorney at law

Hamelton O'Toole stood up quickly, downed his coffee and screwed on his hat tightly. He dropped two dollars on the table then turned to leave the dining room. Anne called out, "Mr. O'Toole, your breakfast!"

"Thanks but I'll have to go without breakfast this morning. I left payment on the table."

"But it's still hot!"

"Sorry. You eat it. You deserve the break!" O'Toole called back over his shoulder.

**Voca, Texas**
**Three days from Austin**

The three riders were just settling down to prepare camp for the night. One of the riders glanced up the trail and gestured with his chin. "Who do you suppose that is?"

Another of the riders stared up the trail at a lone rider approaching. A huge smile formed on his face." Well, I'll be a knobbed kneed jack-ass. Don't you know who that is?"

"If I knew, I wouldn't be asking."

The cowboy who had recognized the approaching rider waved. "Hey! O'Toole! Come on in!"

O'Toole spurred his horse into a fast trot and rode into the camp. It was Danny and Marty Collins and Red Sands.

"Glory be! Howdy, boys!" exclaimed O'Toole. "Now who would have figured!"

"Just fixing to start supper. How the heck have you been? Talk about small worlds!" said Red Sands.

"Tell you the truth, I've been bored out of my mind. I've been work-ing as a bartender in Mule Shoe. At the Crystal Rose."

"Might have figured you'd end up there. Coffee?" asked Red.

"Don't mind if I do. Ya, it's a living but not for me," said O'Toole.

"What brings you this far south?" asked Marty Collins.

O'Toole reached into his shirt pocket and pulled out the letter and handed it to Red. Red took the letter and read it. "Kid's got a way with words, don't he?" Red chuckled.

"He probably figured that would be sufficient and he was right," smiled O'Toole "What brings you saddle bums this way?"

"Saddle bums? We are on our way to Austin. Some fellow named Ainsworth is hiring range hands for some company called Asbury and Benson," explained Danny Collins.

"Good! I'll have company then. I'm going to Austin as well. Caleb sent for me. Apparently he's got some troubles," replied O'Toole.

"Sure would be nice to see him again," said Danny Collins.

"Then we'll have a regular family reunion," said O'Toole.

The four men sat and ate and talked all through the night. They laughed and toasted to memories past and to fallen comrades. Finally, they all bedded down for the night.

**Austin, Texas**

William Asbury was perplexed. His sheriff had suddenly left town. Three men had been killed in a botched raid and Ainsworth was starting to get too darn cocky, running roughshod over the merchants and other citizens. That attorney, Caleb Parker, was too smart for his own good. Nothing had been going as planned. Now the governor was sticking his nose into their business.

"This is all your doing. It was you who hired that weasel Ainsworth. You take care of him. Or I'll be forced to," said William Asbury to Theodore Benson.

"You? Take care of Ainsworth? That's a laugh. William, you worry too much. Because of Ainsworth and his crew, we are this close to controlling all of the commerce south of Austin. Soon we'll have control over all of the water and mineral rights as well. So what if a few folks get banged up in the process," said Theodore Benson.

"Don't be so sure just yet. You're forgetting one little problem. Senora Kataryna Peña Parker and her sons. We have nothing as long as the Peña Ranchero exists," said Asbury.

"I'm already working on that. Don't you fret," said Benson.

"I thought we agreed not to move on the Peña Ranchero until we were certain that Governor Davis had disbanded the Texas Rangers once and for all. You idiot!"

"I'd be careful who you called an idiot, if I were you," said Benson.

"What's that supposed to mean? By going after the Peña Ranchero, you could tip public favor towards them and by doing so the need to re-commission the Texas Rangers. Drew Parker is one of the legends of the Texas Rangers. He alone has heavy clout by being the grandson of the late Don Miguel Peña and is the new patriarch of the Peña ranch. Their political connections extend from both sides of the border as well as in Washington D.C."

"That was before the war. Things are different now. Like I said, you worry too much," said Benson.

"You don't understand politics very well, do you? The government, especially in Texas, needs folks like the Peña's for diplomatic reasons."

"Not if they're dead," replied Benson.

**Peña Ranchero**
**Uvalde, Texas**

Johnny and Jeffrey were riding the north range. Since the end of the war, cattle left unattended were allowed to go feral. The Peña Ranchero stock had not. However, this did not prevent wild Longhorns from mingling and breeding with the Peña cattle. It was these offspring that the two young men were looking for. Their idea was to round up as many of these wild Longhorns and put their brand on them and begin their own herd. They had done fairly well over the past few weeks with nearly 800 head already cut out from the others. They had driven them to the west side of the north range. It was today that they had chosen to spend the next few days branding their cattle. They had chosen the brand "P" over "JJ" which they would register their brand on their next trip to Austin.

"There they are. You ready to get started?" asked Johnny.

"Sure enough. But don't you think we should wait until morning? It's getting late and we haven't even decided on a campsite yet and I'm getting hungry," complained Jeffrey.

"Me too. Alright then. Let's start in the morning. I'll set up the camp and get a fire going. I think there's a watering hole just on the other side of that ridge. We'll camp there. You can look after the horses and fetch the water," said Johnny.

Jeff agreed. The two young cowboys were just settling in and about to have their meal of bacon, beans and coffee when Johnny perked his head up. He whispered, "Hear that?"

Jeff stood up and strained his hearing. "Sounds like cattle bawling."

"We better go take a look see," said Johnny.

They sat on the horses and trotted to the top of the ridge that hid their campsite. They had just barely crested the top of the ridge when Jeff jumped down from his horse, leading it by the reins back down the ridge. Johnny followed.

"Rustlers," said Jeffrey.

"And they're rustling our cows!" Johnny hissed.

"We better hightail it back to the ranch and fetch some help," said Jeff.

"It's too far. By the time we get back, they'll have moved those beevs to another range and started putting their brand on them," said Johnny.

"Well, we sure can't fight them. There's way too many of them for just us two," replied Jeff.

"I know. But we can slow them down for sure. We worked too long and too hard to just let those varmints just waltz in and take those cows pretty as you please," scowled Johnny.

"I hear what you're saying and I'm with you. You know that for sure. But how?"

"We'll let them get good and comfortable with those cows. We'll hang back then when they bed down, we will make our play," suggested Johnny.

"What about the nighthawks? They're sure to have at least two or three watching the herd."

"When we are done there will only be one. Maybe none."

"What you mean?" Jeff asked.

"I figure we let the main bunch get settled into sleep good and tight. Then stampede the herd. We can take out at least two of the nighthawks in the process."

"Kill them? In cold blood?" asked Jeff.

"They're stealing our cows. They're rustlers and murderers, Jeff. They wouldn't think twice about killing us and probably will if they catch us. So it isn't in cold blood. Chances are they're part of that bunch that jumped us on our way to Austin. Maybe even salted the waterhole."

"Well, I'm with you, sure, but if I shoot anyone, it will be in self-defense," said Jeffrey.

"Let's hope it doesn't come to that because we'd be in a hell of a lot of trouble. Okay, we won't plan to shoot anyone. We'll just stampede the herd and skedaddle muy pronto."

The sun dropped over the horizon, a yellow orange glow was all that remained. Blue gray shadows haunted the landscape as the rustlers began to settle in for the evening. Only two men rode nighthawk. Johnny thought to himself, "They're either very confident in themselves not being caught or this is some kind of trap."

"I don't like it, Jeff. Those hombres are acting as if they are the only people in the world. We best not have a fire. It isn't going to be that chilly tonight anyway," said Johnny.

"Well, it's a good thing we set up camp when we did. At least we'll have something to eat and coffee should stay hot enough. I suppose we could let the fire burn out. You think they saw us?" asked Jeff.

"Not likely or we'd be crow bait by now. But they're sure acting like they haven't a care in the world. That's for sure."

"That is about to change," said Jeffrey.

The two young partners finished their supper, gulped down the last of the coffee and broke camp. Jeff sighed. "Ready?"

"Ready or not, we got to do it and we best do it. I'm not about to start putting up with cattle thieves," Johnny claimed.

"Hey! I've got an idea. You reckon we can wait just another hour or so. Or are you in a hurry?" asked Jeff.

"Not particularly but if I dally too long I might get a change of heart. What's on your mind?"

"Just sit tight. Oh! You have any rawhide strips?"

"Yeah but I was saving them to use for a piggin strings," said Johnny.

Jeff disappeared into the dark. About a half hour later he returned with one long mesquite branch and about six shorter ones and a pouch full of egg size stones.

"You're planning to play David and Goliath with those?" asked Johnny.

"Not a bad idea. I've killed many a rabbit with a sling. No, I'm thinking to make a bow and arrows. Those stones tied to the end instead of arrowheads. Can you imagine being clunked on the head with one of those?" Jeff said.

"Are you any good with one of those?"

"I could knock a pigeon out of the air with one. It's how I fed myself for a long time before I could afford a gun," smiled Jeff.

"You better be," Johnny replied doubtfully.

The rustler's camp was ghostly quiet when Johnny and Jeff crawled up on top of the hill overlooking the herd. The two nighthawks were talking in a low voice as one of them lit a cigarette. Johnny and Jeff lay flat on their bellies and waited impatiently. Jeffrey whispered, "I sure wish they'd get on with watching our herd. This ain't gonna work if they stay together."

"Relax, they'll separate soon enough," said Johnny. "You having second thoughts?"

"In a pig's eye! But the less shooting the better," whispered Jeff.

Johnny smiled. "Yeah. We'll go with that."

Jeffrey smiled. "Yeah."

The two nighthawks started to go separate ways. Jeff got up in a crouching position on one knee. He fitted an arrow and pulled back on the bow. He released the arrow and the bow went thwong! The arrow struck the nightawk in the back of the head like someone slapping a ripe watermelon. The rider leaned forward and slid to his left out of the saddle and plopped motionless onto the ground.

"Holy smokes! You can use that, can't you?" whispered Johnny.

"Now what?" asked Jeff.

"Reckon you can get two for two?"

"Only one way to know for sure," said Jeffrey.

They waited for another hour. It would be the routine for the nighthawks to check in with each other. Things were going according to plan when the second nighthawk was approaching. Jeff was getting into position to pick off the rider. Jeff released the arrow at the same time the two young partners heard the crack from a rifle. The bullet whined passed Jeff's head.

"Whoa!" exclaimed Jeff.

"It's their reliefs. Darn! We took too long!" said Johnny.

"Shoot back! And let's get the blazes out of here!" said Jeffrey.

Johnny snapped off three quick shots from his revolver.

"There they go!" shouted Johnny as the cattle started to run.

They had just made it to the horses when they heard several more shots. The two young partners spurred their horses and the horses leaped forward into a dead run. Bullets whizzed and buzzed past them. The young cowboys rode at hell bent for leather speed for nearly two miles. Johnny started to slow his horse and looked behind him.

"I think we lost them. It's too dark for them to follow us far," said Johnny.

"Ya," said Jeff then slid off his horse falling to the ground.

"Jeff! Are you hurt bad?"

Jeff lay motionless. His breathing was quick swith sharp gasps. Johnny took off his vest to fashion a pillow out of it and laid Jeff's head upon it. Then Johnny quickly began to examine Jeff. "This is all my fault. God help us!"

Jeffrey had taken two rifle slugs in the back. His shirt was wet with blood. Johnny rolled him over onto his side. One bullet was high and below his right shoulder blade. The second looked like it may have been a lung shot though Johnny was not certain.

"Hold on, Jeff. I'll get you cleaned up then I can see how bad it is. I need to get a fire going. I can't see," said Johnny nervously.

"No! No fire. Get me on the Colonel. I can ride," protested Jeff in a raspy voice.

"Jeff, I can't. You've lost a lot of blood. The ride might kill you. Let me get a fire started."

"Doggone it, no! Better to die trying than to wait here and be butchered. Get me on my horse, you stubborn ass!" said Jeffrey.

Johnny got Jeff's horse and helped him back into the saddle. The two young cowboys rode steady all through the night.

"Jeff, how are you holding up?"

"I'm thirsty. Is it getting light out?"

Johnny stopped their horses and gave Jeff a drink of water. "Here, but just a little one, okay? I'm not even sure I should be letting you have water. Yes, it's starting to get light out. We're almost there. Hang on. You are tough, son," said Johnny.

"Yes, sir, Lieutenant. Right away. Hey, Sarge, what time is it? Yanks! Yankees, boys! Damn, I am getting cold." Jeffrey was becoming delirious and Johnny was getting scared.

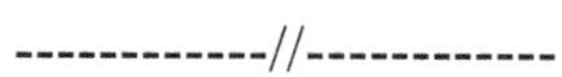

"Come and get it!" yelled Juanita from the veranda of the Peña hacienda.

"Well, I'm not waiting," said Sally. "I'm hungry. If they want to spend all morning wearing their bottoms out busting horses, let them. Let's eat."

"I agree. Let's eat, shall we?" said Senora Kataryna.

"I suppose you are right," said Nancy.

"Me too! I am right. We eat," piped in Miguel Andrew.

"Such a good boy!" said Senora Kataryna as she kissed her grandson's forehead.

"Love, love, love," said Miguel Andrew. And all the women laughed.

"That's enough for now. Paco, Mike, Tiny. Get that second string in the corral after you have eaten. We'll work on them later," said Jack.

"Si. Madre e dios! Look!" gasped Paco. The men all turned around and looked in a direction Paco was pointing.

"What happened?" asked Drew as he rushed to get onto his horse. Jack was the first to reach the two young cowboys at the entrance gate.

"What happened?"

"Rustlers."

"Tell me later. This boy is hurt awfully serious. Drew! Hermano!" yelled Jack.

Drew waved in acknowledgment and turned and yelled, "Mike! Get the buckboard! Hurry!"

"Yes, sir!"

Immediately the women took charge over Jeff until the doctor could be reached.

"So what happened, son?" asked Jack.

"Like I said, rustlers. Jeff and me had built up a nice herd of cattle just north of here. Near that old dried up lake where you and Drew once said you killed that cougar. We were going to start branding them and start our own herd. We spotted them and waited till dark and tried to stampede the herd and get them away from the rustlers. They spotted us as we were about to take the second nighthawk. We forgot how long we were taking and their relief showed up."

"Second nighthawk? Speak plainer," said Jack.

"Man! You should have seen Jeff at work with that bow and arrow he made."

Drew snapped at Johnny. "And a fine job too! You fool young'uns. That boy is in bad shape! May even die! What on God's green earth were you thinking, Johnny?"

Johnny looked at Drew. The hurt and remorse were clear in his eyes and face.

"You're right. This is all my fault. Jeff said we should ride for help. But I would hear no part of it."

"Why?"

"Because they were our cows! I figured you and Jack would have done the same. I wasn't going to ask anyone else to fight my battles. I'm sorry! Alright? I was wrong!"

Senora Kataryna came walking into the parlor where the men were all clamoring. She was carrying a large white stone vase. "Johnny, por favor, fill this. Then take it to your mother in Jeff's room," she said passionately.

"Yes, ma'am," said Johnny.

"Gracias, Johnny," she said. After Johnny left the room, she turned and lashed out at Drew and Jack.

"Just what do you suppose you were doing yelling at that young man, Drew? Jack?"

"What has come over you, Mother? There is a young boy in there filled with bullet holes. Those two could have been killed," said Drew.

Senora Kataryna glared at Drew with a look he had not seen in many years but recognized all too well. "I can remember as if it were yesterday. Two young men took it upon themselves to go hunt a wild cougar. If memory serves me, one of those young men was badly wounded and a broken leg in the process."

"Mother! That was a completely different situation. That was a cougar. Not a bunch of armed rustlers," said Drew.

"Cougars, rustlers! Same thing, mijo. You could have been killed. Dead is dead whether by guns or cougar or falling from a cliff. Dead is dead! Can't you two thick heads see that that young man is hurting enough already? Do you have to add to his pain?"

"Mother, if it will keep him alive, I'd break both of his legs!" exclaimed Jack.

"Jack, that is the most stupid thing I have ever heard come from your lips! He's a man! A young man, yes, and he made a mistake. A mistake that could have lost him the life of his best friend. What he needs is understanding and guidance not humiliation and scorn! Your grandfather wouldn't have acted so. Or have you two so quickly forgotten?"

Drew and Jack stood silent. She was absolutely correct. "That young man has to carve his mark someday. He was attempting to do so then. Both of them. Just as you two have done. If I recall correctly, you were not much older when you became a Texas Ranger." With that Senora Kataryna left the parlor.

"I hate it when she's right," said Drew.

"Yeah. I suppose I have some apologizing to do," said Jack.

"Just go easy on him, Jack. He's beating himself up enough for both of you. Remember: Experiencia ensena sabiduria. Experience teaches wisdom. I believe this is one lesson he will never forget," said Drew.

"I hear you. Just remember that when Miguel Andrew is this age," said Jack.

Johnny was sitting on the veranda rolling a cigarette when Jack walked outside and slowly approached him. "Have enough for two?"

Johnny held out the tobacco pouch and handed it to Jack. "Since when?" asked Jack referring to the cigarette smoking.

"Not long," Johnny replied.

"You feel like having company?" asked Jack.

Johnny shrugged then lit his cigarette. "Sure, I guess."

"He's going to be fine. La Abuela says so and if anyone would know, it would be her. Believe you me. Whew and how!" assured Jack.

"Jack, I mean Pa, if you're here to try and cheer me up, it ain't going to work. I was a danged fool and we both know it."

"I wouldn't go that far. You have to forgive Drew sometimes. He has always been quick with his tongue. It's his Spanish temper. That and having always been the one burdened with being in charge all of the time for so long."

"It ain't that." Johnny was reaching way down with in himself to explain.

"Go on. I'll listen," encouraged Jack.

"It's just that I want something that I can call mine. Something to be proud of. You know? Something that's part of me. Something that I can hold my head high for. We worked so hard gathering that herd. Jeff and I. I see now that we should have gone for help."

"Go on, you're doing fine," said Jack.

"I thought I'd be looked upon as weak. Not man enough to handle my own affairs. I didn't want everyone to lose respect for me."

"So, that's it. You actually thought Drew and I would see you that way?"

"You, Drew and the fellas. Mostly you. But I don't know how I'm going to be able to face the fellas now. Not after this."

"I see. I sure know that feeling but I can tell you you're wrong. The men have grown to respect you all the more. The way you stood up for what was yours and the way you looked after Jeff and brought him home alive. I'd say that the men in the bunkhouse and those with families are mighty darn proud. They know that you're the kind of man they can trust and depend upon. That you would not let them down in a fight. I'd say they rate you pretty high in their books."

"Any man who would run out on a friend is no man at all. He's lower than a snake's belly," sneered Johnny.

"Johnny, do you think Drew and I are any less of a man because we have so many men to fight at our sides if we need them?"

"Why, shucks, no but I'm not sure where you're going with that."

"These men that work and live here are not just our employees. There almost as much of our family as if they were our brothers or cousins. What's more is that each one would not think twice about laying down his life for our family. Because they know we would do the same for them. In fact, so many of those men are second or third generation here. They grew up here."

"I'm not following," said Johnny.

"What I'm saying is, it doesn't make any less of a man to ask for help now and then. Especially when protecting his family or property. Take for instance this new ranchers and farmers coalition. Do you think those men are any less of men because they joined together to help one another?"

"No, but that's just it. They're protecting what's theirs. That's the difference. Sure the Ranchero is a great place. But it's yours. I want something I earned with my own sweat and blood and blisters that says Johnny Caldwell Peña built this and folks can look at me as an equal."

"And you feel that being part of this Ranchero doesn't make you their equal?"

"Honestly, I love this place but I came here only because you and Ma got married. I don't really have any right or claim on any of it. No disrespect meant."

"I understand. So tell me. Where are you two going to run this herd of yours?"

"Well, there's a nice spread of land southwest of here. Not far from the border and the Rio Grande. But we were hoping to stay here on the Ranchero until we sold enough cattle to buy the land."

"I see. Sounds like you two have thought things out pretty well."

"All but this. Now it doesn't seem all that important."

A voice spoke out in the dusk. "I think maybe you should ask Jeff about that," came the voice of Sally. "He's asking for you. Seems he's more concerned about you and those cows than he is his own well-being."

Johnny stood up suddenly, crushed out a cigarette on the ground with the heel of his boot then briskly walked inside. "Thanks Sally," he said as he walked past her.

Morning came with the sound of magpies squeaking and squawking. The morning sun shone a long wide beam of yellow light down the main street of Austin. In the distance could be heard the Ting! Ting! Tang! Tang! of the blacksmith hammering out a band of steel. He had chosen to get an early start this particular morning. The stagecoach had suffered a busted wheel and he was nearly finished with fashioning a new wheel. He was determined to not be the reason for the stagecoach not being able to make its run on time.

In the morning breeze, one could smell the bread being baked at Letterman's Bakery and Pastry Shop. Caleb's stomach growled. He was standing in front of a mirror that hung on the wall above the table that held the washbasin. He had washed his face and slicked back his hair and was now tying his tie and cursing himself in frustration. "Confound it! Can't you even dress yourself?"

A knock came to the door of his room. Caleb froze suddenly and paused a moment in silence, listening. The knock came to the door a second time. "Who is it?"

"Senor Caleb? It is me, Paco."

Caleb's eyes went wide. "Paco? Paco Montoya?"

"Si."

"Come in, Paco, and welcome."

"Gracias, Senor." Paco entered the room and removed his sombrero.

"What brings you into Austin, Paco? Business or pleasure?"

"Wish it was for pleasure," Paco reached into his sombrero and took out an envelope and handed it to Caleb. "But alas, it is not."

Caleb looked in Paco's eyes and could see the forlornness and sadness. "Well, what is it? What's in the letter?"

"I do not know, Señor. It was given to me by Senora Kataryna. She say ride hard. Do not stop until I see you. So here I am. I would not dare open the Senora's letter."

"No, I suppose you would not. You're an honorable man, Paco. But you know something and you are not telling me, si?" asked Caleb.

"I think it is best to read the letter, Señor."

Caleb sat on the edge of his bed, opened the letter and began to mumble as he read. Then he looked up sharply at Paco. "How was he when you left, Paco?"

"The women were tending to him. They say he is very strong young man and should be okay. But I am not sure because I leave with this letter from the Senora. I do exactly as she ordered. I ride and only stopped to rest my horse. I cannot say if Jeff is okay or not. Only what she say before I leave."

While Paco was talking, Caleb quickly finished getting dressed forgetting the tie and tossing it onto his bed.

"Are you hungry? We can get something to eat downstairs and if you like you may sleep here and use my bed."

"Gracias, no, I am not hungry but I could sleep," said Paco.

"Bueno. Feel free. There is fresh water in the pitcher should you want to get some of the dust off first."

Paco yawned. "Si, gracias. I would like that very much."

Caleb left the room and went downstairs to the hotel lobby. He also chose to forgo breakfast. Caleb stepped out onto the hotel's front porch and stared up the street toward the governor's mansion. Then another thought entered his mind. Caleb turned and walked over toward the newly built livery stable. There he rented a horse and rode north of town out of Austin. Two hours later Caleb was riding on to a small but very elegant looking ranch. Then up to the two-story brick and wood home of Colonel John Salmon Rip Ford. Caleb dismounted his horse and tied him to a wrought iron hitching post next to a stone and mortar watering trough. He proceeded to dust himself off as he climbed the 14 steps up to the home's front porch. Caleb was just about to knock when a tall, slender, gray-haired old man wearing a butler's uniform suddenly opened the front door. "May I help you, young man?"

"Yes. I am here to see the Colonel. It's urgent business."

"Who may I say is calling?" asked the butler.

"Please tell him that Lieutenant Caleb Parker is here to see him."

"One moment please. Please, wait here," said the Butler.

Ten short minutes later, former Colonel John Salmon Rip Ford himself came trotting down the hallway. His eyes fell upon Caleb.

"Caleb, my boy! What a pleasant surprise. Come in, come in." Col. Ford led Caleb into a large combination library and parlor.

"You must be tired. Can I offer you a brandy?"

"That's most kind, Colonel. But if you have something a little wetter?"

John Rip Ford laughed. "Absolutely. I remember now. You never were one to indulge in the hard stuff." Col. Ford called to his butler. "Alex! Please see if there is some tea or maybe lemonade in the kitchen and bring Lieutenant Parker a glass. Would you please?"

"Right away, sir," replied the butler.

"So, son. What brings the Lieutenant out this way?" Caleb proceeded to explain to John the nature and seriousness for his visit and gave him the letter from Senora Kataryna.

"How was the lad? What was it he was so affectionately called by the men, Tin Soldier?"

Caleb smiled. "That's close, Colonel. It was Toy Soldier. I can't say for sure about his condition. Only that which I gather from the letter and a vaquero from the ranch. He delivered the letter."

"That's too bad. He was such an inspiration, that lad. Heck of a soldier too."

"Yes, sir. But he's no boy now. He's close to eighteen. Colonel, it would do him a heap of good if he could see you. He thinks the world of you. Still has your horse you gave him. He calls it Colonel," said Caleb.

"Yes, I remember. Gallant act on the part of that lad. May have even been the reason for our victory. But I don't know what good I can do him now."

"The young Corporal may be dying. I don't know for sure. I'm certain no matter what the outcome, your presence will mean more to him than anything. You may even be the medicine that saves his life."

Colonel John S Ford rubbed his chin and stared out the window. "Well, I think I could take a few days away. I'll just have Alex run things for a while. Besides being my butler, he's actually a good cattleman and foreman when need be. Okay! When do we leave?"

"Is now too soon?" asked Caleb.

Colonel John Rip Ford laughed. "That's what I always liked about you, Lieutenant. You never dallied. Okay then. I'll be packed and ready to ride within the hour."

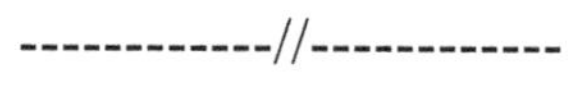

**Uvalde, Texas**

Uvalde was just waking up when Caleb, Col. John S. Ford and Paco rode through the town on the way to the Peña Ranchero. Stopping in town only to eat, rest and feed their horses, they were on their way once more. By noon, the three men were riding up to the Peña hacienda.

Drew was standing on the veranda sipping a cup of coffee when he saw the riders approaching. Drew raised his left hand high.

"Hello, Caleb! Hello, John! Hola, Paco! Please come inside. How are you, John?"

"I'm fine as snuff and twice as dusty," chuckled John S. Ford.

"I'm certainly glad you came, John. We've had some difficulties, you might say," said Drew.

"So I have heard. But actually I'm here to see the young Corporal Jeffery Boxer. I hear he is in a bad way." Marjorie Parker entered the kitchen. She had overheard Colonel Ford's comment. "Well, I'll say! If you call eating a pound of bacon, a dozen eggs and a mountain stack of flap jacks in a bad way. Chances are he'll explode before those bullet wounds kill him."

John S Ford stood up straight and removed his hat. "Beg your pardon, ma'am."

Drew smiled. "John, let me introduce my beautiful wife Marjorie. Marjorie, let me introduce to you the famous John Salmon Rip Ford. A gallant soldier and the best Texas Ranger in Texas. Next to me, that is."

"So pleased to finally meet you, Mr. Ford. I have heard so much about you. One would think you could walk on water given the stories I have heard. Although you are much shorter than I had pictured."

"Oh? How so?" inquired John Ford.

"To hear these men around here talk one would think you were ten feet tall and wide as a barn door with Gabriel's sword in one hand and wings on your back," laughed Marjorie.

John Salmon Rip Ford found himself quickly liking this woman. He smiled.

"Well, I have been known to wield the sword. But as for the wings, certainly not. I regret to say."

"Ha ha ha ha! You certainly have earned them in my book. It's a fine thing you have done. Coming all this way to see Jeff. I see now why he reveres you so. Please come with me. I'll take you to him. You know he named his horse after you."

John Ford found himself bewildered. "What kind of people are these folks?" Never before had he seen such devotion to one another and to take in the boy and accept him as if he were one of their own. Toy Soldier must be one special kid.

As he entered Jeff's room, Jeff was laying in bed sleeping. Senora Kataryna was sitting at his bedside as was Sally, Nancy and Jenny. The women all looked up at John with inquiring eyes. John Ford smiled and waved his hand in a casual manner to set the women at ease. "If only every man could have such angels hovering about him. I'll just come back later. Let him sleep."

Three days later and still weak in recovery from his wounds and under much protest from the women, Jeffrey Boxer got out of bed slowly and determinedly and made his way to the parlor where he now heard the voices of all the men. Mostly serious in tone but now and then the sound of laughter. Whiskey Jack was the first to see Jeff come through the door.

"Well, it looks like our young cowboy's going to live after all!" said Jack.

"I just couldn't take being coddled and confined to that bed one more minute. Howdy, Colonel! I was told you was here. Good to see you, sir," said Jeffrey.

"Corporal, it's an honor to see you again," said John S. Ford as he stuck out his hand.

Jeffrey shook hands and with a serious look in his eyes said, "So when do we ride?"

"Ride? Good Lord, son. You can barely stand on your own two feet. What do you mean when do we ride?"

"I'll be just fine. You did come here to go after those rustlers?" asked Jeffrey.

"I came to see you, Corporal. When I heard you were injured I packed up and rode down here. But I'd be proud to join any posse you men may be organizing. One thing I know for sure, it'll be legal," said Col. John Salmon Ford.

"I'm sure, sir. But legal or not, I aim to get my cows back. I mean our cows. Sorry, Johnny."

"Heck, don't worry about it," replied Johnny.

"It's just that we worked so dang long and hard to form that herd. This time by cracky, I won't be so blamed generous! No prisoners by God! You were right, Johnny. We should have killed them right off. I aim to..." Jeffrey was cut short in midsentence by Col. John Ford.

"Now hold on there, son! Do you want justice or revenge? If it's justice as you're after then I'm with you. But revenge can spoil a good man's blood turning it colder than a January freeze. Believe me, I've seen it happen."

"Yes, sir. I reckon I see what you're saying. But ain't this case a might different? After all, these hombres salted one of our watering holes, stole our cows, definitely nearly killed me. Don't you believe they deserve to die?"

"Sure, son. But only if convicted by a jury and in the case of self-defense. Meaning if they shoot at us first."

"With all due respect, Colonel, those are nearly the exact same words I used and you can see where it got me. Besides this jury you're talking about will come from where? Most of the folks from Laredo to Austin are either in the pockets of Asbury and Benson or just too dang frightened to fight back or simply not strong enough or too poor. Those of us who will and can are being blocked by crooked politicians, bankers and lawmen. Show me the people and I will acquiesce. Those hombres deserve good old-fashioned western tit for tat frontier law and I aim to see that they get it."

"Johnny, I understand what you are saying believe me I do. I wrestled with those same thoughts and emotions on my ride here. Maybe in my old age I'm getting softer, I don't know. I would like to think I'm getting wiser though. But you can't buck the law. I know for certain that for every crooked politician and lawman there are equally as many good and honest ones. Putting that aside, consider this. There are factions that want to dissolve the very existence of the Texas Rangers. Now how would it look if an Army of Texas Rangers, many who were Confederate soldiers went on a killing rampage? You could toss any hopes of having the Rangers reinstated right out the window. We must first act with common sense and good judgment. We will have our justice, I assure you. But when the killing time begins, we as Texas Rangers will have right on our side. We must!"

"The Colonel is right, Jeff. If we go off on some sort of vigilante style hunt those who oppose us will have us right where they want us and Texas, as we know it, will be lost forever. Texas has her flaws, always will. But justice and truth and giving men a fair chance to take the right path must always be our priority. Remember the old battle cry: All for Texas!" said Caleb.

Johnny knew they were right. He had been around Rangers and knew the life of the Texas Rangers most all of his life and was the son of a Ranger. "That may be so, Caleb, but there must be some balance to the duties of any lawmen. Especially Texas Rangers. What about those times when it is impossible to wait on a judge or jury? Caleb, you know as well as I do that sometimes a lawman, especially a Ranger, must act swiftly. To wait could be your very undoing. I've seen it! With you, Drew, Jack and all of the boys."

Caleb knew Johnny was right. His mind went back to when he himself was just becoming a Ranger in the days of Muleshoe before the war.

In fact, one of those times it had been Johnny himself that the Rangers were trying to rescue and it was the Texas Ranger Major Drew Parker who decided the fate of those involved. Johnny was right. To hesitate sometimes meant your own direct destruction in one form or another. Caleb looked at John S Ford. “Well, Colonel, I can’t dispute that.”

The women had been sitting in the parlor listening to the ensuing debate. Senora Kataryna was the first to speak out. “Yes, Colonel, I’m interested in how you feel in that scenario myself.”

John Ford was a tiger against men but against women he knew better and held his tongue. Especially Senora Kataryna Louisa Peña Parker. She continued. “We go back a good many years. You know how fond I am of you. Like a brother.” She pointed out the huge parlor window. “Do you know what I see when I gaze out this window, John? I see the future; I see Texas’ future. I also see the past. Do you see that row of small cottages? They house the married hands of this Ranchero and their children. Over there? That’s the bunkhouse for the rest of our vaqueros and cowboys. And there, near the flower garden is the chapel. We hold mass there when the Padre can make it here. Nearly two generations of Peña’s and their employees were either married or baptized there. I also see what it took to build and to keep this Ranchero and make it what it is today. Those men who work for us as well as their families are more to us than just mere employees. They are family. Almost as much a part of this family as my own flesh and blood. You see? Now we, the Peña family, do not boast very often about our good fortune. Mostly because it did not come to us of our own volition. It came at a price. A very high price. But I will boast this one time nonetheless. We have money, as you know, and quite a bit of it. If men such as Asbury and Benson can buy their own law and politicians I suppose we can too. In the meantime, we have over 200 loyal employees. Who will be around to protect our neighbors when they are being either shot up or burned out? Most of whom we have known for more years than I can remember. It is the duty of the strong and the God-fearing to protect and help their less fortunate neighbors in their time of need and distress. My father believed this and his before him. You once held those same beliefs and visions. Or have you forgotten? Gabriel believed that as well. It was for this belief that my husband died. I can say this with all certainty: My father, Don Miguel and had he lived, my husband, Gabriel, would look at you and say that you were wrong. They would not tolerate men like Asbury and Benson and those who work for them. Not simply for what they have done to Jeff but because of loyalty to our neighbors as well. Don Miguel and Gabriel felt it was their God appointed duty to protect those who cannot protect themselves."

"Those are fine words, Senora Kataryna, but times are different now," said John Salmon "Rip" Ford.

"No, times have not changed. Only man's sense of morality," replied Señora Kataryna.

"You are one of a kind, woman! I can see how Gabriel fell so hard in love with you. As did we all," laughed John Ford.

"So you have not forgotten your vision. You must do something. You must help. Go see the Governor. I know you can convince him to take the appropriate actions," pleaded Señora Kataryna.

"That's a great idea. I'll ride with you, Colonel!" said Jeffrey.

"Now, not so fast, Corporal. You best take another day or two to heal. I do not think you are fit to ride just yet."

"No, he is not," exclaimed Sally. "I swear it's a wonder how Texas got as big as it is. It seems all the good men keep getting shot up or killed."

The women all looked at Sally. They had no idea she had any feelings for Jeff until now. Marjorie was shocked as well. But in Sally's defense, she agreed. "Yes, Jeff. You should rest and this time, Nancy, will you please change Jeff's bandages?" Changing bandages up until now had been Jenny and Sally's responsibility.

Austin was bustling with busy people. Wagons and people going in every direction. The town clock struck 1 o'clock as the four riders rode into town.

"That's the place all right. It has his name on the door. Caleb Parker, Attorney-at-Law," said Hamelton O'Toole.

"Has it been that long? Why just yesterday he was a snot nosed young Sergeant in the Texas Rangers," chuckled Red Sands.

"It has been a while! But he was never snot nosed that is for sure," said Marty Collins.

"No, I guess not. Had to grow up fast he did," agreed Red.

A dainty, elderly woman wearing a white maids bonnet answered the door to the building Caleb had set up an office in. "May I help you gentlemen?" she asked pleasantly.

Hamelton O'Toole took off his hat before speaking. Then he inquired about Caleb and explained their relationship to him. "Of course! Sergeant Major O'Toole. I should have guessed. You are exactly as he described you. A fine Irish specimen you are!" teased the elderly woman. She continued. "Master Parker has gone to Uvalde. It would seem someone shot his Toy Soldier or something. Imagine a man of his age getting all worked up over a toy soldier." She laughed. "Takes all kinds, I suppose."

"Are you sure he said toy soldier?" asked Hamelton O'Toole.

"As sure as you are standing there. Would you gentlemen care to come in?"

"No, thank you, ma'am, I reckon we'll be on our way. We will call on him at a later time."

As the men left and were walking down the street back into the center of town, Danny Collins looked over toward O'Toole with curiosity. "So what does toy soldier mean? Is that some kind of code talk between you two?"

"You might say that. I'll explain on our way."

"On our way where?" asked Red.

"Uvalde and the Peña Ranchero," said O'Toole.

As the four men rode out of Austin, Hamelton O'Toole began to explain what toy soldier meant.

"Lord have mercy! You say he was only 13 years old?" mused Danny Collins.

"Yup but a finer soldier you will never find. For a kid. He took a lot of razzing from the men. But he took it well. At times, I think he actually enjoyed it. Eventually every man in the regiment grew fond of the boy. Jeffrey Boxer his name was."

"Here you tell it ol' Caleb sort of adopted the kid. If so, I can bet my saddle, Caleb is hopping mad," replied Danny Collins.

"Most likely, I'd say. I'm fairly certain the whole Parker and Peña clan is in a fighting mood. That is if Caleb hadn't already spoiled the fun and gone and killed the one who done it," said O'Toole.

"You got that right. The boy is followerin' the captain's footsteps all the way, I'd say."

"He ain't a Captain anymore. During the war he became a part of the Frontier Regiment. Though usually he and Whiskey Jack worked alone. So they went and tacked the rank of Major to him. So I reckon he's still called Major Drew Parker," said O'Toole.

"And Jack? Is he still Capt. Whiskey Jack?" asked Marty Collins.

"I reckon he is," answered O'Toole.

"You sure are quiet, Red. What's got your tongue?" asked Marty.

"Hmmm? Oh, nothing much. Just thinking."

"Thinking! Ain't that a dangerous thing for you to be doing?" joked Marty Collins.

Red smiled. "These days I reckon so. Is it just me or do you fellas get the feeling like you're getting old?"

"Lord above! Old! I'm just getting up in my prime. Old!" exclaimed Danny. He went on. "Yup. Sometimes. Sometimes."

"What brought that on, Red?" asked O'Toole.

"All this reminiscing about Caleb, the Captain and Whiskey Jack. Dang! I miss the boys. Wouldn't it be something if they reinstated the Rangers and we could all get together again? The old company D?"

"Boy, you betcha! Why outlaws would be making water and scooting for Canada or even China! Ha ha ha. Ya, boy!" laughed Danny Collins.

"I wonder if she still remembers?" mumbled Red.

Marty overheard Red mumbling to himself. "Who?"

"That little Sally girl. Remember her?" asked Red.

"Why sure I do! What you thinking?" said Marty.

"Oh no! I am old enough to be her father. I was thinking, that's all. After all, I kind of took her in my heart as an adopted sister or daughter.

Marty! Good grief! You should wash your mind out for thinking and your mouth out for saying such a thing," exclaimed Red.

"Get over it! I was just joshin' you and you know it. We all liked her and her folks. God rest her Pa and brother and sister. I hear tell her Ma may be gonna have another baby soon," said Marty.

"Gonna?! Boy howdy, you have been gone too long. Why she had the handsomest little boy. Looks just like the Major. Named him after Don Miguel; Miguel Andrew Parker. Yes, sir. And, boy, is he a handful! Whew!" said O'Toole.

The four friends and former Texas Rangers rode on in silence for the two hours. Then Red Sands piped up breaking the silence. "So, how old is this boy now?"

"Oh, about 26, I guess," said O'Toole. Red looked at O'Toole, confused and bewildered.

"Say what! How?"

O'Toole broke in with a crackle. "Oh! You mean the Major's baby boy."

"No, you dunder head. I was talking about the governor. Of course, the baby. You haven't changed much, have you?"

"Nope. Not one little bit. Ha ha ha ha. Oh, I'd say around four or five. Not much past that."

"Five years?" said Red sorrowfully. "That long?"

**Two days later**

The four friends rode up the long road through the entrance to the Peña Ranchero. When they neared the huge front porch of the hacienda, the four men reined their horses to an abrupt halt. A small boy of about five years of age was pointing the barrel of a hand carved wooden rifle right at them.

"Stick 'em high!" said the boy with great authority.

"Ain't huntin' trouble, mister," said O'Toole. "We come in peace."

"What you want round here?" asked the boy.

"We're friends, honest," said Marty Collins.

"I said what you want?!"

"We come looking for Major Parker and a fella named Caleb. Are they here?" asked O'Toole stillll holding his hands high in the air.

"I'm Major Parker. I don't know you!"

"You're the famous Texas Ranger? Golly. We meant no troubles." O'Toole was having fun.

"Major Parker, sir, can we put our hands down now? My arm is getting powerful tired," said Danny Collins.

"Yup. Put 'em down. No funny bizziness. Hear?"

"We hear," said Danny Collins. The four men were having the time of their lives when a woman's voice called out. "Miguel Andrew! Where on earth are you?" Marjorie stood there stunned, her eyes wide and her mouth open wide as well. Then she almost burst into tears. "Oh, my dear precious! Drew! Come quickly!" Marjorie was trembling as she ran off the porch towards the four men.

"Well, get down so's I can get a look at you!" Then she hugged and kissed them calling them all by name. "What a wonderful surprise. How I've missed the lot of you."

Drew came running to the front of the house accompanied by Caleb, Jack, Johnny and John S. "Rip" Ford. All of them expecting and prepared for trouble, guns drawn.

"Marjorie, what is it? Is Miguel okay?" Suddenly, Drew froze in his steps almost as astonished as Marjorie had been when she saw them.

"I don't believe it. Miguel, why didn't you shoot these hombres?" Then he laughed. "How the heck are you, boys!" Drew smiled shaking each man's hand and saying hello for the first time in nearly 5 long years.

"Please, everyone. Come inside. I'll fetch some lemonade from the kitchen," said Marjorie.

"Lemonade?" exclaimed Drew. "I'm sure what these men want is a bit stronger than lemonade."

"Actually Major, I wouldn't mind some lemonade myself. Ma'am, I'd be pleased," said Marty.

"I always liked you, Marty," said Marjorie as she wheeled around and left the room to fetch refreshments.

There was much catching up to do and everyone was cackling like turkeys in a pen when Caleb asked, "So you got my letter I take it?"

"Yes. I found these three vagabonds on the way. Caleb, how's Jeff?" asked O'Toole.

"How did you know? Miss Abernathy! Bless her heart. Can't keep a secret to save her life. Why don't you see for yourself?" Caleb pointed behind them.

O'Toole turned around and glanced at a tall, masculine young man of 18, standing in the doorway of the parlor. "Where is the lad? Where's that pesky toy soldier?"

"Howdy, Sergeant Major," said Jeff with a mile wide smile.

"Jeff? Saints preserve us! How you've grown. It's the Irish in ya! I've always said the Irish are a breed apart. We heard you'd been been shot and were dying," said O'Toole.

"He was," said Marjorie as she reentered the room carrying a large tray with several glasses and a large pitcher of lemonade. "But it was the Lord who saved him. Not any Irish blood, Hamelton O'Toole," She said smiling.

"Yes, Mum but I do believe the good Lord is quite Irish himself," chimed O'Toole.

"Be that as it may, I think you're to give Him the credit," said Marjorie.

"Amen," came another woman's voice. "Hello, Ham." It was Nancy Caldwell Parker Jack.

O'Toole looked sheepishly at Nancy and then at Jack. "With your permission, Captain Jack.

"I reckon this once," smiled Jack.

Hamelton embraced Nancy and kissed her forehead.

"I do believe I have died and gone to heaven. Everyone dear to me in one room at the same time," O'Toole sniffled and then cleared his throat. "A toast!"

"A toast? To what?" asked Red.

"Oh, he's Irish. He'd toast the morning if you let him," said Marjorie teasingly.

"A toast to dear friends united and to those gone on," said O'Toole.

"Here, here!" said all in the room.

"Hello, Red," said a voice like that of an angel.

Read turned around and was nearly eye to eye with the loveliest woman he had ever seen. She was full figured with sparkling sky-blue eyes, her nose turned up ever so slightly at the end and her lips were red and full. Her chin was slightly round and complemented with plump, rosy cheeks. Her hair was strawberry blonde and curly. Red swallowed. "Sally?"

Sally pursed her lips teasingly. She was aware inwardly of how long it had been since he has seen her. "Don't tell me you have forgotten me?"

"No way in heaven did I forget you, you little minx!" Red reached out with both hands and grasped her at the shoulders and turned her around and around. "Look at you. A woman and a fine filly at that. Tell me, Drew. What do you feed these youngsters?" Red reached into his pocket. "I have a surprise for you. Close your eyes."

Sally closed her eyes tightly and giggled. "What is it?"

Red took her hand and placed a small but overly stuffed envelope in her hand. "I had no time to wrap it properly."

"Oh, wrapping, napping. Who cares!" Sally tore open the envelope and gasped. "Mama! Look." Inside the envelope was a locket that opened up. Inside was a picture of her and her mother on the day she was released from the hospital many years ago. Also inside the envelope was a tightly rolled band of red and gold bordered ribbon.

"Oh, Red, you really shouldn't have!" said Marjorie.

"Okay, I'll take them back then," teased Red.

"You will not! I will wear this always. Until my dying day," Sally threw her arms around Red's neck and kissed his cheek. "My gallant, Ranger!"

**Fort Sill, Oklahoma Territory**
**October 1870**

Quanah Parker accompanied by Dancing Crow and 30 warriors rode up to the gate of the 24 foot high wall that surrounded Fort Sill. They had come in peace but not in trust. Unbeknownst to the soldiers in the Fort an additional 700 warriors, Quahadi Comanche and Kiowa waited just out of eyesight from the Fort and were hidden by the crest of a hill that was forested by juniper and scrub oak as well as waist tall grass.

They were speaking to Col. William Mitchell. Once more, Quanah would seek a peaceful agreement and treaty with the white eyes. Dancing Crow, though a prominent figure among the Comanche, stood behind Quanah and not alongside him. Because of his ailments, Dancing Crow himself chose Yellow Pony to take his place as the second leader of the Comanche. Dancing Crow would only act as advisor and witness to the events.

The reception received by Quanah Parker and the others was to say the least less than gracious. The Comanches were greeted on both sides and from behind by armed soldiers.

"We have walked straight into the lion's mouth. This looks a trap," said Yellow Pony to Quanah Parker.

"It could be but we will not act as though this bothers us. Let the Colonel Mitchell make the first move. We will hear what he has to say," said Quanah.

"More lies. That's what he has to say," replied Yellow Pony.

Col. William Mitchell stepped out from the office of the commanding officer and out into the parade ground to meet Quanah Parker and the others. He did not hold out his hand in greeting. Rather in a very staunch sort of manner he called for Lieutenant Baines. "See to it that our guests are taken to the ballroom. We will talk there. See to it that they have something to eat and drink. Lord knows what they eat."

"Yes, sir! This way, Indians," said the Lieutenant.

The Comanche had beans and fried beef and water to drink under armed guard. Dancing Crow chuckled. "I don't think they trust us."

"It's been two hours. Do you think they are planning to kill us?" asked Yellow Pony.

"He may wish to but he is too smart to kill us here. The Great White Father might get suspicious. He knows we would not be foolish enough to come here unarmed. If Colonel Mitchell wishes to kill us it will be outside of the Fort with no witnesses to say that we did not start it," stated Dancing Crow.

"You are right, Dancing Crow. I think by making us wait, he is telling us that no matter what those white papers say, he does not plan to honor their words," said Quanah.

Colonel Mitchell entered the room accompanied by his clerk and Lieutenant Baines then proceeded toward a large dining table surrounded by chairs.

"Gentlemen, shall we proceed. It is getting late and I have more pressing business to attend to." Col. Mitchell read the agreement, or rather the ultimatum, to the Comanche. "In conclusion, it is the decision of the United States government and Department of Indian Affairs that all of the Quahadi Comanche be placed on the reservation near Fort Sill. All provisions will be provided including food, lodging, blankets and medical care. All Comanche will surrender their weapons to the commanding officer of Fort Sill upon entering the reservation. Furthermore, all Comanche must agree to learn the practice of farming and all children under the age of 16 must attend school. The leaders of the Comanche will comply with any and all regulations stated by the Department of Indian Affairs and shall be accountable to the Indian agent assigned in charge. So forth and so on. Now gentlemen, if you will just sign your name or place your mark at the bottom of the agreement."

"This reservation. It is occupied by Apache, the Wichita and Kiowa?" asked Dancing Crow.

"That is correct," affirmed Col. Mitchell.

"The Comanche and Apache do not get along together. What will become of a Comanche if he is found fighting with an Apache?" Dancing Crow continued.

"We will appoint reservation police made up by members of each tribe. It will be the reservation police's responsibility to keep order and handle disputes," explained Col. Mitchell.

"A Comanche taking orders from an Apache? This will not work. I would rather die," said Yellow Pony.

Col. Mitchell spoke out. "Quanah Parker, I trust I can depend on you to keep the Comanche under control. I do not want any trouble. Especially from any hotheads. This reservation is a good thing for all of the Indians regardless of their tribal relations. I assure you that troublemakers will be dealt with and punished accordingly. Please, do not force involvement by the United States Army."

"There will be none from the Comanche, Col. Mitchell. Any trouble from anyone Indian or white will be dealt with accordingly. Please, do not force me, Quanah Parker and the Quahadi Comanche to get involved."

Col. Mitchell got Quanah's meaning loud and clear. Quanah would cooperate but he would be watchful. He was giving Col. Mitchell his own warning.

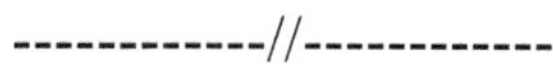

**Lytle, Texas**

The men were having a good time reminiscing and telling jokes which actually had the ring of the truth within them. Whiskey Jack turned and looked at Red Sands. "So Red, what brought you out our way anyhow? Not that I'm not pleased, of course."

"Actually, Danny, Marty and I were riding to Austin to begin a new job we would get when we met up with Ham on the way. He said he was going to your spread in response to a letter from Caleb about young Jeff. So we gladly came along."

"A job? Now that is interesting. There hasn't been any jobs in Austin for over a year or more. Wouldn't you agree, hermano? What kind of job? If you don't mind me asking," said Jack.

"Not at all," Red reached into his vest pocket and pulled out a piece of paper that he had folded and kept.

It was a help wanted notice. Strong able bodied men interested in range work. Pays $40 a month, horses and ammunition provided. Good chuck and friendly atmosphere. Duties include normal ranching chores, bronc busting, gathering wild steers, roping, branding and trail riding. Inquire Austin, Texas, Asbury and Benson Company. Sounds like a right nice steady job wouldn't you say?" asked Red.

"Have you spoken to these people?" Jack asked with a serious tone.

"No, like I said. We detoured and rode to your ranch with O'Toole. Why do you ask?"

"I hope you boys reconsider. You see, these are the very people we are fighting with now. Your job will also include the burning and shooting of a lot of families off of their property and homes. Not to mention stealing cattle and horses. This is a bad company, boys. Muy malo."

"Well, I'll be tied! Thought this sounded too good to be true especially when they said good chuck. When has anyone ever eaten good chuck on a cattle drive or roundup? Are you sure these are the people behind everyone's troubles?" asked Marty Collins.

"Pretty sure you'd be with some mighty rank hombres," said Whiskey Jack. Jack went on to explain the raid on their own cattle, the bridge being sabotaged, the warehouse fire, about their neighbors being threatened and the cattle being stolen after which Jeff was shot.

"I don't understand. If what you fellas is saying is true and I have no reason to believe otherwise then why hasn't anyone gone and done something? Seems to me you've got more than enough reason," said Red Sands.

"Well, Red, that's just it. The knowing is easier than proving. Asbury and Benson have been too smart to let themselves be implicated in any way. At least when it comes to any of the dirty work they have been able to, by all outward appearances, make everything look legal. Don't forget, they practically own the law. My guess is that they have also padded the judge's pockets as well. It wouldn't surprise me if their reach of influence hasn't reached that Gov. Davis himself. If not, at least his staff or a member of it," replied Caleb.

"Watch where you're going with those words, Caleb. I do not want to start getting suspicious. To accuse the governor or staff without having a real good reason would not go well for us. Especially with us pushing to get the Rangers reinstated," said John S Ford.

"Is that what I was doing? I surely wasn't trying to bring an indictment against the governor. A lot goes across his desk it would be very easy for someone on his staff to slip something past him without his knowledge. That's all."

"Just the same. Let's not get carried away. We have a strong case in our favor. If we need to bow and curtsy to get on his good side, that is exactly what we shall do."

"Yes, sir. I suppose you're right. Just galls me that's all. Especially with Jeff being shot up and just pure luck that he lived. That and the good grace of God. I'm pretty riled up," replied Caleb.

"I've got to agree with the Colonel. Caleb, my being shot was really due to my own thickheadedness. Johnny said we should have of gone in guns blazing. But I said no. Johnny was right and we ain't truly positive that those hombres worked for Asbury and Benson or not," said Jeffrey.

Drew said little. He mumbled something in Spanish. Whiskey Jack looked at Drew and laughed.

"What did he say?" asked Jeffrey.

"He said, Un hombre es conocido por la compania que mantiene. A man is known by the company he keeps. Though of whom he was talking, I do not know," said Whiskey Jack.

"I meant this: If Gov. Edmund Jackson Davis is in any way friendly with Asbury and Benson or that no good Harvey Ainsworth in my book, he is just as guilty as the whole lot of them. You lawyers have a saying that you love to use: ignorance of the law is no excuse. I have one for you: You can't walk into an outhouse and not know what the other fella was doing!" argued Drew.

"That is all well and good, Drew, but right now we have neither the outhouse nor the someone. All we do have is the other," said John S. Ford.

"If you choirboys are done, it's getting late so we best make camp soon. We will be in Austin about noon time tomorrow," said Whiskey Jack.

After they had made camp and eaten supper, the men, for the most part, were quiet. John Rip Ford sat whittling on a piece of kindling firewood. He paused and looked over at Drew.

"Drew, I've been thinking. I can see that you hold some reservations as to my stand on reinstating the Rangers. I assure you, as a former Ranger myself, I want nothing more. Texas needs the Rangers and probably will need the Rangers until the rapture comes."

Drew chuckled. "You? Thinking? Now I am worried. John, I do not doubt your integrity but you have changed. There was a time when you would have saddled up armed to the teeth and with 40 or so men, rode hell bent for leather and would have shot dead or hung every one of those hombres."

"You're right. I would have and would still if the Rangers were in active authority and acting in total compliance with the law but we are not. Therefore I must use other avenues to achieve the same goal. But never mind that for now. Drew, there is someone I desperately would like you to meet, when we get back to Austin. Maybe by meeting him you will know I am sincere in my claims to bring back the Rangers."

"Who is that?" asked Drew.

"A man nearly your age. A former soldier of the Texas 5th Cavalry. A lot like you in many ways. His name is Leander H. McNelly. Something tells me you two are going to get along splendidly."

"McNelly. Seems I've heard of him. But the when and where escapes me now," said Drew.

Drew was unusually irritable for some reason though he could not explain why. Jack and the others noticed this as well. Those who knew him well enough that is. "You all right, hermano?" asked Jack.

Drew was deep in thought. "Oh. What were you saying, Jack?"

"I asked if you were all right. You seem distant. Something eating at you?"

"I'm not sure. I just can't get my finger on it. Hasn't it raised your curiosity that so far our ranch is the only spread that hasn't been hit yet? Sure we had that watering hole salted and Johnny and Jeff had that tangle with rustlers. That doesn't add up to too much. Except trouble as usual."

"Ain't that enough?" said Jack. "I hadn't given it much thought more than just being fortunate."

"That's just it. Why should we be so fortunate? We had the biggest and the best spread around. Why leave us alone?"

"I don't know. Maybe because we have 200 ranch hands working for us. To some that adds up to a small army. Or it could be as I said, we've been fortunate."

"Jack, remember when we was kids and you had your heart set on starting that circus?"

"Ha ha ha, oh boy, do I." Jack reflected.

"Why would you think of that now?"

"You were going to have every wild animal in North America. Remember that mother cougar and her four cubs? You didn't want to kill her. But you did want those cubs."

"Ya! Never did get those cubs. I tried everything I could think of."

"Including trying to lure her away long enough to snatch up those cubs. Turned out she was luring you away instead," said Drew.

"Who would believe that she would out right ignore a whole ham? But she did. Where is all of this leading up to, hermano?"

"We shouldn't have both left the ranch. I'm bothered by it. One of us should go back. I've got this chill up my spine that we've been duped."

"I know. I've had that same chill. You thinking that those who stole those cows were sent to draw us out?" asked Jack.

"Very well could be the case. Only that they didn't figure on Johnny and Jeff. That changed everything. Because we didn't go out after them. But I don't think they went for it. Likely as not, they are holed up somewhere and have been watching us like a hawk after a jack rabbit," said Drew.

"And Harvey Ainsworth?" replied Jack.

"He didn't stick around. He figures himself big bull of the herd. So most likely he rode back to Austin. That is if he even took part. Either way, he most likely left instructions to have a messenger. Thing is I just don't know and that rankles me."

"So now what? We draw straws to see who goes back?"

"No. In the morning you go back and explain to everyone my suspicions. Tell Marjorie it had to be this way. No doubt she will be upset that the two of us didn't come back. Can't say that I would blame her either," said Drew.

"Are you certain this is how you want it?"

"Yes. But if you get word that I've been arrested, you'll know I've shot the governor," smiled Drew. "Jack, take Johnny and Jeff with you."

"It will be done, hermano. Do you think Rip will be able to sway the governor?"

"I don't know. In spite of what he says, I'm not sure his heart is in it."

"I wouldn't be so sure. You didn't see the look in his eyes when he saw Jeff laying there in that bed. If you asked me I'd say his heart is well in it. I just think he's one of those types that have a hard time coming around to things."

"I suppose. If you do happen to tangle with Ainsworth or any of his men, try and take prisoners. But for heaven's sake make sure they can talk," said Drew.

"You don't ask for much do you? But I'll try."

"We need them alive, Jack. If the Rangers have a prayer left, we need them alive."

"I know but I don't have to like it. Not after what they did to Jeff. We sure owe them for that."

"True but just alive and even he admits he can identify his shooters. We're walking on eggshells, Jack. So watch that hot head of yours."

"Hot head? Look at the pot calling the kettle black," replied Jack.

**Austin, Texas**

It was a hot dry afternoon when Caleb, Rip Ford and Drew rode into Austin. A strong high breeze swept through the town blowing in from the east like a blast from a furnace. Caleb reached for the blue neckerchief around his neck and tugged at it.

"Whew! I give almost anything to sweat right now. I am dry as John Brown's bones," said Caleb.

"I'll just settle for a cool beer. If there is such a thing," laughed Drew.

"It's going to get a lot warmer before the day is through," said Rip Ford.

"I don't think you're just referring to the weather. Let's hope it's not that hot," said Drew.

A tall lean figure of a man with slightly curly brown hair and a mustache that hung low at the corners of his mouth and deep dark brown eyes stood at the top of the steps leading onto the porch of the governor's mansion. He was neatly dressed, wearing a lavender color shirt with sharply ironed creases and a dark brown cow hide vest. He wore brown corduroy pants also sharply creased and a pair of .45 caliber colt revolvers with polished walnut pistol grips that hung low at his hips. He wore a well cleaned Confederate cavalry hat with the right side of it curved up. He smiled as the men came walking up the steps. "Looks like we may have some trouble, John," said Drew as he nonchalantly untethered his pistol in its holster.

"Hold on, Drew. No trouble here. Hello, Leander!" said John Salmon "Rip" Ford.

"Colonel, how are ya?" said the man.

"Fine! Just fine. You sure are all gussied up. You going to a party or something?"

"Not at all. I was hoping more in the way of a coronation. I'm going with you to see the governor," said Leander McNelly.

"Good! Glad to have you along. Drew, this is the man I've been wanting you to meet. Drew meet Leander Harvey McNelly. Leander, Andrew Parker or Drew Parker as he is most referred to as."

Drew stuck out his hand in welcome friendship.

"I have heard a lot about you. Glad to finally meet you," said Drew.

"And I of you, sir. The famous Major Drew Parker. Your reputation precedes you, sir," said Leander H. McNelly.

"The pleasure is all mine. Though I would hardly call myself famous."

"Oh, contraire mon ami. I believe we have a mutual friend in Abilene. Marshall P. C. Baird."

"P.C.? Well, I'll be. You have certainly surrounded yourself with good company. P.C. and I go a long way back," replied Drew.

"Well, gentlemen, shall we proceed?" said John Salmon Ford.

**Uvalde, Texas**
**Peña Ranchero**

Whiskey Jack, Johnny and Jeff were nearing the entrance to the Peña Ranchero. A charcoal color blue gray sky loomed just north of the ranch. Streaks of bright white and orange lightning flashed in the distance. A cool warm breeze swept across the prairie toward the Peña hacienda.

"Don't know whether that's a good sign or bad," stated Johnny.

"Both," answered Jeff. "We need the rain for true but as dry as it has been. The lightning could be a problem."

"Speaking of problems. Who's that at the hacienda?" said Johnny.

Six men sat horseback out front of the hacienda. Whiskey Jack, Johnny and Jeff were yet too far to hear what was being said. Yet Jack did recognize the man on the tall bay gelding horse. It was none other than Harvey Ainsworth.

"Ainsworth," Jack scoffed. "What does he want?"

"I'm just doing my job, ma'am. It is none of my concern whether you stay here or not. My job is to collect what is owed in back taxes," said Ainsworth.

"Yes, I am sure. As I have already told you. What property taxes we may have owed have already been paid. Though I must say, you show great pleasure in what you do. We have also appealed to the governor to have those taxes exempted. You see, this land was awarded to us many years ago. It was added to the Luis Baca land-grant of 1600. If anyone should be paid, it should be us, as you might say, a toll?"

"Ha ha ha, Senora, I am no fool. The Luis Baca land-grant was for land in Colorado by the king of Spain. Not in Texas," said Ainsworth.

"You are partially correct, Senor. I said it was added to the land-grant. You seriously do not believe that the King of Spain owned only Colorado land? How do you suppose he got to Colorado? The Spanish and Mexico conquered and explored land from Florida to California," said Señora Kataryna Louisa Peña Parker.

Little Miguel Andrew had been playing in the back portion of the veranda when Harvey Ainsworth and his men arrived. Jenny was coming from the kitchen area on to the veranda. "There you are, young man. Playtime is over. It's time for you to take your nap." Miguel Andrew had been playing with his toy wooden rifle. Jenny took the rifle and sent Miguel into the hacienda. "Juanita! Would you please make sure Miguel Andrew takes his nap?"

"Si," said Juanita the kitchen maid. "Come on, little one."

Whiskey Jack mumbled to himself. "It's downright spooky that's what it is."

"What did you say?" asked Johnny.

"I said I don't know how Drew does it or how he knows. He said something was wrong and looks like he was right. Again. Downright spooky that's what he is," replied Jack.

"Ya, I've heard of folks like that. Clairvoyant I think they call it," said Jeffrey.

"Well, whatever it is. I'm glad he has it. But it still gives me the heebie jeebies," said Jack.

Jenny was just rounding the corner of the hacienda when two of the men with Harvey Ainsworth spotted her. She had given no thought to the toy rifle she was still carrying.

"Marjorie! What's going on out here?" Jenny called out not knowing that Harvey Ainsworth and his men had been there.

One of the gunmen saw Jenny and he saw the rifle. Lightning fast the man drew his revolver. "Gun!" he yelled. Then fired.

"No!" screamed Senora Kataryna.

Everyone but Harvey Ainsworth and his henchmen ran over to where Jenny had fallen. She was shot just above her left breast.

"Dios mio! You shot her! I'll see you die!" cried Señora Kataryna.

"She had a gun!" yelled the shooter.

"It's a child's toy! You bloodthirsty moron!" cried Marjorie.

As if someone would poke a stick into an anthill, cowboys, vaqueros and the women from the employee homes came running. Almost instantly, Jack had heard the shot as well and spurred his horse into an instant full gallop his pistol drawn and poised to kill.

"Ainsworth!" cried Jack and fired. The bullet forming a red purple hole between Harvey Ainsworth's eyes. Harvey Ainsworth sat staring at Jack for a good five seconds then leaned to his left and fell to the ground. "Mother!" cried Jack.

"I am all right but Jenny has been shot!"

The other five men with Harvey Ainsworth did not have time to make their escape. Nor did they have time to draw their weapons. All that is but for the man who shot Jenny, a barrage of gunfire filled the air as if a storm has suddenly let loose with 1000 thundering bolts.

Five men, including Harvey Ainsworth lay motionless on the ground. The sixth man was weaving round and round and side to side on his horse then finally gave up any hopes of making a getaway. He threw his hands up high in the air. "Don't shoot! Dear God in heaven don't kill me!" The man wept.

A cowboy at the ranch, Tiny, reached up with a huge thick hand, grabbed the crying henchmen by his belt and yanked him from his horse. "I'm going to crush your skull into mush!" threatened Tiny. As he palmed the man's forehead with his huge hands the gunman cried out "Uughh! Oh God! Someone!" Tiny was filled with blind and deafening rage. He could not hear Whiskey Jack's commands.

"Tiny! No! I said stop!"

Jack picked up a large piece of fence railing that had been discarded for firewood and struck Tiny in the back of the head. The big man crumpled to his knees freeing his captive in the process. The big man was down but not out. Tiny shook his head and with glassy eyes looked at Jack. "Why'd ya slug me? I wasn't really going to kill him. Shucks, there be women folk around. "

Jack stood there in disbelief. He had just hit this mountain of a man with nearly all he had in him yet he was still conscious? Jack swallowed then lied. "Heck, Tiny, I didn't hit you that hard. I just wanted you to stop before you popped his head like a plum."

Tiny stood up and smiled. "That's okay, boss. I probably was a might miffed. Besides, it didn't hurt much."

Jack rolled his eyes in both disbelief and in relief then he turned to the others. "Some of you men take those bodies down to the root cellar and take this piece of cow dung to the smokehouse and lock him up. I'm leaving you in charge, Tiny. If you don't mind."

"It would be my favorite chore. Boss, if little Jenny dies, can I kill him?" asked Tiny.

"One thing at a time, Tiny. One thing at a time."

When Jack entered the hacienda it was almost reminiscent of an auction house. People were all talking and jockeying around to and fro. Señora Kataryna was like an Army general pointing here and there and giving orders. She noticed Jack entered the room. "Oh good! Mijo, you will ride at once and fetch Andrew and Caleb. Now!"

Jack did not speak, he did not hesitate. He rather spun around and briskly walked through the kitchen area grabbing a sack and filling it with bread, roast chicken, several very hot baked potatoes and shoved them into the sack. Then poured himself a large tall glass of lemonade and chugged it down.

"Oh, Senor Jack! That was to be supper," said Juanita.

"Still is mine!" said Jack then he left the hacienda, mounted his horse and was gone.

**Austin, Texas**

Drew, Caleb and Leander H. McNelly were sitting at a table in the back of the saloon, getting acquainted.

"Have another beer? This round's on me," said Leander McNelly.

"Not for me, thank you. Three is my limit," said Caleb.

"Not mine. I'll have another," said Drew.

"Sure! Be like that. But I need to have my wits about me tomorrow. The governor is going to be a hard nut to crack. So if you fine gentleman will excuse me, I will say good night," said Caleb.

"It is a real pleasure to have met you," said Leander.

"The pleasure is all mine," said Caleb then he turned and left the saloon.

"He seems to be a right fine young man," said Leander looking at Drew.

"One of the finest," replied Drew.

"Are you related to him? I only ask because of the last names you both share."

"No, but he may as well be. You might say we go back a ways."

"I see you've taught him well," said Leander.

"You could say we taught each other. Thank you for the flowers anyway," said Drew.

"I wonder what ol' Rip is saying to the governor? He sure has been in his office long enough," said Leander.

"I have no idea but it must be good from the hollering that was going on when we left," replied Drew.

"Ya, that didn't sound very diplomatic to me."

"John never was one to mince words," said Drew.

"You would know that better than I. I think I too shall call it an evening. If you will grant me leave, sir, I will see you in the morning," said Leander.

Drew gulped down his beer. "Hold on and I will walk with you and thanks for the drink."

Drew was awakened by commotion from out in the street as well as much vigorous talking in the hallway outside of his hotel room. He sat up on the edge of his bed and growled. "What in the blazes is all the ruckus?" Drew slipped on his britches and peered out his window and saw Whiskey Jack and seven of the ranch hands in front of the sheriff's office with five bodies draped over horses backs. Drew quickly finished dressing and scrambled downstairs and across the street to meet Jack. Jack saw Drew approaching and took a deep breath.

"Jack, what is this?" asked Drew.

"I tried. I really did. By all that's holy, I really tried," replied Jack.

"Slowdown and start from the beginning." Jack explained every detail to Drew.

"Will she live?" asked Drew

"I'm not sure. When I left all of the women were tending to her. Hermano, this is bad. Really bad."

"Mother?" asked Drew.

"Madre e dios! Hermano, I've never in all my days seen her like this. She was like a mad woman. Hermano, she used the Lord's name in vain. Twice. Then she ordered me here to get you and Caleb. I was frightened by her."

"The prisoner, where is he?" asked Drew.

"Under guard in the smokehouse. Mother ordered it. She has Tiny watching him. Something has happened in Mother's mind," said Jack.

"Jenny is the daughter mother never had, Jack. But it isn't mother I'm worried about right now. It's Caleb. I'm not at all sure how he is going to react when he hears the news. I only pray Jenny lives," replied Drew.

Orrin Bell, the newly appointed sheriff, came down the street toward his office. He was accompanied by John S. Rip Ford and Leander H. McNelly. "This ought to be interesting," said Jack agitatedly.

"You keep your trap shut. Else we'll be hanging you before sundown," said Drew.

"I'm not worried about me. But one thing is certain, hermano. I don't know who but someone is going to hang or whatever. Mother will see to that if we don't first," replied Jack.

Drew knew Jack was right. Senora Kataryna Louisa Peña Parker had just drawn a line in the sand. Now there was nothing left to do but choose which side of that line you will stand on.

"What has happened here?" asked Rip.

"They hit our ranch. Apparently to collect on some back taxes. Which had already been paid. Asbury and Benson sent them. They shot Jenny. Then they died. Any words of wisdom, Colonel?" said Jack sarcastically.

"Now just what is that supposed to mean?" answered John S. Rip Ford.

"You said we should not act without proof. Well, there is your proof! Oh, don't worry about whether or not you'll get any confessions. We have one of them back at the ranch. My guess is he's singing like a choir boy right now," said Jack.

Jack was not about to sit quietly by and say nothing. This was too much. Besides he was not as diplomatic as Drew. Drew was very much aware of the fact and in spite of his pleading earlier, Jack was fed up. Diplomacy be hanged. Drew rolled his eyes but said nothing.

"I would say that they got proper justice. Are you going after Asbury and Benson?" asked Leander McNelly.

"No he is not!" said Drew. "We will go to the governor one last time."

"For all we know he may have known about this while he sat and talked to you. He may be in on it!" shouted Jack.

"I certainly hope you're wrong. Colonel, are you coming?" said Drew as he checked his revolver. He did so more to incite John Ford than for any other reason. That he would actually use his revolver on the governor was doubtful but John S. "Rip" Ford did not know this and was not about to chance anything.

"I am and this time he will act," said John S Ford matter-of-factly. "Caleb, when do you plan to tell him?"

"In due time. For now I just want one more chance to speak to the governor," replied Drew.

The next morning the streets of Austin were a buzz with talking and joyful jubilation by most all of the citizens. The headlines of the Austin Gazette read: GOVERNOR EDMUND JACKSON DAVIS

Re-instates the Texas Rangers

Effective immediately Gov. Davis has reinstated the Texas Rangers. Naming former Colonel John Salmon "Rip" Ford as Senior Captain of the Texas Rangers. His second in command of the Rangers, Gov. Davis has appointed Leander H. McNelly. When asked if he had anything specific to say. Capt. Leander H McNelly had but one comment: "All those who defy the laws of God and of Texas, leave Texas now. There will be no quarter."

Major Andrew Parker has been reassigned to full duty and command of the Texas Ranger Company D Uvalde, Texas. As adjutant to Senior Captain John S. Rip Ford, the Governor has requested formerly retired Ranger Capt. Charlie Welch.

Rangers John S. Ford, Leander H. McNelly, Drew Parker, Whiskey Jack and Charlie Welch were having a celebratory toast and congratulating one another in the newly established headquarters in Austin when a knock came to the office door. It was Caleb.

"What brings you here?" asked Jack.

"I have come to re-enlist," said Caleb. His expression was one of determination and seriousness.

"And what of your law practice?" asked Drew.

"Be proud to have you, Caleb, but don't you feel you would be more help by keeping your practice going?" asked Leander H. McNelly.

"Caleb, maybe you should give this more thought. Jenny is going to be all right. Maybe you should take the time to see her and talk to her. Perhaps you will see things differently once you have had the time to cool down. Revenge should not be your motive for being a Ranger," said Drew.

"You of all people should know me better than that. Texas is my home, Captain. This is bigger than me or Jenny or you or any man in this room. This is about our children's future who are the future of Texas. No one will come to my house for a free meal then tell me how to cook! Captain, this is not revenge. Those who shot Jenny are dead. Revenge would be futile," replied Caleb. "Besides until I know whose law I am actually defending I think it best to put my practice on hold."

"You sure have me convinced. You were a Sergeant as a Ranger, were you not?" asked McNelly.

"That is correct. But rank is not important to me. I have learned from the recent War Between the States rank does not make you bulletproof. I saw officers die just as easy as the lowest ranked enlisted man."

Leander McNelly could not help but admire Caleb. In him he saw a man of true integrity and honor. In him he saw what he hoped would be every Ranger. "Then raise your right hand and repeat after me."

Drew smiled, shook his head and congratulated him. "I had hoped that age and all that schooling would have made you smarter. But I see you're still the same ol' knob head just like the rest of us. I'm proud to have you with us. Now if church is officially over, I am long due to be getting home. I have a prisoner to tend to as well as a wife and son."

"Ha ha ha. Don't forget Grandmother. I'm sure she will have a few words for you as well," said Caleb.

"Don't remind me. But my guess is that she has calmed down some. That letter Dave brought from her sounded as though she had anyway. It would seem that Jenny will be just fine. The bullet was too high and went clean through. Although I'm certain she will be mighty sore for some time."

"It's going to be good to see her. But like you I'm interested in what the prisoner has to say. To say the least, it ought to be informative," replied Caleb.

**Uvalde, Texas**
**Three days later**

"Sure, Major Parker. I was with them. I was just hired on a week before. I had no idea things would turn out the way they did. Honest. Now I'm not trying to weasel out of anything you understand. It's obvious I was with them."

The prisoner, Wally Morrison, reached into his shirt pocket and pulled out a folded piece of paper and handed it to Drew. "You see, I thought it was just a regular range job. But I also knew we were supposed to be collecting back property taxes too. I did know that. But I had absolutely no idea I was riding with skunks. If you want me to plead guilty I will. But I ain't no killer, Major Parker. No sir, especially of women folk and kids. As far as everything else you got me. Yes, sir," said Wally Morrison.

"And rustling? We had..." Drew was cut off by Morrison.

"Hold on! What is this? Mister, I never stole nothing in my life. Not so much as a gumdrop! What's this about rustling? I just told you. I hired on a week ago!"

"Easy now! Or you'll bust a cinch. I was only asking. We had some cattle taken in which one of our men was shot up pretty bad. I was mostly curious as to whether or not you heard any mention of it by them that are employed by Asbury and Benson. That's all," said Major Drew Parker.

"No sir. But I will tell you this. If I had heard such talk I would have been gone like a shot! Pay be damned! I ain't no saint. I will be the first to tell anyone that. But I try every day to live a good Christian life. I take a drink now and then. But I don't go whoring and I don't play cards. My Ma, God bless her, raised me proper and I'm proud to say it. I want nothing less I earned it. Like the Good Book says: If a man does not work then he should not eat. That to me means earn what you get. Anything other than a gift is stealing."

Caleb sat back in his chair. "By God! Major Parker, we can't punish this fella. I honestly believe him! And remember Red and the Collins brothers Danny and Marty? They had one of those papers too. This kid was just in the wrong place at the wrong time with the wrong bunch. He's innocent, I'd say. It's but by the grace of God he wasn't killed along with the others."

Senora Kataryna entered the room. She had been eavesdropping from the hallway. "I believe you are right, Caleb. May our Lord forgive me for how I treated him and how I wished his death. I did not know that Red and the Collins brothers had similar papers. Madre e dios! It could have easily been them. I'm so thankful that young man was spared. You know that Tiny almost killed him? At that time, I would have done nothing to stop him either. Sweet Mother Mary, forgive me."

"So all is forgiven of him? You want him set free?" asked Drew.

"Yes. Him I forgive. You I do not."

"Me! What did I do?"

"You knew of our trouble. Yet you stayed in Austin. Jack told me everything..." Drew interrupted. "Mother, I stayed only to..."

"Coward," interjected Señora Kataryna.

"I was trying to get the governor to... Oh! Never mind and I'm not a coward. I'm just..."

"Just what?" asked Senora Kataryna.

"Smart enough to keep distance from you when you are angry. Jack said you swore. Twice! And using the Lord's name too."

"So you're a smart coward," said Senora Kataryna trying not to smile as she spun around and left the room.

"Just what did you say to the governor to cause him to change his mind?" asked Caleb.

"That is between me, the governor and God. I will never tell and I seriously doubt the governor will either," Drew said smiling.

"Oh, brother! No forget it. On second thought, I don't want to know," said Caleb.

"Neither do I. I would hate to have to possibly arrest a fellow Ranger and a Captain at that." It was Capt. Leander H McNelly.

"Leander? What brings you here? Don't you have much to do in Austin yet?" Drew was surprised to see that McNelly was there.

"I suppose I do. Which is precisely why I am here. We already have a mission and I need the three of you posthaste. We have to form a company of Rangers right away. I will need your help in recruiting men," said McNelly.

"So soon. What happened? Asbury and Benson kill the governor?" said Drew humorously.

"That's not funny. It would seem that the Yankee Army has done it again. Quanah Parker and Yellow Pony along with some 600 Comanche braves have jumped the reservation. They left Fort Sill and headed west. They have hit camps of settlers heading west to Utah as well as several small ranches just outside of Muleshoe and west. The Governor wants Quanah stopped."

"That's some mission all right. What do you suppose set Quanah off? He's one of the good Chiefs."

"I'll explain on the way to Austin," replied McNelly.

"You will not. You will stay the night," said Señora Kataryna who had just reappeared.

"I don't wish to impose and we really would do well to get into Austin as soon as possible," replied McNelly.

"Nonsense. You will make much better time well rested. You and your horses. I won't take no for an answer."

"In that case I'm much obliged to you. Of course you are right. That old horse of mine certainly could use the rest as well as the chance to fill up on those oats. Thank you."

"So what do you suppose set Quanah on the war trail?" asked Drew again.

"Hunger. It would seem. That and, in my way of thinking, some crooked dealings by the Army and a weasel of an Indian agent. For some reason, and I have yet to figure out Yankee logic or justice, it was decided that the Indian Agency was to be moved from Fort Sill to Wichita Falls. That makes it pretty near impossible for the Comanche as well as Kiowa to keep constant food supply levels now that they have to travel so far for their rations. It is no secret that Commanding Officer Col. Mitchell is no sympathizer of the Indians. From what I have heard, his treatment of Quanah and Yellow Pony was less than hospitable. He merely went through the usual formalities. To my way of thinking, had Dancing Crow not been there Yellow Pony would have mutinied against Quanah and attacked the Fort. But it would seem that time and the thought of his people starving has forced Quanah into a corner. I can't say that I truly can blame him. I would probably do the same thing," said Leander H McNelly.

"I agree. We had our difficulties with the Comanche in the past before the War between the States. But we certainly had a better relationship with the Indians before the Yankee stuck their big feet in the dance. You would think that they wanted war with the Indians," said Drew.

"Yes, one would think that, wouldn't they?" replied McNelly sarcastically.

"Are you suggesting that that's what they're trying to do? Incite the Indians into a war?"

"I'm not saying anything. But no one wanted that land they call a reservation before. But since the war ended lots of businesses have been seeing the land become profitable. It wasn't fit for jack rabbits to live on then. Since Dancing Crow encourages Comanche to take up farming they've made the land green. They'd do just well enough to grow some corn to grind, a few turnips, tomatoes and a little wheat to get through the winter. But now with having to travel all the way to Wichita Falls for food rations of beef and for blankets and such, they have been spending more time going back and forth and they hadn't done much farming."

"Why do you suppose that the government saw fit to move the agency headquarters so far from the reservation and Fort Sill?" inquired Drew.

"As I said, I have yet to figure that out. If you can come to some conclusion, I would like to hear it."

"Matter of fact, I may have. This reminds me of a situation back in Muleshoe long before the war. A case that took some doing to figure out."

"Oh?" asked McNelly.

"I'm just guessing here.You cannot foreclose on a reservation. But in any war that could give reason to relocate the reservation. If the Comanche broke the treaty agreements it would require the Indian Agency to request action from the Army and in turn would make reservation land up for grabs. Anyone with enough money and backing could scoop up that land for pennies on the dollar then sell it at a nice profit," explained Drew.

"I see. Such as an enterprising Army Col. and Indian agent? I would hate to think that were so. So far that's the only peg that fits in the hole. As much as I despise the Yankee Army I would much rather think Col. Mitchell was an unknowing pawn in someone's game. I surely would," said Leander H McNelly.

"Whatever the case, we will have plenty of time to sort that out as we find the men for the job. Lucky for you, Leander, I just so happen to know of two. To tell you the truth I'd rather find Quanah and Yellow Pony before the Army does. Maybe we can convince them to return to reservation. We may stand a good chance if Dancing Crow is with them."

"I will certainly consider that hope. Meantime, I am getting tired and ready for sleep. Good night, Major Parker," said McNelly.

"Buenos noches," replied Drew.

## TWO WEEKS LATER

Austin seemed as if the very birds that took residence on rooftops and trees throughout the town knew something was about to happen. For the town seemed unusually still for a Wednesday afternoon. Something was about to happen. There was a change in the air and the Texas Rangers were about to become the most feared lawmen in American history.

They came in twos and threes. Some young, some old. These were men who desired something. A home, a family, a business or land. But all a future. Mostly these were men who desired freedom. Freedom to worship their God. Freedom to build a life with their own two hands. To look upon with pride and satisfaction the fruits of their labors and sweat and blood. These were men wanting to build a nation. These men were wanting home. That home and nation for them would start here. In Texas. These were the Texas Rangers.

By evening, nary a hitching post or support beam of any building on one side and down the other of the main street of Austin, had at least two horses tied. The hotel was so full, men paid to sleep on the porch. The saloon also made use of its tables, bar and billiard tables as well as its floor to accommodate the steady influx of men. Nearly 700 men had come to Austin to answer the call that Capt. Leander H McNelly had issued in flyers to every town and community he could think of. "ALL FOR TEXAS!" Texas is in need of honest, God-fearing, honorable men to ride for law and order. No questions asked. Your word as a man is enough. Must be able to ride, shoot and fight. If you are looking for a start or a fresh start, the Texas Rangers want you.

**Capt. Leander H McNelly**
**Texas Rangers**
**Austin, Texas**

They came all right. Some 700 or more some wanting to turn over a new page in life. To go straight to live inside the law not outside of it. Some were thrill seekers. Some were honest men. Mostly single and young. It was as though Texas took a deep breath and pushed giving birth to a new breed of men and a new beginning.

"Leander, have you taken a walk through town lately? I was nearly tripping over bodies out there! You asked for men and I believe you got 'em. We're bound to find the right men out of that lot," said Major Drew Parker.

"Yes, I was out there. The sight brought tears to my eyes. Since before the recent war, never have I seen such a glorious sight. You know, I believe we are witnessing the dawning of a new era. I believe I recognize some of those faces. We've got us some men, Drew! Hallelujah! We're Rangers again! And this time, come hell or high water, we're here to stay. Look out there! Don't it make your heart swell? God bless Texas!" exclaimed Leander H McNelly.

The next morning. Capt. Leander H McNelly stood on the balcony of the Austin Hotel. He raised the shotgun high above his head and fired. The sound of the shotgun blasts brought men running from every direction. Most with weapons of their own. They stopped when they saw Leander H McNelly and he began to address the crowd.

"I am Leander H McNelly. Captain of the Texas Rangers. This man at my side is Major Drew Parker. Welcome! Welcome! All of you. This afternoon at 1:30, we will be seeing what you are made of. We will be meeting on the south end of the holding pens just outside of town. Bring your horse, your guns but mostly bring your grit. Because you're going to need it! Now, all of you are welcome courtesy of Gov. Davis to a free breakfast at the railroad yard depot. Be kind, boys! The women who fixed your meal may be fixing you someday. We wouldn't want to start off on the wrong foot now, would we? Besides they are all good shots themselves."

"HOORAH! HOORAH! For GOVERNOR DAVIS! HOORAH FOR THE TEXAS RANGERS!" rang up and down the street.

As the crowd started filtering down the street to the railyard, Drew looked at Leander McNelly. "I don't recall the governor mentioning a free breakfast."

"Yeah but the jackass was counting on a lousy turnout. This'll learn him. Never take a Texan for granted." Leander began to laugh and Drew joined in.

"You sure got that right!" agreed Drew.

It was no easy task for Captain Leander H McNelly and Major Andrew Parker to decide among the 700 as to who would or would not become members of the Texas Rangers. Every one of them could indeed ride well and shoot. There were farmers, miners, schoolteachers, ranch hands, ex-cons, riverboat and saloon gamblers and former soldiers, both North and South. Then there were the all willing but just too old. When the final tally was read 647 men were recruited into the Rangers. The 53 not accepted were sworn in and then promptly released with one month's pay. It was the least that the Texas Rangers could do to show their respect and gratitude.

"Ranger Maxwell!" hollered Capt. McNelly.

"Yes, sir!"

"Pass the word. I want all Rangers to meet at 06:30 sharp. I will then address them and give them their first assignment. Until then they are free to take care of any unfinished business they may have."

"Right away, Major, sir," said Ranger Maxwell.

"Ranger Maxwell."

"Yes, sir, Major."

"You can dispense with all that sir nonsense. Just a 'yes, Major' or 'no, Major' will do. "

"Major Parker," said McNelly.

"Yes, Captain," said Drew.

"I will be assigning young rangers Jeffrey Boxer and Johnny Jack to your command," said Leander McNelly.

"That is a fine gesture, Leander, but I must decline. I will have no accusations of preferential treatment. They're Rangers now. They will follow orders and go where they are most needed," said Major Drew Parker.

"I will assign them to company A."

"And whose company might that be?"

Coughing and clearing his throat, O'Toole spoke. "My command, sir."

Drew looked in awe at both Leander H McNelly and Hamelton O'Toole.

"O'Toole! Leander, on second thought, I want my boys back!" said Major Drew Parker laughing. "Well, what do you know! When was anyone going to tell me?"

"Just did. Rip sent me a message by courier. It was his idea and I agreed."

"So do I! Things are shaping up fast that's for certain. You know, the Texas Rangers just might become something at that. What d'ya know. Congratulations, Capt. O'Toole. Wait till the rest of the boys here this," said Major Drew Parker.

"Most of them already know. Actually they took it pretty well," said Capt. O'Toole.

"That's not good. You can bet they're up to something. Mark my words," teased Drew. Drew put his hat on and looked at O'Toole. "Well, come on. Let's go."

"Go where, sir?"

"It's an old Ranger custom that all newly appointed captains must buy the Senior Officers a drink," Major Drew Parker reminded him.

"Aye! I knew I was going to like this job," said newly appointed Capt. Hamelton O'Toole.

The following morning showed signs of rain. East of Austin, a large blue-black sky slowly crept its way toward Austin. Like a slow puddle of water someone would have made on the floor by accidentally kicking the mop bucket. Pink white fiery flashes of lightning lit up the horizon. The wind was starting to pick up in strength. Capt. Leander H McNelly stood tall on the high catwalk that bordered the holding pens. He was accompanied by Major Drew Parker, Capt.'s Hamelton O'Toole, Whiskey Jack and semi-retired Capt. Charlie Welch.

"A fine looking bunch of men. What say you, Capt. McNelly?" asked Capt. Hamelton O'Toole.

"I would but they haven't been put to the test yet. Capt. O'Toole will sort the men from the boys."

"I was sort of hoping Ol' Rip would be here. I believe he would be proud," said Whiskey Jack.

"Yes. Well, perhaps he will be here. At present, Capt. John Salmon Rip Ford is conducting business with the Governor," replied McNelly.

"I'd love to be a fly on the wall right about now. I can only imagine what Rip must be saying," laughed Drew.

"Ya, I can hear him now," laughed McNelly.

"Well. Shall we begin?" said Capt. O'Toole.

"I suppose so. We best hurry. Looks like it's going to be mighty damp shortly," said McNelly.

McNelly waved his hat in the air high above his head and fired a shot in the air from his colt revolvers. The humming of men talking quickly died down. Everyone was looking in McNelly's direction. McNelly yelled as he began to address the crowd of newly sworn in Rangers. "I hope you're all you profess to be. For surely this day, you are needed. As many of you may have heard, the Comanche are on the prowl and are causing somewhat of a fuss up north. The governor has ordered every Ranger to proceed posthaste to put an end to the Comanche raids. So! If any of you are going to have second thoughts of being a Texas Ranger leave now. You will not be thought ill of. But if you choose to stay, listen to me and listen well!! Once we leave Austin, you are officially a member of the Texas Rangers! Each of you have been assigned to a company. You will assemble with that company at daybreak tomorrow morning. I do not want to start our first day riding in a storm. It's bad luck." The man chuckled and jeered then McNelly continued. "Understand this! Any Ranger who deserts or runs from a fight will be shot! You are Texas Rangers! A Ranger never quits; never runs; never goes back on his word! You are more than lawmen. You are brothers. Now I don't know about you but should anyone harm my brother I will hunt him down to the very fires of Hell! I give you that same promise. One more thing by God Almighty, you best remember this if nothing else: I hate a traitor! I promise you any man who betrays his fellow Rangers will be treated worse than the lowest scum of the earth! I want every man armed and ready to ride at 05:30. Make sure you have plenty of ammunition and are well healed. Be here sober! No drinking tonight, boys! McNelly ended his speech with "ALL FOR TEXAS!" and firing his revolver into the air. The men responded in kind.

## "ALL FOR TEXAS!"

Three days later and one day's ride from Abilene, the small town of Juniper gave the Rangers their first clue to the seriousness of their mission. Juniper stood smoldering. People were walking around in a daze gathering and loading charred timbers and a buckboard wagon. A small gathering of men was busy with burial detail at the local cemetery.

"You're late," said a sad looking old woman.

Capt. McNelly removed his hat. "I am heartfully sorry, ma'am. We left as soon as we could. Can any of my Rangers be of assistance to you?"

"You're Captain McNelly?" she asked.

"That is correct, ma'am."

"I'm glad the Rangers are back. Many a good people died here, Captain McNelly. Perhaps you could have stopped the killing perhaps not. But I'm glad we have the Rangers with us again."

"Are you okay?" asked Capt. McNelly, gently. He had noticed the sad look of loss in her eyes. "You look in need."

"The Lord meets all my needs, Captain. It's the people of this town I mourn for," said the old woman.

"Just the same, ma'am, I am going to lend you a small handful of my Rangers. They are under your command," said Capt. McNelly.

The old woman smiled up at Capt. McNelly and said, "God bless you."

"Thank you and God bless you, ma'am."

The Rangers busied themselves with helping the town. By the end of the day a large portion of cleaning up and giving medical and food comfort to the town had been completed. Though their spirits were still low, they had the look of determination and hope in their eyes. Capt. McNelly instructed his men. "We will leave at first light."

"Capt. McNelly, maybe we should send out a couple of scouting parties ahead of us. Could be that the Comanche are miles away by now but it also could be that they aren't too far away either. Either way we will at least save ourselves from being surprised," said a young sergeant Rodney Allen.

"You may have something there. Are you by any chance volunteering?" asked Capt. McNelly.

Sgt. Allen smiled. "Are you volunteering me, Captain?"

"Nope. I let the volunteering up to the individual."

"I reckon I ought to seeing's it were my idea in the first place, sir," replied Sgt. Allen.

"Good man. Sgt. Capt. O'Toole will accompany you with a few of his men. Capt. O'Toole?"

"Aye. We will meet you north of here about a full days ride. Near the salt fork of the Brazos. I do believe Major Parker is familiar with the area I'm talking of," said Capt. Hamelton O'Toole.

"Pass the word around, Major Parker. I want every man rested and fed as well as all the mounts. Check your weapons and ammunition," instructed Capt. McNelly.

The morning sun was just making its debut. An orange, pink, and blue array of colors painted the horizon. A chilling breeze swept across the plains. Ordinarily a cowboy would give the breeze no thought at all but the threat of attack from Comanches added to the chill making it more eerie, than cold. A chill one ran up Ranger Tom Crawford's back sending goose pimples up and down his arms. He glanced to the West and something caught Tom Crawford's eye.

"Smoke, Capt. O'Toole!" said Tom Crawford.

"Aye! I see it," said O'Toole. Then yelled, "Troop halt!"

"Are we going after them, Captain?" asked Ranger Rodney Allen.

"I suppose that would be the thing to do, Ranger. But we're only 46 men. Quanah has over 600," O'Toole pointed.

The horizon showed a long high ridge about a mile away dotted with moving figures.

"I think they already know we're here," continued Capt. O'Toole.

"Now what?" asked one of the Rangers.

"We have little cover except for that small goalie yonder. Standby your horses. We will make our stand there. If we're lucky, we can hold out until Capt. McNelly and the others get here," ordered Capt. Hamelton O'Toole.

"If we can't?" asked another of the 46 Rangers.

"Then we get the hell out of here and fast!" chuckled Capt. O'Toole.

"But Captain McNelly..." started yet another Ranger.

"Captain McNelly what?" interrupted O'Toole.

"Capt. McNelly said a Ranger never runs from a fight," stated the young Ranger.

"What's your name?"

"Paul Carpenter, sir."

"Well, Ranger Paul Carpenter, the way I see it, I don't think this is exactly the circumstances Capt. McNelly was referring to. We won't be running from a fight. I am fairly certain the fight will follow along with us. We will only be regrouping in a different place."

Ranger Paul Carpenter smiled. "Yes, sir! That's exactly the impression I got from that as well."

Tom Crawford yelled. "Here they come, Capt. O'Toole!"

"Stand by your horses! Hold your fire!" shouted Capt. O'Toole.

Silently, the Comanche rode swiftly to just outside of rifle range and stopped.

"Well, I'll be! That's the red devil himself. Quanah and looks like he's carrying a white flag. Could be a trick, Captain," said Ranger Rodney Allen.

"No, it's a parlay before the fight. Hold your fire, men!" ordered Capt. O'Toole. "Ranger Allen, you and Ranger Crawford will accompany me. Let's go see what he has to say."

The Comanche leader, Quanah Parker, was a tall, muscular man with wide shoulders and thick chested. His face was painted for war. Yet his eyes seemed to show regret and compassion for those he was about to kill. He also showed an obvious intelligence, not common among many Indians, of schooling in the white man's way. Not to say that the Indian was not intelligent only that few had education from the white man school. Yet his knowledge of the plains and the desert could not be surpassed.

Capt. O'Toole and the others came to a halt in front of Quanah and seven of his Braves.

"Yah ta hey, Quanah," said Capt. O'Toole.

"Yah ta hey, Ranger," said Quanah Parker.

"I am Capt. Hamelton O'Toole, Texas Rangers. With an open and sorrow filled heart, I welcome Quanah Parker, great chief of the Comanche."

"I am Quanah, chief of the Comanche. But I do not know you. I have heard that the Rangers of Texas were back. Why are you here, O'Toole Ranger?"

"We have come to put an end to the killing and raiding by Quanah and his Comanche. It must stop. It must stop before the Comanche are no more," claimed Capt. O'Toole.

Quanah laughed. "O'Toole Ranger and this little band of O'Toole Rangers think you can stop us? Go back! Go back now or die! You want Comanche to stop killing and raiding. Comanche want whites to stop stealing, lying and killing Comanche. You say you are here because Comanche have taken from white eyes and you feel it is just that you come to stop us! You are all hypocrites and two-faced dogs! Why is it different that Comanche should fight for same reason?"

"We are here to help you, Quanah, great chief of the Comanche. Not to fight or kill anyone. But like you, we will fight. At this very moment, more Rangers are coming. Not to kill but to protect the Comanche."

"Protect!" Quanah laughed again. "You mean to lie and lead us into a trap! Why should the Comanche believe O'Toole Ranger? What can Rangers do? Steal more food from the mouths of our women and children? Make drunkards out of our young men? Treat our women as pieces of meat and corrupt them?"

"No, Quanah. Please hear me. The Texas Rangers know how the Comanche feel. As you know, the white eyes have not long ago fought a Civil War because whites from the far east and north of here were doing the same to the whites in the South and in the West. Is Quanah aware that Yankee blue coats are at this very moment riding to wipe you out? Please, do not give them any more reason," said Capt. O'Toole.

"I almost believe you, O'Toole Ranger. But we have come too far. How can I look my people in the eyes with dignity? While the stomachs of their young growl with hunger and shiver in the cold because they have not enough blankets? Our old are dying; our young are dying.

Better to die with pride and fight as Comanche than to die like hungry dogs in the streets."

"This is very true. Perhaps Quanah will listen to Dancing Crow. Maybe Dancing Crow will remember Capt. Parker of the Texas Rangers," said Capt. O'Toole. "You know this Capt. Parker?" asked Quanah.

"I do. I rode as one of his Rangers many years ago when Dancing Crow, great leader of Comanche, was chief."

"I have heard many stories about Capt. Parker. Dancing Crow used to tell around the fire when I was young. He was an honorable man. But Dancing Crow is old now and sick. He has grown weary of war. No, Ranger O'Toole, go back now. I give you this warning only one time. I will respect the honor of your Ranger Capt. Parker and of Dancing Crow. I will give you until the sun touches the hills. If you do not go you will all die," Quanah and his seven warriors wheeled their ponies around and rode away to the top of the ridge with the other Comanche.

"Four hours," mumbled Ranger Allen.

"Four hours is a long time. I have a feeling this is going to be the shortest four hours in creation but it does give us time to prepare," said Capt. O'Toole.

"Prepare, sir?" said Ranger Allen. "What happened to getting out of here?"

"Not a thing, only we aren't in a fight yet. Therefore, we have no reason to go anywhere. Relax, Ranger. It's only 600 or 700 of them. I faced greater odds during the war," said Capt. O'Toole.

"Semantics. Why do all Captains have to use semantics?" smiled Ranger Allen.

"It's better than lying?" commented Ranger Tom Crawford.

"Oh, thanks! That makes me feel much better," laughed Ranger Allen.

The Rangers worked feverishly. Stacking stones for barricades as well as any old dead tree limbs. They dug holes to crouch lower in, as the protection of the gully was not deep enough. They gathered dead brush and sticks for a fire. They were not running.

"Fools! All of them fools! Who are these white rangers to think that they and only 46 men can defeat us?" scowled Yellow Pony.

"They may be only 46 men. But fools? No, Yellow Pony. I will remember them as the bravest enemy I have ever fought," said Quanah.

"I have seen the blue coats with twice as many men flee like quail kicked out of the brush," retorted Yellow Pony.

"They are not blue coats, Yellow Pony. They are Texas Rangers. Do not take them lightly, my bloodthirsty cousin, or else you may lay among their dead."

"Ppffft! You talk as if you felt sorry for them."

"I do," said Quanah.

"Captain, might I ask a favor?" asked a young Ranger.

"Yes, what is it?"

"I can't read, sir. So could you read a fitting word from the Good Book for me, sir? I'm not skeered of dying but if I do, I want the good Lord to know He was on my mind before I died."

"He knows that already but aye, I will read to you," Capt. Hamelton O'Toole read the 23rd Psalm out loud for all to hear.

"Here they come, Captain!" warned Tom Crawford. A chorus of amens went up to heaven as Capt. O'Toole yelled, "Steady men! Hold your fire! Let them get closer! Make every shot count!"

The Comanche came at devilish speed. Yelling, whooping and painted for war. The tips of their lances glittered in the sunlight flashing threats of death. Arrows soared overhead and all around. Bullets from those who had rifles buzzed and kicked up rock and sand all about. The sound of horses hooves beating the earth grew louder and louder. Soon the Comanche were just 70 yards away. The ground shook beneath them.

"Let 'em have it, men! Fire!" yelled Capt. O'Toole. Guns blazed. Smoke filled the air and stung their eyes and nostrils. Within what seemed mere seconds, all became quiet.

They're gone, Captain! I think we whooped 'em," yelled one of the Rangers.

"They'll be back. This was just a warning. Quanah is giving us one last chance to run," said Tom Crawford.

"Aye! But he will soon learn it takes more than a few screaming painted aborigines to scare off the Texas Rangers," boasted Capt. O'Toole.

"Begging the Captain's pardon," said one of the Rangers. "I'm pretty scared right now and don't mind saying so."

Everyone laughed. "Aye but the trick is not to let them know it. That is true bravery."

"Guess that makes me the bravest of them all," said the young Ranger. "Because my fear is running down my leg."

"As long as it's your fear running and not you," chuckled Capt. O'Toole.

"Here they come again, Captain!" warned a Ranger

"Get ready for a fight, men!" yelled Capt. O'Toole.

"Ain't they something?" said a Ranger.

Soon the men were entangled with Comanche warriors. Guns firing, hand-to-hand fighting. Screaming, moaning sounds were everywhere.

"Look out!" yelled a Ranger as he pointed a double barrel shotgun and fired killing a Comanche brave who was just about to thrust his lance in Tom Crawford's back.

"Thanks, Ranger! Now my fear is leaving me!" said Tom Crawford.

As with the first attack, it was over as quickly as it began. Capt. O'Toole looked around at the bodies on the ground. Suddenly, a hand from a supposed dead Comanche twitched. Capt. O'Toole fired his shotgun at point-blank range. The Comanche raised as one would do if doing a push-up then plopped flat faced into the sand.

"Is everyone all right?" asked Capt. O'Toole.

"Look around, men! Some of these braves may be playing possum," ordered Tom Crawford.

"Excuse me, Captain," said an older Ranger. "You are needed over yonder." The Ranger pointed to a couple of men hovering over another. It was the young Ranger who had asked to be read to. Capt. O'Toole kneeled down at his side. The young Ranger looked at Capt. O'Toole. "We whooped 'em this time, didn't we, sir?"

"Aye and we couldn't have done it without you. I'm very..."

"No need to give any voice of grief, Captain. I know how bad it is. But you know? I feel good. Oh, look! Isn't it beautiful?" The young Ranger pointed to the sky. He gasped, "Momma?" then died.

Another Ranger came and stood next to them. "Excuse me, Captain, but you asked for an assessment?"

"Aye, I did."

"Fourteen dead, eight wounded and they killed most of our horses, sir."

"That was to keep us from going on," mumbled Capt. O'Toole.

"Going on, sir?"

"Yes! Going on after them. Those of us who can ride and fight. The rest will wait here for Capt. McNelly and the others. Tom, pick out a few men to stay behind and help with the wounded. Mount up!" ordered Capt. O'Toole.

"Irishmen! I'll never figure them out. What's the reason to go on? The Comanche have left. No reason to chase 'em until Capt. McNelly and the others show up. Why push on?" complained a weary young Ranger.

"I can give you fourteen good reasons why, son," said Tom Crawford.

It was three days later when Capt. McNelly and the others finally caught up with Capt. Hamelton O'Toole and his Rangers. Capt. O'Toole had been having a steady hit-and-run fight with the Comanche. The Comanche were strangely but most assuredly heading north toward the Red River.

"I don't understand, Leander. Quanah knows that we're on his back trail. He also knows that the Army has patrols north of here. Why would he knowingly ride into a trap?" asked Capt. O'Toole.

"Quanah is no fool. But I can't answer that either," said Capt. Leander McNelly.

"Could be he's homesick. He and his warriors have been away from their families for some time. They are no different than any other man. Besides, I'm sure they have gathered quite a haul of food, blankets and other items to distribute among his people," said Major Drew Parker.

"Could be. But God help him if they run into any Army patrol," said Whiskey Jack.

"From what we have seen and have contended with I'd say it was the Army who should be worried," said Tom Crawford.

"Ordinarily, I would agree. But the Army has a new weapon. Some kind of fast shooting cannon," commented Whiskey Jack.

"I think they call it a Gatling gun. It can spit out over 400 rounds a minute. The Army doesn't need to provide as much manpower anymore. Not with that contraption. They'll cut those Comanche down like a scythe cutting winter wheat," said Tom Crawford.

"Well, if that's the case then what side do we protect? That could explain why the Army hasn't pressured Quanah as hard lately. They know he and his men must come home at some point. They'll just lay in waiting and wham! Close the trapdoor. It'll be cold-blooded murder," said Ranger Rodney Allen.

"He's right. Captain McNelly, it looks like, whether we want to or not, we have to side with Quanah against the Army on this one. With Quanah and nearly all his braves wiped out, it'll be easy as pie for those land speculators to just waltz in and take all that reservation land away from the Comanche. Not to mention the healthy profits some would gain from it. I wouldn't be surprised if some of them would be connected to or still in the Army," said Sgt. Caleb Parker.

"Does that mean we're going to be fighting the Yankees again?" asked Ranger Jeffrey Boxer.

"Just the corrupt, greedy, warmongering Yankees," said Ranger Red Sands.

"That's not exactly how I would put it in my report to the governor, Ranger Sands. But for lack of better phrasing, looks like we are, Jeffrey," said Capt. McNelly.

The Rangers caught up with Quanah Parker and his Comanche near Rock Canyons. The Comanche had been caught completely off guard as they were also growing weary and figured themselves safe in Rock Canyons. Had it not been for Major Drew Parker and Capt. Whiskey Jack the Comanche would not have been discovered. But previous years experience with Peta Nacona and those with Dancing Crow had given the two Rangers as well as those who had been with them some knowledge as to where to look.

It was just breaking daylight and the Comanche were beginning to stir from their sleep. Those who had been on guard were slowly meandering their way back into the camp. A light flurry of snow was starting to fall and the wind was in favor of the Rangers. The Comanche remuda of ponies did not catch the scent of the Rangers as they started breaking off into groups to surround the Comanche.

It was understood that the Rangers wouldn't show their positions and strength until given the signal by Capt. McNelly. The signal was, that Capt. McNelly would remove his hat and wipe his forehead with a red bandana.

The look on Quanah Parker's face was a mix of surprise, admiration and anger. When Capt.'s McNelly, O'Toole and Major Parker along with 12 other Rangers including Red Sands, Caleb and Jeffrey Boxer came riding into the Comanche camp as bold as brass and holding a white flag of truce.

Many of the Comanche began to gather weapons and were in outrage ready to kill.

"No!" ordered Quanah Parker. "They come in peace. They did not kill me when I rode into their camp. Let them be."

Yellow Pony was sick with anger. He wanted blood. "You are fool!"

"You are not yet chief," reminded Quanah.

The Ranger stopped at Quanah's feet. "We come in peace, Quanah," said Capt. McNelly. "Yah ta hey."

"Yah ta hey," answered Quanah. "You are either very brave or wish to die yourself. Why are you here?"

"To warn you and to help you, Quanah. You are in grave danger. Let us work together for peace so your children and our children may have a tomorrow," said Capt. McNelly.

"Tomorrow? Tomorrow is what tomorrow is. We will face it when it comes. That is the Comanche way," growled Yellow Pony.

"Is that why the Comanche have gone on the war trail? To give hope for tomorrow? Or do you fight for all the yesterday's that will never come back? Yellow Pony only wants to fight because he enjoys it. He wants to be the big man in front of all the young warriors. Too young to die for a lost cause. But Yellow Pony would sacrifice 1000 warriors to become chief. Tell me I lie!" scowled Major Drew Parker.

Yellow Pony lurched forward. He wanted to kill Drew and the others.

"Stop!" ordered Quanah. "Or is there truth in what this Ranger says? You are too quick to anger my young cousin."

"Quanah is very wise. He knows he cannot go on fighting forever. Let us, the Texas Rangers, help save what remains of the Comanche nation. For as we speak, the bluecoat Army lays in wait for your return. They have set a trap for you. They have a new gun that spits fire and bullets like rain from the sky. Let us help you. If you choose to go on alone we will not stop you. Nor will we help you. You will force us to take the side of the blue coats. This I do not wish to do. I have heard of the many wrongs done to the Comanche. I can put an end to these things if you will cooperate with me. I can protect you from the blue-coat Army," said Capt. Leander H McNelly.

"What makes you think you will ever leave here alive?" snorted Yellow Pony.

Capt. McNelly slowly took off his hat and wiped his forehead with his red bandanna. "Look around you, Yellow Pony. You are surrounded by 700 Texas Rangers. We do not fight like the blue coats but very much like the Comanche. It was from the Comanche we learned," McNelly was not just warning Yellow Pony, but was hoping Quanah would hear the compliment and what he had said. Quanah did hear. He looked at Hamelton O'Toole and smiled. "I remember you. You are O'Toole Ranger. You fight well. I am sorry many of your men had to die. They died a good death. They fought well."

"Aye, and you too. You lost many good men. I have never met a finer adversary. You can be proud and honor their names," said O'Toole.

"Words! Words!" shouted Yellow Pony. "How do we know you are not part of this trap? Remember Ranger it has been the white man's words of promise that we fight now. No white man can be trusted to keep his words."

"This white man can. If you choose not to heed them, fine. And when all of your young braves lay dying and your wives and children starving do not say this white man lied to you. Go. Go on to your deaths. All of you! My conscience is clear. We will leave you now, Quanah. God be with you."

**FOUR DAYS LATER**
**Fort Sill, Oklahoma Indian Territory**

"What in blue blazes? Corporal of the Guard!" shouted the tower century at the gate of Fort Sill.

"What is it, Lipitz?" replied Corporal Joshua Barnes.

"Indians. A whole passel of 'em. But that ain't all. Look!" said Private Otis Lipitz pointing.

"Well, I'll be! Sound assembly! Bugler!! Someone get the colonel," ordered Cpl. Barnes.

The look upon Col. William Mitchell's face was one of dismay, disbelief and wonder which quickly turned to embarrassment, anger and jealousy. Before his eyes were the Comanche and Quanah Parker being led under escort by nearly 700 Texas Rangers with Capt. Leander H McNelly in the lead. The Texas Rangers had managed to do in just a few weeks what Col. Mitchell and his whole battalion could not do in four months.

"Open the gates!" ordered Col. Mitchell.

Yellow Pony and 200 other warriors refused to go to Fort Sill.

Upon seeing Quanah Parker and coming to the realization the Comanche were still all armed, Col. Mitchell became enraged.

"Lieutenant Howard, disarm those men!" ordered Col. Mitchell.

Upon hearing the order to disarm them, the Comanche began to get nervous and concerned.

"Belay that order!" yelled Captain McNelly.

"Capt. McNelly! I will remind you that you are now in my jurisdiction. Namely this outpost!! Those Indians will surrender their weapons!" scowled Col. Mitchell.

"With all due respect, Colonel Mitchell. I gave my word to Quanah and his men they could keep their weapons and that no harm would befall them should they come in peaceful and voluntarily. They keep their weapons!"

"That may be how you do things in Texas. But this is not Texas nor some ragtag on discipline haggle of vigilantes calling themselves Texas Rangers! This is the property of the United States and the United States Army which gives me full responsibility and authority. They will surrender those weapons or I will have every one of you corralled if need be and placed under arrest and under armed guard," claimed Col. Mitchell.

"Col. I think that if you look hard enough, you'll find that we have done a pretty fair job at handling ourselves in dealing with the Comanche, Kiowa, Apache and from time to time, the Mexicans. But to say undisciplined, wow, that just cuts me to the quick. Colonel, we may not wear a pretty blue uniform and parade around like marionettes but we hold our own. As for discipline, you could be right. You see we value a man's word and his honor before discipline although discipline has its place. Mostly around women. I gave my word, Colonel," said Capt. McNelly.

Quanah was getting suspicious of Col. Mitchell and the soldiers at the Fort. He had been listening intently to the exchange of words between McNelly and Col. Mitchell. Quanah slid down from his pony and softly walked up to Col. Mitchell. A look of apprehension came upon the Col.'s face.

"I give you my weapon but not my respect." And with that Quanah laid his rifle on the ground at Col. Mitchell's feet. Soon all the braves followed Quanah's example.

"I don't give a damn about your respect so long as you obey," said Col. Mitchell.

Capt. McNelly raised an eyebrow. "Colonel, you have much to learn about the Comanche and about honor out here in the West."

"I need no lectures concerning honor, Capt. McNelly. I'll have you know I am a decorated officer and served with Gen. Sheridan in a recent war."

"I have no doubt, Colonel. But yours is Yankee honor. The kind you pin on your chest where and when it suits you. Out here, honor is pinned to your heart. It is in what you say and do and how you live. Out here when a man says I will, he keeps his promise. Even if that promise is to his worst enemy. Yes, sir, you have much to learn," replied Capt. McNelly.

Quanah Parker will go on to live as an influential leader for the betterment of his people, the Quahada Comanche. Because of his mixed blood, his mother being white, he gained the trust of many white settlers and ranchers. He was instrumental in the securing of property boundaries and protecting cattle. He and some of his Comanche were listed as "cattle police."

Quanah Parker would also play a huge role in the formal education of many of the younger Comanche children for many years and also in the economic development of the Indians in Oklahoma. As time went by Quanah Parker would become a well-known and wealthy rancher. His home was named the Star House. But as with all societies, some Comanche would choose to live in the old ways and live the war trail such as Yellow Pony. The future would still hold more trials for the Comanche.

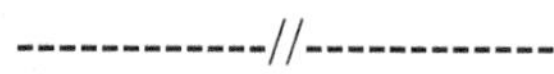

November on the plains was brisk and wet. Rain would fall causing the ground to become so soft that wagons would bog down. Horse's hooves would make sucking sounds as they struggled to make their way. Such was the way that caused many small towns to spring up out of nowhere. Too tired and too poor, many settlers would settle where their wagons stopped in the mud. Such a town was Happens Chance. It had sprung out of the earth seemingly overnight. The town of Happens Chance became home to many years before the War Between the States.

**Austin, Texas**
**Company A Texas Rangers**
**Ranger Headquarters**

"More coffee, McNelly?" asked Ranger Jeffrey Boxer.

"No, Jeff. I've about had enough thanks."

"Are you sure, Capt.? I went and sweetened it a little. Made it a tad strong to boot."

"Well, maybe one more. Since you sweetened it. Kentucky sweetener, I'm sure."

"Yes, sir. Just the way you like it."

From the room next door to Capt. McNelly's office came the tapping of the telegraph machine. A stout balding man with huge forearms and thick neck came trotting into Capt. McNelly's office. "Bull, what is it?" asked Capt. McNelly. "Trouble, Capt. As if we ain't got enough already. I swear..."

"Bull!"

"Oh, yes sir. The town of Happens Chance near the upper Llano Escatado. Bank Robbery, $27,000. The town sheriff is dead. A young kid, Clinton Cutter is acting Sheriff. It was this Cutter fella that sent the wire. Or had it sent I should say. Captain, what are we going to do? By cracky, every Ranger post we own is up to their belly buttons with jobs already!" said Bull.

"Settle down, Bull. We'll think of something. And no, you can't go!!"

"But, Captain, I'm getting cabin fever sitting around here. I was meant to ride the trail. Not stare at some metal and wire contraption all day. I need to feel a horse beneath me. Sleep under the stars. I need to Ranger!" said Harvey Bull Madison.

"Good Lord, Bull. At least let me think!"

"Yes, sir," Bull walked away mumbling to himself. "Sitting in a danged chair all day. Maybe you like it but..."

"Bull!"

"Oh! Yes, sir, I'll hush."

An hour went by and Capt. McNelly sent a reply to Happens Chance.

"Jeff!" called Capt. McNelly.

"Yes, Captain."

"Go fetch Sergeants Caleb Parker and Tom Crawford. They should be in the barracks."

When Caleb and Tom entered McNelly's office, McNelly was reading a piece of paper. "Aahh! Sit down you two. Looks like I've got a job for you. Caleb, you boys ever hear of a town called Happens Chance? It's not too far from a town called Muleshoe. I know you've heard of that," said McNelly.

At the mention of Muleshoe, Caleb's eyes lit up. "Can't say that I have. How about you, Tom?"

"No. But I sure remember Muleshoe. Fine town. Real nice folks too. I wonder if Jake Randles is still marshaling there?"

"Never mind that. Happens Chance's bank was robbed of $27,000. Also the sheriff was killed. The deputy, kid named Clinton Cutter, is now the town's acting Sheriff. He has wired the Rangers for help. At least we know the kid has a head on his shoulders," said Capt. McNelly.

"Did anyone get a description of the outlaws?" asked Caleb.

"Yes, plenty," replied Capt. McNelly

Capt. Charlie Welch stepped out from behind his desk on the opposite side of the room. He was carrying a fistful of papers.

"These are copies of the descriptions of the three men suspected of robbing the bank of Happens Chance. I'm sorry, there are no sketches."

"Hmmmm, not much to go on. Just their names. Jason Brickman, 23 years old, Thomas Brickman, 22 years old and William Brickman, 18 years old. All having blonde hair. Jason Brickman about 5'9", 180 pounds, brown eyes," Tom Crawford continued to read. "Captain, this is going to be a tough nut to crack. These descriptions fit nearly every cowhand and drifter in Texas. Is there any more to go on?"

"I'm afraid not, men, which, is why I'm charging you two to assemble a detail of nine or 10 men and ride out to Happens Chance. I will wire that Sheriff Cutter that he can be expecting you. If you avoid towns and saloons, you should be there in five days unless you run into trouble," said Capt. McNelly.

"Yes, sir," said Caleb.

Bull stood at the door almost panting for the opportunity. "Take Bull with you," sighed McNelly.

"Thank you, Captain, thank you. I won't..."

"Bull! Get out of here before I change my mind."

"Yes, sir," said Bull then rushed out of the room.

It had actually taken six days for the Sergeants Tom Crawford and Caleb Parker and their detachment of 10 men to reach the town of Happens Chance. They had to stop along the way to assist a farmer whose barn had accidentally caught fire.

When the Rangers finally rode in to Happens Chance, one would never have guessed that little more than a week and a half ago their bank had been robbed. Every where you looked, it was business as usual. The Sheriff's office was a cinch to find. It sat in the middle of the road at the north end of town resembling a blockade. As the detachment of Rangers neared the Sheriff's office a tall, slender built, young man of about 19 or 20 stood in the door's opening.

"Howdy! Can I help you, boys?" asked the young man.

"I'm Sgt. Caleb Parker, Texas Rangers. We're looking for a Sheriff Clinton Cutter. Might you be him?"

"If I ain't then this has been one awfully long nightmare. Yup, I'm Clinton Cutter. Y'all come in and lite. I just put fresh coffee on the stove. You boys are in luck. Miss Polly, our baker in town just brought over a basket filled with day-old bear claws. Help yourselves!"

"Thanks, don't mind if I do," said Sgt. Tom Crawford.

"I reckon you fellas want to get right to it."

"Not so fast, Sheriff. We want to help, sure enough. But we've had a long few days gettin' here. I would imagine most all of us would like to get a bath and a hot meal," said Sgt. Caleb Parker.

"Of course! Only one place for all that in town. The Wagon Wheel Hotel. Right yonder across the street on the right. Miss Polly owns that too."

"She sounds like a right enterprising woman. This 'Miss' is it? Miss Polly?" said Bull teasingly.

"Reckon you could say that. She also happens to be the Mayor," chuckled Clinton Cutter.

"A woman mayor? I ain't ever heard of such. How?" asked Bull curiously.

"Her pa, ol' John Polly, was founder of Happens Chance. When he died, Lizzy just naturally took over. The folks in town thought it only right. No one has ever wanted to run agin her. Reckon that might change now with the bank and all."

"Lizzy?" asked Bull.

"Elizabeth. Folks round here just call her Lizzy seeing nearly all of them practically grew up with her. The older folk that is," explained Clinton Cutter.

"I see. So she's not married?" inquired Bull.

"Nope. Never found a man that could suit her. She is what you call tough and runs a mighty tight ship so to speak," said Sheriff Clinton Cutter with a dare you to try smile.

The following morning the Rangers were all assembled in front of the Sheriff's office waiting for orders. "Are you coming along, Sheriff Cutter?" invited Sgt. Caleb Parker.

"I want to, Ranger. But I'm all the law this town has right now. I don't think it would be prudent for me to leave. Especially now."

"I understand. We'll be seeing you. All right, Rangers! Let's ride," said Sgt. Caleb Parker. The Rangers rode west in the last known direction that the Brickman brothers were known to be seen traveling. They picked up the trail of the Brickman brothers almost immediately. Though the trail was old and growing cold as last year's turkey dinner. The Rangers did find some old shoe prints that their horses had left. Chance that to luck and that it hadn't rained in quite some time. Also because the Brickman's carelessness of not removing evidence of a campfire.

"These boys must want to be caught," laughed Tom Crawford.

"Perhaps. My guess is these hombres planned this out long before they robbed the bank. I'm guessing that they were counting on the posse not to follow far. They knew their escape would be an easy one. What they forgot to plan for was us. Once we catch up to them they'll start being more crafty and dangerous," explained Caleb.

"Could be. But how long is that going to take?" questioned Tom Crawford.

"Good question. But we'll catch up to them or bust a cinch trying," replied Caleb.

**Uvalde, Texas**
**Texas Rangers**
**Headquarters Company D**

Major Drew Parker was sitting at his desk rummaging through a stack of papers and sorting old wanted flyers from the more recent when a small but growing commotion caught his attention. Drew stood up and walked to the window and looked out into the street. A crowd was hovering and making its way closer to the Ranger headquarter's front porch. The crowd was hovering around someone. Major Drew Parker stepped outside onto the front porch.

"Major Parker! Come quick. It's Todd Cummings of the Aces over Kings Ranch! He's hurt bad," yelled a man from the crowd.

Drew leaped down from the porch and ran to Todd Cummings side. "Todd, what happened, man? Someone get the doctor," yelled Major Parker.

"He's on his way now!" answered someone else from the crowd.

"Take him inside and put him on my bed," instructed Major Parker.

Todd Cummings looked up in a daze and in shock. "Drew? O merciful Lord."

"Easy, Tom, take it slow. Here, have some water."

Todd Cummings sipped the water and began to speak. "They hit us around high noon time. Must have been 60 maybe 70 or more. Wife, kids hidden in the old wine cellar. Shot to hell. My boys. The men."

"Easy, Hoss. Slow down. Your boys? Are they okay?"

"Not sure. So much shooting. Not all Mexicans. Comancheros maybe. Drew! My wife and kids! Please," Todd Cummings passed out.

"Here's the Doc, Major," said one of the now present Rangers. The Rangers were relaxing in the bunkhouse barracks when they too heard the commotion and came to investigate.

Doctor Paul Aston, new to Uvalde, made his way through the crowd. "Okay folks, let me by. Can someone start some coffee going? Let me look at this fella. He's in pretty rough shape. You'll have to wait until I'm done examining him."

After about two hours, the doctor came out from Drew's bedroom. "I've done all I can. The rest is up to him."

Whiskey Jack came barging into the headquarters. "What's wrong? What's happened? Where's my brother?"

"Over here, Jack. I'm fine. It's Todd Cummings. He's been shot up pretty bad."

"Shot where?"

"He'll be fine. At least that's what the doctor says," replied Drew.

"What happened?"

"I'm not absolutely sure but it sounds as though Comancheros hit his spread. That's about all I can get out of him," explained Drew.

"His wife and the little ones?" asked Whiskey Jack.

"He said he had them in the old wine cellar. I think his boys are dead. Todd was babbling too much so I'm not clear on that either."

"We best assemble men and ride out there right away. We need to know just what did happen," said Jack.

"My thoughts exactly."

When the Rangers of Company D arrived at the Aces over Kings Ranch they could hardly take it in. Barns and outbuildings were smoldering, the big two-story home was a pile of charred timbers. Survivors were meandering about trying to bring order back to what remained of the Aces over Kings. Bodies were neatly laid out in a row. Rebecca Cummings was standing next to one of the bodies accompanied by three little children and a 16-year-old son.

"Rebecca?" said Major Parker gently. Rebecca looked up mournfully at Drew.

"Chip. They killed my boy, Chip. Why?"

Charlie Cummings, known by the nickname Chip, was her oldest son at 23 years old. He had been a hard-working, cheerful young man who would go above and beyond to help others. A happy-go-lucky redhead who was a contradiction to his red hair. He had not an angry bone within him. He loved to read the Bible. Joshua was his favorite next to Christ.

"I'm sorry, Rebecca. I swear to God. I'm sorry. Todd is all right. He brought word and we came as soon as we could."

"What do I do now?" asked Rebecca.

"I'm going to have you and the children escorted to the Peña Ranchero. You will stay there until all of this is sorted out."

Rebecca nodded. "I'm grateful to you. To you and your mother. Todd fought as hard as he could," said Rebecca. "He did not want to go."

"Yes, ma'am. Why are you telling me this?" asked Drew.

"I just wanted you to know."

"Rebecca, I know the caliber of your husband. I never once entertained Todd would have left you unless he knew you were safe."

"Just the same, I want all of you to hear me. It was by my insistence Todd came for you. I know there will be some who will question but my husband is no coward," declared Rebecca.

"Well, that's fine for them but I'm going after those hombres. So you best be counting on company. Cuzz I'm going! With or without you!" exclaimed Christopher Cummings, the younger son.

At the Peña Ranch the mood was a somber one. "I have had my fill of death," said Marjorie Parker.

"I agree. But I'm afraid there will be more. These are some very bad men. Muy malo," said Senora Kataryna.

"Yes, they are. Which is why I am going to send some men to guard you here. Just in case," said Drew.

"No, mijo. The men we have will be sufficient. We will not be caught by surprise again. Besides you will need every man before this is over."

The sun was beginning to disappear over the horizon when a shout came from one of the cowboys perched above the main entrance gate to the Ranchero. "Riders coming!"

Drew stood at the edge of the veranda and strained to see. Trying to identify the riders. "How many?!"

"Twenty five or 30, Major!"

"Sound the alarm. But no one shoots unless I say so."

"Yes, sir. Unless you say!"

Drew held his old 1855 repeating rifle at the ready. Many of the Rangers had the newer model Winchester repeating rifle and so did Drew. But the cold repeating rifle had always been his favorite. It felt comfortable and the sentimental value would help. It had been a birthday gift from his Grandfather. Don Miguel had given it to him on his 20th birthday.

"Major! It's Capt. McNelly and a whole passel of Rangers!" yelled the guard.

"Let them in! False alarm! Go back to your families or to doing whatever it was you were doing," explained Major Parker.

After having eaten that evening, all the Rangers retired outside; all but Capt. McNelly. He had stayed behind to talk with Drew and Jack.

"This is bad, Drew. Things are getting plum out of hand and I'm getting downright sick of it. It's almost conspiratorial like. Ever since the Rangers were brought back into power there has been outbreaks of trouble scattered all around Texas. I've given it some serious contemplation and I've concluded that I'm right. These outbreaks and raids along with cattle rustling, is in my opinion, an attempt to scatter Rangers out so thin that it is almost as if there were no Rangers at all. Up until now, I have held back the full range of power of the Rangers. Partly due to what that cupcake of a Governor Edmund Davis calls proper protocol. I'm saying here and now, hang protocol and hang Edmund Davis. From now on, there will be no quarter for the outlaw. We shall hunt them down relentlessly," said Capt. Leander H McNelly.

"I'm awfully glad to hear you say that, Leander. To tell you the truth, I had been giving thought to resigning. The Cummings are fine people. Honest hard-working folks who would not think twice about helping a neighbor. They are also good Christian folks. Rebecca Cummings is a fine woman. She has always helped Mother at Christmas time with the baking and preparing sleeping quarters for the kids from the orphanage. Her husband is one of the finest men you'll ever get to know. He raised two fine sons. Their oldest son was killed in the raid over on their spread. Most all the folks around here are just the same way. I can't stand sitting on my backside with my hands under me because some softheaded weak kneed Governor hasn't the backbone to do what needs to be done but would rather try pandering negotiations with big bankers and corporations. You can see for yourself where that's gotten us."

"Which is why I'm here. We are going to start to do some raiding of our own. We will hunt down and raid every outlaw hideout we can find. We will give no quarter. If a man surrenders, we will show him mercy. But if a man chooses to fight then we will fight until someone dies. Them or us."

"I hope you mean that. Because that is exactly how I feel and see it," said Drew.

"I do and I'm giving you until noon tomorrow to have all of Company D present and ready to ride with me and my men."

"I don't believe that will be a problem. They've been spoiling for a fight. It's high time they get it and my men are just itching to show them who's who. There comes a moment in every man's life when he has to make a stand for something. You're either right or you're wrong. Some men are wrong thinking they're right. But most men who are wrong know they are wrong. Therein lies the difference between outlaw and someone being misguided. But most outlaws know."

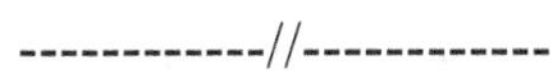

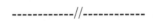

Somewhere about 10 miles south of the red bluffs along the Pecos River, the Rangers led by Sgt. Caleb Parker and Sgt. Tom Crawford, got a break at a small trading post called Yancey's owned by Otis Yancey. It just so happened that the Brickman brothers had left there the previous morning after a four day drinking spree and some time with a few Yaki Indian girls.

"They was here all right. But I never would have guessed they are outlaws. Robbed the bank, did you say? Coulda fooled me way that older brother was pinching his pennies. Said they was going to Utah to start a cattle ranch. Too bad. They seem like right nice young men," claimed Otis Yancey.

"Utah, you say?" asked Tom Crawford.

"That's what they said."

"That's a fair piece from here sure enough. Reckon they headed west toward El Paso Way?" asked Caleb.

"Shucks no! They went north to buy some cattle near Santa Fe and drive 'em into Utah. The oldest was a shrewd one he was. Never did talk much," explained Otis Yancey.

"The smart ones rarely do. It's the quiet ones you have to look out for," said Bull.

"So I've heard say," replied Otis Yancey.

"We'll be staying long enough for supper and to replenish our supplies. Bull will give you a list of all we need. What's for supper anyway?" asked Caleb.

"Sarge, you figuring on traveling in the dark?" asked one of the Rangers.

"Yes. I don't want to give them fellas any more of a start than they already have. I want to be on their trail as soon as possible," replied Caleb.

"Ya but ain't that a might risky for the horses I mean."

"Normally I would agree. But Sgt. Crawford and I have been in this country before. Way back before the war. Remember Slow Water, Tom?"

"Yup. Only back then we was chasing and running," replied Tom.

"Chasing and running? That don't make no sense. How can you chase and run at the same time?" questioned the Ranger.

"It was like this. We were chasing some pretty mean hombres while at the same time trying to stay distanced from Dancing Crow and his Comanche who were chasing us," explained Tom Crawford with a giggle.

"Is that why you figure to move at night. Stay clear of any Injuns?"

"No, I've already told you why. But it doesn't hurt to steer clear of any Indians especially the Apache," said Sgt. Caleb Parker.

"How long do you suppose to catch up with these fellas?" asked the Ranger.

"If luck holds out early tomorrow or at least before dark," replied Sgt. Caleb.

Otis Yancey was bringing out their supper and overheard part of their conversation. "You shouldn't have much trouble finding them.

They took three bottles of Tennessee whiskey. I reckon they'll figure they was scot free. But then like I said before that older one's smart and probably won't take chances."

"I'll keep that in mind. Thanks," replied Caleb.

An hour later, the Rangers were back on the trail. "Hey, Sergeant Caleb?" called out a Ranger. "How do you know we're on the right trail? It's getting dark and I can hardly see the rocks on the ground much less any sign of tracks."

"I know where they're going. They'll stay close to the Pecos River for as long as they can. So will we."

"What makes you so certain?"

"That's easy. Water."

"Reckon you're right. But Injuns will be near the water too, right?"

"Maybe. But worry about that if and when it happens."

"About two maybe three miles ahead is that old place were Major Parker rode that buckskin mare. Remember that?" asked Sgt. Tom Crawford.

"Like it was just last week," chuckled Caleb.

"I don't know who was the more impressed or ornery for that matter. The Major or that mare," said Tom.

"I'd say that mare. Can anyone else ride her? Not to this day. The Major wouldn't have it any other way either," replied Caleb.

Major Parker must have been one heck of a man back then to hear you two talk," said Bull.

"Still is. Don't think for one second that Major Drew Parker has slowed down any. I'd rather have Satan himself on my trail than Major Drew Parker," said Tom Crawford.

Caleb chuckled. "Ain't that the truth. At least the devil gets tired from time to time. The Major? I don't know where his grit comes from. But I've never seen him tired."

They set up camp in the same spot as so many years ago. The old make do corral was still partly standing. So they repaired the fallen down pieces and corralled their horses. Caleb was sitting on a large rock, sipping on a cup of coffee and staring out onto the water. Tom Crawford came walking up to him.

"I set two men to nighthawking and watching the horses. What's on your mind?"

"Nothing much. Just thinking back. I guess it's this place. I was wondering what my life would have been like had I not become a Ranger. I was a poor sight when Drew first found me," smiled Caleb.

"No one ever really knows the answer to questions like that I suppose. Only I have a feeling you'd still have turned out right. You were dead set on being a lawyer even then as I recall. Now look at you. A lawyer and a Ranger. I would like to believe that God was guiding you all this way. I know He has me. Lordy! If I had to depend on just my own dumb luck to get by in life I'd be hung or shot by now. But I truly believe the Almighty does guide us. Thing is, whether we choose to follow or not, now I ain't saying I'm some kind of saint because I ain't by a long shot but I tried to keep my ear to the ground so's I can hear trouble coming. An ear to the ground and my eyes on the cross. It seems to have worked for me thus far. I just can't overcome my temper nor my liking for fine whiskey."

"And the women," laughed Caleb.

"Yeah, maybe. If the Almighty wouldn't have made them so danged awful pretty! So, I reckon that ain't too bad a weakness," Tom Crawford joined in with his own laugh.

"Good book calls it a sin but I know what you mean. Too doggone many to choose from!" replied Caleb.

Dawn was starting to cast shadows from the trees and boulders around the Rangers camp. A quail made his first morning whistle.

"Up and at 'em! Come on you farmers! Get a move on!" hollered Caleb.

"Farmers? Heck if I were, I'd be up already. I'm just lazy!" said one of the Rangers jokingly.

"Hodges, start up some coffee, will ya? And get some breakfast started," said Tom Crawford.

Slim Smith came riding into the camp at a slow walk. "Nothing out there. I rode for nearly two miles upstream on the side and back on the other side. If they went this way, they left little to no sign that I could see."

"Don't be bothered by it. We'll catch up to 'em. They went this way. I can promise you that," said Caleb.

"You got this look about you," said Tom Crawford. "You look just like Major Parker when you're worried or when you're up to something. So what's on your mind? You think they saw us and might be waiting to ambush us further upstream?" asked Tom Crawford.

"Something like that. I'd almost bet one if not all of them doubled back to see if they were being followed and spotted our camp last night. Now they're out there waiting on us."

"These men are too green to be rushing headlong into what we know might be a trap. I say we cross the river and go up on the other side."

"That might work. If anything it could give us at least a few extra minutes to spot them. That is providing we are right."

"Too bad though. At least one of them have brains. Seems a shame to have to kill them. Would've made good hands had they not gone bad," said Bull with a tone of regret in his voice.

"Reckon that could be said for almost every outlaw, Bull," replied Caleb.

Three hours later, hot, weary and frustrated, the Rangers got the answer they were looking for. Ranger Bill Sharp shouted in fear as his hat flew off his head followed by the loud cracking report of a rifle. "Yee ow! Holy God! Where'd that come from?"

"Up there! Along that ridge yonder!" yelled Ranger Tall Hammer.

The Rangers all dismounted as if on cue and had taken refuge among the rocks and scattered junipers and scrub oaks. They began to return fire knocking chips of stone and dust into the air along the ridge. The shooting from along the ridge started up again. Back and forth as if taking turns and on occasion firing in unison at one another. The shooting only lasted for about 30 minutes though it seemed hours. Then as suddenly as it had begun, it stopped.

"Hold your fire! I think they've gone," yelled Caleb.

"No disrespect but I'm going to keep a bead on that Ridge. They just might want us to think they've gone," said Tall Hammer.

The Rangers waited 20 minutes. "All right. Anybody shot or dead?" asked Tom Crawford.

"Nope! Just my hat. Dang it! I just bought that hat, too." said Ranger Bill Sharp.

"Maybe that's why they shot it off your head. Maybe they was just having fun," said Joe Denton.

"Fun! They almost took my head off!"

"I ain't so sure. I believe they wanted to scare us hoping we'd get scared and run just long enough for them to skedaddle out of here," claimed Joe Denton.

"You could be right. But they figured wrong," said Tom Crawford.

For two days, Rangers caught up with the Brickman boys. Seven times they caught up and shot it out. Luckily for both sides, no one had been shot. On the third day along the New Mexico border and in the Guadalupe Mountains, the Rangers had boxed them in. The Brickman's had made a run for it up a canyon that quickly narrowed and dead ended with 1000 foot cliffs on all three sides and the only way out was the way they came. And that way was now blocked by the Rangers.

"Come on out! We're Texas Rangers and you're all under arrest for robbing the Happens Chance bank," yelled Caleb.

"Nothing doing, Ranger! You'll have to come in and get us," answered Jason Brickman.

"Is that you, Jason?" questioned Caleb.

"Yeah. What of it?"

"Maybe you should talk it over with your brothers. William is barely 18. Are you willing to get him killed too?"

"We have and it's unanimous!" Jason replied with a rifle shot. The bullet struck the tree trunk just inches above Caleb head.

"Geesh!" Caleb gasped and dove to the ground landing flat on his belly. "That wasn't nice! Wasn't smart either, Brickman!"

"That was just to let you know I mean business! We can hit what we shoot at if we want," claimed Jason Brickman.

"You don't have to worry about that. The way I figure it you might have water for one more day. We have water, food and can wait as long as it takes. Which shouldn't be long!" replied Caleb.

The next morning about two hours before sunrise, Jeffrey Boxer and Slim Smith were on night duty and were alerted by the snickering of horses. The horses had caught sense of something and had perked their heads up and her ears pointed forward. Jeff cautiously and quickly went over to where Caleb was sleeping and nudged Caleb with the toe of his boot. Caleb set up abruptly. "What?"

"Not sure. Something's got the horses spooked. I think our rats are trying to sneak away."

Caleb nudged Tom Crawford. "Get the men up. We may have trouble."

Within a matter of minutes, the Rangers were up and ready for action. Jeff and Slim were correct. The Brickmans were trying to slip past the Rangers in the cover of darkness. Caleb stood next to Jeff.

"Out that direction," whispered Jeff. "Did you hear that? I could have sworn I heard a horse snort."

"Sshhh," Caleb raised his rifle. He had heard it too. Pointing his rifle in direction of the of the sound and taking a gamble to frighten the men moving in the dark, Caleb squeezed off a shot. The gamble paid off. Almost immediately the Brickmans returned fire as they scurried to make their getaway. Caleb and the others immediately spotted the muzzle flashes from the Brickmans' weapons and and were upon them before the brothers could make a clean getaway. Shouting and shooting, the Rangers circled and surrounded the brothers.

"Alright! We give up. Don't shoot anymore," yelled young William Brickman. His brother, Thomas, lay bleeding on the ground at William's feet.

"Is he hurt bad?" asked Caleb.

"I'm not sure. It's too dark to see and I wasn't going to light a match. Not with you Rangers throwing lead like that," said William.

Johnny and Joe Denton dismounted and walked over to where Thomas lay.

"Ain't too much we can do for this hombre, Sarge," said Joe Denton.

"Do what you can. At least make him comfortable," said Sgt. Tom Crawford.

Joe walked over to his horse, pulled out a half full bottle of rye whiskey then walked over to Thomas Brickman.

"Here, help yourself," offered Joe Denton.

"Much obliged. Say, Ranger. Could you roll me a smoke? Got fix-in's in my vest pocket."

"Sure enough," replied Joe.

Joe Denton, rolling a smoke for the dying brother, when he heard Thomas Brickmund gasp, sucking in a shallow breath and then exhaling a long drawn out breath. Thomas Brickmund had died. William Brickman went to his knees and, lifting his brother's head, held him close to his breast and sobbed uncontrollably.

"Stop your whimpering. Dang you! I knew I should have left you behind. Danged baby! Crying won't bring him back," scolded Jason Brickman.

Joe Denton stared hatefully at Jason Brickman. "Shut your trap. It's a long ride back to Happens Chance and I pray to God you try to escape."

Joe Denton was a medium built man for hard in the ways of the trail. He had worked mostly as a cattleman. He drifted from ranch to ranch. He was loyal and rode for the brand. He was no stranger to death. He had seen men killed by stampede and Indians as well as rustlers. He had also done his fair share of killing. But all were righteous in the commission. He hated killing. But now somewhere deep down in his soul he knew he would enjoy killing Jason Brickman.

Bull walked over to his horse and retrieved the shovel that had been tied behind his saddle. He tossed it at William Brickman's feet.

"He's your brother. You bury him and bury him deep. I want you to think with each shovelful of dirt how all of this could have been avoided if only you hadn't robbed that bank. Think hard. While you're at it, you may want to make things right with your Maker."

Jeffrey Boxer looked at Bull curiously. "What about this one? Why not make him dig?"

"I don't trust him," said Bull.

"You reckon we should hang 'em?" asked Slim Smith.

"No. But don't think I haven't thought about it. If they hang, it will be by a fair trial in Happens Chance," said Caleb.

"Except for what they spent at Yancey's trading post," said Tom Crawford. "I say all the money is here."

Later that day, after William Brickma buried the body of his brother, the Rangers were making their way back to Happens Chance. Jason Brickman began to laugh. "You'll never see me hang! Doubt you ever get me before a judge. First chance I get I'm going to get free. When I do there's going to be a few less Rangers in Texas. Yup! Yes sireee. If I do get a trial, bank robbery is a prison sentence and not a hanging offense."

"So? What does that mean?" asked Ranger Tall Hammner.

"Oh nothing," Jason Brickman said smugly.

"Just keep this in mind. You haven't made it back to Happens Chance yet. If we took a mind to we could hang you here and now and it would be all legal. You shot at not just one Texas Ranger, but 10. That is a hanging offense! We could hang you 10 times over just for the hell of it," said Caleb.

"I say we should hang him anyway. I'd love to put my rope around this hombre's neck. Maybe the air will smell better," said Slim.

William Brickman, sobbing as he wiped the sweat from his brow said, "I can't do it. I dug the hole nearly 6 feet. But I can't put him in it! You Rangers are going to have to do that. I can't bring myself to do it to my brother."

Joe Denton handed William the whiskey bottle. "Here. Take a few pulls off of this and sit down. I'll finish it up."

"Much obliged to you. I ain't ever seen a dead man before. Especially kin," said William.

The Rangers were given a warm welcome back as they rode into the town of Happens Chance. A mob was forming as he escorted the two prisoners to the jail. Sheriff Clinton Cutter stood on the front porch of the jailhouse with a double barrel shotgun in hand and his revolver hanging in his holster up on his hip.

"Let's hang 'em now! Hang the vermin!" Shouts came from the mob. Sheriff Clinton Cutter held up his hand to quiet everyone.

"Nobody's hanging anyone! At least not today. These boys are going to get a fair trial. Go on homenow. Let the law work its course," said Sheriff Clinton Cutter.

"You little snip! We'll show you law. Our law!" a drunk man yelled from within the crowd.

"Now, Ray, I know you didn't mean that and it's just anger and too much liquor talking. But you press me and I'll lock you up in the hoosegow along with these two. Now go on home, you hear?" said Sheriff Clinton Cutter.

"We pinned that badge on you. We can just as easy unpin it!" growled the man called Ray.

"You sure can. Let's wait till after the trial. Who else of you would take this job? I didn't see you running for any horse and gun when I was asking for posse volunteers, Ray."

Big Bull stepped up on the porch next to Sheriff Cutter. "I've heard about all I want today about hanging and pinning badges! Now I'm giving all of you ten seconds to start disappearing or I'm going to start putting my boot in some hind ends! One! Two! Three! Four!"

Bull never got to five. The crowd started to dwindle like sand from an hourglass.

"Thanks, Ranger," said Sheriff Clinton Cutter.

"Awh, heck. Think nothing of it. I knew you could handle it. But now and then you have to spice up the chili. Make it hot enough and you find out who the men are," chuckled Bull.

**One week later**

"I sentence you, Jason Brickman, to five years in prison at hard labor in the state penitentiary at San Antonio. And you, William Brickman, you are a very fortunate young man to have been given leniency at the bequest of so many Texas Rangers. William Brickman, I sentence you to one year hard labor in the Happens Chance jail. Are there any questions?" said the judge.

"No, your Honor and thanks," said William Brickman.

"No thanks from me! How is it he gets off so easy and you throw the book at me?" argued Jason.

"You did get off easy. I could have given you the full 10 years. The reason your sentence is harder is because you are the eldest and an influential figure. Who should have been setting a proper example for your brothers? You did not. As a consequence one brother is dead. Need I continue?" asked the judge.

Jason Brickman stood silent.

"Court is hereby adjourned," said the judge as he banged his gavel.

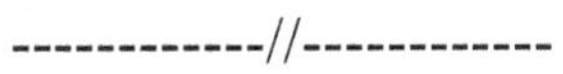

Every town in Texas that had a newspaper read nearly the same.

Hoorah For McNelly and the Texas Rangers!<br>
Cleaning up in Texas!<br>
Texas Rangers giving quarter to no outlaw!<br>
The Texas Rangers Little McNelly's<br>
All For Texas!<br>
McNelly tells outlaws, "Leave Texas!"

The name "Little McNelly's" stuck with the Texas Rangers after a shootout between the ranchers and a gang of 14 men from allegedly Black Lick, Arkansas. Their leader was a homicidal maniac and woman beater by the name of Bob Miriam. The Rangers had cornered them in a small town near Beaumont, Texas. A reporter allowed to accompany the Rangers coined the phrase "little McNelly's" after a mocking comment from Bob Miriam when he peered out from the loft of a barn and yelled to McNelly. "I see you brought your "little McNelly's" along. I don't see any way out of this but a fight to the last man standing."

It turned out that was to be the way it was and how it ended. Fourteen men lay dead after a bloodied two hour shoot out. This day would spark fear in many of the outlaw gangs throughout the western Texas and southern portions. Word of the gun battle spread like wild-fire. The number of dead being grossly exaggerated in every tale. It was also during this gun battle that young Wayne Adams, 19, was killed.

New to the Texas Rangers and a young man who, in McNelly's eyes, had shown promise of becoming a great lawman. Wayne Adams made the fatal mistake of approaching a presumably dead outlaw when the man quickly rolled over and shot young Wayne Adams through the heart. The death of Wayne Adams ignited an anger within McNelly. Not simply because the young man had been killed. That was true enough. Capt. Leander H McNelly had encouraged and recruited the young Adams to become a Ranger. Death was to be expected in the life of any lawman. This had not been the first time a Ranger had been wounded or killed by such a deception. "From now on approach every dead body as if it were still alive! If a man falls, shoot him again before approaching. Leave nothing to chance. I want this to be standard procedure with every Ranger," said Capt. Leander H McNelly. And so it was to be in future gun battles.

The reporter had no idea that the phrase "little McNelly's" would catch on so quickly or become a label of pride among the Rangers. He had actually meant to humiliate the Rangers by poking fun. But in southwest Texas one man did not see the humor in the nickname "little McNelly's" at all. That man was outlaw King Fisher. A man who would become a thorn in the side of Leander H McNelly for many years. The two would grow to hate each other like fire hates water.

Winter winds blew harshly across the plains. The wind cuts through you as a cold that causes every joint and muscle to wrench and shiver so that a man's pain is almost enough to make him forget the cold. Almost.

"Come on, Sam! We gotta keep moving."

"I'm so cold,

Danny. I'm cold into my guts. Let's find a place to stop."

"Stop? Stop where? Just a little while longer, Sam. I promise. As soon as we find a good place."

Sam and Danny Waters were trying to make it into Colorado. Their mother and sister waited near Sand Creek. The two young brothers had taken 150 white faced Longhorn steers into Amarillo to sell at $20 a head. That money would secure the mortgage on their homestead and provide enough provisions to last well into spring. That was until Brett Lasadore absconded with all of their money. Then Sam and Danny

Waters went after him. Brett Lassiter was supposed to be in love with Gail Waters, Sam and Danny's little sister. Brett had signed on for the drive. He was a good cattleman, handy with a gun and a rope and in the six months that they had known him, he seemed an honest man.

The Waters brothers caught up with Brett Lasadore in a saloon near Wichita Falls which ended up in a sudden gun brawl between Sam Waters and Brett Lasadore. The killing was a righteous killing. But the Waters brothers panicked and now they were wanted men. Wanted mostly for questioning though they did not know that at the time. Now with the reward on their heads, all the brothers wanted was to get home. But getting home proved to be near impossible.

"Oh Danny, I've gotta stop! I'm so cold."

"I know, Sam, I know. Up there in those bushes. We'll make camp there."

The newspapers of the shooting had reached Ranger headquarters in Austin. Semi-retired Ranger Capt. Charlie Welch took it upon himself to investigate.

"Something just doesn't add up. Why put a bounty on two young'uns if the shooting was a righteous one?"

"Apparently, it's the question of the money that the Waters boys had taken off of Lasadore. Nearly $3,000," said Ranger Ed Lamb.

"How come no one saw fit to tell me about the money?" asked Charlie Welch.

"Heck, Charlie, don't go yelling at me. I figured you knew. You being so smart and a Captain and all," said Ed.

"Which way were the Waters boys supposed to be heading?" asked Capt. Charlie Welch.

"Last report was west, Charlie. The sheriff in Wichita Falls mentioned that apparently these Waters brothers and the late Brett Lasadore had driven 150 head of steers from Colorado into Amarillo and Lasadore took off with the money. That's the story anyway," said Ed Lamb.

"Then why in blazes put out Dodgers on the boys? Just let them go. That's what I would've done," replied Charlie.

"I don't know, Charlie. But he did and that's that. Now we have to honor it until the sheriff of Wichita Falls calls them in."

"It ain't right! Those two young men are going to get killed by some rambunctious young lawman or bounty hunter and for what? I'm going after them before they end up dead. If they ain't already," exclaimed Charlie Welch.

"You? At your age? Charlie, be serious."

"I am serious and what about my age?'

"Nothing. When do we leave?" asked Ed.

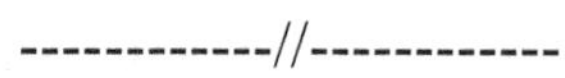

**Uvalde, Texas**

The morning sun was warm on the face. The air was crisp and chilling as Paco topped the hill and suddenly reined his horse to a halt. "Madre e Dios! Banditos, amigo. We better get a closer look," Paco whispered to his gray Appaloosa mare. At a closer look, it was only a small thicket of mesquite and deer brush for cover, Paco counted at least 25 men. "This muy malo. I wonder what they are up to? No time to find out. We better go tell Senor Major Drew."

Paco slowly led his horse through the thicket and over the hill. Then mounted his horse and spurred her into an instant gallop.

Capt. Leander McNelly cursed as he read the letter that had been brought to him by messenger from Austin. "Blast that Welch! Of all the..."

"What's the problem, Leander?" asked Drew as he stepped out onto the porch of Ranger headquarters. He was holding two hot cups of freshly poured coffee and handed one to McNelly.

"Awh! That awful old man Charlie Welch and Ed Lamb. Here read for yourself." McNelly handed the letter to Drew. Drew read the letter mumbling softly as he read it. Then smiled.

"Well, I can see how you might be upset with the headquarters in Austin being shy of him. But I reckon he knows what he's doing."

"Of course he knows what he's doing. But at his age the question is, can he do it? And with only Ed Lamb for company. It's been years since he's been on the trail," said Capt. McNelly.

"Of course he can. But I wouldn't question his age. Not to his face anyway," chuckled Drew.

The two men were standing there sipping their coffee and talking when Leander caught sight of someone on horseback riding hard and kicking up dust like a fury. Leander McNelly pointed with his coffee cup. "Isn't that one of your ranch hands?"

Drew stared down the street at the rider. "Yes. It's Paco."

"Señor Drew! Señor Drew!" yelled Paco.

"What's going on, Paco?" asked Drew. "That horse looks near dead."

"Si, she is tired. Banditos, Señor! Veinticinco, maybe more. Es muy malo."

"Banditos? Where?" asked Capt. Leander McNelly.

"Near Señor Johnny's land," answered Paco.

"Johnny's land? Did they see you?" asked Drew.

"No. But they're trouble. They were getting drunk and their fires were high. They didn't appear to be in any hurry to go anyplace," explained Paco.

"This could be the very bunch that raided and burned the Aces over Kings. Todd Cummings spread," suggested Drew.

"Si, Major," replied Paco.

Major Parker yelled. "Red!"

"Yes, Major?" said Ranger Red Sands.

"Get the men rousted up and ready to ride. We leave at first light tomorrow morning."

"Yes, sir!"

"It's getting dark. Too dark. To leave now would be pointless," explained Drew looking at Capt. McNelly.

"I agree," said McNelly. "A good night's rest would be to our favor."

"Paco, can you ride if I give you a fresh mount?" asked Drew.

"Si. I can ride."

"Pick a horse from the corral and ride back to the Pena Rancho. Alert the men but quietly! Do not alert the women. I don't want them to be frightened. Have all the men armed and ready. Be on the watch! But try to make it look like business as usual. Comprende?"

"Si, Señor Drew. It will be as you say."

"Good man. Vaya con Dios, amigo," said Drew.
"Vaya con Dios," replied Paco.

It was full light in the morning when the Rangers of Capt. Leander H McNelly's Company A and the Rangers of Major Drew Parker's Company D topped the hill from which Paco had first sighted the banditos. The banditos, still half-drunk from the night before, had just begun to stir. A few cook fires were casting small thin streams of smoke into the air when one of the banditos spied the Rangers at the top of the hill.

"Awhee! Tejas Rangers! Tejas Rangers!" he shouted alerting the camp.

Instantly, the banditos were scurrying about grabbing weapons and mounting their horses.

Major Drew Parker shouted, "Company D, let's ride! Rangers! Charge!"

And at that command 21 Rangers of Company D descended from the hill at a half gallop, side-by-side, shouting a long rebel yell sending fear and panic into the spines of the banditos.

Almost in unison and right behind Company D rode the Rangers of Capt. McNelly's Company A. "No quarter, men! Shoot and shoot to kill!" shouted Capt. McNelly.

The banditos rode southwest toward the Rio Grande and Eagle Pass. Shooting behind them as they rode to make their escape. They were about a mile south of Eagle Pass when the banditos fanned out and took refuge on a boulder covered hill near a trail that led into the valley and along the Rio Grande. The Rangers of Major Parker's Company D stopped just outside of range from the rifle fire of the banditos.

"What now, Major?" asked Ranger Rodney Allen. "If we ride into that trail, we'll be like plates at a carnival shooting gallery."

"Yes and the others will be making a clean getaway across the river," said Ranger Kyle Wiggins.

"I'm counting on them thinking the same thing, Ranger," said Major Drew Parker.

"Counting on it? I don't understand. You want them to pick us off?" asked one of the Rangers.

"No. I want them to think they have us in a tight spot just the same," explained Major Parker.

"I'm curious as well, Drew. What do you have in mind?" asked Capt. Leander McNelly.

Drew looked at his brother. "Jack, what was the name of that little village not far from here? Remember we nabbed that Army traitor there?"

"Casas Siete? Yes, that's it!" exclaimed Jack.

"Capt. McNelly, if we took about five or 10 men and snuck out using our rear flank, whilst you and the others kept them preoccupied we could circle around Casas Siete and attack from behind," suggested Drew.

"Sounds like it may work."

"Casas Siete," said Jack.

"Yes. Are you certain it is there?"

"Absolutely sure," said Drew.

"Good. Then get started. We'll keep them busy here for sure," said Capt. McNelly.

The Rangers opened fire upon the banditos and made taunting advances forward then hastily retreating. Keeping the banditos busy and hunkered down themselves as well.

It took Major Parker and 10 of his Rangers a little over one hour to circle around the banditos by skirting the village of Casas Siete. Using the cover of the thick mesquite and dry washes they snuck up behind the banditos before they ever had the chance to be spotted.

The Rangers opened fire mercilessly. The banditos, shooting in two directions, began to scramble. Capt. McNelly noticed the confusion from the banditos and ordered his Rangers to advance. Within a half hour those banditos who had not escaped lay dead or dying. Capt. Leander H McNelly, shotgun in hand, approached a dying bandito.

"Por favor, don't shoot. I am unarmed," said the bandito.

"Let me see both hands. And do it slowly like," said McNelly his shotgun aimed at the bandito who held up both hands as he sat propped against a boulder. "Agua, por favor?"

Capt. McNelly called for water to give to the man who from the looks of things had not long to live. The bandito drank. "Gracias, you Rangers would make good banditos. You shoot straight."

"Who is the leader of your band?" asked McNelly.

"You do not know? Then why did you come after us?" asked the bandito.

"You men raided and burned down a ranch not far from here," explained Major Parker.

"Si, some of us. But I was not part of that. His name is King Fisher. I only took the cat," the bandito took a deep breath, exhaled and died.

McNelly cursed. "King Fisher? Have any of you ever heard that name before?"

None of the others had ever heard of him.

"Maybe not. But I think we are soon to learn of him pretty well," said Whiskey Jack.

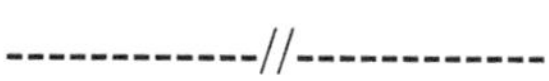

**North West Texas, near the Brazos**

Capt. Charlie Welch's teeth chattered so much that even his jaws began to ache. The cold wind howled, sounding like 100 starving wolves. The cold was cutting through his heavy wool lined coat. Capt. Welch wrapped the reigns around his right hand. So cold they were that he could scarcely move his fingers.

Ed Lamb yelled so that he could be heard above the howling wind. "Don't you think we should look for shelter? It's sure they won't travel too far or fast in this weather. We sure as hell haven't. No need to assume they would either!"

"You're probably right and I'm certain any posse or bounty man has already hunkered down as well. Looks like snow's a coming," replied Capt. Welch who was glad it was Ed who suggested stopping first. The Captain's pride forbade him of it though he was close to abandon that pride if it got any colder.

They found a small ravine which offered some relief from the howling wind. With 14 feet embankments on either side and plenty of dead wood for a fire the ravine became a little quieter and the two men could talk without yelling.

"Bring the horses in closer to the fire. I sure don't want them to grow stiff- jointed overnight," said Capt. Charlie Welch.

"Nor you either, right?" chuckled Ed Lamb.

Charlie raised an eyebrow and looked at Ed. "Listen here, young sprout. It was you who suggested we stop. Not me. I could have gone on another five miles or so," Charlie Welch stretched the truth.

Ed Lamb grinned. He knew the Captain was done in and he knew Charlie's pride wasn't going to let him admit it. "Ya, I reckon you got me there, Captain."

"Just you don't forget it. Why is it that you youngsters think just because a man has a little gray hair that he's lost his usefulness?"

"Now, I never said such. I was only thinking."

"Well, stop! I'm Captain here and I do the thinking and you do the listening."

Ed Lamb grinned. It pleased him to see the old Captain still had his vinegar. He knew better than most how tough the Captain could be when it counted.

"Yes, sir. More coffee?"

"I can get my own, thank you."

"Captain, you reckon we're on a vane chase? I mean, those youngsters, if they ain't been caught yet are most likely to freeze to death. Besides, how are you so sure they ain't made it into Colorado already?" asked Ed sincerely.

"To tell you honest, I hope they are in Colorado. But as for being caught already, I doubt it. Most bounty men are lazy and a posse is only apt to just go so far from home and then turn back. I sure hope they were smart enough to carry warm clothing. Being from Colorado you would think they would."

"I would agree. But kids don't always do what makes common sense," said Ed Lamb.

"If they make it through the night, they'll be fine."

"Why do you want them to get away? Ain't we out here to bring them in?"

"Now, Ed, did I ever say that I was going to arrest them and bring them in?"

"No. But now I must admit, I am confused."

"That's because you're reading too much into a thing. You're thinking! I said that this whole mess never made much sense from the start. If the killing was righteous and Brett Lasadore was in fact trying to abscond with the money, then why put dodgers out on them youngsters? It sure as heck ain't for questioning. If you asked me, that only spells one thing in my book. That low down sheriff wants that $3,000 for himself."

"Okay? Suppose that's so. Then why put out a bounty? If I were a bounty man, I'd just make off with the $3,000 and be done with it," said Ed.

"That's the one thing I can't figure out either. So I'm going to make sure these boys don't wind up dead. I want to hear their end of the story. If necessary, we will personally escort them right to their front door. The bounty don't make sense. Probably every coyote from Wichita Falls to Montana has heard of that $3,000 by now. It'll be like taking candy from a baby. Literally," said Charlie Welch.

"So, we're actually on a rescue mission," said Ed Lamb

"By God! You figured it out. Why you just might make a good Ranger someday," Capt. Welch said satirically.

"Why I'm glad I have such high approval from you," laughed Ed.

Morning came and the wind had ceased. The sky was clear baby blue and the sun was beginning to melt the crystal shards that had shot up through the ground. Capt. Charlie Welch was standing next to the fire, a steaming hot cup of coffee in his hands. Ed Lamb was preparing a breakfast of bacon and biscuits with gravy.

"You were right, Captain. It is a nice day. We should make good time in this weather."

"As long as we get to those boys first," said Capt. Charlie Welch.

"You're still worried, aren't you?" asked Ed Lamb.

"Like you said. We should make good time in this weather. Trouble is, so will everyone else," replied Capt. Charlie Welch.

The two men had eaten and were fairly warmed up from coffee. Then they headed straight for the salt forks region of the Brazos.

"You seem mighty sure they went this way. Why?" asked Ed.

"If I was a young lad, scared and innocent, with a crooked sheriff and his bounty men after me, I'd be looking for the most direct and fastest way home. I'd go toward the Canadian and then turn west right quick."

"And you're figuring everyone else is thinking the same way?"

"Yup," sighed Charlie Welch.

"You know? You act as if you know those two boys. You don't, do you?" asked Ed.

"No. But I was a boy once believe it or not. I wasn't born a Ranger. I was an adventuresome, wiry, young kid at one time. I didn't always have this cherub like demeanor you're so accustomed to."

Ed laughed. "You don't say! I'd never have thunk it."

The next day, the two Rangers were nearing the Cap Rock canyons region. They had rode long and into the night, the night before and rose early before daybreak on this particular day. Their hope was to cover as much distance as possible without wearing out or killing their horses and to get ahead of the posse.

"We're going to have to stop somewhere soon, Charlie. These horses need rest and a good day of grazing," explained Ed.

"Ya, I know. Blast it! I can almost feel it. I know we're close to those two young'uns. I just know it!" said Charlie Welch.

"I don't know, Charlie. Those boys should be halfway to Utah by now. In the time it has taken us to ride clear from Austin to here. Ya, I'd say if they aren't in Colorado, they're..."

"Don't you say it. They are not dead. And how can you be so sure? For one thing, they left in a hurry. No food, little water and obviously not prepared for the weather. Their horses must be plum wore out from dodging posses and bounty men. No, they haven't gone too far. My gut says they're holed up somewhere on the Canadian River. Don't ask me how I know. But I just do!" said Charlie Welch.

"I'm with you no matter what. But don't get down on yourself iffen we are too late. That's all," replied Ed.

## Palo Doro Canyon

"Danny, I think I'm dying. I'm so cold all the time and my body is so stiff I can hardly stand. Oh God, Danny! I don't want to die! I'm scared, Danny, I'm so scared," whined Sam Waters.

"Sam, shut up that talk. You hear? You ain't going to die. Not today or tomorrow. Not if I can help it. So hush!"

Danny was scared too. He was lying to his brother. Sam was awful sick and Danny, only 17 years old, knew nothing about caring for a sick person. Especially his brother who was only 14. Truth was, Danny was thinking Sam wouldn't make it through the night. But Danny kept hoping for the best. He made a bed of juniper branches and using one saddle blanket and bed roll for a mattress and covered Sam with the other bed roll and horse blanket. "You lay quiet, you hear?"

"Danny?"

"What?"

"I'm hungry."

"See? You're hungry. That means you ain't gonna die. That's good!" said Danny.

"Maybe but we ain't ate in two days," Sam whined again.

"You lay quiet and rest. I'll look around. Maybe I can shoot a rabbit or two. Okay?"

"Ya, that'd be great," said Sam, very weakly.

Unbeknownst to Capt. Charlie Welch and Ed Lamb, they were about 3 miles south of the very spot in Palo Duro canyons where Danny and Sam Waters were camped when Ed spied three figures on a hill about a quarter mile away east to the right.

"Charlie?"

"Ya, I see 'm. They've been shadowing us for two hours now," said Charlie Welch.

"Two hours! And you failed to tell me. Why?" exclaimed Ed.

"I didn't want to scare you. You being so young and all. I was just looking toward your best interest."

"Gee. Thanks. So what do we do now, Grandpa?" said Ed sarcastically.

"Nothing. They're not a threat to me. So long as I can see them," said Capt. Charlie Welch.

"Any idea what they want?"

"My guess is the same thing we want. Those two kids."

"How'd they find us?"

"They didn't. We just happen to be going in the same direction. Which means we are on the right trail," said Capt. Charlie Welch.

"Danged if I don't believe you're right. Which means we best find those two boys first and muy pronto," said Ed.

"That's how I see it too," replied Charlie.

About an hour later, the two Rangers heard a gunshot coming from almost straight ahead. Charlie looked at Ed, his eyes wide and hope on his face.

"Come on! We gotta tear up real estate!"

The two men were in the full gallop. They would have ridden past the two young men had they not heard the second gunshot. Had Danny Waters had more experience and the presence of mind to reload his revolver, either Capt. Charlie Welch or Ranger Ed Lamb may have died. As the two Rangers came riding into view Danny Walters, in a state of fear and panic, aimed his pistol and squeezed the trigger twice. But the sound of an empty cylinder was all he heard. The revolver was completely empty. Danny's face went pale and his eyes widened. Almost at the very same instant, Ed Lamb dove from his saddle and tackled the young man. The two of them wriggling and seething like two snakes in a fight to the death.

"Stop fighting, you danged fool! We're Texas Rangers. We are on your side. Will you hold still!"

"Let me up! You old fart!" cried Danny.

Charlie Welch burst out laughing.

"What's so darn awful funny?" said Ed Lamb.

"How does it feel to be called old?" laughed Charlie Welch.

Ranger Ed Lamb got to his feet and lifting Danny up by his shirt collar yelled. "Look! Kid! We are on your side! Do you get that?"

"How the heck am I to know?! We've been chased and shot at by men with badges for nearly a week. How we stayed alive, I don't know.

But there's a couple of them that felt my lead. That's for sure!" snapped Danny Waters.

"I'm sure of that! Where's your brother? Come on, kid, you best tell us now because my guess is at any moment now we're going to have company. Like we said, we're here to protect you. So out with it. Where is he?" said Ed Lamb.

"Up in those bushes on that hill yonder. I was hunting us some food. We ain't had a bite to eat in two days and Sam is awful sick. I think he's dying," said Danny Waters trying hard not to break into tears.

The three went into the camp the boys had made. Capt. Charlie Welch was impressed at how well Danny had hidden his brother, Sam, and at the care he had given thus far. Capt. Welch knelt down and examined Sam. "My Lord! This lad is nearly to having pneumonia. Ed, get that whiskey bottle from my bags."

"No, sir! He's too young and we don't drink whiskey," declared Danny.

"You do today. At least your brother does anyway," said Charlie Welch.

"Is there anything I can do to help?" asked Danny.

"Ya. Grab my rifle and go to the top of that big boulder and look for company coming. Shout when you see anything move," said Capt. Charlie Welch.

"I've got some willow bark in my bag. I brew it into a tea. It helps my bad teeth. I can't see how it would not help him with his fever," said Ed Lamb.

"Yes, go on. Make it strong and clean and make a soup of those two rabbits. The kid has to eat. How are you feeling?" asked Charlie Welch.

"Name's Sam. That's Danny, my big brother. I'm feeling a lot better now that you're here. Mister, I'm powerful scared. I don't wanna die."

"You ain't gonna die. At least not for another 70 or 80 years if I can help it," smiled Capt. Charlie Welch.

Evening was fast approaching. The sky was painting itself black, purple, orange, and blue as the sun was starting to set. A coyote howled out on the prairie. Ed Lamb slowly walked up to the boulder where Danny sat watching diligently for any sign of movement.

"Anything out there besides the normal?" Ed asked.

"Not that I could see. I'm sorry about earlier. If I had only known..."

"Forget it. Besides, given your predicament, I'd most likely have done the same. Only my gun would have been loaded. Lucky for us, yours wasn't."

"Some big brother I am, huh? I damn near got my brother killed."

"You're learning from it, aren't you? That's all that matters. Might have been's are just that. Let's concentrate on what the will be's. Okay? Besides I'd say you've done a fair job up to now. You can be proud," said Ed.

"How could I have been so stupid? That no account Brett Lasaodore! I'm glad I killed him. To think, all this time he was playing us! What am I going to tell Gail? She's our sister. They were gonna get married. She's going to hate me for sure," said Danny.

"Let's cross that bridge when we get to it. Right now, Sam is our concern. Sam and those chasing you. I reckon they'll be surprised that there's four of us now. I'm hoping they'll consider that and turned back, $3,000 or not," said Ed.

Danny's head snapped up and fire shot from his eyes as he glared at Ed Lamb. "That's what you want? I might have known. I am a darn fool."

"You best rein up some. We don't want your money. We're gonna make certain you two hang on to it, believe you me," said Ed.

"I'm sorry. There I go again! Of course you don't want the money else Sam and I would be dead already. I'm beginning to hate that money," said Danny.

"Son, you best get some sleep. Maybe a good night's rest will help put things back into perspective. Ol' Charlie and I will take over from here. There's fresh coffee a brewin' if you're interested," said Ed.

Morning came. The smell of bacon frying in the skillet and coffee brewing woke Danny and his stomach growled. "Holy smokes! It's still dark. What time is it?" Danny asked as he rubbed his eyes.

"5:30. What are you talking about early? We let you sleep an extra half hour," joked Ed.

"You're joshing me. Nobody gets up this early. Not even farmers," said Danny.

"We do," interjected Capt. Charlie Welch.

"How's Sam doing?" asked Danny.

"See for yourself," said Charlie.

"Hey, Danny," said Sam.

"Hey, you look a lot better. How do you feel?"

"Better. But Ranger Charlie, I mean Capt. Welch said one more day's rest," said Sam.

"One more day! We can't. We can't stay. You have got to try. If Ma don't show up at the bank that snake Mr. Yant will kick her and Gail out into the cold and not even bat an eye," said Danny.

"Not if I can help it. I'll be speaking with this Mr. Yant. I'm sure he'll listen to reason," said Capt. Charlie Welch.

"I sure hope you get the chance to, Charlie," said Ed Lamb. He pointed to the four riders who were making their way in their direction.

"Damn!" cursed Charlie Welch. "Well, we're just gonna have to make our stand right here."

"Here? But we'll be like fish in a barrel. I say we get going. Find higher ground or at least someplace better than here," said Danny Waters.

"I can ride. We don't have to stay here on my account and I'm a fine shot with a rifle. Never was too good with a six shooter," said Sam Waters as he crawled out from his bed roll.

Charlie was amused by Sam's attempt at being tough. "Alright then. You two gather up your belongings. Ed, ride up this ravine aways. See how long we can stay in it before there's a chance of us being seen. I'm afraid we're going to have to face these hombres before the day is over."

"I'll be okay, Captain Welch. You don't need to worry about me!" said Sam.

"Son, I'm afraid you're too late on that. I won't stop worrying until we get you boys home. Or those hombres are dead. I doubt very serious that they'll give up and turned back."

Ed Lamb returned as Capt. Charlie Welch and the Waters brothers were making their way up the deep ravine. "We've got about a quarter-mile of cover. Then it's open, wide open. We're going to have to bust out of this ravine like scalded hounds and keep on riding hard and as fast as we can. Maybe we can put some distance between us before they catch sight of us. Maybe," said Ed Lamb.

"Alright then. You three go on ahead of me. I will lay back some and lay down any cover fire should they spot us," said Charlie.

Ed looked at Capt. Charlie Welch with concern. He didn't like the idea but for now it was the best one. "Charlie, I've got the best horse here. Why not you's three go on? I'll bring up the rear? No offense, Captain, but I'm also a better shot."

Capt. Charlie Welch was in no mood to argue the matter. Time did not permit it and the simple truth was, setting his pride aside, Ed was right. He was a much better shot especially at long distances.

"Alright. You give us a head start. Say five minutes and you come as fast as you can. If we don't hear from you or we can't see you in about an hour, we'll ride back for you," said Charlie.

"You'll hear me alright. I'll be the one praying out loud. But don't you slow up much. I'm liable to pass you by," said Ed. Capt. Charlie Welch and the Waters took off at a full gallop. They had ridden about 5 miles when Capt. Welch started to notice the change in the landscape. Small hills giving way to larger ones, scrub oaks and deer brush and the occasional Joshua tree. The terrain became more rocky and scattered with boulders.

Looking off to his left he spotted some higher hills with vegetation and straight cliffs on one side as if someone took a knife and cut them in half. A long switchback trail used by wild horses and elk led to the top of one of the hills. Capt. Welch turned his horse and proceeded to head for the trail. The young Waters brothers followed silently. When they had reached the top, Capt. Welch reached into his saddle bag and retrieved a pair of field glasses and began to scan their back trail. "Come on. Where are you?" mumbled Capt. Welch to himself. Seconds later, Sam Waters spoke out.

"Hey Capt. Welch. That him?" Sam was pointing.

"Yup. That's him and he's burning up the trail too! He doesn't know where we are."

Capt. Wells pulled out his rifle from its scabbard and fired a quick shot into the air from his .52 caliber Smith & Wesson repeating rifle. Ed

Lamb reined his horse to a halt and began looking around. Capt. Welch fired another shot. Immediately, Ed began to ascend up the switchback trail. Soon he was with the Captain and the Waters brothers.

"Happy to see you! Best get ready," said Ed. "Company's coming."

"How many?" asked Capt. Charlie Welch.

"Four. I stood them off for about a good half hour. They apparently spotted you fellas right off and took out after you. Reckon they forgot about me," said Ed.

Sam gasped. "Sir, you've been shot!"

Blood was trickling down his left arm and down his fingertips. "Shucks, tain't nothing. Just a flesh wound. Why I've cut myself worse shaving," said Ed.

"Never mind that now. There they are!" warned Danny Waters.

"Good! I'm tired of running," said Ed.

"Okay. Ed, you and Danny take to them boulders yonder next to that dead Joshua. Anyone tries for that trail up here, stop'em! Sam, you and I will hunker down next to these cedars. We'll stop anyone from trying to climb up the side."

"Yes, sir. Captain Welch?" said Sam.

"What is it?"

"Does it hurt much? I mean, getting shot. Does it hurt much?"

Capt. Charlie Welch studied the young man for a second or two then punched him in the arm knocking Sam heals over head backward. Sam sat up and looked at Capt. Welch questioningly. "About that much," lied Capt. Welch. This was no time for the kid to become hysterical with fright.

"Ow! I see. I can stand it," claimed Sam.

"Good! I never had any doubt. Here take this old colt Patterson and hunker down behind that boulder."

"Captain?"

"Yes?"

"I ain't never shot a man before. I don't know if I could kill another man." said Sam.

"You don't have too. Just aim for his knees. That'll stop'em."

Suddenly without warning, the air was filled with the sound of gunfire. Bullets twanged and zinged overhead. A rapid thwack, thwack, wazong! popped over Sam taking down a tree limb from the cedar tree.

"Yeowwee!" screamed Sam.

"Are you hurt boy?" shouted Charlie Welch.

"I'm fine but..."

"But what? What is it?" asked Charlie Welch.

"I think I wet myself."

Charlie wanted to laugh but at the same time recognized that this was a 14-year-old boy. It would not do him well to give friendly chiding. "It happens, boy. Now and then, it happens. Now start shooting back!"

Soon it became silent again. A voice yelled out from down below the caller hidden somewhere among the boulders.

"Danny Waters! This is Sheriff John Strap! I've come for the money. Just toss it down and you and your brother can ride out. As for your friend with you. I'm placing him under arrest for murder."

"Murder? Of who?" yelled Danny.

"He shot and killed one of my posse. Edgar Plumb," answered the sheriff.

"It wasn't murder, Sheriff. It was self-defense. Him or me. You know that," hollered Ed Lamb.

"I say it was. Who are you to say different?" asked the Sheriff.

"My name is Ed Lamb. I'm a Texas Ranger. With me is Capt. Charlie Welch also a Texas Ranger!"

Everything became silent for 15 minutes. Then, "How do I know you're really Texas Rangers and not partners with that kid?"

"Think, Strap. Don't be an idiot. Up until now you were chasing two kids. How is it you supposed we showed up? News travels fast these days, Strap. Let me suggest you toss away that star you're wearing and ride out for a new career," called out Capt. Charlie Welch.

"I've got a career. A good one too. Though I think I'll keep the star. It's simpler just to kill all of you and be done with it!" replied Sheriff John Strap.

"And become $3,000 richer as well. Right?" replied Capt. Charlie Welch.

"Seems like the thing to do. Now especially. And with you dead, my job is safe and secured!"

"Just one thing wrong with that, Strap!" yelled Capt. Charlie Welch.

"Oh ya! What's that?"

"We ain't dead yet!! That's gonna take some doing," replied Capt. Charlie Welch.

Several moments went by in silence. A magpie squawked in defiance to something and a prairie dog barked his squirrel like warning. Then as if lightning in a thunderstorm without warning, the silence was put to an end by the sound of bullets as they chipped pieces of boulder, bark and dirt all around.

Ed Lamb began a rapid firing down the trail leading up to where he and Charlie and the Waters brothers had traveled.

"So they think this is going to be easy?" said Charlie Welch. Charlie watched the brush and boulders down below. A movement caught his eye. Then a piece stuck out from behind a large boulder. Charlie raised his .52 caliber rimfire Smith & Wesson repeater and took aim. He waited. Then the man leaned forward to take a look. Charlie Welch squeezed the trigger. The .52 caliber roared. Boom! The man behind the boulder fell backward and lay motionless.

"Danged fool. Serves him right," muttered Capt. Charlie Welch.

Sam had seen the top of another man's hat bobbing through the brush. Sam fired the old Colt Patterson revolver in front of the hat. Kapow! Kapow! Kapow!

"Aaugh!! I'm hit! I'm hit!" yelled the owner of the hat.

"Nice shooting," Capt. Welch said to Sam approvingly.

"Thanks. I guess I just got lucky," said Sam his hands trembling as he tried reloading the revolver.

"Let me help," said Capt. Charlie Welch taking the revolver from Sam's hand.

"Thanks again. I just could not get my fingers to do what my mind told them," said Sam.

"Breathe deep and think of these hombres as if they were after your folks. Because they are," said Capt. Charlie Welch to Sam.

"Yes, sir. I'll sure try."

A voice called from the brush below. An argument was ensuing among the posse members. "The hell with this, John. I'm done with it. We've two dead already and them Texas Rangers with those kids."

"Anyone of you who tries to run out now I will kill. You won't have to worry about any Rangers. You're in this to the end," argued Sheriff John Strap to his posse members. "It's only two men and two boys. We ain't leaving until I have that money."

"There were more than four of them. The others must have shown up after the shooting started," Capt. Charlie Welch thought to himself. "It won't work! May as well turn back now while you can! Strap, you're a fool. We can hold you boys off till Jesus comes. From up here, we can spot your every move. It's going to get dark soon and mighty cold too," yelled Capt. Charlie Welch.

"Never you mind about that. Maybe it's you who should be concerned about the dark!" replied Sheriff John Strap.

Capt. Welch did not reply. He was in fact worried about the dark. Strap and his men could easily sneak up on them in the dark. By the time they were spotted it would be too late.

"Sam, I want you to crawl back behind us and gather a couple arms full of firewood. Be careful not to be seen and watch for snakes. Do you think you can do that?" asked Charlie Welch.

"Yes, sir," replied Sam.

"Good man and while you're at it, feed and water the horses. I've got some oats in one of my bags."

Charlie motioned for Ed lamb to come forward. Ed eased his way over to Capt. Welch. "See something?" asked Ed.

"No. But we're getting out of here. We'll set up what looks like a camp and as soon as the sun disappears, ride out. Tell Danny. Until then we best give Sheriff Strap and his minions something to be concerned about. When I start shooting, you and Danny join in. Shoot where you're sure you saw them last."

"Right," said Ed. Then he turned and asked, "Which way? In the dark it's going to be mighty risky and I don't know about you but I don't know this country."

"Don't you worry. I've got all that figured out," replied Capt. Charlie Welch.

Ed Lamb reached his previous spot next to Danny and waved to Charlie. Charlie Welch raised his rifle and aimed at a spot where he last saw movement and began to shoot left to right and right to left. Ed Lamb and Danny joined in the shooting. Soon the posse began to return fire. With the darkening and long shadows being cast by the setting sun, the flashes from their muzzles could be seen with each and every return of fire. Charlie started firing at the muzzle flashes. Then suddenly as it began, it stopped. Charlie motioned to Ed and Danny and the three of them made their way to where the horses were tied.

"Sam, get the fire going. Make it a big one. So's they can see its glow," said Charlie.

With the fire built high and Sam having fed the horses and saddled them, Charlie said to Ed, "If I recall correct, this here hill stretches out about a half a mile east of here then levels flat. We will head east. Let's swing around behind Strap and his men. With luck on our side, we just might be able to scatter their horses. The way I figure it, they'll be too busy trying to sneak up on our camp. They won't leave anyone behind to guard them. So it should work. Then we'll head north. By the time they figure out what has happened, it'll be too late and they'll be all the morning long rounding up horses. They won't be searching for them in the dark, I hope," explained Capt. Charlie Welch.

"That's pretty good thinking, Captain," said Ed.

"When you've rangered as long as I have, you learn a trick or two," said Capt. Charlie Welch.

They lead their horses for about 200 yards before mounting. They rode east until the ground leveled out then swung slightly north then west. Just as Capt. Welch had figured, the posse left no one to guard the horses. Then off in the distance someone yelled. "Blast their hides! It's a trick, they're gone!"

Charlie Welch yelled at the horses as he and Danny untied them from their picket lines slapping the horses on their rumps and shooting into the air. "Heeyah! Heeyah! Git up!" The horses took out on a run.

"The horses! They're stealing the horses!" someone yelled from not too far away. The flash of a pistol being fired could be seen. But the shooter was shooting blindly and did not come close. Capt. Welch, Ed Lamb and the two Waters brothers headed north. About two hours later, they made camp and slept soundly for the remainder of the night.

The large gray three-bedroom house stood proudly out on the prairie. A large windmill groaned as the windmill's propellers turned. Water trickled down a long trough into a big tank with sides about 3 feet high. A barn with a roof in need of repair still welcomed mainly with its large corral supporting four fine looking Appaloosa mares and two fine looking foals. A garden nearly one acre in size lay between the house and the windmill. Charlie Welch was amused at the site of the windmill.

"A windmill," explained Sam.

"I know what it is. Only we don't see so much of them in Texas. A few but not many," said Charlie Welch.

"Pa had it shipped piece by piece all the way from Kansas City. Took him two years to get it all together and raised," said Sam.

"Sounds like your pa was a fine man," replied Capt. Charlie Welch.

"Yes, sir. I reckon so. He died when I was 10 years old. Pneumonia."

A tall slender woman and a young girl almost as tall stood on the porch of the house trying to make out the men who were coming.

"Ma!" yelled Sam.

The woman stood smiling as they rode up to the steps of the porch.

"Howdy, ma'am," said Capt. Charlie Welch.

"Hello," said the woman. Discernment was in her eyes as she glanced first at Danny and then back at Capt. Welch. Danny, sensing the question in his mother's eyes answered. "Ma, this is Captain Charlie Wells and Ed Lamb. They are Texas Rangers. Fellas, this is my ma and my sister, Gail.

"How do you do?" said Gail.

"Ladies," said Capt. Charlie Welch tipping his hat in respect.

"So, how is it my sons got escorted by Texas Rangers? What sort of trouble did they cause?" asked the woman.

"Now that's a complicated question. But I assure you, your sons are not in any trouble with the law," replied Capt. Charlie Welch.

"So, it's customary for Texas Rangers to escort young men home even if that home is two states away? I'm afraid you have me at a disadvantage, Capt. Welch," said Mrs. Waters.

Capt. Welch smiled. He was starting to like this woman. She had spunk and a sense of humor. He also could sense that this woman ran a strict household when need be.

"Not customary, ma'am but there are times," said Capt. Charlie Welch with a smile. "Mrs.?"

"Amanda Waters. Please forgive me. You men can put your horses in the corral. There's hay and oats next to the tack room. Gail and I were about to have supper. You and Mr. Lamb are welcome to join us if you like."

"I'd be very honored. But we don't wish to impose, ma'am," said Charlie Welch.

"No imposition, Capt. Welch. It would be nice to have company. There is also a vase and washbasin in the tack room. You men can wash up for supper."

They ate heartily a meal of pot roast with potatoes, carrots, onion, cornbread and peach pie for dessert. Over supper, the Waters brothers told their adventures to their mother and how it was that they came into the company of the two Texas Rangers. Capt. Charlie Welch also explained.

"Well, I am certainly in your debt, Capt. Welch," said Amanda Waters.

"Not at all and please, call me Charlie or Charles."

Amanda Waters blushed. "Okay, Charles. More pie?"

"Oh, no, ma'am. One more bite and I will pop a button on my shirt. That sure was a fine meal. I will, however, have another cup of coffee. If you don't mind?"

"Of course. It's been so long! I love to watch a man eat," said Amanda Waters.

"A finer meal I cannot recall. I'd like to repay you for your hospitality."

"Nonsense! I will hear no more about it. You brought my sons home safely. That's payment enough."

"I noticed the roof on the barn is in need of repair. Some of those horses could use shod also," replied Charlie Welch.

"We had a bad storm a few days ago I'm afraid. The wind blew some of the boards off of the barn. We usually have the blacksmith in town shoe our horses. We have fallen behind on some of our chores I must admit."

"Think nothing of it. I say for two ladies alone you've done quite well. Ed and I will get to that barn first thing in the morning."

"I don't know what to say. Thank you but how can I repay you?"

"Won't cost you more than another peach pie," smiled Capt. Charlie Welch.

**Uvalde, Texas**
**Ranger Headquarters Company D**

Leander H McNelly stood staring out the window, watching the sunset. He lit his pipe and turned to look at Drew and Whiskey Jack.

"I hate to leave you fellas with all this mess. But if I don't get back to Austin that Governor of ours might declare me a deserter or something. And there needs to be someone looking over his shoulder to hold him accountable."

"I'm not going to say you won't be missed. But I believe we can get by. In fact it's going to be nice to have my chair back. That is if you haven't taken a notion on packing it with you," said Drew humorously.

"Don't tempt me," smiled Leander H McNelly. "While I am in Austin I'm going to see what I can learn of this King Fisher fella."

"He's going to be a handful," replied Whiskey Jack.

"As if we haven't enough to do already. Oh! And when you get back to Austin, give this envelope to Caleb and Johnny. It's from my mother," said Drew.

"You bet. You've done well by those boys. They've become fine men," said Capt. Leander H McNelly.

Four days later Drew Parker, his wife Marjorie, Whiskey Jack and his wife Nancy were having a dinner at the Opal Palace in Uvalde. They were there to see a play at the Palace Theater. It was a welcome event and it had been much too long since they had any alone time together. They were just leaving the theater when the evening stagecoach came bouncing into town swerving left and out of control. A young cattleman leaped from his horse onto the stagecoach, took the reins and brought the stagecoach under control and to a stop.

"Hey! Someone get the doctor. Barney's been shot six ways to Sunday!" yelled the cowhand.

Barney Feldman had been a stagecoach driver for the Butterfield Overland Stage since after the war. He was senior chief driver from Austin to Abilene mostly carrying mail on his return trips. On this particular trip from Abilene, he was also carrying three passengers. One of them the new vicar to the Presbyterian Church newly established in Uvalde as well as mail and bank notes and Army payroll bound for Brownsville.

"What happened?" asked the new Sheriff Waylon Pencott.

"We were about 10 miles from town. They wore bandanas so we could not make out their faces. Barney went for his shotgun and a dish shot him! They laughed as if it were some funny joke," said a male passenger.

"One of them slips of the tongue I'm sure. Called another Frank," said the vicar.

"I'll need you to come over to the jail and write out a statement and to give as much detail as possible," said Sheriff Waylon Pencott. Sheriff Pencott was newly appointed since the previous Sheriff had decided suddenly to retire.

Try as he had, Drew Parker wanted to avoid getting mixed up in this at least for a day or two. Too long and too many times had he promised Marjorie a romantic weekend with just the two of them. No rangering, no ranch talk just the two of them together now this. "Just can't seem to catch a break," sighed Drew.

"You're not reconsidering? Oh, Drew. Let the sheriff handle it. At least for now. I'm certain he will call upon you if he feels the need. Please?" pleaded Marjorie.

Drew smiled and pulled her close to him. "You're right. After all, he is the sheriff. He has to get his feet wet sooner or later."

"I'm hungry!" said Nancy.

"Hungry? Jumpin' catfish! We ate just two hours ago," said Jack in amazement.

"Nonetheless," snapped Nancy humorously.

Marjorie gave Nancy a questioning stare. Nancy looked at Marjorie smiled and nodding ever so subtly. Their evening ended and Marjorie and Nancy walked ahead of Drew and Jack. The women were giggling and recounting the evening's events and the play, Romeo and Juliet by William Shakespeare. Drew was silent for the most part. Jack chuckled and said, "You just can't help yourself, can you?"

"Help what? What are you talking about?" asked Drew.

"Nothing. Forget I said anything," said Jack referring to his brother's hunger for being a Texas Ranger. Though Jack found it hard to comprehend at the same time, it was a quality he admired in Drew. Though a man who stood for justice and truth and believed in it as well, Jack could take off the Texas Star and be content to just being a rancher. Drew was not like that. Drew lived to be a Texas Ranger. Drew was never more alive than when he was on a case.

The following morning was cool and a steady breeze blew west to east. There was something about fall and winter weather as if Mother Nature herself had put on a new perfume. At times Drew would have sworn he caught the scent of cinnamon. The buckboard wagon bounced merrily as the two couples made their way home.

"It was a lovely weekend. Thank you, Drew, but I must admit I miss my little major," said Marjorie in reference to Miguel Andrew, their son.

"Don't be upset if he acts as if he wasn't aware you were ever gone. Mother has doubtless spoiled him to no end," smiled Drew.

"She is a loving grandmother. Women such as she should have many grandchildren. Don't you think so, Marjorie?" asked Nancy.

"Without a doubt," smiled Marjorie. She shook her head while thinking that men could be so slow to pick up on things happening right in front of them.

Sheriff Pencott's posse suffered heavy casualties. They had followed the outlaws about 15 miles northwest of Uvalde. The outlaws had camped along the Nueces River. Sheriff Pencott, not wanting to risk the lives of any more men, turned his posse south and headed home to Uvalde. Immediately, the sheriff sent word to Ranger headquarters in Uvalde. Major Drew Parker knocked at the door of the sheriff's office. "Come in," said Sheriff Pencott as he slid the deadbolt and opened the door.

"Waylon, what's with the locked door?"

Sheriff Pencott shook his head in shame. "I just needed to be alone, Drew. Some sheriff I turned out to be. I failed Drew. I'm just thankful no one was killed."

"It's a tough and thankless job at times. But to say you failed? I don't think so. I've not heard anything in town to make me feel that way either. If you start pouting and feeling sorry for yourself then you might as well say so. Those men knew what they were up against. Most of them have ridden in posses before. If you want my help you've got it. My first advice would be to shake it off and make yourself seen. Self-pity is not what the folks in Uvalde will understand. Like you said no one died and most of those men have been shot before. If you have their respect I can promise you they'll be in the next posse and the next. But they do not understand or respect self-pity," lectured Drew.

"I don't understand. The people hired me to protect them. All I've done is botch things up. How can they respect a man like that?" said Sheriff Waylon Pencott.

"They hired you as sheriff to uphold the law but they also know you're not God. Son, you place too much on your shoulders. These men can protect themselves very well. Your duty is to uphold the law and keep order in the town. Does that mean facing gunslingers and hunting down rustlers and bank robbers? Yes. But the men of Uvalde know that you can't be everywhere at once. And like them, you're just a man. You will make mistakes, you might even get shot now and then. It's confusing and always complicated. Which is why you were hired. You are not doing yourself any good nor the town by locking your door and sulking.

You have to show them you have grit and you'll have their support and respect for as long as you live."

"So what do you suggest? I throw a party for those who got shot for getting shot?"

"Sort of. Go out into the town. Make yourself seen. Visit the men who rode with you. Congratulate them for being men. And buy a couple rounds at the saloon. Let them know that Sheriff Waylon Pencott is no fore flusher. Let them know that you are there for them and that they have your word and your devotion. By doing that you'll have theirs," explained Drew.

"I'm not sure what you're trying to say. But it does me good to know that you believe in me. What you say we go get a drink? On me. Besides, I've got rounds to make and a new posse to round up," smiled Sheriff Pencott.

"There you go! Now that's the start. Give it time, Waylon. You'll figure this job out. You'll make a fine sheriff."

At the saloon, the men of Uvalde were having a talk mostly concerning the recent events with the posse. "Seems to me the sheriff has a lot to learn. Maybe we chose someone too young and green," said one of the men.

"Oh, I don't know. I reckon we ought to take some of the blame. After all we've all been in posses before. Sure the sheriff is young. But he's got guts. We should have known better than to ride into a pass like some circus parade. You ask me, the sheriff's all right. We could have advised him," said another man.

The talk was buzzing and fell suddenly silent when Sheriff Waylon Pencott and Major Drew Parker walked into the bar. Sheriff Pencott strode up to the bar and ordered a beer. Then after taking a long drink, he set his mug on the bar and turned to face the crowd. "That was one hell of a reception we got today, wouldn't you say so, boys? But I'm grateful to you for riding with me. Now I'm asking for you to do it again. This time the surprise will be on them. To show my gratitude, I'm buying the next two rounds for the house!"

The saloon exploded with excitement. "Yeehaw! Let's drink to our Sheriff!" "Yeah, you've got sand, Sheriff, that's for sure!" "I'll ride with you, Sheriff!" "Fellas, looks like we hired a real man for the job!" "You can count on me, Sheriff!

"Men! Men! Please! I sure do thank you. You have no idea what this means to me. But this time, I'm hoping things will be different. By now those outlaws have moved on. We will need a tracker and some help from someone with more experience than me. I'm asking help from Major Drew Parker and his Texas Rangers. If you're going to learn, you might as well learn from the very best. How about it, Drew?" said Sheriff Waylon Pencott.

Drew looked around the room and back to Sheriff Pencott. He stood silent for a moment. "Yes, I'll help."

Someone in the bar shouted. "Hoorah! A toast to the Texas Rangers!"

"See! I told you that sheriff had a head on his shoulders!" said one of the other men in the bar.

"Took guts to ask for help. I'll say that for him. That took guts."

"Took a lot of wisdom too. He's going to shape up into quite a lawman!" said an elderly gentleman.

"Stop the jawin' and let's drink!" said yet another. The fire crackled and popped as the three men sat around passing a bottle whiskey.

"This would be easy, you said. We'd be long gone before they could pick up our trail you said," growled Pat Sigel.

"Oh shut up! You got your money," replied Frank Hazen.

"I told you we should have killed them all. Now look at us. Running like scared rabbits," said Forrest Cook.

"Kill a preacher?! Yeah, that would've been smart. Besides I ain't no murderer," replied Frank Hazen.

"You didn't have any problems shooting that stagecoach driver. I reckon we killed him sure enough," said Forrest Cook.

"Danged old fool. He shouldn't have gone for that shotgun!" said Frank Hazen.

"Maybe. Still, how do you suppose that posse caught up with us so fast?" asked Pat Sigel.

"Lucky, but I reckon we cut their luck short," said Forrest Cook.

"Don't you bet on it. They'll patch up their wounds, give us a day or two. But trust me, they'll be back!" said Frank Hazen.

"You talk as if you admire them or something. Maybe you should just turn yourself in. Ease your conscience if you think so highly of them," sneered Forrest Cook.

"I do admire them. I respect them too! Maybe you should as well, Cook. You don't know the caliber of men such as them. And if they get the Texas Rangers involved we are in trouble. We'd be better off in Bolivia or China. Because the Texas Rangers don't quit. As for that matter the men in that posse are all ranchers and farmers most likely. They fought Indians, Mexican bandits; some may have been in the recent war. These are men who don't go halfway with anything. So you better not be taking them lightly," said Frank Hazen.

"Texas Rangers! Why would the Texas Rangers waste their time on us?" asked Pat Sigel.

"That's a fool question. Why would they not? We not only robbed a stage but we shot a man. Maybe even killed him. Take that and add that Army payroll. Why wouldn't the Rangers get involved?" said Frank Hazen.

"You call that a payroll? Five hundred Dollars! There was supposed to be $23,000. What happened?" said Pat Sigel.

"We got stupid and greedy! That's what happened!" said Frank Hazen.

"That danged paymaster! He fooled us, that's for sure! And as for the Rangers? Not only are we outlaws wanted for robbery and maybe murder, but we are Army deserters as well. I'd be more worried about the Army than I would the Rangers," said Forrest Cook.

"Why don't we just go to Mexico? The Army can't touch us there," said Pat Sigel.

"Maybe not but the Texas Rangers can. Then turn us over to the Mexican government," warned Frank Hazen.

"You seem to know a lot about these Texas Rangers," said Forrest Cook. "Why is that?"

"I've heard of a Ranger who followed a man clean up to Oregon just for robbing a hardware store," said Frank Hazen.

"Oregon? I don't believe that," said Pat Sigel.

"I don't rightly care if you believe me or not. But when that Ranger found him, he killed him."

"Who was this famous ranger you're talking about?" sneered Forrest Cook.

"I never met him but he goes by the name Whiskey Jack," said Frank Hazen.

The Pecos River was nearly dry. The past year had not given much rain and now winter was coming on. In the spring, its banks would be nearly cresting by the melting snow from the mountains in New Mexico and Colorado.

"They crossed here, Sheriff. Their tracks headed south and crossed here. Wonder where they're going?" mused Matthew McDonald. Matthew McDonald was reputed to be the best tracker south of San Antonio. He had been hired by the Butterfield over Lynn Stage to hunt down the outlaws. But when he learned that the Texas Rangers were working with the sheriff of Uvalde and pursuing the same outlaws, Matthew McDonald decided to join in.

"El Paso," guessed Major Drew Parker. "Maybe into Sonora."

"Sonora? What's in Sonora?" asked Sheriff Pencott.

"Not much. But it does offer a safe haven for outlaws on the run. The Mexican Federales will turn a blind eye as long as there is a profit in it for them," replied Major Drew Parker.

"But we can't go into Mexico. We have no jurisdiction," stated the Sheriff.

"Then we had better not let them get into Sonora, had we?" said Drew.

They were half a day's ride from the Chalk River. When Drew came galloping, Sheriff Pencott called the posse to a halt.

"We're gonna have company," said Drew.

"Company? I don't understand," replied Sheriff Pencott.

"I think the Ranger is referring to Indians," explained McDonald.

"You would be correct," said Drew.

"I know I am. I'm guessing 35," said McDonald pointing over Drew's shoulder.

"We better get ready, men. This is just as good a spot as any. Dismount and take the horses behind those mesquite and boulders," ordered Major Drew Parker.

"Apache?" McDonald asked of Drew.

"Apache. We still have the element of surprise. I doubt they know how many of us there is," said Major Drew Parker.

"Fourteen men against 40 Apache?" said one of the posse members.

"Well, we sure can't run. Smaller forces have often become victorious against larger. Just hold your fire and your nerve," instructed Major Drew Parker.

"You reckon that the men we're after ran into this bunch?" asked McDonald.

"It's possible," replied Drew.

The Apache started to fan out. As soon as they were noticed, they vanished into the landscape.

"Stand by your horses. McDonald, take three or four men to our right over there on that potato hill covered with boulders. Sheriff Pencott, you take another four to our left in that stand of junipers and deer brush. The rest of us will line up here in his goalie. Keep your horses close! We may have to ride sudden like," instructed Major Drew Parker.

The air was still and the sun high. Drew took a swallow from his canteen of water. He poured water onto his bandana and washed the nostrils of his buckskin mare then poured water into his hat for her to drink all the while surveying the landscape all about and before him with an eagle eye. A small covey of quail flew up from inside a clump of deer brush and cactus. Slowly, Drew raised his rifle and aimed for the center of the deer brush and squeezed off a shot. Suddenly, a loud yell filled the air as an Apache stood up, took several retreating steps then fell face first into the sand and gravel. At that moment the landscape gave birth to dozens of screaming Apache.

"Fire at will, men! Make your shots count!" yelled Major Drew Parker.

The air became filled with gunfire and screaming Apache. Two Apache had made their way to within 15 feet of Drew and charged at him. The glimmer from a large bully knife flashed in the hand of one of the Apache. Seeing the flash, Drew swung his rifle around and fired point-blank at the oncoming Apache. The Apache flew backward as those snatched by the scruff of the neck and yanked backward. At that same instant, a second Apache pounced upon Drew, clipping the back of his skull with his tomahawk. Drew rolled quickly to his left drawing his revolver at the same time and fired three rapid shots. An Apache warrior jerked and twitched with each shot. Suddenly, the firing ceased and all became silent.

"Reckon we whipped them, Major Parker?" asked a posse member.

"Nope. They'll try again. Count on it." Drew called out. "Be ready on the right and left flanks! This ain't over, men!"

The sun was becoming brutally hot. If there were more Apache in the area, all they needed to do was send a warrior for help. With the only water available being that in their canteens, the Apache only had to wait the posse out.

"What are we going to do?" asked Sheriff Pencott.

"For now, we sit tight where we are. We don't want to give away our strength. Chances are, based upon the last attack, they didn't see all of us. They probably believe us to be about five or six men. If we can hold them off until dark, we may have a chance to get out of here," explained Major Drew Parker.

"Captain!" yelled McDonald. "Looks like they're fixin' to try again. On horseback this time!!"

"Kill the horses! No mercy, men. Your scalps depend on it!" ordered Major Parker.

Drew reached inside his bedroll tied behind his saddle and pulled out a double-barreled 12 gauge shotgun. He took a handful of shotgun shells from his saddle bag.

When the Apache came riding at a full gallop, they tried to throw the posse men into a panic with their screams. The whooping sent chills down the spines of many in the posse. A young posse member stood up from his hiding place behind a boulder to shoot and an arrow went halfway through the muscle just above his right collarbone missing his neck by mere inches.

"Oh! Dear God, they got me! I'm dying! Jesus, I'm dying!" cried the young man.

Drew took the butt of his shotgun and clubbed the young man knocking him unconscious then swung the shotgun up to his shoulder and fired. One shot at the neck of a charging pony. The Indian pony stumbled tossing his rider flying forward like a hawk with his wings stretched wide. Drew aimed and fired as the Apache warrior scrambled to his feet and charged at him. Drew fired and ripped the warrior's chest wide open.

As Drew reloaded his shotgun, another Apache came charging up to him, his lance drawn back preparing to thrust it into Drew's back. Matthew McDonald, seeing the sight, quickly fired two rounds from his Colt repeating rifle. The warrior dropped in midstride. Drew spun around quickly waving his shotgun left to right. But the warrior was already dead. The air grew silent.

"How many hurt?" called Drew.

"Only this young'un, Major. Though I say this goose egg on his head is going to hurt worse than this arrow," said Matthew McDonald.

"Sorry but it was for your own good," said Drew.

"I'm the one should be apologizing. I reckon I sort of panicked. Ain't never been in an Injun fight before. I got rattled," said the young man.

"It happens," said Drew. He let the matter go.

"Major, this time they're sure enough leaving," said another posse member. "Look yonder."

"We best be leaving too and muy pronto. I've a feeling we haven't seen the last of those Apache!" said Major Drew Parker.

"What? After the lickin' they just took? You're telling me they'll be back?" exclaimed Sheriff Pencott unbelievingly.

"They'll lick their wounds. Pick up some reinforcements. Then get after us sure enough," said Major Drew Parker.

"The hell with this!! I'm for going home. Chasing outlaws is one thing. But you have to plow through bloodthirsty Apache to do it? Not me, brother. They can have the danged money. I'm truly sorry about ole' Barney Feldman. But I've had it. I ain't even getting paid for this.

I've got a wife and kids who need me. Sorry, Sheriff," said a posse member named Bob Jenkins.

"You don't have to apologize, Bob. I understand. Anyone else who feels the same as Bob can go as well. No ill feelings," said Sheriff Pencott.

Now, there were three. The others did turn back leaving Drew, Sheriff Pencott and Matthew McDonald.

That was two days ago. The three lawmen camped along a ridge littered with large stone and boulders along with an array of cactus, mesquite and deer brush and a few scattering of Joshua trees. Their fire was hidden by the ridge top on one side and the thick mesquite and boulders on the other. They were somewhere southwest of the Davis Mountains area. The night sky was a smoky gray mixed with black, purple and a hint of fiery orange streaks crisscrossing the horizon.

"Funny, ain't it? We roast during the day and need a fire to stay warm at night. I'll never get used to it and I've lived in Texas all my life," said Sheriff Pencott.

"It does boggle the mind," joked Major Drew Parker.

"Why do you do it, Parker? What makes you Rangers so bent on capturing a man that you'd go through hell to get him?" asked Sheriff Waylon Pencott.

"I've often asked myself that same question. I suppose it's because someone has to. A belief that one day this planet will be a fine place for folks to live. I guess also because like any other man, I want a future for my children. A chance for them to live free and to forge a worthwhile life for themselves. The criminal minded must be taught that as long as there are men like the Texas Rangers, their deeds will have to be paid for. That if you break the law in Texas, you will be held accountable. Texas is a huge land. Lawmen cannot be expected to do it all. Texas needs the Rangers to go as far as it takes, as long as it takes, to apprehend them. Someday, maybe the Rangers will not be needed."

"It sure is a lonely job. I don't know if I could do it," said Sheriff Pencott.

"Oh, I don't know about that, Waylon. After all, you're here. You could have turned back with the others and given up the chase. Why didn't you?"

"That's an easy question. They killed Barney Feldman. He was a fine man. But an old man. They didn't have to kill him. No, sir, they didn't have to kill him. For that alone, they need to pay."

Drew smiled. "See what I mean? You sound just like a Ranger."

"Well, if you asked me, I'm just plain crazy. I haven't yet figured out why I'm still here. I suppose is just plain stubbornness. I hate to leave a job undone and I figured it ain't right that you go after these hombres outnumbered," interjected Matthew McDonald.

The men talked for a while until they finally drifted off to sleep.

Three days later and about 12 miles east of Sierra Banca, the three lawmen rode into the small town of mostly Mexican population, Tres Buttes. Happy to see a town and all three craving a good meal and a hot bath. The three lawmen nearly forgot what they were there for. After taking a bath and getting a fresh haircut and shave, the men decided to have a good meal. Refreshed and feeling more human, the men strolled over to Ariannas Café and Cantina.

"Buenos dias. How can I help you, gentleman?" asked the 17 year old woman. Her eyes darted nervously as she looked over the three men surveying them for signs of trouble.

"Buenos dias, senorita. I'd like a steak, potatoes, beans, greens and a tall cold beer por favor," said Drew.

"And you, gentlemen?" She asked of the other two.

"That sounds good to me. The same for me," said Matthew McDonald.

"Keep things simple. I'll also have the same," said Sherriff Waylon Pencott.

The girl smiled brightly. "Bueno. Food ready un poco. Have beer now?"

"Si, por favor," replied Drew Parker.

An hour later the three lawmen stepped outside of the cantina and started for the only hotel in town. When Matthew McDonald spotted a yellow tag peeking out of the corner of a saddlebag on a gray Appaloosa tied up in front of the hotel. He stopped and, looking at Drew, gestured with his head and eyes toward the horse.

"What is it?" asked Drew in a low clear voice.

"That saddlebag on the Appaloosa. The yellow tag. That's the same sort of tags sewn on the payroll bags used by the Army. They usually scribble the Company or Battalion on it," said McDonald.

"Are you certain? I don't see any writing on it," replied Sheriff Waylon Pencott.

"Probably because it was only one. Most of the time, they send two or more in one shipment. Especially if there are more than one or two stops. Most payrolls are sent by railroad. This must have been something out of the ordinary," explained McDonald.

"Well, now. This could be one of them," said Drew.

"Unless it was a decoy," replied McDonald. "Meant to distract any possible hold up men from the real payroll shipment."

"Only one way to know for sure. Listen, here's what we're going to do..." Drew explained a plan to find out the identity of the three outlaws. It was clear that somewhere along the way the outlaws had either bought or stolen horses.

"Sounds like a right fair plan, Parker. But in the meantime, that leaves only two of us if any gunplay starts. I mean, at least for a few minutes until the other of us get into position," said Sheriff Pencott.

"If I figured this right all three of us will be just where we need to be if any shooting starts," said Drew.

"If," nodded Sheriff Pencott. "If."

Drew and Sheriff Pencott walked casually into the hotel lobby. To the right was a small bar area and six tables situated throughout the rest of the room. Two men were standing at the bar while another three sat at a table in the far back, playing cards. The bartender seemed friendly enough but showed signs of some agitation as though he would like to close up and retire for the night. Drew nudged Sheriff Pencott and the two men started laughing out loud as though one of them had just told a joke or was recalling a funny situation. Then the two men strolled over to the bar. "Dos cervesas, por favor," said Drew with a wide carefree smile. Suddenly, a man burst into the lobby from out in the street.

"Hey! If any of you gents own a gray Appaloosa, you don't no more! Some Injun just stole him and hightailed it north out of town!" The man shouting out this piece of news was Matthew McDonald.

The three men at the far table looked at each other and then after a second of realization, one of them exclaimed in a panic, "That's my horse! Oh, no, the money!" The three men shot up out of their seats and rushed for the door. Major Parker took four quick strides and was standing next to Matthew McDonald. The two lawmen blocked the door.

"Hold it right there, boys! I'm arresting you three for the robbery of the Butterfield Overland Stage near Uvalde, Texas and for the murder of the driver, Mr. Barney Feldman," said Major Drew Parker.

The three men froze in mid-motion. They looked first at each other and then toward Drew and Matthew McDonald. "That's my horse that was stolen!" shouted Frank Hazen.

"All three of you, drop your guns and do it slowly," instructed Major Drew Parker.

Frank Hazen wasn't quick to let the subject of the horse go. "My horse was stolen!"

"It hasn't been stolen. The horse is fine. Now drop your guns. I won't say it again," warned Drew.

Frank Hazen's hand slowly drifted for his six-gun and froze at the sound of a rifle being cocked. Sheriff Pencott had made his way behind the three outlaws.

"That wouldn't be a smart thing to do because if I don't get you, that rifle behind you surely will," said Major Drew Parker.

Frank Hazen's eyes glared an evil smile and the corners of his mouth went upward to form a devilish smile. "So, you think you can take me, do you? That'll be the day. You're just an old man. Worn out and slowing down. I saw how you leaned against the bar. Like some welcome friend."

Frank Hazen's face grew red with anger, from his neck to his forehead. His eyes began to dance glancing from Drew to Matthew McDonald and back. His two compadres were motionless and silent. "Don't do it. I would hate to have to kill you," threatened Major Parker.

"I sure am glad to hear that. But I'd love to kill you, Ranger!" Frank Hazen's hand went quick as lightning but as he was clearing his pistol from its holster, his face grew suddenly pale white as he saw the barrel of Drew's Navy Colt. He saw the fiery sparks explode from its muzzle. But he never heard the loud bang. He never heard the scream from the young barmaid. He will never hear anything ever again. Frank Hazen's head jerked backward as the 36 caliber bullet of Drew's Navy Colt slammed into his forehead charring a half dollar size hole as it exited the back of Frank's head. Frank Hazen fell backward sprawling flat on his back onto the floor. Drew quickly slung his revolver in the direction of the other two outlaws.

"Easy, Ranger! I ain't in this," said Forrest Cook with his hand high in the air.

"What about you?" Drew said to Pat Sigel.

"I'm out of it. For now."

"That's a smart move. Now, with one hand still in the air, slowly reach down and unbuckle those gun belts. Slowly! Remember, I'm an old man. I might make a mistake and innocently move for a draw. You know, my eyes and all."

"That were Frank said that Ranger. Not me, but I must say anyone who could out draw Frank is a man to be reckoned with," said Forrest Cook.

"Frank? Is that his name? What are yours?" asked Major Drew Parker.

"My name is Forrest Cook. Look, you gotta believe me, Ranger. I never shot that stagecoach driver. I ain't no murderer."

"What about you? What's your name?" asked Drew of the other outlaw.

"Go rope a duck!" said Pat Sigel not revealing his name.

"Okay. Mr. Go Rope A Duck. I reckon we'll just have to write that on your marker after we hang you in the morning," said Major Drew Parker nonchalantly.

"Hang me! Without a trial? You wouldn't dare!"

"Oh? What now? You forget I am a Texas Ranger and we're miles away from Uvalde. I am authorized to act as judge, jury and executioner if, in my own judgment, the situation warrants," explained Major Drew Parker.

"You damned Rangers! You're like a thorn in a man's hind end. Sigel! Pat Sigel. You happy now?"

"Nope but it's a start."

"You might as well hang me. Because I'm never going to let you take me back. You best hope I don't get free. Because I meant what I said. I'm out of it. For now."

"Don't make me nervous, Sigel. You may get your wish," warned Drew.

"Ha! It would be the first time any lawmen ever did me a favor."

Drew motion for the two men to step backward. Then stooped down and picked up the gun belts. "Alright. Let's go."

"Go where?" asked Pat Sigel.

"To the sheriff's office," replied Drew.

"That's a laugh!! There ain't no sheriff's office. Why do you suppose we came here?" sneered Pat Sigel.

"No sheriff? Alright then both of you sit back to back in those two chairs," Drew motioned to a table and chairs to their left. "We'll just keep you here."

Matthew McDonald tied the two securely and the three lawmen took turns guarding their prisoners until morning.

**Austin, Texas**
**Ranger Headquarters Company A**
**Capt. Leander H McNelly Commanding Officer**

When Caleb and his patrol arrived in Austin they had all but depleted their provisions. Among the nine men, they had seven biscuits, eight strips of beef jerky, enough coffee for one pot and half a bottle of Kentucky "Red" Whiskey. To say the least, they were glad to be back. That was yesterday.

As morning broke through the windows of the barracks bunkhouse. Tom Crawford swung his feet around and on to the bunkhouse, floor. He scratched his head, stretched and yawned long and hard. "Wake up, you good for nothing saddle bums! It's 6 o'clock in the morning!" he shouted.

"Saddle bums? Look who's talking. At least my toes ain't poking through my socks," joked Tall Hammner.

"Thems only my sleeping socks," smiled Tom.

"Thems your only socks I'll bet," laughed Bill Sharp.

The clanging of the cook's dinner bell rang out. "Breakfast, you coyotes. You've got 10 minutes else I'm throwing it out!"

Moxie Gunn, the cook for the men of the Company A was a tall gray-haired, old black gentleman from North Carolina. He had come West after the war. Moxie Gunn, was one of the many black men who in 1864 enlisted into the Confederate Army in the 1st South Carolina Infantry under Maj. Patrick Clayburn. He and his fellow black confederates were fortunate enough not to see any combat. Gen. Robert E Lee surrendered in Appomattox before they could have the chance. Moxie moved west to seek adventure and fortune and instead wound up as cook for the Texas Rangers of Company A in Austin, Texas. Moxie was well-liked by McNelly as well as all the Rangers. Because of certain prejudices McNelly and Moxie thought it prudent that he would not engage in any Ranger activities. Moxie was more than content to be just a cook and a finer cook they never knew. Not since Juan Martinez.

"You want that I should help you with the dishes, Moxie?" asked Jeffrey Boxer as he carried dishes to the cooking area.

"Why, thank you most kindly but I believe I can handle it."

"Just figured I'd offer," replied Jeffrey.

"You figured on skipping out of mucking out those stables. You ain't fooling me, Ranger Boxer," said Moxie with a mile long grin.

As if from a bolt of lightning, the window behind Moxie shattered. Moaning, Moxie spun around like a top, fell to the floor.

"Moxie!" Jeff ran to his side and knelt down next to him. "Are you hurt bad?!

"No, boy! I do this every day. It's an old African ritual. Of course I'm hurt! My shoulder. I think my arm is broken."

"Let me see." Jeff rolled Moxie over on to his right side. "Awh! It ain't that bad. Went clean through," Jeffrey reassured Moxie..

Shooting had erupted outside. People were yelling, women screaming.

"Go on, Jeff. They need you," said Moxie. "Oh and Jeff, sorry I yelled at you."

"Heck. Think nothing of it. I've heard men say worse when they was shot. Believe me."

Jeffrey grabbed his rifle and stuffed a handful of bullets into his pant's pocket and rushed outside.

"Jailbreak!" someone yelled.

Joe Denton and Slim Smith came barreling out from the horse barn on horseback shooting at the 25 outlaws racing up and down the street. Shooting everything in sight whether it moved or not. "It's that damned King Fisher and his gang!" yelled Bull.

Jeff was standing behind the wagon load of straw. He had taken down two outlaws. Whether they were dead or not, he did not know. Then almost as quickly as it began, it was over. Jeffrey ran back to the bunkhouse.

"Is Moxie okay?" he asked as he came in through the doorway without even checking who was in the room. Moxie was alone.

"I'm okay. You was right. It went clean through," said Moxie.

"Your arm isn't broken?" asked Jeff.

"No. Just banged it up some. Probably when I fell." Rangers started gathering back into the bunkhouse. Some asking questions, some cursing.

"Captain McNelly says saddle up. We're going after them," said Tom Crawford. The men looked at him still dazed and somewhat confused. "Move!" he yelled. The men scrambled as if kicked in the behind. Tom Crawford's yelling had brought them back into reality.

"Darn it!" cursed Steve Hodges. "I ain't even had a chance to eat yet."

"I'll pack you something. Now get," said Moxie.

"Thanks, Moxie," replied Steve Hodges.

"Beats me how we could have lost them but we did. There are so many tracks going every which way, it's hard to tell whose are whose," said Joe Denton.

"We'll split up. It's certain they went south. Whether south east toward Brownsville or southwest toward Mexico by way of the Eagle Pass area. We'll meet in three days near Uvalde.You men head southeast. If you don't find any sign, swing west. If you do find their trail send for us." Capt. McNelly was instructing Caleb and Tom Crawford. "I will do the same. But in any case, by nightfall if you do not find their sign, head west."

Four days ago, Capt. McNelly and 12 of his Rangers had arrested King Fisher for rustling. King Fisher and nearly 20 of his gang had taken cattle near Gonzales and were attempting to push them east toward Galveston.

McNelly and his little McNelly's intercepted King Fisher along the Colorado River. After a three hour shoot and run battle King Fisher had lost four men and was captured in an old barn with three others from his gang. The Rangers were able to recover 80% of the cattle. Unfortunately most of King Fisher's gang had escaped. Now they had ridden into Austin, bold as brass and busted King Fisher out of jail.

"We'll run 'em down! That son of a coyote has pulled his last hoorah with me! I won't rest until they are all in jail or dead!" cursed Capt. Leander H McNelly.

Later that morning, 47 Texas Rangers of Company A rode south out of Austin.

"Something told me we should have stayed in Happens Chance," mumbled Bull.

"What was that?" asked Caleb.

"Happens Chance. We should have stayed a few days longer. At least we could have gotten some rest."

"You have a point there," chuckled Caleb.

"You reckon we'll catch him?" asked Jeffrey.

"We'll catch him. Or bust a cinch trying," replied Capt. McNelly.

Jeffrey replied, "Yes, sir. They're most likely halfway to the Mexican border by now, Captain."

"Maybe but I'm betting they'll stop and try to set up an ambush for us," replied Capt. McNelly. "We will separate at Gonzales. Sgt. Caleb, proceed south. If you reach West Bluff and have not yet spotted them or any sign of them, head to Uvalde."

"Yes, sir, but..."

"But what, Sergeant?"

"Do you plan on joining forces with Major Parker's men?"

"It had crossed my mind."

Caleb wasn't objecting to the idea of more men but as it stood, Uvalde and the neighboring ranchers have already had their fill of trouble. The Aces over Kings Ranch was struggling to rebuild. Charlie Owens was struggling on his farm. There allegedly had been raids and rustling by Asbury and Benson's hired men. Capt. McNelly may need Major Parker and Company D but Uvalde needed him more.

At Gonzales, the men divided. Caleb chose to keep those who had gone with him to Happens Chance.

"What are we doing, Sergeant?" asked Tall Hammner.

"What do you mean what are we doing? We are chasing King Fisher and his men," replied Caleb.

"That's the story anyway. But I'd bet my saddle against a biscuit we are chasing nothing but time. Fisher and his men didn't come this way," stated Tall Hammner.

"I know. Capt. McNelly thinks he's outwitted me. But I read his sign right off. He's hoping before we reach Uvalde that he'll have King Fisher pinned down and we'll hear the shooting and come running in from behind King Fisher and his men."

"Like Chickamauga! Well, I'll be a three legged billy goat!" said Tom Crawford.

"Yup. That's what I figured too."

"So you plan on getting there first?"

"That's right. If I have King Fisher figured right, he and his men will stop near Big Wells. With all those hills and thick mesquite and cactus it's the perfect ambush. Capt. McNelly will have nowhere to go but retreat. And he ain't about to retreat," explained Caleb.

"But that's crazy! They'll be chopped to pieces," said Jeffrey.

"Not if we get there first." Caleb called out. "Johnny!"

"Yes, Caleb, I mean, Sergeant," replied Johnny.

"Do you reckon you know the area well enough to scout without getting killed," asked Caleb.

"Shucks, I can sneak up on a coyote and cut his tail off before he could turn around. Yup. I know that area real well. So do you. That's where we trapped those rustlers with our cows remember?" said Johnny.

"Yeah but you're forgetting one little detail," replied Jeff.

"What's that?"

"I darn near got killed," said Jeffrey.

"Yeah but this time, we will have the advantage. They won't be expecting us and we have more men with us," said Johnny.

Jeffrey raised his eyebrows then rolled his eyes. "Oh, Lord! You are trying to get me killed, ain't you?"

"You coming or not?" laughed Johnny.

"Lead the way!" said Jeffrey. "But if I die, I'm gonna haunt you all the days of your life."

The two young men rode out ahead of the patrol. By now the sun was beginning to set. It would be getting dark soon. The sky was turning pink and purple. White and charcoal gray clouds dotted the horizon like cattle grazing on a prairie.

"Reckon we should set up camp and wait on the others?" asked Jeffrey.

"Yeah, I suppose. Seems the thing to do. Let's look for a good spot. If I'm thinking right, there's a small creek about a mile north. Plenty of cover too. So I doubt anyone looking would see our fire. You ride back and bring the fellas in," suggested Johnny.

"Sure enough. Oh! I like my coffee strong," pestered Jeffrey.

"Will you git?" smiled Johnny.

An hour later, Jeffrey returned with the rest of the patrol. "I smell coffee," said Caleb as he audibly breathed in.

"Yup. It'll be ready shortly. Got some biscuits in the pan too. Just set them on the fire."

"You're going to make some woman a real prize catch one day," joked Caleb.

"Oh, shut up. Where is your coffee cup?" replied Johnny.

"When do you plan to turn north?" asked Tom Crawford.

"First thing in the morning. If I have Fisher figured out right, they're already across the Rio Grande into Mexico. But if he stopped along the way, he and his men will be camped along the Nueces River. Or close by it. Whiskey Jack mentioned a small village of mostly Mexican folk called Casas Siete. It's possible they could be there. But I doubt it. I figure they're in Mexico," Caleb explained.

Johnny noticed Caleb thumbing something in his hand. At a closer look he recognized that it was rosary beads. He smiled and said, "You still have them."

Caleb looked up at Johnny. Puzzled but only briefly. Then looked down into his hands and smiled, "Yup, don't go anywhere without them."

"You miss her, don't you?" said Johnny.

"Miss who? Oh! You mean Grandmother Kataryna. Yup. But that's not why I saved my rosary. I kind of got into the habit you might say. Makes me feel good."

"I miss her too. Her and Ma and Jenny. All of them really. even Tiny. Clumsy ol' galloot. Grandmother couldn't buy a better guard dog."

"Guard dog? More like guard grizzly. He sure is faithful to her."

"I wonder how it is he came about to work on the ranch?" wondered Johnny.

"I'm not sure really. My guess is, he is either one of Abuelo's or Abuela's converts. Or maybe he grew up on the ranch. Who knows? But a better man is hard to find," replied Caleb. Johnny and Caleb were interrupted by Tom Crawford's calling.

"Are you two schoolgirls going to jabber jaw all night? Supper's ready."

That night just as they were bedding down, except Tall Hammner who had drawn first watch, and all was graveyard quiet, out from nowhere, Jeff piped up, "I wonder if she has a beau?"

"What? Who?" replied Caleb startled from a deep sleep.

"Sally. Does she have a beau?"

The camp rang out with laughter.

"Good night, Jeff!" said Caleb.

The camp grew still again. Only the occasional pop and crackle of the fire or snort from one of the horses could be heard.

Morning came too soon. Caleb was still asleep and Jeffrey decided to play a joke on him. "Up and at 'em, boys! We got Yankees on our flank!" Jeffrey cried out.

Caleb sprang to his feet,"Yankees!" Jeff started laughing hysterically. "That'll learn ya! Now we're even."

"Even for what?!" replied Caleb.

"For poking fun at me last night. T'weren't funny," said Jeffrey.

Whiskey Jack was sitting out on the veranda, smoking a cigar and having coffee. He stood up slowly and stared out toward the entrance gate of the Ranchero.

"Hermano!" he called out.

Drew came out onto the veranda. "Looks like Capt. McNelly and all of Company A.

"Yup, looks like he's got his dander up again. Wonder what it is this time?" replied Jack.

Capt. McNelly drew his horse up to a halt at the veranda wall. "Good morning, Captains."

"Morning, Leander. What is it this time? Please get down and join us for breakfast. You men can get in line with the others over yonder by the bunkhouse," said Drew. Capt. McNelly explained the details to both Drew and Jack outside over coffee and before going inside for breakfast. "I didn't feel it prudent to talk of this in front of the women. But there you have it. I'm fed up, Drew. I'm going to snag that coyote and skin him alive!"

"Well, I certainly understand how you feel, Leander. Just thankful no one was injured," said Jack.

"Yes, well it's just pure luck that they weren't," replied Capt. McNelly.

After breakfast they were on their way again. Stopping in Uvalde, at headquarters for Company D, Drew had chosen the following men to ride along:

1. Red Sands
2. Danny Collins
3. Marty Collins
4. Guadalupe Mendoza
5. "Buckshot" John Stiles
6. Mike Gertles
7. Ray Jorganson
8. Rodney Allen
9. Joe Hawker
10. Kyle Wiggins
11. Terrence "Slim" Todd
12. Johnny Brown
13. Jerolde Oaks

And, of course, Whiskey Jack.

Capt. Leander McNelly looked up at Drew, somewhat puzzled."That's it? You're only bringing 14 men?"

"No, 21 actually. I want my boys back. You have Caleb, Tom Crawford, Johnny and Jeff," replied Major Drew Parker.

"That's 18. Who were the other three?" asked Leander H McNelly curiously.

"I'd also like Joe Denton, the one called Tall Hammner and Bull," said Drew.

"Bull? Now see here! I can't let Bull go. He's my best clerk," argued Capt. McNelly.

"He's a better Ranger. He craves the job. I want him and any of the others that choose to come I'll take as well."

"Why you Shanghai Pete! Next I reckon you'll be wanting my horse or maybe my job as well!"

Drew laughed. "Nope, you can have your job and keep it. Though you are a pretty good judge of horse flesh you can also keep her."

"Thank God! Anything else?"

"Nope. I just want my Rangers back. The men who paved the way for you to Austin. They deserve to stay together. Would you agree?"

"Oh, I see. Your precious 21 Rangers. I suppose so but I've a feeling it wouldn't matter to you if I agreed or not."

"You've got that right," chuckled Major Drew Parker.

It was nearing mid-afternoon when a small Army of Texas Rangers noticed a rider tearing upside as he rode his horse to near death speed.

The rider, seeing the formation of Ranges, began waving his sombrero and yelling, "Major Parker! Major Parker!"

Capt. McNelly called the Rangers to a halt as the rider came closer.

"Why, that's Pete Homer! What in heaven's name?" said Drew.

Pete Homer came to a stop in front of Drew's buckskin mare. Pete's horse was soaked with lathering sweat and panting so hard he wheezed.

"Pete! You've nearly killed that horse! What in the name of Texas is wrong?" asked Drew Parker.

"It's the High Solara, Major! Bandits! Ol' Jack Bartlett sent me for help. He said he believes it's that outlaw King Fisher and his bunch. They're putting up quite a fight. Thank heavens you thought to send some of your Rangers to warn us," said Pete.

"Rangers? What Rangers?" replied Drew.

"Sgt. Caleb and his men. You mean you didn't know?" asked Pete.

"I did not," replied Drew looking sternly at Capt. Leander H McNelly.

"I hadn't figured they would make such good time, Drew. They're a day ahead of plans," explained Capt. Leander H McNelly.

"Maybe so. But you could have at least mentioned it. So help me Leander, if anything happens to one of my boys!"

"No need to worry about that, Parker. At least I don't think so anyway. Why when I left they had those outlaws thinking twice about hitting the High Solara. That Sgt. Caleb was shouting out orders like ol' Bobby Lee but I am not sure how long they can hold those outlaws at bay. That's why they sent me. We drew straws and I lost," said Pete Homer sorrowfully.

Major Parker called for another horse for Pete as they prepared to ride for the High Solara. Capt. Leander H McNelly turned in his saddle and shouted. "Alright, Rangers! Remember, no quarter! Make every shot count!! All for Texas!"

Smoke could be seen off in the distance where the High Solara should be. As the Rangers neared the High Solara, Capt. McNelly called the Rangers to an abrupt halt.'

"Major Parker, you take Company D to the east. I will take company A to the west and we'll circle around them. Your men clockwise, we will circle counterclockwise and close in tighter with each time around the clock. We'll choke them into a bunch. Tight like a clump of grapes. Then smash them. Only do not kill that King Fisher. I want him. He will hang. But I want him to suffer his defeat," ordered Capt. Leander H McNelly.

"Right you are!" replied Major Drew Parker. "Company D," he shouted. "Take your weapons! Let's ride!"

Whether it was luck or some devilish sixth sense, King Fisher managed to slip through the trap that McNelly had fashioned. Like a steer just one step ahead of the lariat's loop.

The outlaws had put up a fierce fight. Showing no remorse nor fear. Either out of pure meanness or because they knew that the Rangers would show no mercy as well. The fighting was so intense that when the shooting was over, McNelly's ears still hummed from the sound of gunfire.

"Boy! Are we sure glad you fellas came when you did!" said Jeffrey. Spinning the cylinder on his revolver, he reported, "Two shots left and one shotgun shell. Now that is what I call cutting it close."

"Are you all right, boy?" asked Major Drew Parker with deep concern.

"I wasn't worried. Much," smiled Jeff with saucer sized eyes.

"I don't mind saying it. I was plumb scared. I'll bet we ain't got 50 rounds among the whole lot of us," replied Johnny.

Caleb was standing next to Jack Bartlett of the High Solara. They were assessing the damages. "Well, all said and done, I say we fared pretty well. Only two of my hands are dead. For that I grieve but only slight fire damage to the barn, a few windows in the house busted out. They sure did a job on my hay but I think we'll manage. Thanks to you, Rangers," said Jack Bartlett.

"Glad we arrived when we did. Looks like ol' King Fisher will be licking his wounds for quite some time. By my count, 16 of his men will be riding another range for the rest of eternity," said Caleb.

"You're taking this too personally, Leander. King Fisher isn't toying solely with you. He's toying with the whole of the Texas Rangers.

He thinks he is pretty good at it but I believe he just sent a message that he didn't want us to understand," explained Major Drew Parker.

"What, pray tell, would that be?" asked Jack Bartlett.

"Jack, why would an outlaw with the whole of the Texas Rangers on his tail stop out of his way and risk capture to hit your ranch?" said Drew Parker.

"I don't know. Maybe because he's a no good skunk. He's an outlaw, Drew. What other excuse does he need?" replied Jack Bartlett.

"Could be he and his men are hungry and also in need of fresh horses. It's for sure he won't find anything in Mexico and I'm fairly sure his guarantee of any protection from the Mexican Federales is growing pretty thin. They'll want the payment for protecting him and his bunch and I'm pretty certain he doesn't have anything for them. He hasn't any money," explained Drew Parker.

"You could be right. If you are then my guess is he'll be forced to cross back over into Texas. When he does we will have him for sure. If you can't pay the Federales, it's sure he can't pay his men and they'll be drifting away mighty quick. Maybe we have squeezed them into a corner at last," said Leander H McNelly.

"Maybe. Only one way to know for sure. We'll have to set and bait a trap for the infamous King Fisher," said Major Drew Parker.

"Bait? What sort of bait?" asked Sgt. Caleb Parker.

"Money of course!" said Capt. Whiskey Jack. "Money is what he needs more than horses."

"Okay. But where are we going to get this bait!" asked Capt. Leander H McNelly.

"Beats me. You're the brains of the outfit. You figure that part out," laughed Major Drew Parker.

"Who says the money has to be real?" piped in Johnny.

"Not real? Are you suggesting counterfeiting money?" asked Jack Bartlet.

"Not at all. I mean, it would be careless to risk actual money. But if we made it look as if we were."

"Explain," said Capt. Leander H McNelly.

"We put out the word then we let them see the money being loaded onto the stage from Uvalde to Brownsville or maybe Laredo. Only it won't be money. It will be a trunk full of paper with a layer of real money on the top. Make sure folks can see it. Then we sweeten it with a trail drive of 20 horses or so from our spread." Johnny suggested looking at Drew.

"That's quite a gamble, Johnny. Especially with our horses," said Whiskey Jack.

"Not really. I mean it isn't really a gamble. Seeing that what we're the ones stacking the deck."

"I like it. It could very well work," said Drew. "How did you become so darn smart and where did you learn about stacking the deck?"

"Good upbringing, I reckon. As for stacking the deck, every man has some secrets he'd rather not divulge," smiled Johnny.

"I reckon you're right. Besides the skill of poker is a handy tool for any Ranger," smiled Major Drew Parker.

This stage would leave Uvalde at 11 am sharp as usual for Brownsville with four stops on the way to Laredo, then from Laredo to Brownsville. It would be a four-day trip to Brownsville by stagecoach figuring 30 miles per day.

The talk was meant to purposely leak out and reached the ears of King Fisher and his men. Not only could he use the money, it was hoped he would not pass up the chance to give Capt. McNelly's pride another black eye. If the outlaws did notice the small guard for the stage, it might embolden them to attack.

"Maybe they have. Who knows? Maybe the Army will meet them on the way," said Tall Hammner.

"Did you see all that money? Enough to tempt any man," said Johnny.

"I hear you. I might be tempted myself, if it weren't for those Texas Rangers. I can handle that Yankee Army. But the Rangers. No sir. Not me," said Red Sands.

The young men were talking loud enough to grab anyone's attention which was their plan.

As the day grew older, the stage was getting closer to Big Wells. By now there were 18 Rangers escorting the stage. They would meet the remaining three Rangers at Big Wells for a total of 21. Their first stop would be at Big Wells. Capt. McNelly had devised a plan that at every fifth mile of the journey the stage would be met by three additional Rangers for escort. As there would be three Rangers escorting the stagecoach out of Uvalde Capt. McNelly had already sent the 18 other Rangers ahead. His thinking was to only draw enough attention to the stage to add curiosity and provide a false appearance of vulnerability. They gave the stagecoach a half-day head start then the rest of companies would follow behind. Meanwhile, Johnny, Jeff, Red Sands, Mike Gertles and Tall Hammner were having a pretend friendly game of poker and purposefully talking louder than usual making comments regarding the stage and that big box full of money.

"Kind of risky if'n you asked me. I would have waited and wired for the Army to come get it," said Jeffrey.

"Maybe we're wasting our time. I half expected to be neck deep in trouble. Surely had King Fisher got the news he'd be upon us before now," said Tall Hammner.

"I reckon Jeffrey wasn't convincing enough," said Johnny jokingly.

"We still have a ways to go. We will make Laredo by 4 pm tomorrow. So don't go get too comfortable," warned Red Sands.

"Reckon I'll get a fire going and get something together to feed all of ya. Someone fetch a canteen or two of water for the coffee," suggested Mike Gertles.

"I sure hope the rest of the fellows get here soon. It may be just me but I've got the feeling on the back of my neck that we're being watched," said Red Sands. "Someone bring those horses in closer. Just in case."

"You're nervous?" exclaimed Ray Burson, the stage driver, "Imagine how I feel. There is supposed to be $23,000 in that box."

Two hours later the rest of the Rangers had found the camp.

"No sign of trouble?" Major Parker asked of Red Sands.

"No sir and it's got me worried. I am glad to see you."

"That is odd. Perhaps that last fight with him had taken some of the wind out of his sails," said Capt. McNelly.

"Perhaps but I wouldn't count on it. If King Fisher is anything in the way of the outlaw I believe he is he will ambush us before we get there. He'll want these horses if not for anything else," said Drew Parker.

"That may be, Major, but from all the gab I've been hearing, he's somewhat of a Robin Hood hero to some of the folks in these parts. He'll most likely have ears and eyes on every boulder and cactus from here to Chihuahua," said Red Sands.

"You could be right. But a Robin Hood? I think not. Just because he doles out a few coins here and there or buys a drink for folks doesn't excuse the fact that he has robbed, killed, rustled and burned the folks out on this side of the border. In Texas, he's nothing more than an outlaw. Although I am concerned by the prospect of his notoriety among the Mexican citizens of both sides of the border. It might be to our benefit to send some ears and eyes of our own ahead into Laredo," said Major Drew Parker.

"I agree," said Capt. McNelly. "We could wait a day or two. To let them settle down some in Laredo. That should give them time enough to learn of anything and then send word back to us. Though I am wanting King Fisher to hurry up and get on with it."

"Be careful what you wish for. I want him too. But not at the expense of losing any men," said Major Parker.

"Neither do I but I am a realist. Losing men or at least having a few wounded is an inevitability that comes with the job. The men know that as well," replied Capt. McNelly.

"True. But I still don't have to accept it. I want us to be the ones with the jump ahead," said Drew.

"If he is around and he does know where we are and hasn't hit us by now could be a sign that he either hasn't the men or fresh mounts. He might not ever attack," said Red.

"If he is around, it's because he plans to hit us. He'll attack sure enough," said Capt. McNelly.

"If he is around I hate to say it hurts my pride some but this King Fisher fella is either part Apache or he isn't in these parts. Because I have yet to see any sign of anything being in these parts for weeks. And I like to think of myself as a good tracker," said Matthew McDonald.

"What if he never was? What if he stayed on the other side of the Rio Grande paralleling us? If he has eyes and ears like you think everywhere he won't have to cross over until he's good and ready," suggested Jeffrey.

"That could be as well. He may already be in Laredo. That's pretty good thinking for a kid," said Caleb.

"Only one way to find out. Forget sending scouts ahead to Laredo. We aren't going to Laredo," said Capt. Leander H McNelly.

"Not going to Laredo, sir? I don't understand," said one of the Rangers.

"No, we're going to chum the water some. Bypass Laredo and continue on. Maybe stop at San Isidro then continue on to Brownsville. We will force him to cross over the border and attack us. His curiosity, pride or whatever it is that motivates him will get the better of him. He will feel I've won and he won't stand for that. So he'll cross, I promise you," said Capt. McNelly.

The ambush came half unexpected. The rarely used road to San Isidro dipped sharply downhill for almost a quarter mile with cactus and a mixture of mesquite and scrub oaks to the right and south and a long sandy hill laden with more cactus, boulders and mesquite to their left and north. Dust filled the air and it became difficult to see. The air became a kaleidoscope of yellow, brown, gray and white as the dust rose high into the sky. The entourage was nearly at the bottom when the first shot rang out splintering the foothold to which Ray Burson had his right foot.

"Ambush!" someone yelled.

"Keep going, men. Yeehaw!" yelled Capt. McNelly.

The Rangers began firing up at the top of the hills and galloping hard behind the stage. The rooster tail of dust was making it hard to see just where they were shooting and making it hard for man and horse to breath. King Fisher had picked a perfect spot for an ambush. The stage was nearing the bottom of the steep downgrade when suddenly a loud roar like thunder filled the air. A shower of dirt and stone rain down upon them. Dynamite! The outlaws had them trapped. King Fisher's men had caused a rockslide. The road was blocked.

"Oh God forbid! They're killing my horses!" cried Ray Burson, the stagecoach driver.

"Cut 'em loose! Someone give him cover!" yelled Major Drew Parker. The air was filled with gunfire, screaming horses and shouting men.

"We'll have to use the stagecoach for cover. We have to roll it on its side. Come on, men!" yelled Major Parker.

Capt. McNelly yelled to the rest of the Rangers. "Take cover in those thickets! You men, get those horses to cover!"

Rodney Allen, Joe Hawker and Tall Hammner quickly drove the herd of horses deep into the thicket of mesquite and scrub oak. Bullets hummed and whined all about them clipping and pruning limbs and leaves. The rest of the Rangers had found cover either around the stagecoach or behind the brush and cactus or behind boulders.

"Well, Leander, you wanted him to attack. Looks like you got your wish!" shouted Capt. Whiskey Jack.

"Oh, shut up! What I want to know is, how he knew when and where to hit us!" exclaimed Capt. Leander H McNelly.

"If we live through this, that's a question I want the answer to as well," said Major Drew Parker.

The shooting suddenly stopped and all became eerie quiet. A voice came from the top of the hill. "The great Capt. Leander H McNelly and his little McNelly's. Looks like the bold gallant Texas Rangers have met their Waterloo! But I am a fair man. Your little McNelly's might have a chance to ride out of here providing you leave the money and horses behind! I also want you too, McNelly. You and that famous Drew Parker. I want you two as well. It's time to see just how brave and tough you two really are!" yelled King Fisher.

"That's a very tempting offer, Fisher. But I'm going to have to decline. You understand," yelled Capt. McNelly.

"Oh sure. I understand. You're not so tough without backup. Oh well, you can't say I didn't give your men an even break!"

"I'd hardly call an ambush an even break. We both know you have no intentions of letting anyone out of here alive!" yelled Capt. McNelly.

"Perhaps! But one may never know now, will they?!" yelled King Fisher.

Jeff stood up and yelled. "Here's my answer, you son of a pig!" He began firing his rifle in the direction of King Fisher's voice.

"All for Texas!" yelled another Ranger and began firing as well. Instantly, every Ranger yelled and began in with the shouting. "All for Texas!"

Surprised and stunned at the reaction of the Rangers and furious at their defiance, King Fisher, overwhelmed with anger, ordered a charge down the slope of the high hill. A mistake he would regret. The Rangers also charged on foot at the sight of the outlaws. The hill being so steep made it somewhat cumbersome for the horses and slowed their downhill descent. On the other hand, the Rangers could move quickly being on foot and could shoot more accurately.

Although the outlaws were no strangers to gunfights and were for the most part good horsemen, they still had a tough go at it this day. The Rangers were mostly all seasoned war veterans. They were accustomed to tough terrains and fighting on foot. Many was the time they had to fight on foot in spite of being cavalrymen.

Red Sands was standing next to Jeffrey Boxer behind the stagecoach. For the moment they had a good spot at the stage's front end section and next to the tongue. They were suddenly distracted by someone calling, "Hey, Jeff, Red!" It was Rangers Rodney Allen, Joe Hawker and Tall Hammner. "Come on! We found a way to get around behind those hombres," said Ranger Joe Hawker.

"One of the horses spooked. As I was chasing him down, I found a way to get around behind them. Totally unseen," said Rodney Allen.

Rodney Allen had found a gully nearly 9 feet deep and over 200 yards in length before it started to level out, almost directly on the road just behind the rock slide. The thicket was so dense, it was hard to be seen even from the top of the hill.

"Well, what are we waiting for?" said Red. "Let's go!"

"Yeehaw! I'm with you. Let's go skunk shooting!" said Jeffrey Boxer.

The battle was intensifying and becoming mostly hand-to-hand. King Fisher and what remaining men he had with him, found it difficult to do much shooting in fear they may kill their own men. Suddenly, the outlaws began scattering. From the top of the hill could be heard more shouting and shooting. Rangers Red Sands, Jeffrey Boxer, Rodney Allen, Joe Hawker and Tall Hammner came charging along the crest of the hill from west to east. "All For Texas! Eat lead!" yelled Ranger Rodney Allen.

Vigor and energy swelled up anew in the now weary from hand to hand fighting Rangers.

"Alright, Rangers, mount up! Let's get after 'em!" shouted Sergeant Caleb.

"Rangers ride! Cut 'em down! One and all!" yelled Capt. McNelly.

When the battle was over and all of the Rangers regrouped the now turned upright stagecoach was refitted with horses. An account was given. Six Rangers dead, four wounded. Nine outlaws dead. The Rangers lost four horses. King Fisher and his men had paid dearly as well and none the richer to show for it. They buried the outlaws where they lay. The bodies of the dead Rangers were loaded into the stagecoach and taken to Brownsville where they were given a proper Rangers burial. King Fisher had once again escaped Capt. McNelly and his little McNelly's.

**December 20, 1871**

Sand Creek, Colorado, had taken on a wintry landscape. Snow covered the planes like a heavy blanket. The scattered cedars and spruce pine drooped cumbersomely with snow laden branches. Charlie Welch and Ed Lamb had never seen such a sight. Sure, they had seen snow before but had lived in Texas their entire lives. Snow didn't last in Texas. As the day drew nigh, Charlie felt overwhelmed by the majesty and beauty of it all. The fading light of day gave a silvery blue tint to everything as the snow reflected the light in all directions.

"I'll be happy to get back to Texas. Won't you?" asked Ed Lamb.

"What's that?" The sound of Ed's voice pulled Charlie from his wintry trance.

"I was saying I can't wait to get back to Texas. How about you?"

"I suppose. To tell you the truth, I sort of like this country. They tell me it's even more magnificent further north," replied Capt. Charlie Welch.

"I'll admit, it does have its charm. But I miss Texas. That Miss Waters is a fine woman, don't you think? Those are two fine sons she has as well. Wouldn't you say?" said Ed.

"Humm? Oh. Yes, yes she is," agreed Charlie.

"You don't fool me, Charlie Welch," chuckled Ed Lamb. "You are smitten with her and you know it."

Charlie grunted. "She is a fine woman that's true. You do have to admit for a widow woman she has done a fair job at keeping her home and raising fine boys. Their Pa would be proud of them. It took a lot of guts and determination to do what they did. Not many boys their age would have even thought of such a venture. Yup, fine boys."

"Ya but they nearly lost it all too. Not saying the least almost getting themselves killed in the process," replied Ed.

"But they didn't, did they? Now that's something to hang your hat on," said Charlie with a hint of pride in his voice.

"Only because we jumped into the mix. Had we not, never know what might have happened."

"That don't figure into it. Not the way I see it. Somehow I have the feeling Sheriff John Strap and his boys underestimated those two youngsters. That Danny has sand," said Charlie.

A voice came from the back door of the house. "Dinner! Ma says she ain't waiting!" yelled young Gail Waters.

"Now there's trouble for you," laughed Ed. "Somehow I think old Brett Lasadore got off easy."

Charlie smiled. "You may be right."

Morning came to Sand Creek. The sunlight beat through the window of the room Charlie and Ed had been using next to the tack room of the horse barn. Charlie wasn't sure if it was because of the openness of the country or because the snow made everything so pronounced as the reflected sunlight bounced all around. Even the air was crisper and smelled and felt fresher and new. He wasn't sure if it was the climate or Amanda Waters good cooking or maybe the working on the ranch or all of it combined. But somehow he felt stronger and full of life. He smiled as he splashed water in his face and scrubbed his face, neck and hands. He dried off with a towel and stared out of the window. Then his smile turned into a frown of curiosity. Three men came riding up the snow- covered wagon road and onto the ranch. They rode up to the front porch and stopped abruptly.

Charlie could see Amanda standing on the porch. She was holding a double barrel shotgun in her hands. Charlie kicked a bed in which Ed was sleeping. Ed sat up with a jerk a questioning look in his eyes.

"Get up. I think we have trouble," said Charlie as he strapped on his gun belt. He put on his wool lined heavy coat and walked outside careful to stay behind the three men and out of sight. The snow was soft and masked the sound of his footsteps.

"You do know that it has snowed, Mr. Grueber. Surely you could have taken that into consideration," said Amanda.

"My job is not to take considerations. Especially with those who were avoiding the bank. I've come to foreclose, Mrs. Waters. You have three days to vacate. I am sorry," said Bob Grueber, the banker.

"Three days! Surely you are joking! Why couldn't you have come here sooner? It seems you have seen fit to do so today? If the matter was so important to you, why didn't you ride out here before now? And with armed escort? You must consider me a real tough cookie," exclaimed Amanda.

"I don't need any armed escorts. These two men are here on another matter. It seems your two sons are wanted in Texas for murder and robbery," Bob Grueber's words were cut short from a voice coming from behind them.

"Sheriff John Strap! Howdy, Sheriff. You working for the banks now? Or have you made a deal with this grub worm or Grueb. What is your name again?" said Charlie Welch.

"Grueber! And no. There is no deal between us," stated Bob Grueber defensively.

"I see. But you somehow saw fit to come out here today coincidently with these two. Come now, Mr. Grubworm. Surely from the looks of things you are not accustomed to spending many hours out of doors and especially out-of-doors in the cold and in the snow as well. Clearly you are not accustomed to riding judging by the way you're sitting. Backside hurting?" Charlie went on.

Grueber was getting angry from Charlie's criticism and implications. "Just who are you, mister? This is no concern of yours."

"I beg to differ. My name is Capt. Charles Welch Texas Ranger. As for young Danny and Samuel Waters being wanted in Texas that comes as news to me."

"A Texas Ranger? Why I..."

"You what?" interrupted Capt. Charlie Welch. "You had no idea or you weren't told I might be here? Hold it right there! Strap," said Charlie. John Strap eased his hand near his revolver while Grueber and Charlie were talking.

"That goes for you too, mister," came Ed's voice from around the corner of the house. He was holding a shotgun and pointing it at Sheriff John Strap's partner or deputy. He did not care which. "One move from you and I'll take your head off!"

"Now see here! Don't you try threatening me!" said Sheriff John Strap. "Those two boys are wanted in Abilene for killing Brett Lasadore and stealing over $3,000 known to be on Lasadore's body at the time."

"Uhuh, their money. And it is not for murder or robbery. At least half the town of Abilene can testify to that. But if that isn't enough, we can get a statement from the buyer of the cattle," said Capt. Charlie Welch.

"If what you say is so, how is it that the Texas Rangers got involved?" asked Bob Grueber.

"What do you care? You have no affiliations with Sheriff Strap anyway. At least that's what you said. Or was I mistaken?" said Charlie.

From the way Bob Grueber was reacting to Charlie's question, it was clear to Charlie that there had been some sort of arrangement made between himself and Sheriff John Strap. Exactly what that arrangement was, was not clear. Perhaps only payment for taking Strap to the ranch or perhaps a cut of the $3,000 that he most likely would never see. John Strap would most assuredly kill Bob Grueber once he had the money. It was also apparent that neither Bob Grueber nor the other man were in any way expecting two Texas Rangers to be at the Waters Ranch. Only John Strap would have been aware of that.

"That's all right, Capt. Welch. I've got the Sheriff in my sights. If Mr. Grueber is looking for easy money, he'll have a hell of a time collecting from a dead man!" Danny Waters was perched in the upstairs bedroom window. The muzzle from his 44 caliber Henry repeating rifle was leveled right at Sheriff John Strap.

"Here's how it's going to play out, Strap. You, Mr. Grueber here and that lackey with you. You're gonna turn around and ride out of here. Tomorrow, Mrs. Waters and I will ride into town and make her payment on her ranch. Then in three days Danny, Samuel, Ranger Ed Lamb and I will head out for Texas. I will personally see that the circuit judge reviews the claims you have on them. If what you say is true then justice will be served. But I think you'll discover that your claims are invalid. After which, if I see you within 1000 miles of Abilene, I will shoot you down like the rabid dog you are. Remember what I said back in those canyons in New Mexico, your days as a lawman are over, Strap. I will send word from Texas to California of what a low down dog you are. Now get!"

Sheriff John Strap's right hand quivered. He had, for just a second, considered drawing on Charlie. But with all the iron pointing at him he'd thought better of it. Besides something about this Capt. Charlie Welch's calmness and matter of factness told him he would not be an easy takedown.

"We're going, Ranger. But this ain't over. Remember, this is Colorado. You have no jurisdiction here without the Governor's request or approval. You're just another man with a gun," replied Sheriff John Strap.

"I could say the same for you, Strap. But if it's a showdown you're wanting, dismount and we'll end it all right here, right now. But Strap let me tell you this, I promise you, you will lose. So what'll it be?" said Charlie Welch.

"I can wait," sneered Strap as he wheeled his horse around and started away from the ranch. Bob Grueber and the other man followed behind.

Capt. Charlie Welch started for the steps of the front porch. When Amanda's eyes grew wide and she gasped. "Charlie!"

Capt. Charlie Welch spun around and in one smooth easy movement his revolver was out and leveled. Sheriff John Strap had wheeled his horse around and was galloping toward the house. His face red with rage and his revolver out and pointing at Captain Charlie Welch. His first shot whined over Charlie's head and striking a porch post. Capt. Charlie Welch crouched to almost a kneeling position from the porch steps and fired two quick shots. John Strap cried out and fell backward in the saddle. His head struck the horses rump and bounced two or three times. Then he slid from his saddle, one foot still in the stirrup, to the ground. His horse dragged him and left a long, dotted red line across the snow-covered lawn. The horse came to a stop within a few short yards of the house.

**Austin, Texas**
**The office of Asbury and Benson**

At the office of Asbury and Benson, William Asbury was furious. He was banging his fist on the top of his desk.

"What in the world is your problem, Bill? I can hear you clean across the hallway. Have you been drinking?" exclaimed Theodore Benson.

"What's my problem? Here. Look at these account statements. We're going broke! That's what my problem is! Those damned Texas Rangers!" said William Asbury.

"We are not going broke, Bill. I have already gone over all of our accounts. As far as the Texas Rangers, we'll just have to ease up a bit. We can wait on a lot of our foreclosures if that's what's bothering you. We'll just have to raise the interest rates on late payments. That's all. It may be to our benefit anyway. Relax else you'll give yourself a heart attack," explained Theodore Benson.

"I'm sure it would just break your heart if I did. You know? Sometimes I wonder whose side you're on!"

"What kind of remark was that? I'm trying to make this company a success. That won't happen if we have Texas Rangers shadowing our every move and hiring paid gun hands to chase off all of our debtors is not going to help any. It's 1871 for crying out loud. Times are changing. Instead of bucking the law why not use it to our benefit? Folks are more likely to cooperate if a lawman delivers papers to them instead of half-drunk happy goons," said Theodore Benson.

"Are you suggesting we hire the Texas Rangers? Huh? That would be a laugh."

"No. But we could hire reputable men. Or maybe an agency like the Pinkertons. We just can't continue to run roughshod over all of Texas. The country's growing, Bill, and so are the Rangers. Not to mention other law enforcement."

"The times are not changing. You are! You've gone soft. Maybe you're happy with being mediocre but not me! Sometimes I wonder why we ever became partners," said William Asbury.

"Ha! That's easy. My old man's leaving me $14,000 when he died. That's how we became partners. That and your scheme to buy up all the land after the war by swindling folks. Just how long did you think folks would sit by and let you walk all over them?!"

"I was perfectly within my right. Those fools could not keep their end of the loan agreements," said William Asbury.

“Especially when you’re hiring men to run off or rustle their stock or arrange for mysterious crop or bonfires. No, they couldn’t keep their end of the agreements. Not with all that going on!”

“I didn’t hear you complaining any! Especially when the money came in!”

“Money from stolen cattle! Or resales on land we stole by cheating folks! No, I guess I didn’t complain. Partly because I didn’t know until afterwards! But that was before the Texas Rangers were reinstated. Just how long do you think it’s gonna be before one of those hired men are called and starts singing like a canary? I’m telling you. The Rangers have done such a thorough job of cleaning house that outlaws are avoiding Texas. Why even the Jansen brothers have said they’d rather travel through Indian Territory in Oklahoma than risk the Rangers coming after them. No, one day this type of business is going to blow up in our faces. Why do you think those men are called outlaws in the first place? If they have no respect or concern for honest working folks, what makes you think they’ll respect you and your orders? Don’t be surprised, my friend, if one of your dogs turns and bites your nose off!” argued Theodore Benson.

“Are you done preaching, Reverend?”

“Go ahead. Poke fun at me. But I’m right. You know it too!” said Benson.

Blake Saunders knocked on the door to Capt. Leander H McNelly’s office.

“Come in, boy, confound it! No need to act like a nervous woodpecker on a fence post !” exclaimed Capt. Leander H McNelly.

“Excuse me, Captain.”

“Did you do something wrong?”

“No, sir.”

“Then there’s no need to be excused is there?”

“No, sir, I reckon not. I’m glad you’re in a good mood. Unfortunately it will be short lived. Someone has stolen our entire payroll, Captain.

I've checked and rechecked and checked again. But the money is sure enough gone."

"What? There has to be some mistake! How can $23,000 come up missing? Check again!" said Capt. McNelly.

Nervously, Blake Saunders took a step backward. "There's no point in it, Captain. I swear I looked everywhere. It's gone sir. We've been robbed," said Ranger Blake Saunders.

"Robbed? How can that be? How am I going to explain how someone stole $23,000 from the Texas Rangers?" exclaimed Capt. McNelly.

"There's one more thing, Captain."

"What?"

"I believe I know who may have stolen it. That weaselly looking clerk, Clifford Thompson. He's nowhere to be found either."

"Thompson? That piss ant? You've got to be kidding. I'm impressed. I didn't know he had it in him. Where was he last seen and when?" said Capt. Leander H McNelly.

"Yesterday, sir. In the accounting room. He's the one who signed for the money when it came in," explained Ranger Blake Saunders.

"Get me all the information you can on Thompson's activities for the past two weeks," said McNelly.

"That could take all day! And he's getting farther away as we speak. But you're wrong about one thing, Captain. Clifford Thompson's no piss ant. He's a dead shot with a six-gun and an excellent horseman."

"So why are you standing there? Get busy! Now!"

"On it, sir!" said Ranger Blake Saunders.

Capt. McNelly mumbled to himself, cursing. "Don't this just take the cake? How in blazes am I going to explain to the governor how the Texas Rangers managed to be robbed of $0.23 cents much less $23,000? I'm getting too old for this!"

Capt. McNelly was still ranting and raving with himself when Capt. Charlie Welch and Ed Lamb walked into the office.

"Ed, something tells me we should have stayed another week in Abilene," said Charlie as he looked at Capt. McNelly. "What in the name of Sam Houston has you in such an outrage, Leander?"

Leander H McNelly began to explain about the money and how the clerk, Clifford Thompson, had absconded with it. Charlie Welch whistled out loud and tried to fight back a laugh. Not that the missing money was a funny matter. It was the mental picture of Clifford Thompson stealing the money and then redness of Capt. Leander H McNelly's face. Somehow the whole thing seemed funny.

"Thompson? My Lord, who would have thought he had that much sand? I don't know whether to be angry or impressed with the man," said Charlie.

Capt. McNelly grew even more outraged.

"Blast it, Charlie, this is no laughing matter! But maybe it is to you. You have resented my taking over of the Rangers right from the start. Maybe you think I'm getting my just rewards?"

"Oh shut up, you billowing bag of wind! I feel nothing of the sort. I retired! Remember? You gall darn idjit!" shouted Capt. Charlie Welch.

Leander McNelly stared at Charlie. Then gradually began to chuckle harder and harder until he burst into laughter.

"The irony of the whole thing is I too was impressed with Thompson. Who would have thought," he gasped, "who would have thought of him of all people," Capt. Leander H McNelly was now laughing so hard he couldn't finish what he was trying to say.

Charlie Welch walked over to a corner table that held a crystal flask of brandy and poured three glasses full. He handed one to Capt. McNelly and the other to Ed Lamb. "A toast! To Clifford Thompson. May he rot in hell."

"Here, here!" chuckled Capt. Leander H McNelly wiping his eyes..

"So naturally we have to go after him. Who do you have in mind?" asked Ed Lamb.

"I've been thinking about just that very thing and I keep coming up blank. Who do you have in mind? If we weren't spread so thin," said Capt. Leander H McNelly.

"Well, me and two other newer Rangers. It's going to have to be in written orders coming from you. As it is, the two I have in mind are in Company D Major Parker's command."

"Major Parker's? You love tormenting me, don't you? Who are they?" sighed Capt. McNelly.

"Two young ornery galloots. They're perfect for the job. They could blend in anywhere and never be suspected of as lawmen. They're good with pistol and rifle, excellent horsemen and conniving as a couple foxes. Rangers Rodney Allen and Joe Hawker. Give me those two and if Thompson hasn't caught a ship to Bolivia by now we'll catch him," said Ed Lamb.

A couple laughs came out of McNelly as he considered that idea. "Bolivia?" chuckled McNelly. "Thompson is not that smart. I hope."

"He was smart enough up till now. Don't sell him short," said Charlie Welch.

"Right," replied McNelly. He chuckled a couple more times.

Ed looked at McNelly then shook his head. He had never seen McNelly find anything so funny before. Charlie Welch looked from one man to the other. He hoped they would have an easy time catching Thompson.

**Four Days Later**
**Uvalde, Texas**
**Major Andrew Parker Commanding**
**Texas Rangers Headquarter's Company D**

"I really appreciate this, Drew. Though I do not want to be in your shoes when you have to tell the men," said Ed Lamb.

"Well, it may sound unfair and it most likely is. But my Rangers' pay will be covered by the Peña Ranchero. We'll be alright. I just hope this doesn't rip the Rangers apart as a whole. It's no easy thing to ask a man to risk his life and not receive pay of some sort. I wish I could do the same for all the Rangers," said Major Drew Parker.

"You got that right. Maybe the governor can authorize some sort of recompense for the others if anything," said Ed Lamb.

Surprised, yet not surprised, Drew Parker was once again reminded of the character and caliber of men he possessed under his command at Company D. Not one Ranger would accept any pay from the

Peña Ranchero. Ranger Red Sands was elected spokesman for the men. "Major, it just ain't fair to the other boys. Mind you, we are truly obliged but we couldn't in good conscience take any money. If one suffers, we all suffer. Like Capt. McNelly once said we are all brothers. Please thank Señora Kataryna for us. We eat well; we have a nice roof over our heads. I reckon we'll get by."

"I'm mighty proud of each and all of you men. I am truly blessed to have such an array of stand-up men in my command. But I will be insulted if you men will not at least accept a case of the Peña Ranchero's finest brandy. From the cellar of my grandfather, the late Don Miguel Peña," said Drew Parker.

Ranger Red Sands cleared his throat. "I doubt any one of us would want to insult you. No sir. We sure wouldn't want to do that," smiled Red.

**Galveston, Texas**

"Just what makes you so all fired positive that Thompson would head for Galveston?" Ed Lamb asked of Ranger Rodney Allen.

"Well, Sarge, didn't you mention Bolivia to the Captain? Besides Thompson craves attention. He likes to be liked. If I wanted to live it up, I'd go where the fun is and women and money are loose. Maybe even gamble on might. If I were inclined to go someplace like Bolivia, Galveston is the logical place. There are ships leaving every other day to Cuba, Venezuela, Mexico and Bolivia. Not only that but Joe here said Thompson mentioned Galveston once in a card game when we was in Austin. So Galveston has to be the place."

"Humm, well it looks like we have quite a task before us. Look at this place! Have you ever seen such a place?!"

"Yup. New Orleans. Remind me sometime to tell you about it. Especially a place called the Top Hat. This looks a lot like New Orleans. I'd say we should look in all of the casinos and body houses first. That's where I'd go if I were Clifford Thompson," said Joe Hawker.

"If you were Thompson? My hind end! You'd go there regardless, you hound," laughed Ranger Rodney Allen.

"Joke if you will but I'll bet we find him there."

"In that case we'll check the docks. Maybe we should find out what ships are due to set sail soon and if Thompson's booked passage on any of them," suggested Ed Lamb.

"Well, Sarge, if he has it's a cinch he didn't use his own name," said Joe Hawker.

"And it's a cinch that a man like him will be flashing money all over the place. I would not be at all surprised to find him dead in some alley. And all the money gone," said Ranger Rodney Allen.

Curiously and with great suspicion in his voice Ed Lamb looked at the two young Rangers. "Just what did you two fellas do before you joined the Rangers?"

"Nothing illegal, Sarge. Honest. But we did get around you might say," smiled Joe Hawker.

"You two head south along the piers. I'll take the north end. We'll meet right here in two hours and don't go getting into any mischief. I'd hate to discover that the two of you went and got yourselves locked up in jail or shanghaied," said Ed Lamb. "Yes, sir, Grandpa," Rodney Allen said teasingly.

"I'm serious. Men get shanghaied all the time. Watch each other's back. Two hours, sir," replied Joe Hawker.

As the Rangers parted ways, they began their search. Joe Hawker looked at Rodney Allen and questioned, "Do you suppose that Thompson has already set sail?"

"Maybe. But I doubt he has had the time. There would have had to be a ship departing the moment he arrived. But it probably wouldn't hurt to ask around if one had."

"Mighty hot. I never could understand how it could be so hot so close to all that water. You would think the water would keep things cool. What with the breezes and all," said Joe Hawker.

"Ya, it is. But we ain't stopping for a drink. I know how that will end. One leads to two then 10. Plus the Sergeant said two hours. So we best get to it," said Rodney Allen.

"You know you're not as fun as you used to be. I think Rangering has gone to your head," smiled Joe Hawker.

"Come on. Let's go," replied Allen.

Two hours later hot, thirsty and with sore feet the Rangers met back at the designated area they agreed on.

"Any luck?" asked Ed Lamb.

"None," said Joe Hawker. "There were only two passenger ships. The Lorena and the SS. Lord Buve. They will not be boarding for three more days. I doubt Thompson will be brave enough to risk hanging around for that long."

"I doubt that myself. The only ship I found was the Bark Iris, a German ship from Bremen, Germany. The Captain, a Mr. Rodenberg, was very accommodating. He said he would keep an eye out for Thompson. I gave Capt. Rodenberg a fairly good description of Thompson," said Ed Lamb.

"So now what?" asked Ranger Allen.

"So now we keep on looking. The day isn't over yet and there are at least half a dozen saloons and gambling casinos. Not to mention them other places," replied Ed.

"Yeah! Ain't it something?" said Ranger Allen with a big wide smile.

"It's something alright. I hope we catch this jasper soon. I'd sure like to do some sightseeing," replied Joe Hawker.

"Alright, rein it in, boys. Now let's see where to look first? There. The Blue Sea Gull," said Ed Lamb pointing to a large nautical looking tavern.

"There? Ha!" sneered Ranger Allen.

"Alright, wise guy. Where then? And why not there?" asked Ed Lamb.

"That's most likely a favored tavern by most of the deck hands. It's most likely a real rough sort of establishment. Not likely a place that someone such as Clifford Thompson would patronize. Especially with all the money he would be carrying. He would most certainly end up robbed or killed or both. He wants to feel rich. Hobnob with high society folk. He'll most likely go someplace sporting and fancy like.

Like the Neptune's Palace. Or the Blue Flamingo or maybe the Black Pearl. At least that's where I'd go if I were Thompson."

"Oh, you would, would you? I'm starting to question my judgment of character. I figured you two to be a bit more naïve. But I'm getting a different picture now," said Ed Lamb with a hint of humor in his voice.

They searched the Black Pearl and Blue Flamingo. Clifford Thompson was nowhere to be found. Ed Lamb questioned the Pharaoh dealer at the Black Pearl giving as close a description of Thompson as he could.

"I seem to recall a fella fitting that description. Nice fella. Friend of yours? Only his name wasn't Thompson. It was Shealy. Ivan Shealy. No, no, Ian. Ian Shealy. That's the name! But you're too early. Things don't liven up around here for another three hours. Yes siree, you come round bout nine 9 o'clock and soon you'd be lucky to find standing room. So? I didn't get your name, mister. Perhaps if I see Mr. Shealy I can give him a message for you."

"No, that's okay. We used to be business partners. Perhaps we'll catch up with him later. Right now, we just want to relax and take in the sights," lied Ed Lamb.

"Yes, sir, and there are plenty of sights to behold! Yes, sir. Okay then, good day to you sir," said the Pharaoh dealer as he returned to his work.

Joe Hawker came strolling across the casino floor toward Ed Lamb. His eyes were wide like a child at Christmas time.

"Whew weee! Ain't it grand, Sarge?"

"I must say. I've only but heard of such places until now. We've found him," whispered Ed Lamb.

"Where's Rodney?" asked Joe.

"He isn't with you? Damn it! I told you two..."

"There he is yonder," Joe motioned with his chin.

Ranger Allen came walking briskly across the open casino floor. "I found him, Sarge. He's registered upstairs in room 304."

"Yeah, I know."

"You know? How?" asked Ranger Allen puzzled.

"No, I mean I know he's here. But I didn't know he had a room here. Good job, Ranger. Oh! Speaking of Ranger. Do not tell anyone you're a Ranger. At least, not yet anyway. Got it?"

"Why sure, Sarge. But what do we tell folks if'n they ask?" asked Joe.

"You're old friends and business associates."

"What kind of business?"

"Money management and livestock," replied Ed Lamb. It was as good an excuse as any and Ed Lamb said the first thing that came to his mind.

"How were you sure it was Thompson? I know he didn't register under his real name. Even he isn't that stupid," Joe asked of Ranger Allen.

"Well, between the desk clerk's immediate recognition of his description and the date of checking in it wasn't hard. Why the desk worker pointed right to him in the book. Thompson made one detailed mistake. He should have bought a new hat. When the desk clerk mentioned his boulder hat and pheasant feathers, I knew then it was him. When we played poker, you could tell when Thompson was bluffing by that hat. Because he always stroked the feathers with his fingertips," said Ranger Allen.

"Hey! You know? That's right! Well, I'll be," said Joe in amusement.

Later that evening after the Rangers had a good supper and bath and a fresh change of clothing, they walked back into the casino ready for an entertaining night of fun. With the room filled with a mix of piano music, smells of whiskey and perfume worn by the casino cocktail waitresses combined with the colorful lighting the two young Rangers found it most difficult to concentrate on the job at hand. Rodney Allen and Joe Hawker were nearly lost in the excitement at the roulette wheel. Both were on a winning streak.

Ed Lamb, standing at the bar, had a good line of vision across the entire casino floor.

Ranger Allen was picking up his winnings when he casually glanced up and found himself eye to eye with Clifford Thompson. Thompson was three tables down from him. He had been trying his luck at the dice table. Allen gave Joe Hawker a quick nudge with his elbow. But when he looked up again Clifford Thompson was gone.

"I saw him I tell you. He looked at me as if he had seen a ghost. He was right there! At the dice table," said Ranger Rodney Allen.

Joe looked around the room. "There! Near the stage floor. See? Look for that hat."

Ranger Allen could see the feather adorned boulder hat bobbing through the crowd. Allen waved to Ed Lamb then motioned toward the stage where the dancing girls were about to perform. Ed Lamb nodded and casually waved his hand at waist level to acknowledge he understood.

Dodging and weaving through the crowd the two young Rangers were trying to herd Thompson away from the stage much like cutting a calf out of a herd until Thompson had but only one exit. There, standing like a large stone statue, was Ed Lamb. "You're under arrest, Thompson. Or is it Shealy?" Ed Lamb's voice was clear and thundering. Almost for an instant, as if the room were totally empty, Thompson started to reach into his coat's lapel for a small handgun he had hidden there. Rodney Allen's hand landed with a solid thump on Thompson's shoulder. Thompson froze instantaneously. Rodney Allen thundered loudly. "Well, I'll be hanged! Ian Shealy! How the heck are you!?" Then in a quick low tone Allen continued. "Go for that gun and you're as dead as last night's chicken dinner."

"Okay, okay. You got me. Now what?" said Clifford Thompson.

"Now you know better than to ask a fool question like that. What do you expect is going to happen? Now move along. Slowly and smile," said Rodney Allen. As he reached into Thompson's coat lapel and retrieved a handgun then he chuckled. "You actually intended on using this? Hey, Sarge, maybe I should have let him shoot you with this. All this would have done is sting the Sarge and piss him off real good."

Joe Hawker laughed "I had one of those when I was 10, maybe 11. Used to shoot rats and birds with it. Why hell! We didn't arrest you. We rescued you!"

Everyone in the room laughed.

**December 24**
**Austin, Texas**

"I can't believe it. What on earth ever possessed you to do such a thing?" asked Caleb.

He and Capt. McNelly were talking in McNelly's office. Capt. McNelly had summoned Caleb to his office for this very reason.

"Ed Lamb had wired me from Galveston. He and two other Rangers trailed Thompson there. And none too soon either. Another day or two later and Clifford Thompson would have been long gone. He had booked passage aboard one of the ships there and was due to set sail. They should be here tomorrow or the day after. They're taking the stage. At least Ed Lamb and Ranger Allen have. Ranger Hawker agreed to bring their horses and rode out alone."

"But it's Christmas Eve! Surely you don't plan to try him on Christmas? But I still don't understand why you summoned me here" said Caleb.

"Oh heavens, no. I'm just bringing you up to date. His trial will be after the holidays. Actually, Judge Currly asked for you. He wants to appoint you as defense for Thompson."

"Me? Defense for Clifford Thompson?! Get out of town! Why? Why me?" questioned Caleb.

"You will have to ask Judge Currly about that. Thompson was a Ranger and it would take too long to fetch another attorney from San Antonio. This is an internal affair and should be handled as such. There are one or two things you need to know. Thompson has agreed to turn states evidence in lieu of a lighter sentence. It would appear he did not act alone," explained Capt. McNelly.

"I'd just as soon we hang him and be done with it. The man's a thief. What's more he stole money from his brother Rangers. Wasn't it you who once said you would show no mercy to any Ranger who betrayed his fellow Rangers?"

"You have a shrewd memory, Caleb. Yes, I said that. Or at least something close to that. But this has turned out to be a bit more complicated. We have just pulled the rug out from under that Asbury and Benson

Company. At any rate, you'll have ample time to prepare your case and interview your client. We need Clifford Thompson. Like it or not."

"Gee, thanks," said Caleb sarcastically.

"Don't be like that, son. Even men like Thompson deserve a fair trial. One bad turn a criminal does not make," said Capt. McNelly.

"Oh. Says who?"

"Perhaps you should have a long talk with Judge Frank Currly."

"I know the story. Maybe I have kicked up some sand. But you're right, Captain. I reckon I just let my anger get ahead of me. I will have to seek counsel myself and talk with Sgt. Ed Lamb and the other two Rangers. I just don't want folks thinking the Rangers are hiding anything. It would not look good for it to appear Rangers get a different style of justice than other folk," explained Caleb.

"I understand. But you're right on one account already. Texas Rangers who go bad will get a different style of justice. We are going to set a precedent with this case. That a Ranger who goes bad will be dealt with harsher than the average criminal. He will receive the maximum punishment allowed by law."

------------//------------

**Uvalde, Texas**
**December 25, 1871**
**The Peña Ranchero**

"It's just not right! Oooooo! That Leander McNelly!" Señora Kataryna was furiously ranting over the telegram she had just read. A messenger from Uvalde had arrived at sunrise to deliver a telegram stating that Caleb would not be able to join them on this Christmas Day. Due to too much pressing legal matters. She had so wished for him to be there.

"Mother? What has you so angry? It's Christmas. You had better be present when the children all opened their gifts. I know how much joy it brings you," said Marjorie.

"Oh, it's that bellowing windbag Leander McNelly! Caleb will not be able to be here for Christmas. He has pressing legal matters. How pressing can it be that it would keep him from Christmas?"

"How awful! On Christmas? Well, if I know Caleb, he most surely put up an argument. I am certain that he would not have stayed in Austin had he not felt it necessary to do so. Please Mother, the children? They are all waiting for you," said Marjorie.

Señora Kataryna stuffed the telegram into the pocket of her dress. Then quickly brushed away the wrinkles as she stood up from the chair in which she had sat reading the telegram. She gave herself a once over glance inspection in front of the mirror in the hallway. "Oh Mother, please! You look gorgeous, as always you do," protested Marjorie.

Señora Kataryna smiled, inhaled deeply and proceeded down the hallway to the large parlor to greet the children.

"What's wrong with Mother?" asked Drew.

"She just received a telegram. Caleb will not be arriving for Christmas. He must stay in Austin. Something to do with urgent legal matters or something like that," explained Marjorie.

"Something tells me this has McNelly written all over it," replied Drew.

"And you would be correct. I, for one, would not want to be Leander H McNelly right now. Señora Kataryna's law is about to trump the law of Capt. Leander H McNelly and the Texas Rangers. I can promise you that," chuckled Marjorie emphatically.

"I have that feeling. Something tells me we are about to go to Austin. The mountain, Señora Kataryna, is about to go to Mohammed. Specifically Caleb," said Drew.

"You can't be serious! Pack up Christmas and take it to Austin? Even she can't be that fanatical about it. Surely she understands Caleb is a lawyer. What's more he is also a Ranger. Surely she wouldn't," said Marjorie.

Drew looked at his wife with one eyebrow raised and his head tilted to one side. "Where have you been living lately? Oh, yes, she would. Thank God I had nothing to do with it. If made angry enough, she can be mighty determined and dead set. She may not pack up everything. But she would most certainly go. Did you see her eyes? There is nothing short of childbearing too important to not celebrate Christmas or Easter for that matter. My mother is solid as a rock in her faith and I'm telling you not to be the least bit surprised if by this time tomorrow we aren't all on our way to Austin. If so, God help Capt. Leander H McNelly!"

**Austin, Texas.**
**December 26, 1871**

"So let's go over this again, Thompson. You say you were hired by Asbury and Benson to rob the payroll. You do know how absurd that sounds? Why Asbury and Benson are sure to have solid alibis against you. Don't you see? You were played, Thompson. They had no intentions of meeting you in Galveston or anywhere else. All they wanted was to humiliate the Rangers. To disperse the Texas Rangers so as to make it easier to petition the Governor one last time to do away with the Rangers altogether. It nearly worked too expect for Ranger Ed Lamb and his two men. So far no one even knows you are here or even that the money is here. Now, tell me again, how do Frank Hazen and Pat Sigel and Forrest Cook fit into all of this?"

"They were meant to draw the Ranger's attention away from Austin. Somehow Asbury was able to persuade an Army paymaster to leak it out that a large Army payroll was secretly being shipped to Brownsville by way of stage. Then they also got the Sgt. at the stockades to look the other way while Hazen, Cook and Sigel escaped," explained Clifford Thompson.

"This isn't going to be easy. I can see that right off. Frank Hazen is dead. Forrest Cook and Pat Sigel are back in the Army stockade. As for those two Army sergeants it's your word against theirs. Asbury and Benson have rock solid alibis. That, my friend, leaves you acting solely on your own," explained Caleb.

"But I'm telling the truth. Look, Caleb, I'm guilty sure enough. But I swear to you, it's just like I said," exclaimed Clifford Thompson.

"Yes. And I believe you but there is no proof. Nothing solid enough to tie everything together. Damn!" cursed Caleb in frustration.

"Not if I'm not caught yet," said Clifford Thompson.

"What?"

"Suppose you could get word to those two Army sergeants that I am still on the lam. That I was seen somewhere around Brownsville. Besides Asbury and Benson, Frank Hazen and Pat Sigel are the only ones who know what I look like. I'm betting on that and that those two sergeants would do most anything to get that money before Asbury and Benson," said Clifford Thompson.

"You're not making any sense. What makes you sure that those two Army sergeants would risk their careers and a court martial based on a rumor? Or for any other reason for that matter?"

"Well, I'm not sure that much is true. But the way I see it, they risked it once already. I don't know if or even how much Asbury paid them. But I'm sure it was nowhere near $23,000. If they did it once they'd most likely do it again. That much money is a mighty powerful temptation. I should know. Plus you could also say that I was wanting to turn myself in. Asbury and Benson would not want me to talk," said Clifford Thompson.

"Suppose I said that could work. There is no way that Capt. McNelly would let you out of jail. Not even to catch the goods on Asbury and Benson. Besides there's Sigel and Cook. They're sure to recognize anyone posing as you," explained Caleb.

"Ya, that is true. I didn't say it would be easy. But I doubt very seriously that they would be allowed more than 10 feet away from the stockade grounds unless under double guards. But still it is risky," explained Clifford Thompson.

"Just one more question, Thompson. Why are you so willing to cooperate? I doubt McNelly will change his feelings. You are still going to do time at the least."

Clifford Thompson, sighed. "Yeah, I know and I deserve it too. But maybe McNelly and Judge Frank Currly would show some leniency and give me a lighter sentence. Plus, I want to get even with Asbury and Benson for double crossing me."

"Perhaps. I'll talk to the judge and to McNelly on your behalf. Maybe I can persuade McNelly. To tell you the truth I wasn't much on your side either," said Caleb.

"And now?"

"I'm a lawyer, Thompson. I'm also a fair man. I believe you're truly remorseful. So I'll help but I can't promise you anything. There is an old Mexican saying, "lo que se hacedebe ser soportado," said Caleb.

"What does that mean?"

"What is done, must be endured," said Caleb.

"Oh, yeah, I reckon. But thanks anyway."

"Don't thank me yet," replied Caleb.

Later that evening, Caleb walked up to the door of Capt. McNelly's office and with much reluctance and doubt sighed deeply then knocked upon the door.

"Come in, Sgt. Caleb."

Caleb slowly opened the door and walked in. "How'd you know it was me?"

"A lucky guess, I suppose." Capt. McNelly chuckled and with a smile continued. "I saw the light on in your office and since I figured I was the only one here at the time. So, what's on your mind, Caleb?"

"Well, Captain..."

"Would you like a drink, Caleb? You seem a bit edgy."

"I'd appreciate that very much. Thank you."

Caleb took the glass of brandy from Capt. McNelly's hand and took a swallow. Soon he began to relax and regain his composure. "Captain, as you know, I was at first set against representing Clifford Thompson," said Caleb. "I am still against it but I've decided to do my best. What I am saying is Thompson ain't all that bad. He's guilty sure enough. Even he admits that but I believe he's most guilty of being stupid and easily influenced. Thompson has never really had anyone's respect and friendship. Sure he was respected as an officer of the state and of the Texas Rangers. But beyond the confines of this building he was just some odd little man that even his fellow Rangers sidestepped. That he was a terrific horsemen and excellent shot with a pistol and rifle was just something most Rangers took for granted. As we are all good shots and horsemen. So when Thompson had found someone who showed him a little respect and attention, though it was all a put on, he took it. Hook, line and sinker. I really believe it was what he wanted more than the money. A man like that could very easily be played and made a fool of," explained Caleb.

"Yes. That is very true. Which is precisely why I chose you to defend him. He will need you to convince Judge Currly and me not to hang him. As you know, I made it clear when I became Senior Captain of the Rangers, of my expectations toward my Rangers. How I would hold them to a much higher standard of morals and obligations than I would of any outlaws. I meant it. Little did I know that I would have to actually uphold that standard. Especially against someone such as Thompson. For you see Caleb what you have now come to realize about Thompson I saw long ago. I thought I was helping the boy by giving him a chance at being a Ranger. I do not want to hang him. But I must. My word and the honor of the Texas Rangers demand that I hang him. Or else every Texas Ranger will think of me as a floor flusher. You, my friend, must not let that happen," explained Capt. Leander H McNelly.

Caleb sat up straight in the brown leather upholstered mahogany chair and took another long swallow of the brandy in his glass. He ran his fingers through his hair, breathing deeply and said,"Yes, sir. Which is why I came to you in the first place. I have an idea or rather Clifford Thompson has an idea. He is of the opinion..." Caleb went on to explain his plan to both bring leniency for Thompson and possibly finally get the goods on Asbury and Benson.

"I know it's risky, Captain. But it just could work. Thompson is, I believe, very sincere and remorseful. I truly believe he wants to help and to redeem himself as much as he can."

"Risky is putting it very lightly. If it works it could also be a waste of time. Asbury and Benson have become very clever not to have their footprints in any of the doings they are suspected of," said Capt. McNelly.

"Yes, sir. But that's what Rangers do. Take risks and the fact that Thompson is willing to risk his life helping tells me it just might work," explained Caleb.

"I must be getting soft in my old age. But I'll allow it. I hope, for both yours and Thompson's sake that this works."

"My sake? I don't understand."

"I just don't want to see you lose. It may be a very hard blemish to overcome."

"Maybe, sir. But that could also happen if I win," said Caleb.

A week later, the prison wagon from San Antonio pulled away from the jail in Austin. Inside the wagon were two prisoners. One man, Walter Dean, sentenced to three years for poisoning another man's cow and Clifford Thompson. Along with the driver of the caged wagon were two guards, Rangers Rodney Allen and Joe Hawker. Ranger Tall Hammner and Caleb would follow a half hour head behind the prison wagon.

The plan was that, hopefully, the prison wagon would be waylaid somewhere between Austin and San Antonio. It was leaked out that Clifford Thompson had not been captured with the $23,000 in his possession. It was presumed that Thompson stashed the money somewhere and had refused to say where. Hopefully Asbury and Benson would either become nervous or greedy or both and would arrange for Thompson's escape or kidnapping in order to get the money and to silence Thompson.

"I don't like this. We're supposed to let a bunch of coyotes jump us and not put up a fight?" said Ranger Rodney Allen.

"I don't like it either. But orders is orders. Hopefully no one will get shot or killed. We're to let them take Thompson. Then we follow them. That's what Tall and Sgt. Caleb are for. They will come to our aid after we are hijacked," smiled Joe Hawker.

"Oh? And just supposing these coyotes take it in their heads to shoot us? What then?"

"Well, again, that's what Tall and the Sergeant are for. To stay just far enough back so as not to be seen. But close enough to help if this all blows up in our face. But, just in case, it sure has been good knowing you," chuckled Joe Hawker.

"Go ahead. Make jokes," said Ranger Rodney Allen.

"Who's joking?" replied Ranger Joe Hawker.

"You know, Joe? I'm starting not to like you so much anymore," said Rodney Allenan.

Forty miles south of Austin, the prison wagon and its escort rode into the town of Nova, Texas. A small town of predominantly Welsh and German immigrants with a booming population of 700 people which included mostly the families of farmers in the surrounding area. With one general store, one saloon, a church which doubled as a school during the week, one livery stable and feed and grain store one would hardly know the town existed had it not been for the stagecoach stop and watering station which it also doubled as Sheriff's office and telegraph office.

"We'll stop here for a couple of hours to switch our horses and have supper," said the wagon driver.

"Okay you two. Climb on out. You can rest yourselves on the front porch. There's shade enough. Come on, come on! Get a move on," said Ranger Rodney Allen.

About an hour later, two more riders came into town. As they tied their horses to the rail in front of the stagecoach stop. The two men seem to be drinking in every detail of the town with their eyes. The tall dark haired rider strode casually in direction of Joe Hawker. "Don't look for any more than grub around here, friend. This place is deader than an Egyptian tomb," said Joe Hawker.

"Only came here to eat anyway," said the young dark-haired man. Then he whispered. "What did you find out?"

"Not much I'm beginning to suspect. This is a mistake. I ain't seen hide nor hair of them," said Joe.

"They'll show. Mark my words. I can feel it in my gut. Just as sure as God made the earth. They'll show."

After watering and feeding their horses, the four Rangers made their way into the stagecoach stop. A man with charcoal gray hair and standing 5'9" tall, his face sporting a friendly smile and hazel green eyes, greeted them as they entered the building. “Have a seat. Dinner will be ready in about 40 minutes. Can I offer you something to drink?”

“Sure thing!” said Tall Hammner. “How about a mug of beer for me?”

“Make it four. All around,” smiled Caleb.

“Hey, how about us!” asked Walter Dean.

“You get coffee or water! And be thankful for it,” said Caleb.

The man running the stagecoach stop came carrying a round tray with four tall mugs of beer. His large hands at the end of thick strong muscular wrists laid the tray down on top of the table and began serving the men.

“Been here long?” asked Tall Hammner as he took a long drink.

“Since Nova sprang up. Just after the recent War between the States,” said the man.

“Nice quiet town. Do you know where we can find the sheriff?” continued Tall.

“Sure enough! Mind if I ask why you need the sheriff?”

“Not at all. Got a couple hard cases outside and it is just possible they might have friends following us who don’t favor the idea of their working for the state of Texas for the next three years,” said Sgt. Caleb.

“Well, now fellas, you’re in luck. Just so happens I’m the Sheriff. I’m also the telegrapher, stagecoach stop manager, bartender and most importantly, the Mayor of Nova. Name’s Gabriel Johnson.”

“Sounds like you have a well-rounded life. Pleased to meet you, Sheriff,” said Caleb as he introduced the other Rangers. Sheriff Johnson sat himself down at the table and he and the Rangers began talking. As they talked a woman with long, blonde, braided hair came into the room. She was carrying a large wooden bowl with a delicious smelling stew. She placed it in the center of the table. Then left only to return shortly with six bowls, spoons and a large round loaf of warm bread. Almost immediately the sound of rumbling stomachs could be heard. Caleb took two bowls of the stew outside for the prisoners then returned to enjoy his dinner.

They were enjoying the dinner and drinks. Tall Hammner raised his head, his eyes holding a curious look about them. Then he began to sniff the air.

"Is it just me or does anyone else smell smoke?"

"Yeah, come to think of it, I do," said Ranger Rodney Allen.

Just then Sheriff Johnson came barging through the back door. "Fire! The barn's on fire!"

The Rangers all sprang from the table to their feet and rushed outside.

"Showtime," said Caleb as he ran outside. "Joe! Stay here. This may not be just any fire."

"Yes, sir!"

As the men rushed toward the barn, Tall Hammner noticed movement from the corner of his eye. Someone was sneaking around the back and making their way behind the other buildings toward the stagecoach stop.

"Hey, Sergeant, look!" yelled Tall pointing.

"He's after Thompson!" said Caleb.

"I can get him real easy like," said Tall.

"No! Let 'em go!"

A shot came from the south. After a second or two, Caleb saw a man's hat. It was bobbing up and down from behind a buckboard wagon. Caleb had been standing near the horse corral when he saw the hat. Carefully, Caleb rested his rifle on the top rail of the corral fence and took careful aim on the hat. Slowly he squeezed the trigger. The bullet found its mark and the hat soared through the air with lightning speed. Caleb chuckled. "That'll put a scare in him."

The tall big bodied outlaw bounded onto the porch where Clifford Thompson and Walter Dean were chained together. As his right foot fell, the outlaw aimed and fired one shot from the double barrel shotgun he was holding and blasted the chain into that had shackled the two prisoners feet together.

"Let's go!" The outlaw shouted to Clifford Thompson. Clifford sprang to his feet.

"Where to?"

"Never you mind. The boss wants to see you."

"Hey! What about me?" asked Walter Dean.

"What about you?" said the outlaw and with the other barrel of the shotgun he blew a hole into Walter Dean's chest big enough to hold a watermelon.

"What the hell? There was no call for that," said Clifford Thompson half frightened and half angry.

"No witnesses," said the outlaw, with a smile.

"God!" exclaimed Clifford Thompson.

"He ain't here!" laughed the outlaw.

An hour later, thinking that they had made a clean getaway, three outlaws and their captive, Clifford Thompson, rode into a large forest thicket of mesquite, cactus and scrub oaks. Deep into the center of the thicket there appeared a large opening nearly two acres in size. In the center of the opening, there was a campfire and sitting near the fire, his back towards them, was a well-dressed man in a suit of clothes a lawyer or businessman or politician would wear. Clifford Thompson did not at first recognize him. Until that is the man turning toward him and still sipping his coffee spoke.

"Took you long enough," said the man.

"Asbury!" gasped Clifford Thompson.

"Hello, Clifford. Have a seat and have some coffee," said Asbury.

"What's going on, Asbury? Why'd you have me kidnapped?"

"Now, Clifford, that's gratitude for you. I would figure you would be glad to see your friends and after we went through all the trouble of getting you free. Cuts me to the quick," said Asbury.

"Ya some friends. You went and used me! Set me up for the fall. You never had any intentions of meeting me in Galveston. Did you?"

"Well, now we never really said that we would. Did we? All you had to do was to get on board that ship and leave. But no, you just had to play the aristocrat. Flashing money around as if you grew it on grape-vines. Speaking of the money. Where did you hide it? We know you didn't have it on you when those Rangers caught you. Else we would have heard it said after they brought you back to Austin."

"It's gone. Seems we all lost on that account," replied Clifford Thompson.

"Gone? What you mean gone?" questioned Asbury.

"Stolen. I figured it was you or at least one of your goons you sent. Ironic, ain't it? We rob the Rangers payroll only to be robbed ourselves. Guess the Almighty saw it only fitting," laughed Clifford Thompson.

"I'll get him to tell us. That money wasn't took. Let me have him boss. He'll talk, I promise," said Forrest Cook.

"Go to hell! And it's taken. The money wasn't taken. Took. No wonder your world is crumbling around you. Again, it's the Almighty passing his judgment on you. You stooped to hiring some of the lowest, dumbest reprobates in Texas! Go on, Cook! Have at me. If I wasn't trussed up like a turkey for market, I'd take you apart piece by piece. You're nothing by yourself," said Clifford Thompson.

"Why you!" Forrest Cook lunged forward to grab Clifford Thompson.

"Settled down! You'll get your moment! Now I'm going to ask you one more time. Then we play rough. Where is the money?" said Asbury.

Clifford Thompson smart mouth reply was interrupted by Forrest Cook's boot in his ribs.

Clifford Thompson sucked in air in shallow draws. Then smiled and laughed a ragged laugh. "Whatcha gonna do, kill me? You dumb idiot! Go on! Get! You'll never know what happened to the money for sure then."

"So! You do have it. Or at least you know where it is!" said William Asbury.

The four Rangers, Caleb, Tall, Allen and Hawker had followed the trail of the outlaws to a long wide, rocky bottom dry wash. Then the trail became difficult. When the outlaws came to the wash, they split up. Some went north. Two went east and two went west.

"Now we've done it! McNelly will skin us alive! We've lost them," said Tall Hammner.

"We could split up ourselves and follow the tracks until one of us spots something. Then meet right here in an hour from now," suggested Ranger Rodney Allen.

"We could. But this could be just what they want for us to do. This could be a trap," said Sgt. Caleb.

"So? Now what? I don't cherish the idea of going back empty-handed. Not only have we lost Thompson but a man is dead as a result. I say we keep looking. Maybe begin in a large circle and keep making it smaller. They have to be close unless they learned to fly," suggested Tall Hammner.

"I'm not going anywhere without Thompson. He is our key witness to possibly taking down that low down company Asbury and Benson. We'll keep looking. My Lord! It is getting hot today!" said Sgt. Caleb.

"Shh hush. Hush!" said Ranger Rodney Allen. "Did anyone else hear that?"

"Hear what?" said Tall Hammner.

"I could have sworn I heard groaning," replied Ranger Allen.

"Come to think of it, I thought I caught the smell of smoke earlier but danged if I can spot any," said Ranger Joe Hawker.

"Come on, Thompson. Be sensible. Without the money there is no crime. If you were captured without it then it's your word against theirs and all you have to say is that you were taking a few days of fun. That it is simply a coincidence that the money came up missing around the same time. Tell me where it is and I can place it in several different enterprises so that it would be near impossible to trace it. You'll be well off financially as well. We all will and not one of us will be able to be implicated beyond mere speculation. I will make sure you do not go to jail and that you get exactly what is due to you," said William Asbury.

"And I'm telling you I can't tell you where it is. I have to show you," said Thompson.

Thompson's four captors were having a little powwow their backs turned toward him. For an instant, he thought about making a run for freedom. He decided against it as he had no horse, no food nor water. More importantly no gun. Suddenly his attention was interrupted as a small stone bounced off his knee. Clifford Thompson looked sharply around into the dense mesquite. Caleb gently wiggled a small branch. Clifford Thompson caught the movement.

Caleb slowly raised his right hand as if to say, "Over here." Thompson coughed loudly."Hey, how about some water? My throat is mighty dry. Come to think of it. I'm awful hungry. How about some grub?"

"Sure! How about I fill your belly with lead?" scoffed Forrest Cook.

"Go ahead. Nothing you can do can possibly be worse than what McNelly has in store for me," laughed Clifford Thompson.

Forrest Cook reached into his saddle bag and pulled out a small orderly brown paper wrapping. "Got hardtack and jerky."

"What? Jerky? I saw some javelina tracks when we came in here. You kill him and I'll skin and clean him. Deal?" said Clifford Thompson.

Forrest Cook looked at William Asbury then to the two other outlaws. "Sounds good. What about it, boss?"

"I must say I could most certainly eat. Yes, it's a deal," said William Asbury.

Forrest Cook and one of the hired outlaws set out in the direction of where the javelina tracks were seen. As soon as they were out of sight and in the mesquite brush, Clifford began to start annoying small talk and references to the skill and determination of the Rangers. "Look, Asbury. Why not just let the money stay where it is? Then once I'm out of prison you and I can go fetch it. By that time the case will be closed and the Rangers will have forgotten the whole matter. You can go on doing business as usual until then."

"I prefer my way. Like they say. If you want things done right, do it yourself."

"Sure. So long as you're talking about horse chewing, mending fences, fixing door hinges and so on. But something as serious as $23,000? You'll have to go to another country. The Rangers will hunt you down until the return of Christ. Especially that Ranger Major. Drew Parker. He once tracked a man clear to Denver, Colorado then dragged him back to Texas to hang the man."

"Oh shut up! You make it sound as if the Rangers were some sort of modern-day Knights of the Round Table and McNelly as Merlin the Sorcerer with some crystal ball," said William Asbury with disgust.

"A crystal ball? Almost. They have the eyes and ears of honest folk. Plus a determination unparalleled by any law agency in the United States maybe even the world. The closest may be the Mounties up in Canada way."

Like I said shut up," said Asbury. "If you're so fond of them then why did you betray them?"

"I have asked myself the same question many times," replied Clifford Thompson remorsefully.

When Forrest Cook and the other outlaw left to hunt javelina Tall Hammner and Joe Hawker slinked back deep into the mesquite and circled around to intercept the two.

Caleb whispered to Ranger Rodney Allen, "We'll wait. Tall said we would know when to make our move. He said he would give his signal. Three rapid shots."

"There ain't no danged javelina around here! These tracks must be two days old," said the outlaw to Forrest Cook.

"Ya. I'm beginning to believe that Clifford Thompson has pulled a fast one on us. Just wait until I get back into camp. I'll stomp mud in his..."

"Hold it right there, Cook!"

Forrest Cook jerked to a sudden stop. Then looked around furiously. "Who's there?"

"Texas Rangers! Don't move either of you. We don't want to have to kill you. But if you leave us no choice, we will," said Tall Hammner.

"Rangers! I ain't going up against any Rangers, Cook! I'm giving it up," said the outlaw.

"Gentry! You yellow belly dog! I'll kill you myself!" growled Forrest Cook.

"Go for that gun, Cook, and I swear by all that's holy, I'll shoot you dead as a rock!" said Ranger Joe Hawker. Forrest Cook's hand stopped with a jerk quivering just inches from his revolver. "I ain't bluffing, Cook! Try it and you're dead," repeated Joe Hawker.

"I'm dropping my guns, Ranger. Don't shoot me. I swear, I'm out of this," said the outlaw named Gentry.

"Awh hell!" shouted Cook then went for his revolver.

"Don't!" warned Joe Hawker then pulled the trigger on his Henry repeating rifle. The bullet found its mark leaving a dark purple hole in Forrest Cook's forehead and a large hole in the back of his head.

Forrest Cook's hand still held the Navy Colt revolver and began to pull the trigger shooting into the ground. Then he fell face first into the sandy soil.

Gentry cried in horror. "Aaah! Sweet Jesus! Don't shoot me!"

"Oh shut up!" said Tall Hammner as he tied Gentry's hands behind his back.

"So, Gentry. That is your name, right? What's your whole name and how did you come into this mess?" asked Ranger Joe Hawker.

"Joe. Joseph Gentry. That conniving Sgt. Black! We was only supposed to get Thompson freed. We was to get $1,000 each. No man ever got rich on Army pay. It seemed to be an easy plan. I didn't know you Rangers were on the job."

"And Pat Sigel? Where's he?" asked Tall.

Gentry looked at Tall Hammner surprised he knew of Pat Sigel.

"Sigel? Why he's dead. Hanged himself."

"Hanged himself? Are you certain of that?" asked Tall.

"I was up until now. Now, I'm not so sure. But as God as my judge, I had nothing to do with Sigel. Cook either. Why I never knew them until a few days ago. That's when Sgt. Black introduced me to that William Asbury fella."

"What about Benson? Where's he?" asked Tall Hammner.

"Benson? Who is he? I never heard of anyone called Benson," replied Gentry.

Tall Hammner held his revolver high into the air and squeezed three rapid shots.

"That's the signal. Let's go!" said Sgt. Caleb to Ranger Rodney Allen.

And with that the two Rangers stepped out into the clearing. Their weapons were already drawn and poised to shoot. Sgt. Bob Black spotted the Rangers a moment too late. "Hey, what's going on?"

William Asbury spun around to look.

"Don't do it, Asbury! On second thought. Go ahead. I'd enjoy nothing more than to blow your gizzard out," said Sgt. Caleb. "Now both of you drop your guns and step back."

"Well, well, if it isn't the Texas Rangers. You obviously know me. Who, pray tell, are you two?" said Asbury.

"Not that it matters. Name's Caleb, Sgt. Caleb Parker Texas Ranger," Caleb looked at Bob Black. "Who are you?"

"You're the Ranger? You fellas are supposed to be so damn smart. You figure it out. Why should I tell you anything?"

"No reason, I suppose. Only it would be nice. That way I would know what name to carve on your grave marker. But I guess rest in peace will suffice," smiled Caleb.

"I've heard about you Rangers. No quarter and all for Texas! You fellas think you're better than God himself!" exclaimed Bob Black.

"No, no. Not at all. You got it all wrong. God is our Commander and Chief. Then there's Capt. McNelly.He talks to God. Then to us. As for no quarter, you're still alive," pointed out Sgt. Caleb Parker.

"Go ahead and make jokes. But you won't be Rangers for long. I'll have your badges. You have no reason for arresting us. I'll sue you for false arrest," said William Asbury.

"You kinda have to be alive to do that. But that's where you're wrong. I'm arresting you for the robbery of the Texas Ranger payroll in Austin," said Sergeant Caleb Parker.

"Ha! With what evidence? We haven't any money. If I recall, it's Thompson you're really after. Wasn't it he who stole the money?" William Asbury was smiling confidently a look of triumph in his eyes.

"Yes, you're right. But how did you know that?" said Sgt. Caleb Parker.

"It was in the newspaper. The Dallas Herald."

"Yes, only that there had been a robbery. Not how much was stolen. Nor did I say who stole it. I should know. But up till now, I couldn't figure out how the Dallas Herald found out about it. And so soon too. Only one other person than Thompson would know that the payroll had been stolen. That would have to be Thompson's accomplice. That accomplice is you!"

Not aware that Rangers Tall Hammner and Joe Hawker had captured Gentry and had killed Forrest Cook, William Asbury mistook the rustling of bushes for Cook and Gentry's return. A smile came to his face. He had the Ranger surrounded, he thought. Without looking behind him to be sure, William Asbury spoke out. "And so what of it, Ranger? No one in Austin other than you two and Thompson here know anything about that. And with you three dead no one will ever know. Kill 'em, boys!"

"What? Kill my Sergeant. Are you crazy?" said Tall Hammner.

Surprised Asbury, spun around quickly. "What in the world?"

"Got one of them, Sarge. The Cook fella tried his hand. Ranger Hawker had to kill him."

William Asbury became confused and desperate. Panic stricken, he dove for his revolver that was laying in the sand. Clifford Thompson dove for Bob Black's revolver at the same time and then grabbing it in his still tethered hands, he rolled over onto one knee and pointed the revolver at Asbury. Asbury was furious and confused. "Thompson! What the hell are you doing?"

"The right thing for a change!" said Clifford Thompson. Then he fired his revolver.

William Asbury fired almost simultaneously shooting Clifford Thompson in the chest. At the same time, Clifford Thompson's bullet struck William Asbury in the throat breaking Asbury's spinal cord killing Asbury almost instantly.

Caleb ran to Clifford Thompson's side. "Thompson! Thompson, are you hit bad? Here let me see."

"Don't! It's no use. I'm done in," said Clifford Thompson.

"No, no. You'll be alright. Just hang on, Ranger," Caleb spoke without realizing that he had called Clifford Thompson Ranger.

"Ranger? I like the sound of that," said Clifford Thompson.

Caleb cradled Thompson on one knee his arm holding Thompson up and in a half sitting position. "Just hang in there. Tall! Can you do something for him?"

Tall Hammner knelt next to Thompson and opened his shirt to see. Then with a sad expression on his face, he looked at Caleb.

"Like I said it's alright. Really," Clifford Thompson coughed. "I know my Redeemer liveth," and with three fingers of his right hand he gingerly stroked Caleb's badge. "Tell McNelly I'm..." and then with a long exhale of air Clifford Thompson died.

"He sure died good, didn't he?" said Ranger Tall Hammner.

Caleb just nodded. Then cleared his throat. "He died a Ranger. In spite of it all. That's for sure. He died a Ranger."

"What's going to happen to us?" asked Joe Gentry.

"Well, we could just hang you at the first good tree. But I reckon we'll take you back to Austin. Could be that the Army is looking for you two anyway," replied Sgt. Caleb.

"Better hang me. Because I'm not going back to any Army court-martial and prison. First chance I get, I'm gone! And if I have to kill one of you doing it so be it," said Bob Black.

"Is that a fact? Well, now. I'll be sure to leave you plenty of chances between here and Austin then. One thing I love more than playing cards is a good challenge," smiled Ranger Rodney Allen. "That and shooting Yankees."

**January 7, 1872**
**Austin, Texas**

"And in conclusion, gentlemen, I would like to reiterate it is true that Clifford Thompson helped to steal the $23,000 payroll of the Texas Rangers but I daresay that Clifford Thompson never betrayed the Rangers. Rather, I would submit that it was the Texas Rangers in its entirety who betrayed a brother, Clifford Thompson. Too many times this young Ranger was shunned by his brother Rangers. Rejected as a Ranger and viewed mostly as an odd peg in a group of pegs. In spite of his dandy dress style, in spite of his refined way of speech, not rough and vulgar as that of his comrades, he was a Ranger. Let me remind you that it was Clifford Thompson who held the record for marksmanship and horseback riding at every Ranger competition. Still he was for some reason not enough to be accepted and included in as one of the boys so to speak. So where did Clifford Thompson turn in his desperate search for comradery and acceptance? Sadly to men such as William Asbury. He made an error in judgment! I am certain that nearly every man in this room would have to admit that somewhere at some time in their life has done something they are not proud of and would rather keep it buried in the past. Clifford Thompson was pushed to the bad by good men. I am not condoning his actions rather than I am explaining them. But I swear to you in the final moments of his young life. Clifford Thompson died a Ranger's death. He died as honorably and as bravely as any Ranger. He died as Ranger Clifford Thompson."

In spite of Clifford Thompson's death, Caleb felt obligated to Clifford Thompson. Caleb insisted that his trial not be dismissed but to be conducted as planned and that he would go on to defend Thompson and clear his name.

**Uvalde, Texas**
**February 10, 1872**

Major Drew Parker was sitting at his desk going over a newly arrived stack of wanted posters when young Matthew Daniels, 14 years old, red headed and freckle faced with deep blue eyes and a lanky 5 feet tall came strolling up to the Rangers headquarters and knocked at that the door.

"Come in!" called Major Drew Parker.

"Excuse me, sir, I have a telegram for you. Mr. Morris said I should give this to you pronto. So here it is, sir."

"Thanks, Matthew. By the way how's your pa doing these days?"

"Fine, Major, thanks for asking."

Three months ago while turkey hunting Jason Daniels had been thrown from his horse when it was spooked by a half blind Brahma bull that had been lost in a large mesquite thicket. The fall left Jason Daniels temporarily paralyzed from the waist down. He had been given very little chance of recovery but by God's will and his own stubborn determination, Jason Daniels walked.

"Tell him I said hello. Maybe I'll stop by to look at that string of horses he has."

"Yes, sir! He sure will be glad to see you, Captain. Gotta get back to work. Mr. Morris gets uppity if I tarry too long. Goodbye."

"Okay then. Scat!" Drew began to open the envelope containing the telegram and began reading it.

"Dear Lord, Dancing Crow is dead," he muttered to himself. The telegram was sent from Muleshoe, Texas. It was signed Mrs. Gloria Martin, editor and owner of Morning Glory newspaper.

Drew suddenly found himself mentally drifting back to the earlier days. The days of Muleshoe, Texas. The days of Comanche raids, the days of Dancing Crow, his one-time enemy who became a lifetime friend and ally.

"I'll go," Drew mumbled to himself. "I could do with a little vacation. Guess Marjorie would like to go as well. Dancing Crow dead. This could spell trouble.

**One week later**
**Muleshoe, Texas**

The stage from Austin to Muleshoe came bouncing up the main street of Muleshoe. The town had grown some since last Drew had seen it. There was a large brick building across the street from the Marshall's office. The sign on the brick building read Paradise Hotel. Next to the Paradise Hotel stood a large blue building with Morning Glory newspaper painted on a large glass picture window on the building's front.

Several newer buildings dotted the upper end of town. There was a new cannery, a feed and grain store, a tailor shop as well as a new mercantile.

"Town's grown some," said Drew as the stage came to a stop next to the livery.

"Yes, it has. It looks beautiful," said Marjorie.

"Well, let's get settled in at the hotel. I could use a good meal. I'm starving," replied Drew.

"You're always starving. I could use a nice hot bath. So could you, Mr. Parker," Marjorie said to the little boy sitting next to her.

"Oh, mama! I ain't dirty. Geez!" replied Miguel.

"Mind your mother, son," said Drew sternly.

"Bull says too much bathing is bad for the constitution," retorted Miguel.

"So is sassing your mother. Now get on. You hear?" said Drew.

"Yes, sir."

After settling in at the Paradise Hotel and having a dinner fit for a king, Drew decided to visit the Morning Glory newspaper office.

A tall red headed 13 year old boy with bright green eyes and a cheerful smile looked up from a large plate to which he was obviously setting to type.

"How can I help you, sir?"

"I'm looking for a Mrs. Gloria Martin. Is she in?"

"That would be my ma. She should be. Her office is over there. Just knock."

"Your ma? I didn't know."

"Yes sir," The boy smiled. "Thomas is my name."

"Pleased to meet you, Thomas. My name is Drew Parker."

The boy leaped from his stool, wiped his hands clean with his apron then he thrusthis hand forward. "Good gosh! Captain Drew Parker?!"

"Major. That would be me. Yes."

"Just stay right there! I'll get Ma."

A few short moments later a smiling and still youthful looking Gloria Martin came bouncing out of her office. "As I live and breathe! Andrew Parker! I knew you would come. It is so good to see you. I see you have met Thomas. Thomas please, don't just stand there gaping. Show Major Parker to a chair. Can I get you some coffee?"

"Coffee sounds good."

"So sad, Drew. Dancing Crow dead. Now I fear that in spite of Quanah Parker's efforts to keep the peace there could be trouble. I fear for the Comanche. The Army has taken the idea that Yellow Pony may start trouble. Actually I believe if there is any trouble, it will be the

Army that causes it. It's only my Christian heart that keeps me from saying what I feel."

"Well, you sure wouldn't be thought less of by me, Gloria. I have dreaded this day. Quanah and Dancing Crow have done the impossible up until now. Though I believe it was more due to Dancing Crow than Quanah. But then, that's just me you understand."

"Yes, I quite agree. Although I will give Quanah his due. His diplomatic ability, probably due to being half white, has made some progress. But it was Dancing Crow's ability to keep the braves in check that truly has kept the cork in the bottle," replied Gloria Martin.

"How is it that you believe the Army may be the triggering factor?" asked Drew.

"Land and the railroad. The railroad and the government had absolutely no interest in that land when they first placed the Comanche there. A dry, rocky and worthless land. But through the efforts of Quanah Parker and Dancing Crow over the past few years and much to the credit of the Comanche they have made it blossom with good farming and some sheep and cattle. The Comanche have faired prosperously as prosperity goes for the Comanche. In spite of corrupt Indian agents now the government says that the land is valuable to the progress of the railroad! Hogwash! Had the Comanche not improved that land the government would still have no use for it. Now the Army is placing restrictions on the land! Slowly boxing the Comanche in and and taking control of the land by marking it with right of way survey markers for the railroad. I fear the worst. I, for one, cannot blame the Comanche for getting angry. I have been writing about it in articles in my paper."

"What are the feelings of the folks here in Muleshoe toward you?"

"Oh, I have no opposition from the town folks. They are mostly in agreement with me. They remember the old days. There have been a few troublemakers. But nothing serious. I believe they may be working for the railroad in some way. Or possibly hired instigators by the Army. But our Marshall has done a good job at defusing any potential trouble."

"Marshall Randles? Jake?" inquired Drew.

"Yes! How nice you remember him. You would do well to pay him a visit. He will be delighted to see you. He does not know you are here. Nor that I have sent for you. He has become a fine lawman," said Gloria.

"I believe I will. Perhaps you, Thomas and your husband will join Marjorie and myself for breakfast in the morning?"

"We adopted him just before the war. Elijah, sadly, is no longer with us. He was taken from us at Bull Run. He and I found Thomas in San Antonio doing odd jobs at eight years old. Elijah took to him right away. As did I. The rest is history."

"He seems like a very fine boy. And a very happy one too," replied Drew.

"I could not picture life without him now. He loves the paper and news reporting."

"Well, it has been a pleasure, Gloria. But I must go. It is getting late and I do not want to keep Marjorie and Miguel waiting up for me."

"It is so good to see you, Drew. I am glad you came."

"I had to. Dancing Crow was a good friend in the end. Though what I can do, I do not know," replied Drew.

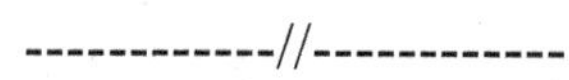

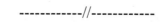

The old yellow painted buckboard bounced aimlessly along the deep rutted wagon trail that led onto the reservation.

"Are you certain we will have no trouble, Drew? I just don't feel we are being wise coming here alone with little Miguel along as well," said Marjorie.

"We will be alright, Momma!" said Miguel showing no sign of fear. "Pa's friends with the Indians. Right, Pa?"

"I was, son. Once upon a time, I was. But you two will have nothing to fear. The Comanche don't take to killing women and children if they can avoid it. Chances are, if anything would happen, you'd become a young brave in time and your Ma, a beautiful Indian squaw," said Drew teasingly.

"You are not funny, Drew Parker," said Marjorie.

"Look! Indians! Oh boy!" said Miguel excitedly.

"I see them. They've been following us for over an hour now," said Drew.

Drew hadn't time to say more when suddenly the yellow buckboard wagon was completely surrounded by Comanche braves all whooping and yelling. Drew held up his hand in a sign of peace, "Ya ta hey! We come as friends! I am Texas Ranger Drew Parker. Who is leader here?"

"I am leader. I am Crooked Nose. I have heard of the Captain of the Texas Rangers. Why has Parker come here?" Crooked Nose stared at Marjorie and Miguel curiously.

"Hi, Indian! My name is Miguel. That's my Pa! Your nose ain't crooked!" announced Miguel excitedly leaping up out of his seat.

"Miguel, shush!" said Marjorie as she pulled him back to his seat. He bounced right back up and she returned him to a sitting position.

Crooked Nose looked at Drew and smiled. "Young Ranger very brave. Speaks from heart. Yours?"

"Yes. Squaw is mine also," said Drew.

"Squaw!"

"Yes, Marjorie, squaw," said Drew very sternly and matter-of-factly.

"You follow," said Crooked Nose. Then he motioned to the other Braves and escorted the Parker wagon into the Comanche camp. Their reception was one to be expected. One of suspicion and loud talking and shouting. A tall, muscular, mean looking man stepped out from a teepee that was centered inside the camp. Immediately, Drew recognized him. "Ya ta hey! Yellow Pony. Old friend."

"Not old. Not friend. Ya ta hey Major Ranger Parker," said Yellow Pony with a wolfish smile.

"I see you're still angry with me. Maybe you want to even the score for that scar on your hip?"

Drew slowly stepped down from his wagon removing his coat and shirt as he stood on the ground. Yellow Pony smiled as he too removed his sheepskin vest type shirt. The two men circled each other warily. Suddenly, Yellow Pony lurched forward. The two men clashed like angry wolves in a fury of grunts and groans. Writhing and twisting rolling one atop the other, Yellow Pony rolled on top of Drew with a look of triumph in his eyes but short-lived. Drew managed to bring his right knee up square into Yellow Pony's groin then flipped Yellow Pony heel over head causing Yellow Pony to land with a thud flat on his back. He groaned. Then Drew pounced upon Yellow Pony's chest pinning his arms to the ground with his knees with lightning speed. Drew pulled his long, wide bowie knife and placed it at Yellow Pony's throat. Then smiled. As he sheathed his knife he stood and held out his hand to help Yellow Pony to his feet.

"You are still a good warrior, my old friend, Parker," smiled Yellow Pony.

"I does my heart good to hear that, Yellow Pony," came a voice from within the crowd. "It would sadden me to shoot my chief of warriors," It was Quanah Parker. He had been watching in case of foul play holding had a rifle in his huge left hand.

"No need for that thing, Quanah. Yellow Pony and I are good friends. This was just our way of saying hello. Isn't that right, Yellow Pony?"

Yellow Pony smiled. "It is so now. But a day long ago..."

"Yes, and a better warrior I have never met. I would not want to have to face Yellow Pony in a true battle. I've may not be so lucky in a real fight to the death," said Drew.

"Who is this with you?" asked Quanah Parker.

"This is my wife and son," replied Drew.

"Welcome. No harm will come to you," said Quanah Parker.

"Pa, are we related?" asked Miguel.

"No. Why do you ask?"

"Well, his name is Quanah Parker and my name is Miguel Parker."

Drew chuckled. "Just coincidence, son. Many people have like names but are not related."

"Oh, I see. I think."

"I will explain later," replied Marjorie.

"So, Major Drew Parker, to what do we owe the honor of your visit?" Though a Comanche, Quanah Parker was half white. Because of some schooling in a missionary school for Indians, Quanah had become very well-versed in the English language. His education and having a white mother he had learned the art of diplomacy. In spite of some opposition from some of the Quahadi Comanche, Quanah had done much to improve their relations between the white man and a Comanche.

"My true reason for coming was to pay my respects to Dancing Crow's family. Dancing Crow and I had become good friends. His passing saddens me. I came with gifts for his family and, if they permit me, to visit his grave and to say farewell," explained Drew.

"It is good. This thing you do for his family. But sadly, I cannot let you visit his grave. No white man can visit the graves of any Comanche," stated Quanah.

"I understand," replied Drew.

"No white man can go into the sacred burial grounds. But he may be allowed to see from afar. Perhaps Dancing Crow's spirit will come to you instead?" said Yellow Pony.

"You would take him?" Quanah asked Yellow Pony.

"Yes, this one time," said Yellow Pony.

"I would be honored. Thank you," replied Drew.

Three days later Drew and his family said goodbye. He had learned much from Quanah regarding the troubles the Comanche were experiencing. It was the same old story. Corrupt railroad officials, corrupt and greedy Indian agents and the U.S. Army. Whether there was corruption within the Army or not, Drew could not say but it wouldn't be the first time that the Army would be used by those within the bureaucracy. They arrived in Muleshoe around noon. Gloria Martin came whisking her way down the board walkway to the hotel. She held a notepad tightly against her chest and a smile on her face. "Major Parker, may I have a word with you!?"

"Of course right after I get my family settled in and then clean up a might. You will allow me that?" replied Drew.

"Of course. How selfish of me. Good day. You must be Mrs. Marjorie Parker?" said Gloria Martin.

"I am. And you are Gloria Martin of the Morning Glory newspaper. I have heard so much about you and Muleshoe. I feel as if I am coming home or at least visiting family," replied Marjorie.

"My! You are as beautiful and charming as the Major said. I have a feeling we are going to get along splendidly. And who is this very handsome young man?"

"I am Miguel. Who are you?"

"Miguel! Mind your manners," scolded Marjorie.

"Nonsense! Manners. You are perfectly within your right to ask. My name is Gloria Martin. I own a newspaper office here in town. Maybe your mother and father will bring you over to visit. Have you ever seen a newspaper office and a printing press?"

"No, ma'am. I don't even know what that paper pushed thing is" said Miguel.

"Printing press," corrected Marjorie. "And I would love that very much."

"Splendid! Then it's all set! You and Miguel, come and we will have tea," said Gloria.

The following morning as Drew stood outside in front of the Paradise Hotel puffing on his pipe and enjoying the warm morning sunlight his attention was quickly averted by the sounds of a commotion just down the street.

"Get your hands off me, you lousy coyote!"

"Why you snot nosed little brat! I ought to..."

"Ought to what?"

The man turned abruptly. He caught the hard gaze of Drew Parker's dark brown eyes upon him. "Beat it, hay seed!" said the ruffian.

"Let the boy go," said Drew in a slow, calm, matter of fact voice.

The young boy having a hard time from the scruffy ruffians was young Thomas Martin.

"I said beat it. This ain't your affair," said the ruffian.

"That's where you're wrong. At any rate let's just say I'm making it my affair," Drew's hand hovered slightly over his holster and revolver while he glared at the young man.

"Just so's I know who I'm about to kill, mister. Who are you?" asked the ruffian.

"The name is Major Drew Parker Texas Ranger."

"Texas Rangers! Now see here, I ain't got no squabbles with the Rangers. And you ain't going to force me to draw on you either," said the ruffian.

"Thomas, come here." Drew's eyes never drifted away from the ruffian and his two companions. "I'm not forcing anyone to do anything. Thomas, what's this all about?"

"These coyotes threatened me and my Ma. Said if we print any more lies about how the railroad is stealing from the Comanche they'd burn down the paper," said Thomas.

"That ain't strictly true, kid. I never said anything about burning down the place," protested the ruffian.

"He said it would be a shame if the newspaper should catch fire. If that ain't a threat I'll eat my hat!" said Thomas.

"Seems to me you three are looking for trouble. My advice for you is to ride out of town. Come back when you're sober. If I see you in town for the rest of the day, I'll have to take your guns and lock you up in jail," said Major Drew Parker.

"That's mighty big talk for just one man agin three. Ranger or no," said one of the bullies.

"He ain't just one man. You best do as the Ranger says and you won't get hurt," said Marshall Jake Randles as he came upon the scene. Drew slowly glanced over toward the voice. A smile of appreciation came upon his face.

"Good morning, Marshall," said Drew.

"Major Parker," replied Marshall Jake Randles.

"You boys still here? Go on now and you can tell Maj. McKinnley I said hello. That is unless you'd rather I told him myself?" continued Marshall Jake Randles. At the mention of Major McKinnley the three bullies seemed to sober up quickly. The leader of the pack grumbled and then spun around on his heels and walked away with his two companions in tow.

"How did you know they were soldiers? You have dealings with them before?" asked Drew.

"Soldiers? More like mercenaries. Their boots, Army regulation issue. But to answer your question, yes. I have had dealings with them before," explained Marshall Jake Randles.

"This is more serious than I thought. I knew there was trouble. But I did not know that the U.S. Army was involved. This Major McKinnley is part of this mess?"

"I don't know. But he is a stern man. Army through and through. If he had any stock in this, it's because he's a man who follows orders without question. The fact that he hates Comanche doesn't help much either," said Jake.

"By any chance has the name Unified Land and Loan Company ever come up?" asked Drew.

"No. Can't say I've heard that name. Isn't that the name of that company we had so much trouble with back when? New Mexico outfit, weren't they?"

"The same. But I reckon they're not in this yet," replied Drew.

"I sort of figured that they went belly up a long time ago after you Rangers cleaned up house."

"Maybe. But they had an office back east somewhere. Pennsylvania, I think. Jake, if you wouldn't be offended, I'd like to send a wire to Austin and to Uvalde. Maybe send for a company of Rangers. I could be wrong but I think I may have happened along just in time. I smell trouble brewing. Maybe we can help you."

"I'm glad you're here. I've had the same feelings. I'd be obliged for the help. It's just a matter time and I'm going to have to face some trigger-happy cowboy and I'm not in a killing mood. Not if I can help it," replied Marshall Jake Randles.

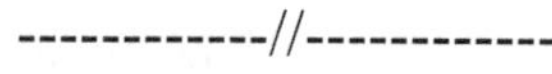

**Uvalde, Texas**
**To Texas Ranger Company D Headquarters**

Bring the men to Muleshoe. Stop. Bring Caleb. He is needed. Stop. Bring your fighting shoes. Stop.

Major Andrew Parker

Red Sands was standing behind Capt. Whiskey Jack and looking over his shoulder as Jack read the telegram.

"Short and sweet. I wonder what troubles the Major is talking about?" asked Red.

"I have no idea. But he said come. Tell the boys we are pulling out. Remember the Major said bring your fighting shoes," said Jack.

Red smiled. "He does have a way with words, don't he?"

"Ya know Red, I'm glad you're on our side. You like fighting too much. I sure would hate to see you turn outlaw," said Jack.

"Not a chance, Captain. I like being on the right side of the law too much. Besides a free Texas is worth fighting for. Wouldn't you say?"

"Oh get! That wasn't what I meant and you know it!"

Red smiled. "I'll have the boys ready in four hours."

"Take your time. I don't want anyone to forget anything. We will leave at first light. Have every man check and recheck their gear. And eat hearty! It'll be a few days before we get a decent meal until we get into Muleshoe."

"Yes, sir."

Caleb was sitting at his desk going over a few depositions when a knock at his office door interrupted him. "Come in," he called.

Two young Rangers entered hats in hand. "Beg your pardon Sergeant. But Capt. McNelly sent us. We are to give you this telegram. And the Captain said we were to place ourselves at your disposal. Whatever that means," It was Rangers Joe Hawker and Rodney Allen.

"Oh he did, did he? First things first. Let me have the envelope," Caleb opened the envelope and read the telegram. He pushed his chair back and ran his fingers through his hair. "Have you fellas ever been to a place called Muleshoe?"

"No, sir." they answered in unison.

"Well, you're about to be. I want you two to pack your gear. Go to the mercantile and buy double your normal cache of ammunition. Pack provisions for one week each. Then meet me at the bunkhouse at 06:00. Got it?"

"Consider it done. That must be one heck of a telegram. Are we riding into trouble, Sarge?"

"When a Ranger gets orders to ride it usually means trouble. Why? Does that bother you?"

"Shucks no! I was just asking is all," said Ranger Rodney Allen.

Caleb put his hat on and smiled. "Still here?"

"Nope! See you! 06:00," said Rodney Allen.

"Hot dog! Finally. I was getting so bored I was about to go crazy," said Joe Hawker.

The old boarded-up building that once supported the Morning Glory News was donated to Major Parker as the new Muleshoe Headquarters Annex for Company D Texas Rangers.

"It certainly is big enough. Maybe too big. Are you sure you want to do this, Gloria?"

"More than anything in a long while. Besides I was thinking Marjorie could make the top floor into a nice home for the time you will be here. I'm sure she would prefer her own place to that one room hotel room."

"I am sure of that. It's a deal then. Rent of $10 a month sound fair? I insist you be paid rent," said Drew.

"Ten? I was thinking more like 30?"

"Thirty dollars?" Drew was cut short by Gloria's laughter.

"Relax, Drew! I was just kidding. Of course that is more than fair."

The afternoon air was warm and the breezes carried small dust cyclones up the street. A woman stood on the board walkway in front of the hotel. Drew noticed the look on her face and heard her gasp and say, "Not again." Drew turned and looked in the direction of the woman's stare. A smile came to his face!

"No trouble, ma'am. Those are Texas Rangers."

"Oh thank the Lord! I was thinking they'd be here to cause trouble."

"That they were rail hands?"

"Or worse, soldiers," replied the lady.

"No, ma'am. These are the best men in law enforcement. I best go meet them," Drew excused himself and tipped his hat.

The small detail came to a halt as Major Drew Parker stepped out into the middle of the street.

"Halt!" shouted Sgt. Tom Crawford. "How to, Major. We left as soon as we got word."

"This is all? I asked for the whole lot of you," said Drew Parker.

"This is all Capt. Jack could spare. Don't worry, there should be a few more coming. Caleb is bringing others with him from Austin."

"You could take the men over yonder to that building. There is room in the back to accommodate everyone. We haven't had time to put in bunks yet. You'll have to use your bedrolls for the time being. No one goes upstairs. My family has already taken that," instructed Major Drew Parker.

"Yes sir. You get the lumber, we will make the bunks. Say! Ain't that the old newspaper building?" asked Sgt. Tom Crawford.

"You have a good memory. It is. Sort of donated by Mrs. Gloria Martin. You can see for yourself. She's grown some. News building is just yonder," explained Major Parker.

"Glad to hear it," said Tom.

After supper, the Rangers settled in. Major Drew Parker filled them all in on the troubles in Muleshoe and with the Comanche.

"Well Major, as always, we're with you," said Shorty.

"I'm glad to hear that. But I'm hoping our just being here will be enough to keep things quiet in town. As for the Comanche I can't say," said Major Parker.

"I don't get it. Who in their right mind would want that useless swath of land anyway? It's bad enough that the Comanche were forced on it. But even the railroad should know it's worthless," asked Jerolde Oaks.

"Was worthless. Dancing Crow and Quanah held the Comanche under control pretty well over the past few years. Those Comanche turned out to be good farmers. They made the land green. Put in water tanks for livestock and drinking water. Now it seems too valuable to pass up. The government wants it now as does the railroad," explained Major Parker.

"Why those dirty, double crossers. I don't blame the Comanche for getting riled. Sad thing about old Dancing Crow though. Now there was a man! One hell of a fighter too!" replied Jerolde Oaks.

"You got that right!" Comments popped up throughout the room from all those who remembered Dancing Crow as a formidable opponent.

Two days later, Sgt. Caleb Parker along with Rangers Rodney Allen and Joe Hawker came riding into town and tied their mounts to the hitching rail in front of the Marshall's office. They walked inside.

"Can I help you?" Marshall Jake Randles looked up from the newspaper he had been reading when the three rangers walked in.

"Hello to you too, Jake," smiled Caleb.

"Caleb? Is that you?"

"In the flesh."

"I'll be. Look at you!"

"Where's Major Parker? And the rest of the boys?"

"Over at Ranger headquarters of course."

"Ranger? I thought this was Ranger headquarters?"

"Ya. 100 years ago!" laughed Jake. "They got their own place now. Hold on, I'll walk you over there. How the heck have you been anyway?" The two old friends talked and brought each other up to date on their lives as they walked over to Ranger headquarters. Drew Parker met them at the door as they came across the street.

It had been two days since Caleb's arrival into Muleshoe. He and Major Parker were walking up the main street after just having left the barbershop. Suddenly an old man came tumbling backward heels over head through the batwing doors of the saloon. A gruff angry voice came from the other side. "And stay out! Lousy Injun lover!"

The old man groaned as he righted himself and dusted off his clothes. An angry look of defiance and a need for revenge was on his face.

Major Parker asked. "Are you alright, old-timer?"

"Old-timer?"

"Easy. Didn't mean any disrespect. Now what happened, mister?" asked Major Parker.

"All I said was there was plenty land and better for a railroad than that of the reservation. And any government crooked enough to steal land from hard-working men, Comanche or not, was a government of skunks and that Quanah Parker and Dancing Crow kept their word and that ought to mean something. Dad burned Yankee soldiers! They think they can walk all over me? I'll show 'em," said the old-timer.

"Now hold on! Don't go getting yourself killed for nothing. I'll handle this," said Major Parker.

"Ya? Well, I've got my pride. Nobody pushes me and walks away! And I fight my own battles thank you!" exclaimed the old-timer.

"Yes sir. I hear you. But you're outnumbered and outgunned. Let the Rangers handle it," said Caleb.

"Alright. But I'm going in there with you. I ain't no coward!" replied the old-timer.

Six hard looking devil may care men wearing civilian clothes could have been mistaken for simple cowhands had it not been for their boots. They were laughing and talking rudely. Their talk and laughter ceased when they saw the old-timer reenter the saloon.

"You again? I thought I told you..." said a large man with curly black hair and evil looking brown eyes.

"To what?" interrupted Caleb.

"Who the hell are you?! You stay out of this, if you know what's good for you," said the big man.

"Ya, squirt.This is none of your affair," said another of the six men.

"I beg to differ," said Caleb.

"Ooo! A fancy talker too!" said the man.

"Thank you. I pride myself on being mannerly. It's a sign of intelligence."

"Are you calling me dumb!?" The man turned completely around. His back was to the bar and he faced Caleb. His hand spread wide just inches above his revolver.

"I didn't say dumb but if you go for that gun you'd be real dumb. I'm a Texas Ranger. I'm advising you men to go back to Fort Sill. Tell your boss or commanding officer or both. Muleshoe is off-limits. You're not welcome here if you're here for trouble. If you are here for trouble you'll find it. You're welcome only if on official Army business."

"One Ranger against six. Now tell me who's dumb?"

"Two," came the voice of Major Drew Parker who had ease his way to the end of the bar and to the right of the six men.

"Make that four," Rangers Rodney Allen and Joe Hawker came forward. They had been sitting at a table in the back of the saloon and were watching the events unfold.

"I wonder why it is that it always takes more than one with some people? Now if you still want to drag arm let's go for it. Otherwise, saddle up. All of you. And ride out of town. If you are here one hour from now. I'll place you under arrest. Understand?" said Sgt. Caleb Parker.

"Arrest? Ha ha ha. What for?" asked the curly-haired soldier.

"We can start with drunk and disorderly. Add assaulting an unarmed citizen. Attempted assault upon a Texas Ranger. Shall I continue? I'm sure if I try I could come up with more," said Major Drew Parker.

"And who might you be, his nursemaid?" said the second of the six men still glaring at Caleb.

"Nursemaid? Not a chance. I'm your guardian angel. I'm Major Drew Parker Texas Rangers. But I think I've told you that once before. You could say I just saved your life and that of your friends. But if you still want to try Ranger Caleb here. You have my word. No one will interfere in any way."

"I don't know about you, Cletus. But I ain't tangling with any Rangers. I say let it go. We'll have our day," claimed a blonde haired cowboy with green eyes and standing about 5'4" tall and medium build.

"You shut up! You've already said too much," said Cletus, the big man with curly black hair.

"Time is running out. You still have 40 minutes or 10 days in the jail," said Caleb.

"Ten days? You ain't got the authority. You ain't no judge. And we ain't on trial," said Cletus.

"I am a Texas Ranger. That's all the authority I need by power of the Governor of Texas. And you don't have to go on trial to do 10 days in jail," said Major Parker. "Thirty minutes. Time is running out, boys."

"Alright, we're going. But Texas Rangers or not this ain't over. I'll be seeing you again, count on it," snarled Cletus.

The six men grumbled and walked out of the saloon to their horses.

"How did you know those fellas were soldiers?" asked Ranger Allen.

"Easy. First off their saddles. They had USA stamped on them. Secondly, their boots. They were Army issued. I'd recognize those boots anywhere," said Caleb.

"Fort Sill is a good three day ride from here even on the best of horses. Reckon why they would come this far? Certainly not for a drink or fun. Not that Muleshoe isn't a nice town. But the kind of fun those fellas would be looking for ain't here," replied Ranger Allen.

"Just getting a lay of the land most likely. Sizing up any sign of resistance. Sort of a reconnaissance mission. That and to silence Mrs. Gloria Martin's newspaper."

"Mrs. Gloria? Why she's just a woman with a young boy. They wouldn't. Would they?" asked Ranger Joe Hawker.

"They would and they will. They've already given her some trouble and threatened the boy," said Drew Parker.

"Then maybe one of us should sorta always be close by her place. Just in case? Threatened the boy? Why, he's as harmless as a kitten," continued Ranger Joe Hawker.

"Oh good grief! Tell me you're not smitten by her. Joe! Dad burn it!" exclaimed Ranger Rodney Allen.

"Smitten? Shucks, no. But she's a fine lady and I like that kid."

"Whatever your reason, your idea is a good one. Perhaps we could post two or three men around her place around the clock. That isn't just her place of business. It's her home as well," said Major Parker.

"I can't place it, Major. Maybe I'm imagining things. But there's something familiar with that big fella. Cletus. Seems I've seen that fellow once before. Oh well, it'll come to me," Said Caleb.

He came bouncing up the road in his blue and red painted buckboard wagon. A large figure of a man with broad shoulders and a thick chest, his brown face sported a wide pearly white smile. On top of his long black braided hair was a new looking brown colored boulder hat. Above his large frame body and fixed with rawhide leather straps was a large blue-and-white laced on umbrella. The kind one would find in the east like New York or Maine. A beach style umbrella.

"What in the name of? What is that?" said Jerolde Oaks. He had stepped outside of the Rangers headquarters and bunkhouse to have a smoke. Red Sands came to the door to see. Hearing Jerolde Oaks' question, Red was just about to say something when he spotted Mrs. Gloria Martin scampering outside of the Morning Glory newspaper and into the street and toward the wagon. The wagon came to a stop.

"Well, look at you! Had I not met you before, I wouldn't have known it was you. Honestly, I envision you riding into town on a painted horse and wearing buckskins," said Gloria.

"I see. I figured as much with many people especially if word had gotten out that I was coming here. There are some who would like nothing more than to see me dead." The man talking was Quanah Parker. He had agreed to give Gloria Martin an exclusive interview in the hope that the more people informed and gave the truths of the plight of the Comanche and their willingness to achieve peace the more chance for success in doing so. Newspapers such as Gloria's were a valued source of communication. Quanah had learned early in life that the white man was more inclined to believe what they read than what they heard through local gossips who get turned around, deleted or added to. But if it is there in black and white to read and if printed in a notable paper for telling the truth such as the Morning Glory then the better his chances.

"Yes. I suppose that does make sense. But that hat you're wearing would be reason enough for some men," said Gloria.

"You like it? It came all the way from St. Louis. Cost me $12.00."

"Please, let's get out of the street. You may hitch your wagon in front of the paper. I will have Thomas tend to it."

Red Sand's curiosity got the better of him and he walked over to the Morning Glory. After all they were to keep an eye on the place and Mrs. Gloria.

After learning of the mysterious visitor and his identity, Red felt it prudent to keep the matter under his hat and to inform Major Parker only.

"Thank you, Red. You're correct in assuming to keep the matter tight. It could mean trouble if the word got out to the right people. Still, I can't see keeping that secret for too long. He does have to eat and he will need a place to stay during his visit here. Perhaps I better go over to the Morning Glory," said Major Drew Parker.

"Figuring on trouble already being here?" asked Red.

"Could be. But that remains to be seen."

"Ya," replied Red. "I'll double the watchmen."

"Good idea. Even if it's nothing at all. It's good exercise for the men."

Quanah Parker's visit was brief. Sensing trouble himself, Quanah departed from Muleshoe sometime in the early morning hours of the next day.

"He left? When? Isn't that his buckboard wagon outback?" Drew asked Gloria.

"Why, yes it is. I traded him my horse for the wagon. He will make better time and a wagon would be just too easy to trail. It is most likely that someone could have recognized him in it and sent word of his whereabouts," explained Gloria.

"Why that sly, old fox," said Red Sands.

"Yes, he is. I wish him well," replied Drew.

But there was still the trouble from the men hired by the railroad. Or at least by those who might have a vested interest in the railroad. It was bound to happen and one afternoon it did. Gloria Martin, of the Morning Glory newspaper, had decided to do an afternoon's worth of shopping. With the day's run of the newspaper already in print and ready for distribution she left Thomas in charge of seeing that all of the orders went out in time and to the cleaning of the floors and machinery.

Marjorie and Miguel Andrew were sitting out on the balcony of their upstairs apartment enjoying the warm afternoon sun. Miguel was sitting at her feet playing with a newly purchased wooden train. Drew came stepping out to join them.

"It's such a lovely day, isn't it? Just smell the air. So fresh and I swear I can detect a hint of lilac," said Marjorie.

"Could be that you do. Yes it is a nice day," replied Drew.

"Look, Daddy! Chugga chugga choo choo. All aboard!" said Miguel. He was puffing his cheeks with air to make the sounds.

"All aboard? Where's your train bound for, son?"

"California! We're going to see the ocean."

Drew was just about to kneel down next to Miguel when suddenly as if magically appearing from thin air there came a group of riders, shouting and shooting.

"Get Miguel inside! Hurry!" ordered Drew to Marjorie.

"But my train!" cried Miguel.

"Get along, son! I'll bring it," said Drew.

A stray bullet struck a clay flower pot that was hanging just outside of the balcony door. The flower pot exploded sending shard's of clay pot, soil and water everywhere.

"Oh! Drew!" cried Marjorie in fear.

Drew strapped on his gun belt. "Just stay inside. You'll be alright. But just in case," Drew handed Marjorie a rifle. "Just in case," he repeated.

Marjorie nodded. "Be careful. Make sure you come back to us."

Drew smiled. "Of course."

Rangers were scampering all about downstairs yelling and swearing. "Where's my boot! What the blazes! Get your guns, boys!"

As Drew ran out into the street he was followed by at least a dozen Rangers.

"Smoke!" someone yelled. "I smell smoke!"

"It's Mrs. Gloria's place! It's on fire!"

Gloria Martin came running down the street screaming like a woman gone insane. "No! Oh dear God, no!!"

Red tried to grab her arm but she broke free instantly. "No, Mrs. Gloria! Don't!"

Jerolde Oaks rushed at her and tackled her to the ground. "No! No! He's in there! He's in there!" Suddenly Jerolde Oaks understood.

"Thomas is in the building!" shouted Jerolde Oaks.

Red Sands dove full-bodied into a water trough then rushed inside. The loud popping and cracking and odor of burning timber filled the air. "Bucket brigade!" someone yelled.

"He's not coming out!" said Jerolde Oaks. Then he too rushed inside the burning building.

Caleb came running from the other end of town. "How'd it happen?"

"I don't know," said Tom Crawford. "But Rangers Red Sands and Jerolde Oaks are in there!"

"What?"

"Gloria's boy, Thomas! They went in to get him!" said Tom Crawford.

"Look!" yelled an onlooker.

It was Red and Jerolde Oaks shielding Thomas from the flames with their own bodies. Jerolde Oak's shirt was blazing.

"Dear God, help us!" prayed Caleb. He tackled Oaks to the ground dousing him with dirt and sand and beating the flames with his hat. Jerolde Oaks lay on the ground. His breathing was ragged and he was moaning in torment. "Get it off!! Get it off!" he cried.

Marshall Jake Randles knelt down next to him and pulled out a Bowie knife. He was about to start cutting away Oaks shirt or what remained of it.

"No! Don't do that!" yelled Caleb.

"He is in great pain," said Marshall Jake Randles.

Caleb kicked the knife out of Marshall Randles hands. "Yes but he'll be worse if you cut that away now. Trust me!"

"Oh God!! Somebody kill me! Please! I can't stand it! Kill me. Kill me!" cried Jerolde Oaks.

"Somebody get the doctor!" yelled Capt. Drew Parker.

"I'm right here. Dr. Walter Gates is the name. Now get this man on a stretcher and into the saloon now!"

"Saloon? He needs a hospital!" said Major Drew Parker.

"Yes, he does but we don't have that luxury! We have to act now! Get him inside lay him face down on the bar," ordered Dr. Gates.

Dr. Gates closed and cleared the bar to all with the exception of his wife, Diana Gates. They went to work saving the life of the man before them.

"How did this happen, Thomas?" Gloria asked.

"I'm not sure. I was sweeping up when I heard a gunshot. I turned around and the entire front of the paper was on fire. I'd have died had it not been for the Rangers. Is Ranger Oaks going to die because of me?" Thomas began weeping.

"Whether Ranger Oaks lives or dies is up to God now. It isn't your fault," said Major Drew Parker.

Shorty came walking down the street his revolver strapped on and tied low. A rifle draped over his back and a double barrel shotgun in his hand. His eyes glared like that of a wild man. "No, kid. It ain't your fault. But I know whose fault it is and I aim to kill every last one of them."

"Shorty! This ain't the way," said Ranger Sgt. Tom Crawford.

"Maybe not the Ranger way. But today I'm not a Ranger. My best friend's life teeters between here and eternity. Now you boys can do one of two things. You can gun me down trying to stop me. Or stay the hell out of my way. Sure as the sky is blue, I'm going to kill those traitors," said Shorty.

Sgt. Tom Crawford looked at Major Drew Parker pleadingly. "Major?"

"You've got to do it but not alone," replied Major Drew Parker.

"We're with you, Shorty! So what's the plan?" shouted one of the Rangers.

"Unless someone has a better idea I'm going to walk into the Paradise Saloon and start killing. Anyone who gets in the way is just unlucky," said Shorty.

"We're going to walk in alright but bystanders have a chance at leaving. We're going to do this right. We will give them a chance of being arrested although they surely deserve to die. But we're not vigilantes. If they choose to fight then all bets are off," said Drew Parker.

They stood at the bar. Five men as mean and as tough as they came. It was obvious by their clothing and their horses outside that these men were not soldiers. Most likely outlaws for hire. Maybe former military mercenaries. They stood laughing and joking as if they were in their own home. It was clear also that it was most likely these men would rather fight it out before they allowed themselves to be arrested. Rangers or not. Drew Parker spoke first.

"You men are under arrest. Keep your hands up high and turnaround. Real slow."

The five men looked side to side at each other. Then slowly they turned and faced Major Parker. Immediately they noticed that there were ten Rangers as well as Marshall Jake Randles. They were undoubtedly surrounded.

A tall, thinly built man with sandy blonde hair and brown eyes that held an empty, eerie stare had a scar on his neck that most likely was a rope burn from a hangman's noose. He smiled an evil smile. "Well, well. If it ain't the town's fire brigade. Obviously, you put it out. I sure hope no one was injured."

"You men. One by one drop your gun belts and kick them forward toward me," said Major Drew Parker. He was in no mood for idle chitchat.

"Not so fast. What's the charge? We haven't done anything," smirked the man.

"The charge? How's discharging a firearm within the town's limits, reckless endangerment, arson and attempted murder for starters?" said Ranger Sgt. Caleb Parker.

"Them's mighty serious charges. Got proof? We ain't attempted to murder anybody. As for arson, well, we ain't. All we was doing was cutting up some on the way in. Since when was that a crime?" repeated the sandy haired man.

"Since there's a big sign on both ends of town that reads NO DISCHARGING OF FIRE ARMS WITHIN THE TOWN LIMITS. Your disregard of that sign resulted in a fire. A fire which almost cost the life of a young boy and a Texas Ranger. Now I'm tired of talking.

Are you men coming in peaceful? Either way makes no difference to me," warned Major Drew Parker.

'Well, now, I ain't quite decided yet," answered the man.

"One thing is certain. You are going to jail," said Major Parker.

The tall blonde haired man grinned devilishly. His hand slowly crept down above his revolver. The other four men began to spread apart. Readying for a fight. Shorty caught the tall blond man's stare. Their eyes locked on one another. Shorty was determined, this man was going to die. Shorty pursed his lips and blew a silent kiss toward the blonde haired man. The man's eyes filled with rage at the insult. His hand fell quickly upon his revolver to draw. Shorty was more than ready. Shorty's hands were lightning fast. Shorty drew and fired before the blonde haired man could clear leather. A sudden but prominent red grew quickly larger at the center of the man's chest. He stared at Shorty bewildered, his lips forming words but no sound. He fell face first onto the floor. Then a thundering of gunfire filled the saloon echoing out into the main street of Muleshoe. The gun smoke so thick in the air that it burned the eyes. When the firing stopped four of the wild bunch lay dead. The other a short, stocky, ashy brown haired man lay badly shot up but alive.

Major Parker cursed. "Damn it all! I didn't want to kill anyone! What set them off?!"

No one spoke. For no one but Shorty truly knew the answer.

"This one's going to live, Major Parker," said Marshall Jake Randles.

"Get him over to Doc Gates. I've got some questions for you, mister. You'll answer too. You better satisfy my curiosity else you may join your friends here at the end of a rope," said Major Drew Parker. The man stared into Major Parker's eyes then shook his head in agreement.

------------//-----------

**Austin, Texas**

"I'm going to miss you, Charlie. You've been a great service to the Rangers. So, what's a retired Texas Ranger do? Got any plans?" asked Capt. Leander H McNelly.

"I've saved up a might of money. That plus my pension. I figure I should be set in a good spot for the rest of my days. I'm thinking of doing some ranching."

"Ranching? Sure! Where?" asked Capt. McNelly.

"Colorado is a mighty pretty country. Saw a ranch there. Maybe I'll buy it. I know of two good hands who will be more than willing," replied Charlie.

Ed Lamb looked up from the newspaper he had been reading and gave Charlie a wolfish smile. "Sand Creek area?"

"And suppose I said yes?" replied Charlie.

"Nothing! I'm just surprised it took you so long to make up your mind," said Ed Lamb.

"Yeah," Charlie smiled. "Reckon sometimes a fella can be mighty slow."

It was the dawning of a new era. A changing of the Guard. Those who had blazed the trail, who had first begun the Texas Rangers, would now hand the torch to a younger breed of men. Men of honor and of justice. Strong and determined. With the wisdom gained from the old and the stamina of youth. These are the Texas Rangers ALL FOR TEXAS.

But peace would not come easy for Texas nor for the Texas Rangers. Treaties would be broken between the government of the United States and that of the Indian Nations. The railroad would bring with it a more cunning and brutal breed of criminal. Oil boomtowns would soon make their debut and with the oil would ooze from the vile craggs of man's soul an evil that man had yet to encounter: human trafficking, drug cartels, illegal land grabbing, cattle wars, the criminal minded would learn to organize and influence politics by whatever means possible. But the Rangers would learn of new weapons in fighting crime: forensics, ballistics and the art of finger printing.

# DEDICATED TO
# MY MOTHER AND FATHER

Donald A Knott Sr.
and Virginia Knott

"Train up a child in the way he should go and
he will not depart from it"
Proverbs 22:6

To all of the men and women in law enforcement
who devote their lives every day to the protection of their
fellow citizens and the pursuit of justice.

"Greater love hath no man than this,
that he would lay down his life for his friends."
John 15:13

CPSIA information can be obtained
at www.ICGtesting.com
Printed in the USA
LVHW040952201119
637825LV00003B/159/P

9 781949 231564